THE MITING

DEE YODER

Kregel
Publications

For Rachel, Maryann, and Matty.
Your journeys are my inspiration.

CHAPTER ONE

Leah Raber sank wearily onto the porch swing, causing the chains to jangle. She leaned her head back, closed her eyes, and imagined herself free—her skirt and apron flung carelessly over the branches of a prickly mulberry, her legs running to the pond, her hair blowing behind her as she leapt into cool, deep waters. She could almost feel the splash as she plunged into the secret world of water and swam among the fronds of the dark pond bottom, the silky liquid sliding against her arms and legs as her feet kicked out, over and over.

A cow mooed, and Leah came up for breath, opening her eyes to the reality of the hot, unrelenting sun.

Leah's gaze traveled around the yard to the barn, where she spotted Benny chasing a few of *Maem's* setting hens away from the road. His laughter carried across the field, his cheeks rosy and his bowl-shaped haircut flopping up and down while he chased the squawking birds. Life used to seem so simple.

From outward appearances, Leah could certainly see why *Englishers* would think her family's life was idyllic. But they didn't have to wear the long skirts and *kapps* and heavy shoes in the summer. They didn't have to follow endless rules . . . forever.

Pressing her feet against the gray boards of the porch, she stopped swinging and thought about going inside to help *Maem* put lunch on the table. With a sigh, she wiped the sweat from her face and stood up.

"Might as well get to it."

The kitchen felt even hotter than outside. *Maem* had started the weekly bread baking before five that morning in an effort to finish the task before the heat of the day, but the wood-burning stove had held its warmth. A fan or a quick-cooling propane stove, anything to relieve the heat, would be so nice in the kitchen.

"Another silly thing the *Ordnung* won't allow . . ."

Maem turned with a puzzled frown. Wisps of damp hair clung to her flushed cheeks, and perspiration beaded over her lips. "Did you say something, Leah?"

"Just . . . oh, nothing."

Maem bustled by to get some of her homemade, sweetened peanut butter spread and sweet pickles from the pantry. Her brow furrowed again, but a smile played at her lips. "I never know what you're going to surprise me with."

Leah reached into the bread box for the only loaf of wheat bread left from last Saturday's baking. Slicing and arranging the bread on a white pottery plate, she hummed a song she'd heard the last time she'd been with her friend Martha.

Martha—against her parents' and the church's wishes—was dabbling in the English world. While some Amish sects turned a blind eye to a teen's running-around years, their bishop preferred that children not flirt with sinful English ways. Just last week, Martha and her boyfriend, Abe Troyer, had stopped by Leah as she walked along the road. They were in Abe's beat-up truck on their way to Ashfield to shop. Country music had blared from the radio, and the joyous freedom emanating from her friends made Leah long for something that seemed just out of her reach. A few of the words she'd heard still stuck in her head.

"Oh, I wanna go to heaven someday—I wanna walk on streets of pure gold—I wanna go to heaven someday, but I sure don't wanna go now."

"Leah!"

Maem's sharp tone brought her back to the present, and Leah's cheeks flushed as she realized she'd sung aloud. Not something her parents would want her to sing, that's for sure.

"Sorry."

Maem lowered her gaze and shook her head slightly, her face drawn.

Lately, Leah couldn't keep count of the number of times a day she made her mother frown. It didn't take much. The set of her jaw showed her disappointment.

Leah slammed the cheese knife down on the counter in frustration. *Can't even sing in my own home—can't sing anything but Sunday singing songs. Boring.* She whirled around to escape back onto the porch, but *Maem* caught her arm and motioned her to the table.

"There's something *Daet* and I want to talk with you about. We're concerned for you. I know it's your teen years and at least one of your friends has fiddled with English ways—"

"*Maem*—"

"No. Listen to me, please, for just a minute. So far, you haven't acted like you wanted to join Martha, but we're worried she's influencing you."

Leah ducked her chin, avoiding her mother's gaze. She'd known this talk was coming. *Best to get it over with.*

"*Maem*, don't you remember your teen years? Don't you remember longing for freedom? Just a little bit of time with no one telling you exactly what to do, what to wear?" Leah lifted her gaze to her mother, willing her to show a glimmer of compassion. *Maem*'s stony face looked back, fueling Leah's determination.

"Didn't you ever wish that you could blend in—that people wouldn't stare at you, point at you, laugh at you? Why do we have to live this way? I want to understand, *Maem*, I really do, but I just don't see what we gain by living this way. So . . . so . . . backward. I could even accept being hot all summer long if I just understood why. So many things are wrong and sinful—too many to keep track of. But some of those same things are okay in other Amish communities. Like being allowed to have a phone shed in the driveway. Why can other Amish have that but not us? *Why?*"

Realizing she had raised her voice, she clamped her jaw shut. She hadn't meant to be disrespectful. *Maem* held her gaze, but her cheeks had gone white in spite of the heat of the kitchen. When she finally spoke, her voice was full of reproach and sorrow.

"You surprise me, Leah. You really do. You've never talked like this before. Your *daet* won't be happy to hear you saying these kinds of things.

And no, I did *not* question the things you seem to be so unhappy with."
Maem swiped a dish towel across the table in frustration. "What's to
question? You have a good home, good family, and a hard-working *daet*
and *maem*. Your brothers and sister are good to you, too. The church—"

"*Maem*, I just want you to understand me. Even if you've never
thought like this, can't you think about what I'm saying? Just let me
have a little breathing room, okay?"

"Breathing room for what?" *Maem* exclaimed. "Putting the light in
your window as some girls do to attract *buves* driving by? Sneaking away
in some boy's sinful car and riding around drinking, smoking all night?
Listening to godless music and wasting your life trying to find out what
the English world has to offer you? Let me tell you this: the English have
nothing to offer you. Believe me. Nothing."

"How do you know that, *Maem*? How do you know! You've spent
your whole life in this place and done everything the bishop and the
church told you to do." Leah jumped up from the table and threw her
hands out imploringly. "I'm not like you and *Daet*. I need some freedom,
and I want to do things other than staying here in this house, on this
farm. I don't want to spend all my time—"

The back screen door banged. *Daet* stood in the kitchen. Sawdust
and small curls of wood covered his face and his blue cotton work shirt.
He undoubtedly had heard her last words, but he silently went to the
sink and washed his hands, then came to the table and sat down next to
Maem. Fear of his reaction kept Leah from storming out.

The screen door banged again as her brothers and sister rushed in for
lunch. *Maem* and *Daet* exchanged a look, then bowed their heads for
silent prayer. When he finished praying, *Daet* pointed to Leah's vacated
chair. She cautiously eased into her seat and took a slice of bread.

"I think someone should catch that mean *hohna*, as soon as lunch is
over." Benny's blue eyes sparkled. "I can do it. I'm old enough now."

Maem wiped a glob of mustard off his cheek. "Being a second grader
does make you old enough to do many things to help out, but I think
you'd best leave that old rooster alone. He'll claw you if you try to catch
him."

"But don't you think he'd make pretty good *bott boi*?"

Ada snickered. "He's ancient. And he's mean, so I vote for *bott boi*, too."

"Pretty much up to *Maem* when a chicken's life is over around here." *Daet* nudged Leah's older brother, Daniel. "But she gets attached to 'em, too. Isn't that why we don't have chicken *bott boi* for *suppah* much, *Maem*?"

"That rooster has much more life left in him. We won't be using him for pot pies any time soon. Now hurry and eat your lunch. *Daet* wants to *schwetz* with your sister."

The siblings' eyes swiveled to Leah. Deliberately ignoring their stares, she scrutinized her uneaten bread, her lips pressed tightly together.

The family finished the meal in silence, her brothers and sister seemingly aware of the awkward strain between their parents and Leah. Benny finished his milk with a long, loud gulp, wiped his mouth on his sleeve, then scurried out of the kitchen behind Ada and Daniel.

Finally *Daet* pushed his plate back and leaned forward, resting his fists beneath his chin. He sighed, and his beard bobbed as he swallowed.

"Leah, I'm sorry to say I have no respect left for your friend Martha—"

"*Daet!* That's not fair—"

He held up his hand. "No. I've thought and prayed about this for a while, and your *maem* and I have talked this over. You're being influenced by her and what she's doing."

His gaze held Leah's firmly, and though he said nothing else about her friendship with Martha, his message was clear: Martha would not be a welcome visitor to their home as long as she was *rumspringen* with the English. She was definitely outside the will of the church and going against the *Ordnung* letter in open rebellion.

"I also want you to consider joining the church sooner—as Daniel did. He didn't have to join when he was only seventeen, but he decided it was best. I think once you've made that decision, all these worries and problems you're having will stop pestering you."

He stood up, signaling an end to the conversation, and went to the back door. As he pushed open the squeaky screen, he looked back at Leah, a tilted grin clearing his face of lingering anger. "By the way, Jacob Yoder is coming today to help me unload and stack lumber. He should be here in about an hour."

An unexpected wave of remorse rolled over Leah, and she moved quickly to her father, giving him an impulsive hug. He clumsily patted her arm before he hurried back to work in his furniture shop.

Leah then offered a look of contrition to *Maem*, who merely pointed to the dishes left on the table, waiting to be washed. Suppressing a sigh, which would only resurrect angry feelings, Leah set about redding up the kitchen. A moment later she felt *Maem*'s hand on her shoulder.

"Leah, you have always been such a headstrong child. Please don't let your stubborn and sinful nature get the best of you." *Maem* softened her words with a smile before reaching down for her basket and garden shears. With one meal over, it was time to start planning for the next one.

"I promise to think about joining the church. Okay?"

Her mother paused and tucked a strand of damp hair back under her kerchief covering. "Don't just think about it. Pray earnestly that your heart turns to *Gott* and that you will do it joyfully. Yes?"

Leah gave a short nod, turning to the table to gather the lunch dishes for washing. She watched through the kitchen window as her *maem* walked slowly across the yard.

Childhood memories of working beside *Maem* flashed through her mind—planting seeds in the spring and later pulling weeds to keep the rows neat; snapping green beans on hot, late-August afternoons; picking apples in the fall. *Maem*'s apron pockets had held secret sweets to reward her back then. Her mother wasn't much for hugs or kisses—it wasn't something her people did. But no matter what happened, *Maem* was always there to soothe away childhood hurts with her work-worn hands.

What kind of *maem* would Leah herself be one day? How would she deal with a daughter who dreamed of freedom and yearned for more than what farm life and rural living could offer? Would she understand a daughter's yearning to shake off the traditions of Amish life?

A long line of ghostly forefathers seemed to hover over Leah's shoulders, whispering their must-nots in her ears the livelong day. She shuddered. She was not rebellious by nature, and it hurt to know she was causing her *maem* pain.

"I really am trying *not* to be difficult," she whispered as she washed. "I just don't know what to think anymore."

Later that afternoon, Leah was in the wood shop helping *Daet* with the billing when she heard a wagon come up the drive. Nervous anticipation fluttered inside her. At the last Sunday singing, Jacob Yoder had shown more than enough interest in Leah, but he hadn't yet asked if he could take her home. Leah did not object to his attentions one bit.

The door swung open, and Jacob stepped in. She tried to control her keen awareness of him by pointing him to the back of the shop where *Daet* worked, but his impish dimple made it clear her nonchalant attitude hadn't fooled him.

"Good afternoon, Jacob," *Daet* called as he strolled out to the front of the workshop.

The men shook hands in greeting.

"Where do you want me to stack this cherry lumber?"

Daet pulled at his beard. "Let me see. I had it over there next to the back wall, but I think, with the order of dining-room furniture I have yet to finish, I'd like it closer this time." He scuffed out a spot to the right of the door. "This should work. It'll be close to me but not in the way of the oak that'll be coming next week."

Daet and Jacob worked side by side for several minutes in silence, while Leah forced herself to focus on the receipts. She could hear Jacob's footfalls as he moved back and forth between the delivery wagon and the shop. Already she recognized his step: quick and sure. He had been bringing supplies to *Daet* for several months, earning extra money for his family. It was a given that, being the oldest son and a good farmer in his own right, Jacob would take over from his father someday. But for now, he was also adding to the family's income by delivering lumber for Jonas Coblentz, the local lumber mill owner.

She glanced up in time to catch his glance as he passed the desk. The roguish dimple flashed as a friendly grin spread over his face. Leah held his gaze for a moment, taking in the broad shoulders, lean frame, and suntanned face. She could feel heat rising in her cheeks as Jacob's eyes twinkled in amusement.

Daet cleared his throat. "Uh, Jacob—"

"Yes?" Jacob broke his gaze to turn respectful eyes to Leah's *daet*.

"What are you and the other teens hearing about Martha Mast and her boyfriend, Abe Troyer?"

Leah's eyes darted up, and *Daet* glanced her way, as if to be sure she had overheard his question.

Jacob shuffled his feet in the sawdust and kept his head down. Finally, he looked at *Daet* and then over at Leah. "We know she's *rumspringen* with *Englishers*, and she's not likely to join the church, John."

"Not going to join the church! You think not?" asked *Daet*, alarmed.

Leah looked at the pile of bills in her hand. *Daet* had thought Martha was going wild, but she knew it had never occurred to him before today that she might leave the Amish for good.

Jacob resumed piling wood. "She says she's not going to join, and Abe's looking into getting a factory job in Richland because he wants to do something other than farm."

"I don't farm either, but in no way would I consider leaving my faith and all I know to be right just to do something different for work."

Jacob shook his head. "Work isn't the issue for him, John. He doesn't like all the rules and ideas of the Amish anymore. He claims he wants his freedom."

Leah watched *Daet* ponder Jacob's words. The community would not consider Abe's actions a simple rebellious *rumspringen*, as some of the less strict, higher church Amish might. He would be seen as a young man with sin in his heart and the Devil's hand on his shoulder.

Daet turned his gaze to Leah. "If Abe has Martha thinking like this, then maybe Martha is putting these same thoughts in your head, Leah." He wagged his finger at her. "You should watch this friendship with her very carefully, Daughter. If she says anything against the church or the *Ordnung*, maybe we should get the bishop involved. Better to cause embarrassment or shame than to risk her soul."

Leah lifted her chin in silent defiance. "I'll remember that, *Daet*."

He nodded, apparently satisfied with her response. "I'll be right back. I have to get a tape measure."

As he passed by her, he murmured under his breath, "A little time alone with Jacob won't hurt, eh, Leah? You should be thinking of your future." *Daet* left the shop, whistling.

The heat from the sunlight coming in the window behind her had nothing to do with the warmth in her face. Jacob kept stacking lumber, but Leah was sure he'd heard some of *Daet*'s whispered advice.

"Being married almost always ensures that the jungen *join the church,"* he'd said many times. He'd even mentioned once, after Benny and Ada were in bed, a *daet* who had gone so far as to allow bed courtship. The father had claimed it "helped" his wayward daughter make up her mind, but Leah's parents didn't think a hurried marriage with an early baby were worth the shame or risk, no matter how rebellious a daughter might become.

Jacob walked over to Leah and leaned casually against the counter. His shirt cuffs were rolled up to his elbows. His face glistened with sweat in the heat of the shop, but he looked calm and collected.

"Your *daet* is really concerned about Martha."

Leah frowned. "He and *Maem* think she's influencing me with her wild ways, and . . . maybe . . . some of that *might* be true."

She leaned in closer to Jacob, glanced at the door, and lowered her voice. "Do you ever have questions, Jacob, about all this, you know?" Her gesture took in the whole place.

Jacob shifted his weight, and when his gaze met hers, he was serious but gentle in his reproach. "Leah, you shouldn't be so worried. Everything is *gut*; your parents have the best in mind for you. My parents do for me, too."

"I don't know why, but I'm restless, Jacob. Feeling trapped, in a way."

His brown eyes looked into hers. He nodded. "It's your age, I think. I went through that for a few weeks, but you'll see. Soon you'll be back to being your cheerful self."

"So you plan to join the church this fall?" Leah asked, as she wiped her clammy palms on her apron. *Can he sense the indecision in my heart?*

"Yes. Probably will. Can't think of any reason not to, you know?"

Jacob twirled his straw hat. His work-hardened hands appeared older than the rest of him. He looked back at her merrily, and she couldn't help but smile. One thing about Jacob Yoder: he could charm a person into anything. His wide, unaffected grin and sparkling eyes were everything friendly and warm. Laugh lines, accented by the tan he carried from being outside, added to his appeal.

Leah arranged the bills in a neat pile and stretched a rubber band around the ones that still needed to be paid. "I guess I should get back to the house and see what *Maem* wants me to do yet today."

He nodded. "Always lots of chores on a Saturday—right? You going into town later?"

"I think so. We have to do some shopping for the singing tomorrow night."

"It's out here?"

"Yes. We offered to host in place of Miriam and Paul. They have church tomorrow, but with their new baby, we thought the young people shouldn't bother them tomorrow night. *Maem* and *Daet* said it would be okay to have it here. You coming, Jacob?"

"You know it." He winked, then turned back to stacking lumber.

As Leah passed *Daet* on her way to the house, he raised his eyebrows, not missing the grin she wore and knowing who was responsible for putting it there.

⚜

The Sunday night singing went as planned. The *jungen* sang their favorite hymns and songs, ate the cookies Leah made, and chatted in the between times. When the evening ended, Leah wished the singing had been hosted elsewhere so she'd have had an excuse to be driven home in Jacob's buggy. She waved to friends as they drove away, some in couples, and some by themselves. Jacob drove off alone. Maybe he'd not be alone after the next singing.

Chapter Two

What do you think about *rumspringen*—not just singings on Sunday night, but going to movies like English teens?"

Leah looked at her younger sister from behind the pants she was hanging on the line and blinked against the sun. "What do you mean? Why are you asking me that?"

Ada shrugged. "I just wondered, is all. I mean, I'm going to be fifteen soon, just one more year. I'd like to know what *Maem* and *Daet* think about it."

Leah turned to hang another pair of denim work pants. She shook out the damp wrinkles and pegged the pants tightly to the line. "Why? Are you thinking of trying it? Sunday singings are okay, but I think you know how *Maem* and *Daet* feel about anything else. No one wants to see their kids go off and do something they don't approve of, and our church doesn't even believe in *rumspringen*—not the way Martha's doing it. What the church doesn't allow, *Maem* and *Daet* certainly won't allow."

Ada's chin tilted down, hiding her expression as she smoothed the wrinkles from a worn shirt she had pegged to the line, then pulled a wet vest out of the basket. "I just wonder sometimes if I could keep going to school."

The wistful expression in her sister's eyes pained Leah. Smart girls like Ada suffered the most when Amish schooling came to an end in eighth grade. But there was no point in discussing it. Railing against the unfairness would not change the rules about school. By next year, Ada would be finished with her education, and there was no chance of studying beyond that. A deep sigh from Ada indicated she had reached the same conclusion.

They worked in silence a few more minutes. "I heard Martha might leave. Do you ever think of doing that?"

Leah glanced away, afraid her expression might reveal too much. Leaving home meant leaving the church, something almost impossible to contemplate. It meant breaking all ties to family and friends and community and bearing the weight of condemnation as the wayward child of John Raber. And *Daet* would suffer, too. Having a child leave the faith automatically lowered the status of the parents in the church community. The knowledge that she would bring such a heavy burden down on her family sat like a stone in Leah's stomach. She recalled the sermons she'd heard: The Devil with his hand on a wayward child's shoulder. The evil in the outside world. The fear of knowing her eternal damnation as soon as she traded her *kapp* for flowing hair and English ways. It all brought home to her the cost of leaving.

"I don't know, Ada. It would be terrible to do that to our parents. We've seen what happens when young people leave. I shudder to think of being under the *meidning*—not being welcome at home anymore."

Ada's eyes swerved to hers. "The miting! You *have* thought of leaving."

"Ada, I didn't say that. I have no plans to leave."

She shouldn't be having this conversation. The very thought of leaving all she cherished twisted her heart. Leah glanced at her sister as she bent over the laundry basket, the grass touching the hem of Ada's skirt. A shaft of sunlight illumined her sister's browned arms, and a lofting breeze tickled a tendril of chestnut hair along her neck. A swallow dipped and trilled his way over their heads, and an almost painful desire for this moment to last forever flared in her being. No. She could never leave. Not her family. Not her life.

Ada spoke, snapping Leah back to the soft summer day that wrapped around them.

"*Maem* would never put you under the miting anyway. She loves her kids too much. But Henry Miller would have no trouble doing it." Ada grimaced, rolling her eyes. Leah ignored the sarcasm directed at their church bishop.

Henry had been a staunchly religious man before he was chosen as bishop, but since that time, his relentless adherence to the *Ordnung* had intensified dramatically, and so had the burden on his church. In exacting strict piety, the bishop declared he was only trying to follow the *Ordnung*, though Leah wondered if he sometimes enjoyed the privations he put on his group. Whatever his motives, he certainly wasn't popular with his people.

The clothes all hung, Leah picked up the empty laundry basket, trapping its woven fibers against one hip as she made her way back toward the house. "Anyway, it's not going to be something you'll ever have to endure, right, Ada? And I don't have any notions about leaving, either. As for Martha, well, who knows about her?"

⚜

The sun had barely risen over the hills Monday morning when Leah pushed open the back screen door. It banged shut behind her.

The sharp, fresh-cut smell of lumber greeted her in the shop. A customer was coming by early to check out the progress on his bedroom furniture. *Daet* was polishing the footboard to the sleigh bed he'd created, ensuring the finish color was perfect. He glanced up as Leah strolled to the desk.

"*Morgen.* Ready for a busy day?"

"*Ja*, sure," Leah said, glancing down at *Daet*'s hands as he rubbed a tack cloth across the footboard to remove the smallest dust particle. His large-knuckled, hard-working hands. *Daet* provided for his family, never shirking his duty as father and protector. His face was lined from years of outdoor work. His eyes, though mature, still had the ability to sparkle with fun, and his deep laugh echoed in her memory. She wondered what her father had been like as a child before the responsibility of family had come. Did her grandmother soothe away his tears when he fell? Did he play like Benny did with the chickens—running to and fro without a care in the world? Her gaze softened at the thought of her father as a vulnerable child.

When he was finally satisfied with his work, he carefully stood the headboard against the wall, examining every surface for flaws.

"What do you want me to do first, *Daet?*"

"I'd like you to add up Ben Hochstetler's bill. He owes me some yet, but I haven't had the chance to get it figured out, and you're better at it than I am anyway. It's this one . . . uh . . . let me find it . . . yes, this one here."

He shoved a worn piece of paper across the desk to her, his stained fingers marking another smudge on the wrinkled corner. Leah positioned the bill in a ray of sunlight streaming through the back windows of the shop and from overhead. *Daet* had installed gas lines for winter lighting, but for the summer, he fitted rows of solar tubes in the ceiling. The light flooding through them reflected brightly over the center length of the wood shop. Most days, sun was all that was needed to see properly.

Leah copied a line of numbers onto a sheet of scratch paper and totaled the sums. She then waded through a lopsided pile of paper bits *Daet* had used to record the work he'd done for Hochstetler. Discovering the customer still owed two hundred dollars, she showed *Daet* the tally.

"That much, eh?"

"Yes, but he's paid steadily, so I don't think you'll have any trouble collecting the rest. It may take him some time, though, now that they've added twins to their family."

The bell over the shop door jingled, disturbed by an English man who entered, smiling broadly under his summer cap. To Leah's amazement, he greeted *Daet* in Pennsylvania-Dutch.

"This is Matthew Schrock," Daet explained. "He's the fellow who ordered the cherry bedroom set. Matthew, this is my daughter, Leah."

"Nice to meet you, Leah." Matthew spoke in English. He politely shook her hand, his pleasant manner drawing her attention.

"Thank you. Nice to meet you."

"Your *daet* does the finest work. He's one of the best carpenters I know around here."

"Yes, and he enjoys everything he crafts."

"Ahh, that makes a man's work more agreeable—enjoying the process as he goes."

The bell jingled again, and in marched Bishop Miller. *Daet* immediately moved to greet him. Leah took note of her father's tight smile as he observed the bishop's gaze fixed on the *Englisher*.

Matthew Schrock greeted the bishop as if he knew him, and Bishop Miller's chilly nod verified the fact.

"He came to see the furniture I'm crafting for him, Bishop." *Daet* pointed to the headboard. He shifted his eyes to Matthew and offered his hand. "Thank you for stopping by. I'll let you know when everything's ready."

Leah saw the *Englisher's* Adam's apple dip as he swallowed. He hesitated, then returned *Daet's* handshake. "*Danke*, John. I'll look forward to seeing your final work." He nodded to the bishop and exited the shop quickly. Silence enveloped the room until the bishop cleared his throat.

"John, it's good to see your business doing well."

"*Ja*, it's going well, thanks to God and the help He gives me in my labor."

The bishop stroked his scraggly beard. "You're doing work for the English now, John?"

"Here and there. Schrock stopped by one day when he noticed my sign."

"Order much, did he?"

"*Ja*, a whole bedroom set—cherry."

"Know much about him?" The bishop took off his hat and toyed with the brim.

Daet paused before he answered, glancing toward Leah as he spoke. "Not much. He speaks Dutch."

Bishop Miller scrutinized a polishing cloth lying nearby. He fingered it, then dropped the cloth into a heap on the shelf. Oily residue glimmered on the tips of his fingers. He took out his handkerchief and rubbed the oil off.

"Used to be Amish."

A world of innuendo in the bishop's declaration wasn't lost on Leah. Implications hung heavy in the air. Just as the bishop opened the door to leave, he turned back. "Schrock left the Amish years ago—became a born-again Christian. He helps the *jungen* leave the Amish."

Daet nodded, his expression grave as he faced the bishop. "I'll keep that in mind, Bishop Miller." He glanced at Leah before returning to work.

That night, Leah propped her pillow against the windowsill. She gazed at the surrounding fields, a bystander watching the darkness spread over the land in slow measure. Its shadows smothered the rolling Ohio hills like a thick, velvety robe. The sounds of large and small creatures swelled in the summer night one last time before they went the way of the slumbering Amish surrounding them.

Her eyes were heavy, but her thoughts fastened on Bishop Miller's last words: *he helps the* jungen *leave the Amish.*

⚜

At breakfast, Leah lingered at the table longer than the rest. Once *Maem* returned to the kitchen after shooing Benny back to his room to wash his ears, she sat down across from her daughter to savor a second cup of morning coffee. Leah wanted answers. *Maem* might give them.

"Bishop Miller told *Daet* that Matthew Schrock is former Amish."

Maem sipped her coffee, offering no acknowledgment of Leah's statement.

"He said Schrock helps *jungen* leave."

Maem pulled the saucer from the bottom of the cup and poured a little of the steaming liquid into it. She pursed her lips and blew across the surface of the coffee, then took a tentative sip, still ignoring Leah's questions.

Leah persisted. "Have you heard that, too?"

Maem set the saucer down hard enough to splash a drop of coffee onto the oilcloth table covering. She touched the drop, smearing the puddle in ever increasing arcs, and sighed.

"Why, Leah? *Why* do you want to know about a man like that?"

"I . . . don't know. But Bishop Miller was angry at Matthew, even though I thought he was a nice man. Matthew was friendly and talked about how much he appreciates *Daet*'s work."

Maem glanced down, pulling at her apron to straighten it before finally answering.

"It would be better for you not to ask anything about him." She tilted her head, gazing at a spot over Leah's shoulder. "But on second thought, maybe you should know what he does in case Martha ever tries to get you to go along with her—though I'm pretty sure Martha won't be going to a Bible study. Still . . ." She fixed her gaze on Leah. "He says he hosts Bible studies, but what he really does, according to what I've heard, is pressure the Amish kids to leave. He gives them worldly jobs to keep them out."

"Bible study?"

"Not only that, he sometimes takes in Amish people who have run away from their faith. He helps them stay away from their people. But he and his wife are blinded, Leah. They know the truth and have decided to reject it. You know what happens to people who have rejected the truth."

"What's wrong with a Bible study, *Maem*?" Leah was truly puzzled. From the way Bishop Miller had spoken yesterday, she'd suspected Schrock was kidnapping Amish youth. Holding Bible studies and taking in runaways didn't seem terrible.

Maem waved her hand. "Of course, learning Scripture is not a bad thing, but placing an interpretation on it that our forefathers haven't sanctioned *is* bad. He has rejected all he knows, and his wife has, too. That, in itself, is sinful."

"But why, *Maem*?"

"Why? You know why. If the good Lord sees fit for a person to be born Amish, they have to die Amish in order to go to heaven."

"Matthew seems like a good man, though. He doesn't seem evil at all."

"Leah—" *Maem* sighed and stood up. "Please, just trust me with this. You ask too many questions, and you'll get yourself and everyone else all stirred up. With this, you have to listen to us. *Please*." She looked into Leah's eyes with a silent entreaty, then turned and poured a cup of coffee to take to *Daet*. The conversation was over.

Through the window over the sink, Leah watched *Maem* walk to the shop and wondered what she would tell *Daet* about the conversation. They were both worried about Martha's influence. Questions about Matthew Schrock could only bring more concern.

Leah lay on the colorful quilt covering Martha Mast's bed, giggling with her friend over silly nonsense. Martha had pulled up in her buggy not long after *Maem* had gone out to *Daet*. Even though her parents had shared their concerns about Martha, Leah couldn't resist the sunny smile and outgoing nature of her wayward friend.

When Leah had stepped to the wood shop door and called to her parents she was going along with Martha to her house for a visit, *Daet* had frowned and shaken his head but had not forbidden her to go. Instead he simply asked, "Is that wise, Leah?"

Pretending not to hear his question, Leah had waved and run to join Martha in the buggy.

Now they were in Martha's bedroom under the eaves of the big old farmhouse that held all seven of Martha's siblings, her *Maem*, and her stepfather.

"I heard Daniel's getting married." Martha absently smoothed the quilt between them, peering at Leah as if she could see the answer inside her head.

Leah smiled cautiously, not wanting to give away her *bruder*'s secret entirely, but also not wanting to discourage Martha's desire to talk about it.

"Well, spill the beans! Is he, or isn't he?" Martha tugged Leah's *kapp*. "Tell me."

"Yes, he is."

"I knew it! Is it Sara Wengerd?"

Leah giggled. Even though members of her community didn't reveal who a girl went home with from singing or admit to a romance that could lead to marriage, it wasn't possible to keep these things secret indefinitely. "Let's just say it's someone who lives near our place and is very sweet."

Martha hopped from the bed. "Yep. It's Sara. There's no one else in the *jungen* right now as pious or sweet as *her*."

Martha's hash emphasis surprised Leah. "But Martha, she *is* sweet. It's not an act with Sara."

Her friend pulled a stack of forbidden jeans from the back of her dresser drawer. "Forgive me if I gag. Anyone who laps up the rules the way that girl does sets my teeth on edge." Her frown quickly changed to a mischievous grin as she threw a pair of jeans at Leah. "Try these on. I think they'll fit you."

Though she was curious about *Englisher* clothing, Leah hadn't thought of actually trying it on. Her fear of what *Daet* would say if he caught her had kept her from even thinking of bringing a pair into the house. But this forbidden fruit was dangling deliciously close. She gave in to the temptation and jumped to her feet. As she yanked the pants up under her dress, Martha laughed.

"Silly! You won't be able to tell how they look if you wear them that way. Take that ugly dress off and try them on the *right* way."

Leah turned her back to her friend to drag the dress and apron up and over her sleeveless, navy blue slip.

Martha snorted. "You're too modest, girlfriend."

She tugged the unfamiliar jeans over her legs and struggled to fasten the metal button at the top, bunching the slip fabric into a ball in order to see what she was doing. The texture of the fabric as it pulled over her calves when she bent to pick up her dress and apron felt a little strange, though the freedom to stretch and bend and sit any way she liked was wonderful. Leah skipped back to the bed, chuckling as she fell onto the bouncy mattress.

Martha hopped onto the bed, too, settling herself against the headboard. She giggled at Leah's uncharacteristic enthusiasm.

Suddenly, she stopped laughing as she shot a worried glance to the door.

Leah followed her gaze and observed the handle on the door slowly turning. When she looked back at Martha, her friend's face was as white as the pillow coverings, and her playful smile vanished as she stared at the knob.

What in the world is wrong? Leah watched as the knob continued to rotate slowly. The door creaked open. All at once, Martha's older stepbrother, Abner, wedged his face between the door and frame. His thick black eyebrows rose when he saw Leah, but he said nothing to either of the girls.

Leah sucked in her breath when she caught sight of the leer on his face. She had never felt comfortable around Abner, ever since Martha's mother and his widowed father had married several years back, each bringing their own children to the newly formed family. But *this* Abner . . . this was a side of him she'd never before seen.

Martha stared at her stepbrother, her eyes wide with alarm and apprehension. Then, like a deer exploding in motion to escape the hunter, she leapt from the bed, landing within a foot of where Abner's face peered eerily in at them. She shoved the door, momentarily pinning his head against the wall. He yelped and grasped the edge of the door with both hands. In a second he had pulled his head free and grabbed at her wrists. Martha jerked from his grasp, slapping at Abner in a frenzy of rage.

"Not when she's here! You go away! Not when she's here, you don't!"

"You *dumme kuh!*" Abner yelled, grasping both of her arms and pinning them behind her back. He shoved hard, propelling Martha onto the bed face down and pinning her with his knee. "Don't you ever pull that again! I'll come in this room anytime I want!" He let go of Martha, but not before yanking her over and giving her face a vicious slap. She covered her head and cried out in pain, her scream echoing through the stark room.

Abner turned his gaze on Leah, who cowered in a tight ball against the headboard. Her heart pounded so hard she could barely breathe.

He sneered, running a look over the shape of her legs in the tight jeans. "*Shenna bee,*" he motioned.

Leah covered her legs with both hands instinctively. His comment forced another shiver down her spine.

Abner turned and sauntered arrogantly to the door; his last glance at Martha hate filled and evil. "I'll be back," he said, his tone carrying unspoken threats as he left.

Martha struggled to her feet, ran to the door, and slammed it behind her stepbrother. One side of her face was already an ugly shade of red, and she turned her eyes away in shame before crawling into a corner and burying her face in her arms.

Leah trembled on the bed, afraid to say a word. Finally, she got up and carefully peeled off the jeans. She quickly pulled her dress and apron back on, and then sat uncertainly on the edge of Martha's bed.

At last Martha looked up and began to wipe her nose and eyes with her apron, her face a tight mask of humiliation and wrath.

"Martha?" Leah whispered, unspoken questions swirling about the room.

Martha shook her head as she carefully pulled her hair back under her *kapp*, squared her shoulders, and averted her gaze.

Leah was amazed at her friend's ability to hide what had happened so quickly, but she would not soon forget the look on Abner's face, nor the terror his violence created. Though he didn't touch her, imagining the kind of touch his eyes conveyed as he looked over her legs made her shiver anew.

And Martha—she glanced at her friend. How could she endure such treatment? How often did she have to put up with that from her stepbrother, and what else was he capable of doing to her?

Martha's *maem*, Anna, stood at the bottom of the stairs, eyeing the girls warily as they descended. Her face wore a hard, spiteful look, and she turned to watch as the friends walked to the front door. Martha frowned but did not stop to talk with her. Leah's heart pounded harder than ever at the strange expression on Anna's face. It wasn't right. *Or am I just overreacting from the fright Abner gave us?*

CHAPTER THREE

Leah clutched the reins tightly, the leather chaffing her palms as she held Sparky back from an all-out trot. She was going to town with Sara Wengerd, Daniel's fiancée, to buy fabric for Sara's wedding dress. Sunlight reflected off the tops of the few cars traveling this back road to Ashfield, and she worried over Sparky's tendency to dance to the right as vehicles zoomed past. The ditch was dangerous, but pulling the horse to the left too far could cause a crash, as well. The road rolled and twisted, making driving unsafe since cars were liable to pop over a rise unexpectedly.

Leah licked her lips, launching into small talk to ease her nerves. "Sara, what color blue are you thinking of wearing?"

"Light blue looks best on me. Daniel likes that color, too. I hope we find something the *Ordnung* will allow." Sara flushed and pressed her feet against the buggy floor. She fingered the edge of her cape uneasily. Conversation lapsed.

Sparky's hooves kept time with the swaying buggy. He flicked his tail from side to side, shooing away flies that zeroed in on his haunches. Farmland dotted with corn, soybeans, and cows sloped gently away from the road. Boys and men tended to animals in barnyards and shoveled manure into wheelbarrows, which they then trundled off to add to compost heaps. The rural scents were common enough for Leah and Sara to ignore, and the beautiful scenery offered an enjoyable ride, if they didn't have to watch traffic.

"How is the house coming along?" Leah tried again to stretch a chatty string between herself and Sara, but her future sister-in-law was shy and didn't talk much.

Sara's family had moved to the area only recently, so she hadn't grown up with the Amish girls in her church. Daniel had spied the timid girl at her first singing. It hadn't taken him long to ask if he could take her home, but she had kept him at a distance for weeks before finally saying yes.

Leah darted a glance at Sara, noticing the lowered chin and flushed cheeks. She was fair and redheaded, freckled and delicate in manner and appearance. Leah had a hard time imagining Sara tending a challenging farm alongside her husband, much less bearing children and handling a home, but she could understand Sara's sweet nature attracting Daniel.

Sara swallowed and lifted her gaze to the road ahead. "Daniel's making progress on it. He had some friends come and help him last week. They painted most of the rooms so the house is ready for our furniture now."

Both girls lapsed into silence while Leah concentrated on a particularly dangerous curve and hill that hid their buggy from any traffic coming upon them. Sara shifted sideways to keep an eye out for fast-moving cars and trucks on the highway behind their buggy, her fingers clenched over the back of the seat. Leah realized her own knuckles were white and forced herself to relax her grasp on the reins.

Once they crested the rise and started down the other side, the remaining route into Ashfield was flat and straight.

Leah sighed in relief. There shouldn't be as much danger now, as long as Sparky behaved himself and cars were careful of them. The locals were adept at watching for the black buggies, but visitors, distracted by phones or unfamiliar routes, sometimes overtook the slow-traveling vehicles and the results could be fatal. On occasion, even the Amish forgot to be cautious. One time, her uncle absentmindedly turned his horse and buggy left into the side of a passing minivan. Luckily, no one was hurt, but his horse suffered an injury that took time to heal. Sharing modern roads with *Englishers* was never an easy situation.

Sara's continued silence brought a question to Leah's mind: Could she have heard about Martha? Had the community gossip caused Daniel's fiancée to wonder about Leah's association with the rebellious teen?

It wouldn't surprise her. Rumors flew through Amish communities quickly, and Leah had no doubt that Martha and Abe's doings provided much fodder for gossip and innuendo. Martha might even be disciplined soon; most everyone had already given up on Abe.

At last the two young ladies reached their destination. The fabric store was busy when they entered. Amish and English women mingled together in the crowded store, their lively chatter creating a loud buzz of conversation. Sara and Leah meandered through the rows of fabric bolts until they found the calicoes and plain fabrics at the back of the shop.

Leah waited patiently while Sara searched through the variety of bolted blues, leaning one against the other while she fingered the heft and weight of the materials. She settled on a plain length of fine cotton in a robin's egg hue.

"This is perfect. I love the feel of the fabric, too."

Leah nodded. The weight of the woven cloth created a lovely drape. To be sure it fit with the *Ordnung's* rule that the textile not be sheer, she stretched the blue fabric over her hand and held it to the light. "See? Nothing shows through. This ought to be okay."

Sara waited for the fabric to be measured and cut, then gathered the tissue-wrapped bundle and followed Leah out the door.

"Do we have time to stop by the grocery?" Sara held the packaged fabric to her brow, sheltering her eyes from the harsh afternoon sun.

Leah considered. It would take another thirty minutes to return home, but the day was still young.

After untying Sparky, they made their way slowly through the downtown traffic, the horse's shoes clopping against the hot roadway.

The grocery parking lot was full of cars, but at the back under the shade of several gnarled maples, hitching posts waited for the horses and buggies of Amish customers.

She hopped down and secured Sparky's reins to the post as Sara headed into the store. The sun shimmered over black asphalt and reflected off metal hoods and trunks, and Leah wiped beads of perspiration from her neck and forehead. Sparky shook his mane free of flies, his haunches quivering from gnat attacks. Leah smoothed his neck, whispering into his ear as he rolled brown eyes toward her voice. "We won't be long, friend." He stamped a time or two, signaling his impatience, as she walked into the building.

The cool air of the store immediately brought relief. Not for the first time, Leah longed for respite such as this at home. Wondered how it would feel driving along on a steamy summer day, passing farm and field, with sweet cool air keeping the journey pleasant. Wondered how it would feel to sleep without her sweat-drenched gown and sheet. Her upstairs bedroom, situated at the back of the house above the woodstove-heated kitchen, was sultry and stagnant by the end of a summer's day.

She glanced at a group of girls who looked to be her age. They wore shorts and sleeveless T-shirts, their hair pulled off their necks and secured with bright ponytail bands, their feet protected only by flimsy sandals that slapped the floor as they strolled. They looked refreshingly comfortable.

She pondered why the Amish insisted on stifling dark fabrics and long cumbersome dresses weighted down by aprons and thick-soled black shoes. They dressed not for season but for modesty, and often, at the end of a blistering summer day, her skin was chafed raw from sweating. She swished her skirt back and forth to cool her legs and blew a puff of air up over her forehead as she pushed damp strands of hair back under the *kapp*.

Lost in thought and eyeing the store aisles for signs of Sara, she was startled when a man spoke to her.

"Hello, Leah. *Wie gehts?*"

She glanced around and met the kind eyes of Matthew Schrock.

"Oh! Hello, I'm sorry I didn't see you. I'm fine, thanks."

Matthew pointed to a petite, attractive woman walking toward him. "I'd like to introduce you to my wife, Naomi."

Naomi Schrock reached out her hand to greet Leah, smiling shyly. "Nice to meet you, Leah."

"You, also."

"I've heard from Matthew about the wonderful work your *daet*'s doing on our bedroom suite. I can't wait to see it."

Leah noticed Naomi's Amish accent. Were the rumors true? Were they both former Amish?

"Thank you. He's skilled at his job."

After chatting about the weather for a couple of minutes, Leah decided that talking too long with them could be construed as a bad thing, if they were the kind of people the bishop insisted they were. As she nodded good-bye to the Schrocks, Matthew stopped her.

"Before you go, would you mind if I give you a brochure of our life story?"

Leah hesitated, not sure how to respond. "Uh . . . I suppose it would be okay."

"It's not a very long brochure, but it will let you know, if you're curious, about our ministry."

Matthew offered a steady gaze. "I'm aware there are many rumors about us, and I thought it might help to explain what we do."

She realized he must know about the bishop's opinion.

"Thank you. I appreciate the information." She took the brochure and hurried to find Sara. Accepting the pamphlet from Matthew felt dangerous. But she was anxious to read about this man and his wife, and perhaps solve the mystery of who they were and what they did with wayward Amish. They seemed so kind and so sure of their decision to leave.

The girls finished their shopping and were soon on their way home. The weight of the brochure filled her apron pocket, but Leah stifled her curiosity long enough to drop off Sara before pulling the buggy to the side of the road to read the material.

The Schrocks had been born and raised Old Order Amish. They had married and joined the church, but a former Amish friend had introduced Matthew to the "life-giving grace of Jesus Christ," and after reading the Bible and learning more about Christ, Matthew had explained what he had learned to his wife.

The pamphlet was sprinkled with Bible verses. Leah was surprised to find them all in English. The Bible used in her Amish church was written in German, and only a few of the words made sense to her when it was read in service.

But this—these words struck her heart. The message in the brochure was of hope and freedom. Incredibly, it did not include anything about obeying the *Ordnung*. No long list of rules to adhere to—nothing about the length of her skirt or the size of the hat band her *daet* and *bruders* wore. She found no instructions about the kind of fabric her dresses had to be made from, or the color, or the amount of undergarments she needed to wear. No directions about securing her skirt and aprons with straight pins. Nothing at all about *verboten* buttons or zippers. There was nothing mentioned about being a certain kind of person in order to deserve or earn her salvation.

Leah furrowed her brows. Could it be so simple? The verses spoke of the futility of living only to do good—of trying to be the best for the sake of showing good works to God, family, and community. She flipped the pamphlet back to the front and read through the verses again. What would it be like to own a Bible she could understand?

She remembered a group of *Englishers* who had stopped by her school one year when she was in the elementary grades. They had handed out small New Testament Bibles written in English. What had she done with the book the Gideons had given them? It had to be among her childhood things somewhere.

She reread the verse on the front: "For by grace are ye saved through faith; and that not of yourselves: it is the gift of God: Not of works, lest any man should boast."

What could that mean? Leah wasn't sure but knew it had something to do with her desire to be free from the *Ordnung*. Could that ever be a good thing? Maybe this was the answer she'd been looking for.

Or maybe Matthew Schrock really was a sinful and treacherous man trying to lead innocent Amish into hell.

❦

Leah carefully carried a frosty glass of mint tea and a neatly made sandwich on a tray to the shop. *Maem* had asked her to take *Daet* his lunch. The gnawing in her stomach reflected her worry that *Daet* had something to say to her.

To her relief, Jacob was working alongside *Daet*. She didn't think her father would air the family's dirty laundry in front of others. She hurried to the counter and placed the food within *Daet's* reach. He looked up, surprised she was there.

"*Maem* asked me to bring your lunch today."

"Yes. I see. Jacob and I have more work to do, Leah, but I'd like you to come back later—in about an hour." He turned his back, dismissing her.

The curt reply in front of Jacob embarrassed her. *Daet* was angry or he wouldn't have spoken like he did, but his censure fanned a spark of her own anger. Impulsively she stopped, hand on the doorknob.

"Jacob, I heard Martha and Abe went to Richland yesterday. They watched every movie at the theater. They spent the whole day there, and then they went to the mall and both of them bought new blue jeans. Martha said they had a great time."

She knew her observation would bait *Daet*. Knew it, and for the moment didn't care. Her only thought was to shock him, to defy him and the rules he represented. "I wonder what a movie is like."

Jacob turned a piece of wood over several times before he met her gaze. Leah hoped he would side with her like any Amish teen would. But he dropped his gaze when *Daet* swung around and tossed a two-by-four onto the pile with a heavy hand.

Daet's eyes scorched Leah like hot coals. He pursed his lips and sighed as he strode across the shop.

"You're forbidden to talk with that . . . that . . . *Martha* again until she comes to her senses and stops this nonsense." He pointed a finger in her face. "*You* want go to a movie, too, eh? *You* want to wear jeans and dress ungodly, too? No more of this! No more Martha, and no more talk of acting like an *Englisher. Verstehen mir?*"

Leah chewed her lip and dipped her chin. Her eyes filled with tears as she fled the shop.

She instantly regretted the humiliation she'd inflicted on herself and *Daet. What have I done?*

In the kitchen, Ada and *Maem* were canning the last of the freezer cherries as preserves. The moist heat from the kettles and woodstove made the kitchen nearly unbearable, but the women worked on.

"Just in time." *Maem* wiped her brow, smiling now that the hard task was nearly over. "Can you stir this while I work with Ada on the rings? We have another few hours to go, and then we'll be finished for another year."

Leah picked up a long metal spoon, its end coated with cherry juice, and slowly stirred the bottom of the pot where the cherries tended to stick. She'd have to say something to *Maem* about going back to the shop.

"*Daet* wants me to come out in an hour."

"Why?"

She cleared her throat. "He . . . wants to talk with me."

Maem squinted. "And?"

"I . . . said something I shouldn't."

Maem groaned. She turned back to her work. "Will you *never* learn? I'm going with you."

Leah spent the next hour helping *Maem* and Ada, but she knew there would be a price to pay for her sassy comments. Ada cut her eyes back and forth from the pot to Leah, trying to get her sister's attention. *What happened?* she mouthed when *Maem*'s back was turned, but Leah shook her head.

At last, they heard Jacob's buggy pull out of the barnyard. They worked a few minutes more, and then *Maem* put down the kitchen towel and motioned for Leah to follow her.

"Ada, please wipe down those jars before you add them to the cooling table, and if you don't hear one ping as they seal, put it aside so I can check it."

When they approached the shop, Leah could hear *Daet* working the lathe; the sharp whir of the spinning machine filled the air inside the wood shop. Leah watched the curls of wood fall to the floor in a pile of rejected shavings. *Like me.*

He glanced up as they entered, finished trimming the piece of cherry with the sharp blades, and then shut off the switch to the gas-powered machine that sat outside. He walked slowly to stand beside *Maem*, but frustration lined his face.

Her parents looked at her steadily for a second before *Maem* sat on the high stool behind the counter. *Daet* motioned Leah to the chair usually reserved for customers as he leaned above her at the edge of the desk. Instead of meeting his eyes, Leah studied the wood shavings that clung to the bottom of his dark pants.

"What you said today in front of Jacob Yoder tells me Martha Mast is no true friend to you."

She cocked her head and drew her eyebrows together. "But *Daet*—"

He cut her off with a wave of his hand. "Otherwise, she wouldn't tell you such things. She wouldn't try to entice you into the sinful world she's playing around with. Satan has gotten a grip on her and Abe Troyer, that's for sure. A true friend wouldn't try to seduce you to the ways of the world. And you're listening to her. *Maem* and I mean to put a stop to this."

He shifted uncomfortably as he fixed his gaze on her. "I've tried to tell you Martha is close to being disciplined, but you haven't listened. Now I insist you don't see her anymore. Not one more time. Do you hear me? If you keep on this way, I will beat the rebellion out of you, if I have to."

Leah's eyes widened, startled. *Daet* had never promised that kind of punishment before. Would he really beat her? He had used his belt on occasion when his kids were younger, but he hadn't swatted even Benny in the last couple of years. Leah rubbed her sweaty hands on her dress. She could feel her whole body shaking.

Daet glanced at *Maem*, and she nodded agreement. He pulled at his beard, his voice softening. "You have to see, Leah, Martha's *rumspringen* is much more serious than the others'. They drink and smoke and maybe party a little, but Martha and Abe . . ." He left the sentence unfinished as he frowned.

"She and Abe are driving their parents to tears and causing them trouble with Bishop Miller," added *Maem*. "The elders and Bishop Miller will be meeting with both families soon to discuss how to discipline them. You can't be seen with her, Leah. You can't," she implored.

"*Maem*, Martha is my best friend. How can I not talk to her? You don't know what she puts up with in that house, too. If you knew what I saw her stepbrother do, you'd have pity on her—I can't abandon her now. She needs a friend—"

"No!" *Daet* banged his fist on the desk, causing *Maem* and Leah to jump, then stood and stalked to the door. "I've had enough of this kind of nonsense. You do what's right, and I mean it! One more question, one more sinful notion, one more sign of disobedience from you, and . . . I'll . . . I'll call the bishop myself."

He pivoted and marched out the door, letting the screen bang shut behind him.

Leah trembled.

Maem played with a paper on the desk. "He loves you. We both do. We're only doing this to save you from the grip of the Devil. You don't want to be like Martha; we know that. Just listen to *Daet. Please.* Go and think about this. Decide you'll settle down and join the church. Please, quit giving us so much grief." *Maem* wiped her eyes with the corner of her apron.

Leah dropped her chin. Tears fell on her cupped hands. She promised to try harder, to not ask questions or see Martha.

Maem nodded and stood. "We need to finish those preserves, and I have to start supper. Come in and help when you've pulled yourself together." She walked slowly to the shop door, her shoulders hunched.

It hurt Leah to see *Maem* looking like that. She knew she had sinned against her parents and the church. She knew the desire to be free was wicked and selfish.

But what really disturbed her was the sinful lie she'd just told to her parents, telling them she would think things through, would think about joining church. Though she truly didn't want to hurt her parents, the pressure to conform to the rules pressed in on her so much that she couldn't breathe.

Leah stared out the window at the summer scene beyond. Birds were singing their songs in hidden nests while a swift honeybee darted between rich-hued violets. The sun shone bright white, and the warm air slowly turned the windmill that brought water to the kitchen pump. Even though it was a beautiful and tranquil summer afternoon, shadows of apprehension clouded her mind and her stomach churned.

She sighed, walked to the door, and headed back to the kitchen. Tonight of all nights, it would be best not to keep *Maem* waiting.

Chapter Four

The summer days passed into autumn. Leaves slowly changed colors and dotted the hills with oranges, reds, and brilliant yellows as the air grew chilly at night. Leah managed to keep her feelings to herself through much of the harvest season, while even the neighbors who didn't farm helped the farmers. Life continued at its own pace. In the meantime, a few older youth in the community settled down and joined the church, though Leah noticed Jacob was not among the new members.

To Leah's surprise and relief, Martha escaped harsh discipline. She had to confess one Sunday to the sin of going to see movies, but the rest of her actions appeared to be ignored. And she seemed to be controlling her worst behaviors, too.

Forgiving those who repent had always been one of the Amish church's most important instructions. Those who confessed their sins before the church were forgiven in glad relief. Martha had done this, but Leah sensed *Daet* didn't trust her confession. Since she had been disciplined and accepted the church's decisions, he reluctantly allowed the visits between the friends to resume. But he kept a polite distance when Martha came by.

One fall day, *Maem*, Ada, and Leah aided in the preparation of food for field workers at the Bontrager barn raising just a few miles from Martha's house. Leah was happy to see Martha there, too, so they quickly became a team. After working diligently to help serve the men, the friends stood in line with the women for lunch. Leah and Martha cooled their faces with paper fans and chatted about the young men they'd watched that morning. Most of the older women sat at one of the long tables, but Martha motioned to a table away from the others. An old, shagbark hickory tree cooled the air and provided much-needed shade.

"Do you think you're ready to join the church?" Leah nodded to a couple of teens in a group nearby. "Tobe and Rebecca are taking instruction right now. They're younger than both of us."

Martha gazed a long time over the surrounding fields before her gaze finally met Leah's. "I don't know. I haven't seen Abe in a few weeks. He took an apartment in Ashfield and is living with a group of ex-Amish guys. He gave me this before he left." She palmed a tiny cell phone, its bright, shiny red color totally out of place against Martha's dark, plain dress.

"Martha—have you been using that?"

She giggled. "Of course, silly. With Abe gone, how else can I talk to him?"

"Then you're not really planning to settle down and join the church?"

She shook her head. "Like I said, I don't know. I don't want to leave my younger sisters, but . . ." She left the sentence unfinished.

After a minute of silence, Martha slipped the phone back into her apron pocket and leaned close. "If I tell you something, will you promise not to say anything to your *maem* or to anyone else?"

"Well—"

"You have to promise." Martha whispered firmly. "I mean it!"

Leah watched her friend's troubled face and, thinking about what she'd witnessed in Martha's room, reluctantly agreed. "Okay. What is it?"

She ducked her chin and fixed her gaze on the tops of her black shoes. "My stepbrother . . . he . . . he's been doing *bad* things to me." Tears gathered at the corners of her eyes.

It took a minute for the meaning to register, but then Leah took note of the flush that had slowly spread from Martha's neck into her cheeks as she told her secret. Shivery tingles covered Leah's body as she recalled what she had seen in Martha's bedroom. Her heart beat faster as her mind conjured up even worse scenarios than she had witnessed.

"You mean—"

Martha nodded.

"Abner?"

Martha glanced around and leaned closer still. *"Ja,* you saw him. It's Abner."

The awful scene in Martha's bedroom suddenly made sense, especially the way her friend had acted, the way Abner had treated her, the things he said to Leah as he left the room. The puzzle pieces came together, forming a terrible picture. Leah's stomach twisted.

She reached for Martha's hand. "You *have* to tell someone."

Tears fell from her gray eyes, but Martha shook her head. "I've told *you,* Leah, so you'll understand when I leave someday."

Knowing now what her friend endured at home, Leah could understand why Martha wouldn't consider staying Amish. Why had she confessed to the church, agreed to all the rules, and stuck around her chaotic family? She had the perfect excuse to get out.

"You should tell on him," Leah pronounced.

Martha shook her head. "No. I'm afraid he'll start on my younger sisters if I tell. *Maem* suspects something, but she looks at me like it's *my* fault. I tried to tell her—I tried, but she turned her head away before she heard everything. She told me I should try harder to be good. *I* should 'be more pure in thought and manner,' is how she put it." Martha swiped tears off her cheeks. Her hands clenched her apron.

"Abe wanted me to leave that night, and I planned to, I really did, but then I saw my little sisters, and well, I just couldn't do that to them, Leah."

"What about you? How are you avoiding Abner? You live in the same house."

"Abe took me to town. I told him I wanted a lock for my bedroom door. Now I lock that door every night."

"You said you're worried about your sisters. Has he bothered them since you've locked him out?"

"They're too young! He wouldn't!"

Leah could see that Martha hoped her words were true.

"If he marries soon, they'll be safe." Martha's voice wavered.

Leah couldn't imagine the pain her friend was going through—

violated by her own stepbrother! How could Anna Mast allow such a thing?

⚜

Everything changed for Leah after Martha revealed her secret. She spent nights wondering how Martha could stand living in her home, day after day after day. She was furious with *Daet* when he showed an unforgiving attitude toward her friend. She fought the urge to scream, *"Don't you know what she's going through?"*

On a day not long after the frolic, Martha dropped off a couple of dozen sugar cookies she'd baked. Leah's family was in the living room when she came, and Leah was dismayed when *Daet* took the plate of cookies without so much as a simple thanks. Even *Maem* frowned as she watched him leave for the kitchen without a backward glance at Martha.

Leah clenched her hands, remembering *Daet*'s rudeness. Sometimes she tried to justify his behavior by reminding herself he had no idea what was going on in Martha's home. Her sacrifice for her sisters by remaining in that home went totally unnoticed by everyone—everyone but Abe and Martha, Leah, and Anna Mast. And Abner.

⚜

One night, as she lay in bed thinking of Martha, Leah remembered the pamphlet she'd been given by the Schrocks. She crawled out of bed and crept across the cold floor to the dresser, rummaging through her drawers until she found the pamphlet. She took it to the window and pulled back the curtain. As she scanned the brochure, she squinted in the dim light to read the paragraphs, looking for a line she recalled reading once before. There it was: *Mission to Amish People provides counseling to those who have been victims of sexual abuse.*

"God, if You hear me, please help me know what to do. Help me know what to say to Martha. Please, God." Tears slid down her cheeks as she slipped back to bed with a strong resolve to tell *Maem* everything tomorrow. She'd promised Martha she wouldn't tell, but she couldn't bear this burden alone. Someone else had to be told what was going on in the Mast home. Surely, the church and the bishop would help Martha once they knew what was happening.

She closed her eyes, but Abner's angry face filled her thoughts. Her heart pounded when she recalled his features as he struck his stepsister. He was evil, and Martha needed her help. She needed *God's* help. "Where are You, God?"

⁓❦⁓

Morning came and, with it, a brilliant sun burning through the limp curtains at her window. Leah squinted as she rolled out of bed. Her limbs were leaden as she slowly dressed, pulling the hot modesty slip on first and then her dress. The straight pins she used to close her dress pricked her shaking fingers, and she sighed in frustration. *What was so sinful about buttons?*

Finally, she had her hair up and pinned smoothly. She pulled the apron over her head last and leaned down to tie the laces on heavy black shoes.

Maem was pulling bread out of the wood-fired oven as she came into the kitchen. The smells wafted over her, her stomach growling in anticipation. *Maem* pointed to two thick pieces of fresh bread, lightly toasted. A pot of apple butter sat nearby, enticing her to spread the thick, sweet confection on the warm toast. Her six-year-old brother, Benny, had finished his oatmeal, and *Maem* rushed him along so he wouldn't be late for school as Ada came into the kitchen to grab her light cape off the hook by the back door.

"Get your lunch, Benny, now hurry!" *Maem* prompted.

The commotion of the departing siblings kept Leah's mind occupied while she slathered apple butter on the toast and poured herself a cup of hot tea. The kitchen quieted. *Maem* stood, waving her children down the drive, and then she came back in, shaking her head.

"That Benny," she chuckled. "He asked if he could take his rabbits to school because they're studying farm animals. He thought it would be fine to keep them in his desk all day. Poor bunnies. It's a good thing I caught him trying to stuff them in a paper bag before he left for class."

Leah chuckled, smothering the laugh with a big bite of spicy apple and crunchy toast. *Maem* puttered back and forth between the table and sink before Leah finally got the nerve to bring up what was on her mind. "*Maem*, could I talk to you for a minute?"

"Sure. Let me finish these dishes and get the counter wiped up. I need a second cup of coffee this morning, anyway."

Leah sat silently while *Maem* quickly did the chores, poured herself a hot cup of coffee, and plopped down with a sigh across from her. "I think Benny being a late baby shows my age more." She grinned. *Maem*'s rosy cheeks and soft brown eyes glowed with love and contentment. "Now, I'm ready. What's bothering you?"

"Someone told me something a few days ago that really shocked me."

"*Ja?*"

"This person told me . . . um . . . they have a problem at home." She glanced up as worry passed over *Maem*'s face.

Maem set down her cup of coffee. "Who is this person, Leah?"

"I promised I wouldn't tell, but this is a bad thing, so I don't know if I should keep the promise."

Maem picked up her coffee, sipped, and winced as she swallowed the hot brew. She fumbled for the cream pitcher and poured liberally, creating a billowing cloud across the black-brown surface.

Leah watched as she stirred the coffee to a light caramel color and then took another careful sip. "Tell me what this person said, Leah."

"She, I mean *they*, said someone in their home is doing things to them that aren't right."

"What kinds of things?" Her eyes widened as she guessed Leah's meaning. "Is this person Martha?"

"Yes. It was Martha."

"Was it some kind of abuse?"

Leah nodded.

"Abuse by beating? Or . . . other things?"

Again, Leah nodded. "And I saw her stepbrother, Abner, hitting her.

He was awful, *Maem*. It scared me. He's the one who is—abusing her—
in other ways, too."

Maem stopped talking and looked out the window toward *Daet's*
shop. In the silence, Leah heard the tick-tick of the wooden clock hanging over the sink. A faint rustle from trees scraping the window reached
her ears, and she turned toward the sound. The tree's shadow created a
pattern of leaves on the clean floor. "*Maem*, was I wrong to tell you?"

Maem shook her head slightly but kept her eyes on the window.
Finally, she faced her. "Why don't you get your inside chores finished so
you can be ready to help *Daet* in the shop today? He has a lot of customers scheduled to pick up their furniture. *Ja?*"

"Shouldn't I do something? About Martha, I mean?"

Maem thought for a minute but shook her head. "I know it's not what
you want, but we have to let someone know who can help her."

Maem motioned for her to get on with her chores.

As Leah reached the stairs, *Maem* added, "We must always be careful
when accusing another, Leah. I'll talk this over with *Daet*, and we'll
decide together what we should do next."

From the bottom of the staircase, she watched *Maem* as she stirred her
coffee over and over, and then closed her eyes.

She wasn't sure *Maem* believed her. Leah knew many in the community didn't believe a thing Martha said anymore, but her word—and
what Leah herself had witnessed—was evidence enough for Leah about
how Abner treated his stepsister.

Maem sighed and rose to rinse her cup at the sink. Leah went up to
her room, walked to the window, and waited for *Maem* to hurry across
the yard to the shop. Her pulse hammered at the thought of how *Daet*
would react.

❧

One afternoon a few days later, Benny begged Ada and Leah to play
Duck, Duck, Goose in the soft grass where the sun warmed the fallen
leaves. As the children's steps crushed the dry leaves, they released a
spicy, pungent aroma of autumn into the air.

Leah's attention was caught by a passing car. A teen girl waved from inside the shiny red auto. What would it be like to be inside with the *Englishers*? Would she love the freedom they seemed to enjoy? If she left her family and the Amish, their times together would be limited, maybe even forbidden. She plopped down in the grass and watched her siblings taunt each other, gazing also at the yard, shop, and house. The familiar corners of *Daet's* shop, the golden swell of the fields behind the house, the barn sitting so solemnly and importantly at the end of the lane—they all became dear and comforting to her in that moment. The thought of leaving them behind grew unbearable. She wondered if her doubts about the *Ordnung* could compare to the comfort of knowing this familiar world would be here now, tomorrow, and into the future. If she wanted it to be.

Leah's thoughts were interrupted when *Daet* came out of the shop, stopping on the threshold to turn back and lock the door for the day. He crossed the yard, greeted his younger son and daughter with a smile, and then turned to her. His smile faded, he clenched his jaw, and a shadow of resentment lit his eyes.

Her heart twisted, the disappointment on her *daet's* countenance dredging sorrow from her very bones. But as quickly as sorrow grew, her own flame of resentment sparked, swelling until it mirrored his.

So this is how it will be? From now on, failure will always be the first thing he thinks of when he sees my face?

"Leah, please come with me to find *Maem*. We have things to discuss." He walked ahead with assurance that she would follow along behind. And she did.

Leah glanced at his cold back and realized that the smiles she'd received from *Daet* in the past were all earned by her dutiful obedience. For the still-obedient Benny and Ada, he had smiles, but for her, only disdain. Apparently his one desire was for her to become a good Amish girl. As her brother had done before her, she was expected to accept her Amish role of church member. Then, as she matured, she would become a supportive wife and mother. *Daet* had never spoken to her of anything else, and indeed, his role as father did not require much more from him than to provide for her, show her the way to Amish spiritual acceptance, and be the final authority for her decisions.

Leah swallowed and hoped *Maem* would intervene. She had always been more attentive to Leah's emotional well-being.

Maem relaxed in the swing on the front porch, a mug of tea in one hand, and the Amish newspaper, *The Budget*, in the other. She looked up as they approached the porch, scooting over to make room for *Daet* to sit beside her. Leah took a seat in one of the two wicker chairs facing the swing.

Daet didn't waste any time. He tented his fingers and leaned forward with his elbows on his knees. "Leah, these accusations Martha is making; who does it involve?"

"She told me a name, but should I tell, *Daet*? She asked me to keep her confidence."

"I just need to know this: is she accusing her *stepdaet*?"

"No. Not her *stepdaet*."

His face relaxed a bit, and she noted his mouth softened, too. "These kinds of things have to be handled privately. First, *Maem* and I will talk with Bishop Miller. We'll ask his advice about what to do next, but I expect he and the elders will take it from there." His eyes squinted against the late afternoon sun slanting its way under the porch eaves. "Now, don't get upset with my next question, but you know Martha's behavior hasn't made her a very reliable source for this story."

She shivered at his words. Could it be that no one would believe Martha's account?

Daet cleared his throat. "Did you know she's been seen with a light in her bedroom window? Inviting boys up to her room?"

Leah shook her head, surprised and confused.

He nodded, smug to see he had surprised her and perhaps relieved she didn't know about *that* part of Martha's activities. "Yes. Evidently she had Abe up there."

"Abe? Why put her lamp in the window for Abe? She could just tell him to come by. Were they—bed courting?"

"No. Well, I don't know for sure, but I don't think so. From what I've heard, I think they sat at the little window seat she has in there. But it's not a good practice. I wouldn't allow *my* daughters to do that." *Daet* glanced at *Maem* and raised his eyebrows slightly. *Maem* momentarily turned her gaze away, her eyes scanning the fields across the road. A pink splotch flushed her neck at the top of her collar.

Leah knew a discussion like this was not something a good Amish mother expected to have in front of her husband. The girls usually learned about that part of life from whispered conversations with each other. Or worse, from the boys eager to teach them what to do. Leah had heard rumors for years about that, and about male family members who sometimes crossed lines with their sisters. Her stomach lurched. This entire conversation made her sweat. Suddenly, she thought of the advice one of her friends in school had been given by her mother about bed dating: keep your dress in place.

"We're hoping the bishop can get to the bottom of this," *Daet* continued. "If it's true, then something needs to be done. But if she's lying about this, Leah, it'll not go well for her with the church." His eyes held a glimmer of suspicion and disbelief.

So, what else is new? Leah squelched the ever-rising flame of anger in her. Why did she even bother telling *Maem?* She *knew* Martha wasn't lying, and if she added to Martha's burdens, Leah would feel awful.

She stood, stressed and tense. "I have a lot to do in my room. I'd better get to it."

As she went in the house, all she could think about was Martha. The possibility her friend might find out Leah had told her secret weighed heavy. And if Bishop Miller came down too hard on Martha or blamed her for the trouble, Leah doubted she'd be able to forgive herself. She wrung her hands, wondering if she'd done the right thing after all.

❧

After supper, Leah went directly to her room to search for the pocket-sized New Testament the Gideons had given to each student in the Amish school. After much digging, she finally discovered it in the bottom of a box in her closet, alongside sixth-grade papers and books.

She stretched out on her bed and opened the book to the first page.

"Matthew 1:1. The book of the generation of Jesus Christ . . ." She soon grew tired of reading the lengthy genealogy of Christ, and skipped to verse 18. "Now the birth of Jesus Christ was on this wise: When as his mother Mary was espoused to Joseph . . ."

Halfway into reading through the book of Matthew, the life of Christ took on new meaning. She didn't fully understand everything and wondered what it would be like to attend a Bible study where she could sit with others to discuss her questions.

Her eyes were gritty from reading in the dim light, so she lay the book aside and turned down the lamp.

As she closed her eyes, she wished the house had electric light to keep reading. She wanted to learn more, but mostly, Leah wanted to block out thoughts of Martha and what the bishop might or might not do.

She pondered the idea of contacting the Schrocks. Maybe *Maem* and *Daet* wouldn't mind if she asked the English couple for advice. And if Leah did her best to follow the *Ordnung*, maybe her parents would also allow her to ask about counseling for Martha and about the Bible study for herself. She yawned. She'd think about asking them. Tomorrow.

⸙

Ada roused her the next morning, but Leah was groggy as her sister perched at the foot of the bed and started to chatter. Ada's lively voice annoyed her sleepy ears. She talked about school, her friends, the coming wedding of their brother, and anything and everything else that popped into her head. Her tactic worked.

Leah struggled up from the covers and moaned, "Please! Stop, Ada. I'll get up, I promise. Just go away. *Please.*"

The girl laughed and pulled the covers off on her way out the door. "Come down for breakfast soon. *Maem's* making waffles. You know Benny will eat all of them if we don't hurry."

Her sister's shoes clattered loudly on the wooden steps as she hurried down to breakfast. Leah wearily wiped her eyes, and sat up.

As she put her feet on the cold floor, she thought of Martha once again. She decided to never tell another soul the secret entrusted to her.

She prayed *Maem* and *Daet* wouldn't mention it, either, or maybe the bishop wouldn't have time to listen to them.

Maybe she could get away to a Bible study, too.

She felt a little guilty for thinking of her own desires in the wake of Martha's problems, but it appeared nothing could stop the deep yearning to know more about God's Word. Whatever happened, she was glad she'd found the little New Testament. She carefully tucked it back into the box of discarded papers and planned to read more of it that night . . . in secret.

CHAPTER FIVE

Leah, what do you have planned for today?" *Maem* asked as they were finishing their last bite of breakfast.

"Nothing special, *Maem*."

"Would you be willing to take Ada into town? She needs to get tablets, pencils, and a folder for school."

"Sure." She looked across the table at her sister. "You almost ready?"

"I want to taste this last bite of waffle." Ada squeezed her eyes shut as she savored the tasty morsel. "Yum. *Maem*, you make the best waffles in the world." After Ada drank her milk and wiped her mouth, she pronounced herself ready and hurried off to grab her purse.

"*Maem*, about Martha," Leah said, taking advantage of the private moment.

Her mother reached a tentative hand to Leah's shoulder. "It's okay. The bishop said he will check into it soon. I think he is planning to head that way tomorrow."

Too late. The bishop is involved.

Leah walked to the barn with shaky knees. Readying the horse for the trip to town gave her time to think and calm her whirling thoughts.

It *couldn't* be bad for Martha to get help, could it? That should bring only good for her. *Please*, Gott, *please let things go well for Martha.*

❧

Sparky was feisty on the way in to Ashfield. Every time a car passed, he skipped to the right a little, and Leah had a difficult time managing him. He also wanted to trot faster than she was comfortable allowing, so she ended up pulling and tugging the reins more than usual. By the time the sisters got to town, Leah's arms ached from fatigue. She guided the horse to a hitching post and looped the reins.

Ada and Leah walked leisurely to the discount store and strolled among the aisles. It was good to be doing something with Ada. They giggled at a pair of silly-looking pens. Wispy hair glued to the top made the pens resemble wild people, and below the hair, googly eyes rolled around and around. It'd be fun to write with these, but the schoolteacher would never allow such worldly items in class.

After Ada chose her supplies, they headed to the checkout, pausing to choose a few candy bars for themselves and Benny.

As they walked back to the buggy, Leah spotted Naomi Schrock getting into her car across the street at the hardware store.

"Wait here, Ada. I'll be right back." Leah made her way through traffic easing past the stores and called to Naomi.

"Naomi! Hi—I have a quick question."

Naomi paused, turning to greet Leah. "Hello. How are you?"

"Good." Leah took a deep breath. "I was wondering about the Bible study. Is it at your house? And what time does it start?"

"Yes—it's at our house. It starts at 6:30. Are you thinking of coming?"

Leah nodded, looking behind her to the parking lot where Ada was watching her every move, pacing to and fro behind the buggy.

Leah swallowed a lump born of anxiety over this bold move. "I'll need to get a ride, but if I can, I plan to be there."

Naomi took out a small notebook and scribbled something on it. "Here's the address. Let me know if you need a ride. Maybe we can arrange something."

"Thanks. I'd better get going." She waved a hand toward her impatient sister. "Ada's ready to go on home."

"Okay. Hope you can make it. Bye."

As Leah sprinted back to the buggy, her mind reeled with what she had just done. She wiped sweat off her forehead and tried to relax her tense jaw. Having untied Sparky, she hopped in the buggy as her sister jumped into the other side. Leah tried to disregard Ada's bemused stare.

Once they reached the outskirts of town, Sparky settled down and trotted along easily. Leah glanced at Ada, who was grinning like Cheshire cat.

"Are you going to go?"

Leah frowned at her sister. "What?"

"Come on. I know why you talked with Naomi Schrock."

Leah shook her head. Trying to get something over on Ada was hopeless. "Didn't take you long to get to the point, did it?" she groused.

"Well? Don't change the subject—are you?" Ada persisted.

"I don't know. I'd really like to learn more about Scripture, and *Maem* says I should read our Bible, but it's in German and I just can't understand it like I want to. It can't be bad to learn about God. Can it?"

Ada shrugged. The Bible was a book to her. Leah could tell she thought there were far more interesting books to read.

They chatted back and forth most of the way home, with Ada cooking up ways they could sneak out of the house and places to meet or hitch a ride. Leah was uncomfortable playing this game, but as the conversation went on, she recognized she was storing away ideas for later. Maybe she *could* use one of these plans to get to a Bible study.

Guilt flooded her heart. Her palms sweat as she considered sneaking off.

As they turned down the road leading to the lane, Sparky sped up, intent on reaching the barn. Leah kept him tightly reined because she didn't want to get home too quickly.

"It must be really hard to be under the *meidning*," said Ada unexpectedly. "Even though they left many years ago, do you think the Schrocks still miss their families?"

She remembered the stories she'd read in the brochure the Schrocks had given her. "I think so. Naomi Schrock said she passed her *maem* on the street once, but her *maem* wouldn't speak to her—just smiled."

"That would be sad."

Leah's mouth trembled when she thought of being shunned. She couldn't imagine what it would be like not to be near family anymore, not to have *Maem* or *Daet* to talk with—or Ada, for that matter. Since the *meidning* extended to all family members, she'd have to sit at a different table away from her family.

But what if she never joined the church before leaving home, would they still shun her?

Once the buggy reached the lane, she let Sparky have his head, and the sisters leaned back on the seat, lost in their own worlds.

Leah was thinking about the Bible study, reading whatever verses she wanted and discussing with others just like her what it all meant. She took a quick look at her sister and wondered if Ada was thinking of going on to high school, maybe even college.

Ada spoke first, "Do you ever think about leaving, Leah?"

Leah hesitated, searching her sister's face to judge what she should share. She didn't want to be a bad influence, but she also didn't want to lie. She swallowed. "Sometimes. I want more freedom—I want to get out from under the rules, but maybe every teen feels that way. Do you?"

"I do. *Ja*, it does annoy me the way we're told exactly what to think and exactly what to do. And I'd love to go to school, maybe study science so I could be a nurse—or a doctor!"

Leah laughed at her sister's growing ambitions. It didn't seem right to keep a girl like Ada from learning everything she wanted to learn. What if she *did* have the ability to become a doctor? Why should Ada have to give that up just to fit in with all the past ancestors? As for herself, she could think of many things more dangerous and sinful than wanting to study the Bible in a language she could understand.

Without stopping to think, Leah blurted out, "I know *Maem* and *Daet* wouldn't like it, but I might call Naomi Schrock so I can go to the Bible study on Tuesday."

Ada turned rounded eyes to her sister. "You'll get in trouble if they find out, Leah."

"I know, but I want to go just once, to see what it's like—after that, I won't go anymore."

Ada thought for a minute and then grinned. "Me, too."

Leah immediately shook her head. "Now Ada—"

"No! I want to go, too, Leah."

"I'll get into trouble, for sure, if I lead you astray right along with me."

"We may as well be in trouble then, for no matter what we do, if we're even thinking of going, we're already in hot water. Being rebellious is a bad thing, you know."

"Rebellious? Who said anything about that?"

"That's what it'd be, Leah. Wouldn't it? That's how *Maem* and *Daet* and, for sure, Bishop Miller would see it."

She stopped talking. Leah didn't think going to a Bible study should be called *rebellion*. That seemed too strong a word for what she wanted to do.

Another example of a senseless rule.

⚜

Once Ada and Leah finished chores, *Maem* called them in to help prepare dinner. "Girls, can one of you bake the pie crusts so I can fill them after supper? Joe-Ida sent a good amount of berries to me today. Won't a piece of pie taste *gut* later? And I need someone to peel these potatoes so they can be boiled and mashed."

Leah placed the pie crusts in the oven, then perched on a stool near her mother. She glanced at Ada, and her sister winked. She'd guessed what Leah was about to do.

"*Maem*, remember when I told you the Schrocks have a Bible study at their house?"

Busy with her work, *Maem* nodded distractedly.

"Um . . . I was thinking . . . that is . . . I was wondering if it'd be okay for me to go—just this once—on Tuesday?"

"Me, too," Ada jumped in.

Maem stopped what she was doing and looked first at Leah and then at Ada. She shook her head in disbelief and frowned. "Why are you bringing this up? You know what *Daet* and I said about that, Leah—and you, Ada! Since when do you know anything about this . . . this *Englisher* Bible study?" Her cheeks reddened below furrowed brows.

Maem placed her hands on her hips. "No more about this now. Get the idea right out of your heads and don't dare bring this up with your

Daet. I'm done dealing with this, and I suspect Martha has been talking to you again, Leah. And one more thing—"

Maem pointed at her. "You have things you don't like about our ways—things you want to do that the *Ordnung* forbids. Go ahead then, do your rebellious acts if you have to, but don't include your younger sister." She glared at Leah and stomped out of the kitchen.

Leah's face blazed, humiliated by *Maem's* unusual outburst. She dropped her gaze to her shoes, trying very hard to control the now familiar resentment uncurling in her heart.

She glanced up at Ada. Her younger sister was peeling potatoes, cheeks slightly pinker than normal, but showing no apparent qualms. How did she did do that? How did she not lose her temper at *Maem's* lecture?

Leah turned away and left the kitchen abruptly. She had to get out of there before she said something she'd regret. For now, she'd drop the idea of going to the Bible study, but in her heart, the longing still burned.

❧

The following Sunday, the community gathered at the Masts' farm for services. Leah saw no sign there may have been trouble with the bishop. She was hoping to have a chance to talk to Martha alone, but she didn't see her friend right away. As families arrived, buggies were unhitched, horses tended, and greetings extended. Leah took her mother's jars of recently preserved bread-and-butter pickles to the kitchen. It was their family's contribution to the traditional church *suppah* of *bubbli* soup, red beets, bread, peanut butter spread, and pickles.

She still had not spotted Martha as the men and boys lined up in the barnyard, preachers and bishop, oldest to youngest, in line and in control. They filed into the machine shed, which had been cleaned from top to bottom and filled with rows of benches.

The women came next, falling into their queue as their husbands, brothers, sons, and uncles had done: oldest to youngest.

Leah studied the room as the women settled themselves on backless benches. Some immediately bowed their heads, showing reverence, while others gathered skirts and children near. Old and young, wide-hipped and slim-hipped wiggled into their spots, hoping to find a position tolerable to the numbing hours ahead. No concession was made for those in their later years; creaking bodies made the same brittle contact with hard unyielding wood as young bodies.

Starched and pristinely pressed *kapps* perched on the heads of women bowed low in preparation for the start of service. Men folded their long legs in against the benches, bare heads and scraggly beards bobbing right and left as they greeted their neighbors.

Many men and women leaned forward, resting their chins on hands supported by their knees. Mothers wrestled their toddlers into a final submission, and a low buzz of voices hummed through the room.

Leah caught sight of Abner on a bench against the back wall among the *buves* who tried hard to suppress their youthful energies. The reverence of their elders was not matched on the faces of these young men. They had spent their morning getting in a last smoke, a last joke, a last burst of joviality before having to endure the three hours of sermons and hymns. Their eyes smoldered with a myriad of emotions: boredom, restriction, strong-armed vigor, resolution, and smugness. Abner stared straight at Leah with spite-filled eyes.

She flinched and jerked her gaze from his malevolent glare. Martha was still not in the room, and Leah fretted something had happened after all. Abner's surly expression cast a shadow over the room like an oncoming storm. Leah locked her gaze on Jacob, and his warm smile calmed her spirit. Finally, Martha sauntered in, settling into the back row of women, her demeanor distant and distracted.

Before Leah had the chance to catch her friend's attention, the first preacher stepped forward and started the service. The rising and falling inflection of his voice lulled Leah quickly into a haze of gloomy considerations.

That morning at breakfast, Leah had sensed her parents were reluctant to go to church at the Masts'. She wondered if they were thinking of the deep shameful sin they feared was harbored in that household. But being the good Amish people they were, they had not wanted to disappoint the Mast family or Bishop Miller, so they came anyway.

Leah contemplated a plan to attend the Bible study, glancing at her neighbors as she imagined their reactions if they knew her thoughts.

The service seemed unusually long, with the preachers dwelling on obedience to the *Ordnung*, of being a help and not a hindrance to the community. They stressed the importance of always obeying parents. Always putting the needs of others first.

Preacher Byler looked directly at the youth during the third and final sermon. Most of the *jungen* missed his pointed stare as they had long since lowered blank eyes to the floor and hunched their shoulders to their ears, shutting out the admonitions with daydreams and strategies.

By the time the service was over, Leah's back railed at the long hours of stiff sitting, and her head throbbed from thirst and hunger. She shuffled through the line and out of the building, looking across the yard for any sign of Martha. Finally she spotted her friend serving mint tea to the men. When Martha walked back to the kitchen to refill the tea pitcher, she waved and waited for Leah to join her. "I can't talk right now, but after we eat, meet me back at the potting shed. I'll give *Maem* the slip while she's busy redding up with her friends."

Leah waited with her mother until the men had their fill, then ate the same church supper she'd eaten her whole life. Martha was kept busy filling cups and passing soup. In a way, Leah was glad not to have her friend sit down beside her. Her parents were already watching the two of them with eagle eyes.

Once *Maem* wandered off in search of Anna Mast to offer help in cleanup, Leah slipped off to the shed, shuffling along in seeming disinterest for anything other than enjoying the crisp sunny day. The inside of the shed carried an atmosphere of leftover fragrances from summer. The push mower and sickle conveyed fragrances of green grass and pungent wild onion cut down in their prime and reluctant to be forgotten. Here and there, Martha's parents had stacked moss-covered clay pots. Peat and potting soil aromas added to the earthy surroundings.

She pulled an old wooden stool out from under the potting table and sat down to wait for Martha. Her gaze drifted to the little square window overlooking the back yard where she could view the assemblage of Plain folk. The men were standing or sitting in groups, discussing their crops or other important issues, and the women held squirming children and shared gossipy stories of the neighborhood. All of them appeared peaceful, calm, and purposeful. She knew, however, the niggling fears many of them carried: fear of breaking the *Ordnung* . . . fear of disappointing their bishops or lay preachers . . . fear of the modern world . . . fear of questioning and of those who questioned . . . and most of all, fear of not going to heaven.

As this thought crossed her mind, she was struck by the blunt truth of it: they all feared not going to heaven.

Now why did I think that? The Amish are known to be the most religious group in America.

Yet she knew she was right. It was fear of falling short. Of not knowing if a person lived right enough or obeyed the rules enough or did enough kind works and deeds to get into heaven. According to the *Ordnung,* no one could know their eternal destination until death, so although death *should* be a happy homecoming for the good Amish person, it was instead a time of dread and fear.

Leah recalled a verse she'd read in her Gideon Bible; something about all falling short of the glory of God. But wasn't there a second part to that verse? Wasn't there something about the gift of God? She scrunched up her face, trying to remember.

She wanted to rush home to read the verse again, but that would have to wait. It was more important right now to warn Martha. She had to tell her friend that she had betrayed her trust—she had spilled Martha's secret to her parents. Leah regretted breaking her friend's confidence and longed to be told there had been no consequences stemming from her betrayal. Martha's actions as she served drinks to the folks in line had seemed calm enough. Maybe nothing had come of Leah's talk with her parents, after all.

"What are you looking so glum about?" Martha interrupted her thoughts as she came into the shed. She let the door bang shut behind her.

"Oh! You scared me! I didn't see you. I was . . . just thinking."

"'Bout what?" She pulled over a companion stool and wiggled onto it with a sigh. "My feet hurt from standing today."

Leah couldn't wait another minute. "I said something to my *maem* about what you told me—"

"What?" Martha's startled face blanched.

"I'm really sorry, but I've been so worried, and I felt like an adult should know about what your stepbrother's been doing—"

"Leah! Oh no. When did you tell?"

"A few days ago. Hasn't the bishop—"

"The bishop?"

"I'm sorry! I told *Maem*, and she told *Daet*. They went to the bishop."

Martha's pale cheeks glowed in the dim light of the shed. Her eyes darkened as she stared at her friend. "Oh no! Now what do I do? Abner— *and Maem*—oh no." She dropped her head in her hands.

Tears stung Leah's eyes as she witnessed Martha's distress. Remorse flooded her body. "So no one has said anything to you yet?"

"No." Martha groaned the word, her eyebrows drawn tightly together.

"Yesterday, *Maem* told me the bishop came by the house and asked my parents questions. He told them he was on his way over here."

"The bishop came here? Yesterday?" Martha jumped up. "Now it makes sense," she muttered as she paced. "I was trying to put the pieces together—the goings-on in my house this morning. Abner glared a hole in me at breakfast. *Maem* slapped my bowl of oatmeal on the table, wouldn't say a word to me. But I couldn't figure out *why* they were acting like that. They must have already talked with the bishop." Martha sat down again, staring into space.

Then she shook her head. "I wonder what they decided to do. Obviously, they didn't make Abner leave the house." She frowned. "Why didn't they talk to *me*? I wonder if that means they don't believe me? Leah!" Martha's eyes widened. "Do you think Abner—I bet he convinced them I lied! Do you think they believe him over me?"

Leah shrugged, guilt landing on her shoulders like a heavy weight. "Maybe they decided to wait until church was over today before saying anything. Maybe they'll talk to you when Abner goes to work tomorrow." Never had she felt more shame. "I don't know. I wish I did know what happened." She raised her eyes to her friend. "I'm sorry. So sorry."

Martha nodded, her voice a whisper as she held Leah's gaze. "I know you meant well, Leah. Maybe this is all for the best. *Gott* knows how often I've begged Him to help me with Abner. I don't know—could this be His way of helping me?" She shrugged. "I'll just have to wait and see, right?"

Silence grew between them. Finally Martha shook her head and rose to stretch her arms high over her head. "Let's talk about something else. How's it going with the Sunday night singings? Any fun coming from that? Any *buve* taking you home in the dark?"

Her voice held a mocking note, and a challenge glittered in her eyes. "No. Not yet. What's it like?"

Martha laughed. "Easy. You hop in a buggy and find a place to neck. No big deal. Any boy will ask you once they know what you're willing to do." When she noticed Leah's flushed cheeks, she pointed her finger at herself. "But I'm different. I don't mind the kissing and stuff. My life is such a wreck anyway, it doesn't matter what the boys think." She giggled and tossed her head. "With your parents the way they are, they'd have a thousand fits if they knew I told you that. What would they say? Tell you to leave me alone?" She squinted, her eyes holding a dare. "What would you say if a boy wanted to bed date?"

Leah swallowed hard, uncomfortable with the turn of the conversation. "I know what my parents think of bed dating—they don't like it and wouldn't allow it in our home."

Martha smirked, a hint of condescension in her expression.

Wanting to meet Martha's unspoken challenge, Leah blurted out her plans to sneak away to a place her parents had forbidden her to go.

Martha sat up straight, intensely interested. "Really? Where?"

Leah scuffed the toe of her shoe into the dirt floor, wishing she had never answered her friend's dare. There was no going back now.

"I heard about an English Bible study. I want to go, but *Maem* and *Daet*—"

Martha burst out laughing, her troubles momentarily forgotten. "Oh, Leah! I should have guessed. You're so funny! You talk of *Bible* studies? Whoa, you *are* rebellious!" She held her sides as more laughter rocked her.

Leah's face warmed, but she chuckled a little at her naive ideas. "You know it's forbidden; even if it is just reading the Bible. It will get me into trouble if I go. It's at an *Englisher's* place, and the Schrocks have a reputation of leading away Amish kids."

Martha caught her breath, slowly sobering. "I know of the Schrocks. They have a phone number you can call if you need help." She wiped tears of laughter from her cheeks. "I've heard of kids who leave the Amish, and the Schrocks try to help them. I've thought of calling them before." She held her finger up in the air. "Wait a minute. Maybe I should go to this Bible study, too. I could check them out—see if they're on the up and up, maybe find out if they can help me."

Was she serious?

Martha continued, "Do you think you could sneak over to Raysburg General Store on Tuesday?"

"I don't know. If *Maem* thinks I'm going there—"

Martha shook away her first idea. "No. Wait. I know something better. You could tell her Sara wants your help with the wedding plans, like the girls are getting together to help her with a quilt or something. Then you could meet me and Abe—he has his truck—and we could go on over to the Bible study." Her eyes lit with excitement.

Leah wasn't as excited as Martha seemed to be about the lies she'd have to tell. But she'd gotten Martha into trouble with the bishop, so it was only fair to help her find a way out. Besides, she could check out the Bible study, too. She chewed her lip trying to decide what to do.

"Okay. I'll be there a little before 6:30. How will you let me know about what the bishop decides, Martha? Can you come by after you hear?"

"*Ja*. I'll need to get the mail at the post office sometime tomorrow. If I know anything by the time I go, I'll tell you."

"And Martha, I really am sorry. I hope it all turns out for the good."

"No matter. Abner has had it coming for a long time. Now, at least, he knows I'll tell on him. Maybe that'll be enough to keep him away from me and from my sisters."

Leah glanced out the window and noticed people were leaving. "I'd better go find *Maem* and *Daet*. Looks like things are breaking up."

She said a hasty good-bye to Martha and slipped back into the crowd.

As she approached her family, *Daet* turned. "Where have you been? We need to get home, Leah." He looked around suspiciously, but as his gaze settled on Martha clearing the tables, his shoulders relaxed.

"I stretched my legs, *Daet*. Preaching goes on so long sometimes." Though she had made a remark against the preachers, she grinned to hide her feelings about lying. To her surprise, *Daet* nodded in agreement.

"*Ja*. We picked a few long-winded ones this time, for sure," he whispered.

On the way home, the family chatted and laughed. It was unusual for *Daet* to be so calm and happy after church—he usually had something to chew over that he'd heard from the other men.

She had a lot to think about as they drove home, so it took her by surprise when *Daet* turned around.

"You might want to make sure you get to the singin' on time tonight. I heard Jacob Yoder say he will be there, and he might be looking for you." He smiled at *Maem*, and she giggled like a girl.

All eyes focused on her. Ada grinned and gave her a friendly slap on the arm, while Benny hooted and kept it up until *Maem* admonished, "That's enough now, Benjamin."

Leah looked out the back flap, and all thoughts of her secret plans with Martha scattered like dust behind the buggy's wheels. All she could think about was tonight. Would Jacob ask to take her home? Could this night be the start of a new life for her? A life that would be satisfying. A life of contentment with her Amish heritage. A life filled with love for Jacob—and his love for her. Could the questions and desires that burned in her be settled by the love of a good Amish man?

CHAPTER SIX

After a relaxing day of reading, playing games, and napping, Leah's family had supper. It had been a typical church Sunday. Visits to family and friends usually happened on the off Sundays—the days when church services weren't scheduled. Most of the time, church Sundays were quiet days.

Leah and Ada washed the *suppah* dishes, and as eight o'clock drew near, Leah went up to her room to get ready for the youth singing. She made sure her *kapp* and dress were wrinkle and spot free, and tucked in a few wayward strands of hair. Finally, it was time to head to the Masts' place again. Daniel took her in his buggy, since he planned to meet Sara there.

A large crowd had already gathered when Leah and Daniel arrived. The church's young people, age fifteen or sixteen and older, gathered in the barn and talked for a while before Anna Mast called them in to the kitchen. They sat across from one another, boys on one side, girls on the other, and sang through song after song. Jacob caught Leah's eye from time to time, and she saw him whisper to his friend John. She wondered if he would send John over to ask if he could take her home.

Though she longed to have Jacob's attention, she was nervous. What if he wanted what Martha did with boys? Leah was sure she wasn't ready for any of that.

As the singing slowed and the popcorn and apples were passed, she watched John head her way.

He grinned as he came near. "Hey, you think you'd like Jacob Yoder to take you home tonight?"

She glanced around, wishing he had waited until they were outside. Right here, in spite of the mingling and loud chattering, she felt conspicuous. "Um . . . I guess that would be okay."

John chuckled. "Just okay? Should I tell him that?"

Leah flushed. "No—I mean, yes, I'd like that."

"Got it. He said to wait for him near the side door, and he'll bring the buggy along."

"Okay."

Nervous energy held sway with Leah the rest of the evening. She didn't know what Jacob's family expected: Did they hold with bed courtship? She was pretty sure most of the church folks in her district did not like bed courtship. Would he expect her to sit on the couch with him and kiss? She had heard such stories from older girls, but now that it was her turn, she was petrified of doing too much or too little. It was just as shameful to back away from courting as it was to go too far.

Maem hadn't been much help. She had never told Leah a thing about dating, courtship, marriage, or even about a woman's monthly cycle. She'd learned it all from friends.

At least when it's Ada's turn, she can ask me questions.

Finally the party broke up, and Leah tried to sneak off to the dark corner of the side door. But as she hurried away, Martha called to her. "Don't stay up too late, Leah. And make sure you keep a light going in the kitchen." She snickered when Leah shook her head. The girls gathered around Martha, gawking as Jacob pulled the buggy alongside her. When they rode off, she heard laughter and squeals from their peers.

The dark lane swallowed them in shadows quickly, and Leah was relieved that part was over.

Jacob reached around her and pulled a sweet-smelling quilt over her lap. So he had prepared. She smiled into the darkness at his thoughtfulness.

"Are you warm enough?"

His voice, deep and friendly, filled her with happiness. "Yes—I'm plenty warm."

They listened to the night sounds, punctuated by Bingo's hooves. He was proud of his rig and his horse. He took care of his animal and was gentle—unlike some she knew who drove their horses too hard and fed them scanty meals. *Daet* said it didn't make sense to treat horses that way: all that did was guarantee the need for a new horse sooner, rather than later. From what she'd seen, Jacob followed the same practice with Bingo.

"I hope you ignore Martha's teasing. And I want you to know up front that my family doesn't agree with bed courtship. 'Course, we don't go around spouting off about it, but none of my brothers or sisters did that. I plan to spend some time with you, get to know you, and leave. I know some people think being against bed courtship is too high church or proud, but my *daet* thinks it's too much temptation for *jungen*." He turned Leah's way. "Besides, I have to get up too early to stay out until four in the morning like some of these fellas do, and I need my sleep." He winked.

Leah breathed a sigh of relief and returned Jacob's smile.

Once they pulled into Leah's lane, the butterflies increased in her stomach. She noticed the lights were out in the house, except for a lone glow coming from the kitchen. Jacob let her off and then walked his horse to the hitching post. True to his word, he didn't unhitch Bingo and lead him to the barn. Instead he gave the horse water and then walked with Leah to the kitchen.

After she poured mint tea for both of them, they sat at the table and talked. He shared his dreams of having his own farm one day, and she listened as carefully as she could.

Every now and then, her heart lurched at his future plans, wondering if he was truly considering her a part of them. But she also knew there was something holding her back.

She still wasn't sure where her future lay—or even if she wanted to be Amish. But there was no denying the attraction she felt for Jacob. He was most definitely a different kind of Amish young man. Warm. Kind. Friendly. Not domineering or coarse. No bad language, and to her knowledge, no drinking or smoking.

As the clock chimed the midnight hour, Jacob scraped back his chair.

"I'd better get going. I'm glad you accepted the ride. See you next time, Leah."

"Yes—thanks for asking me."

She walked with him, and as he held the screen open for a minute, he seemed to consider something, but then grinned, put on his hat, and turned to leave. At the last minute, he leaned close and gave her cheek a quick kiss.

Out he flew into the barnyard, unhitched Bingo, and hopped into the buggy. Smiling, she waved him off, and closed the door. *That wasn't so bad. Made it through my first buggy date.*

⁂

All day Tuesday, Leah waited for Martha to send word about what the bishop and the elders had decided to do with Abner. She did her chores, went to the shop, helped *Daet* put his accounts in order, and prepared lunch, but still had no word from Martha.

At lunch, Ada kept looking at her but not saying anything. Once the dishes were put in the sink, and Ada began helping Leah clean them up, Ada leaned close and whispered, "I want to go, too."

Leah shushed Ada and frowned, ignoring the remark.

"Leah, I want to go with you tonight."

She shook her head, pressing her lips together firmly.

"It's not fair," Ada whispered fiercely. "I'm old enough to decide what I want to do—next year, I'll be out of school. I don't see why you won't let me come along tonight. It's just a dumb old Bible study."

Leah folded the damp towel neatly over the towel bar to dry and turned to face her sister. "Just how do you know I'm going? And why do you want to go if, as you say, it's a dumb Bible study?"

"I don't know—just want to is all. And you told me, remember? You told me the day and everything." She shrugged. "I just figured you'd find a way." She wrinkled her brows. "How are you getting there, anyway?"

Leah was annoyed. "Martha's boyfriend has a truck."

Her eyes widened.

"Now stop talking about it. *Maem* has already said I'm a bad influence for you. You can't come with me because I'll just get into the biggest trouble ever."

Ada rolled her eyes and gave up begging, but Leah wasn't so sure she'd really given in, and wondered what would happen when—or if—Martha came by with news. Would Ada try to figure out where they were going to meet?

Later that afternoon as Leah walked back from the mailbox, she spotted Martha on her bike. Her hair was covered with a work kerchief, but a few strands here and there pulled loose in the breeze and created a halo around her face with the sun behind her. Leah waved and smiled as her friend approached. When Martha didn't smile back, she feared the worst.

Martha brought the bike to a stop at the edge of the road where the driveway met the pavement. She leaned on the handlebars. Small sweat beads lined her face, and she tented her hands over her brows to shade her eyes from the bright sun. "He's going to be banned for six weeks, Leah. Then he'll be allowed to come back to church. Six lousy weeks—that's all they're going to do to him. And he looked at me like the cat that swallowed the canary." She was breathing hard, and tears rimmed her eyes.

"Not good, Martha. What do you think he'll do once the ban is lifted?"

"I don't know, but I'm sure he thinks he got away with it. I hope he doesn't start on my younger sisters. I just couldn't handle that."

She lifted her gaze to meet Leah's. She sniffed and wiped her angry tears. "But I can't do anything else, and at least the bishop knows now what to look for. The bad thing is they acted like I was lying. It took me several minutes to convince them." She sighed, her gaze resting on the surrounding fields. "They don't like me, Leah. I'm too rebellious—not Amish enough anymore."

She shrugged, but her eyes revealed her pain.

A buzzing sound interrupted their talk, and Martha reached into her apron pocket to flip the cell phone open, fully confirming what the church leaders suspected of her.

"Hi, Abe. Yep, it's over. I'm here at Leah's. We're talking about what the bishop decided. Uh-huh—he's banned for six weeks from church. That's all—yep. I plan to stay away as much as I can." Martha glanced at

Leah, then looked away. "She said she'd meet us at the general store in Raysburg, okay?" She turned back and whispered, "Six thirty?"

Leah hesitated, then nodded. The decision was made. She tried not to think about lying to *Maem* and *Daet*. The memory of *Daet*'s joke and *Maem*'s laughter from Sunday flashed through her mind, but she shoved the happy moment away. She'd never go through with it if she thought of things like that.

Martha flipped her phone shut and shoved it back in her apron pocket. "I gotta get going. *Maem*'s already hopping mad at me about Abner. She told me I had no business airing the family's dirty laundry. She said all girls have to put up with a little bit of uncomfortable attention at one point in their lives—better it comes from a brother than a stranger. Can you believe it?" Martha's face showed her disgust.

"How awful! Why would she say that?"

"I think she had it happen to her, too. She just doesn't know any better, I guess." Martha clutched the handlebars of the bike tighter. "It doesn't make sense. How can people be Christians and *do* stuff like this? Y'know?"

"I don't know."

Martha got back on her bike. "I'd better get going. Anyway, I'll see you tonight, okay?"

"Yeah. Six thirty. I'll be there."

She pushed off toward home but turned back once and waved. Leah waved to her and shuffled wearily back to the house. She was nervous and hoped anxiety didn't show on her face. As she entered the kitchen, Ada hurried over and repeated, "I'm going with you, Leah."

"Ada—"

"No, I mean it. I don't want you to get into trouble by yourself. If it happens, then it happens."

"It will be worse for me if you're along."

"I'll tell *Maem* and *Daet* it was my idea."

"For the last time, Ada, no! I mean it. Leave me alone, please. This isn't easy, and I'm not doing this just to disobey like you seem to want to do." She gave her sister an annoyed frown and walked away. Ada backed off, but Leah knew it wouldn't be the last time Ada would try to go along.

After supper, Leah sat on the porch swing for a while with *Maem*. The chill in the air made her think of Daniel's coming wedding, which led to the first lie of the evening.

"*Maem*, Sara might want me to come over and help her with some of the wedding things tonight. Is it all right?"

Maem stretched her tight muscles, nodding absently. "Sure. Just be careful coming home—it's dark earlier now. Are you taking Sparky out?"

"Naw, it's just a mile or two down the road. I'll walk."

"Be sure you stay well off the road. The drivers won't be able to see you. Maybe you should walk in the ditch. It will be dry."

"Okay, *Maem*."

"What time do you think you'll be back?"

"Oh, about nine, I guess. I don't know for sure."

Maem nodded, rising from the swing with a yawn. "I'm mighty tired, and I still need to nudge Benny to work on his school project and get ready for bed. Have a good time, Leah."

"Thanks, *Maem*."

After *Maem* went inside, Leah sat in the growing darkness thinking about what she was about to do. Her stomach rolled as she tried to justify her deception. She didn't know if she could keep this up. Lying and sneaking around were not part of who she was. If she lied, though, and died tonight, she'd go straight to hell; that much she knew.

She shoved the swing back and forth, back and forth with the toe of her shoe. The squeak of the hinges and the accompanying clang of chain against chain set a steady rhythm. She stopped suddenly, ready to get on her way. Just as she stood up to go inside, Daniel came out on the porch.

"What're you up to, Leah?"

She sat back on the swing, resumed swinging, and tried to sound nonchalant. "Oh, getting ready to take a walk."

"In the dark? Hope you're careful." He dug into his bowl of ice cream.

To change the subject, she asked Daniel about his plans for the evening.

"I'm going to go visit Sara, and then we're heading to her grandparents'.

They asked us to come over so Sara can choose a quilt from the ones her grandma's already finished."

Leah stopped swinging, a solid lump of fear filling her stomach. If *Maem* found out Sara wouldn't be home tonight, she would know Leah had lied. She couldn't go in and give *Maem* a different story now. She'd have to hope her parents never found out about Sara.

"Well, have a good night, Leah," Daniel said as he placed his empty bowl in her hands. "Mind taking this in for me? I'm late already."

"Sure."

"*Danke*, Sis." Daniel jumped from the top porch step and disappeared toward the barn.

She sighed and stood up. As she carried Daniel's bowl back into the house, her hands felt clammy at the notion of disobeying her parents.

The *Ordnung* stressed children should always obey their parents, not only while they were young, but for the rest of their lives—even when they were grown and married. To disobey them now would be a bad path for Leah to head down. But somehow, she couldn't ignore the urge to discover what the Bible study was like.

She'd burst from curiosity until she knew what went on. Maybe after tonight, her mind would be settled and that would be the end of the deceptions. She hoped so anyway.

Her hands shook as she rinsed Daniel's bowl. One thing was sure: she wasn't cut out to be conniving.

Chapter Seven

The yellow glow from the windows of Raysburg General Store fell across the ground in geometric patterns as Leah approached. She burrowed her hands beneath her cape to keep out the crisp autumn air, her shivering no doubt also brought on by nerves at her first outright rebellion.

A group of boisterous youth hung around the front door to the shop, but none appeared to be Amish. She walked to the building and carefully pulled open the heavy wooden door. The jangle of the bells over the door startled her. She entered and made her way to the candy aisle, glancing around to see if Martha was waiting.

She didn't see Martha or Abe, so she wandered back out to the benches that squatted under the shelter of the old building's eaves. She peered up and down the road, and just as she was beginning to think they weren't coming, she spotted Abe's old blue truck pull into the far end of the parking lot. Leah's heart pounded as she hurried to meet them.

"Hey there!" Martha greeted her. "Get in. This old truck will get you where you want to go, even if it doesn't look pretty."

"Okay." Her voice wobbled, uncertainty crowding her every thought. She climbed into the truck beside Martha. "Thanks, Abe, for taking me to the Bible study. I appreciate the ride."

He glanced her way as he pulled out of the parking lot. "No problem, Leah. I hope you have a good time." He snickered as if he'd made a joke.

It was clear Abe thought her rebellious trip was not worth the potential punishment, but Leah shrugged him off. She remained quiet the rest of the trip into town. It was only fifteen minutes later that they pulled into the Schrocks' driveway.

Several cars were already parked in front of the house. Her eyes widened with apprehension. Before she could change her mind, the side door of the house opened, and Naomi Schrock came out to the driveway. She waved to Leah and leaned over to smile at Martha and Abe. "Come on in, Leah. Your friends are welcome to come in, too."

Leah eyed Abe and Martha, but their disinterested faces gave the answer without having to ask them. Disappointed, she guessed Martha had already changed her mind about asking the Schrocks for help. "Martha, please, I'd love to have you come in with me."

Martha avoided Leah's eyes and shook her head quickly.

Abe leaned over, clearly pleased with Martha's response. "So what time do you want us to pick you up?"

"I'm not really sure, but how about an hour or so?"

"Okay. See you then."

"Thanks." Leah gave her friend's hand a gentle squeeze, then went to greet her host, a tentative smile on her face.

"Leah, don't worry. We're all friendly in this group."

"Thanks. I was hoping my friends would come in, too. Especially Martha. She needs help, but I guess she'll think of another way." Leah glanced down at her Amish clothing. "I feel kind of funny wearing these clothes."

"Remember, most of us once looked just like you. No one will judge you. It'll be all right."

She followed Naomi into the house, where Matthew Schrock greeted her. His broad smile put her at ease, and the other former Amish in the living room also greeted her warmly. Naomi led her to the kitchen, offering coffee and brownies. Leah poured coffee, adding lots of sugar and cream into the cup. As the milky concoction steamed, the scent of the coffee beans filled the room. The cloudy brew reminded her of *Maem*. *Better to not think of that now.*

The rest of the visitors found their seats, and Leah sat between Naomi and another girl who looked to be younger. The girl introduced herself as Mary. Her enthusiasm as she gave a testimony about God's grace to her during the week impressed Leah. Mary's face glowed with joy as she recounted her experiences.

"I tell you, if it hadn't been for the Lord, I just don't know if I could have left my family the way I did. But I felt I had to go back once to try to set things right with *Maem* and *Daet*. They weren't happy to see me at first. They told me I couldn't read my Bible at the table in front of my brothers and sisters, but I let them know I always read Scripture first thing in the morning. It sets my day off right."

"How did they take that news, Mary?" asked Matthew.

"They weren't happy for about a week, but then they calmed down. Before I left, *Daet* actually took the German Bible out and read it to the family at night."

"Do you think things were better when you left the second time?" asked Naomi.

"I like to say that when I left the first time, there were tears and nobody was happy, but the second time, everyone hugged and said good-bye. So I left with smiles the second time."

"Sounds like you did the right thing when you went back to try to make things right," said one of the young men sitting to Leah's right.

"Yes. I definitely think so, and now I have a *gut* relationship with them again. The Lord can do miracles with our families if we just let Him."

As she soaked in Mary's experience, Leah wondered if she would ever have the chance to make her parents understand what she wanted from attending Bible study. Would she also have an enhanced relationship with her parents if she understood God's Word better?

After the testimonies of a few of the other young people, Matthew led them in prayer, and then the Bibles were opened and the Scripture study began.

Matthew started off talking about the ABC plan of salvation. "The plan of salvation is really very simple. In the first step, the letter *A* stands for admit. Admitting that we are all sinners is the first key to salvation. Romans 3:23 says that 'all have sinned, and come short of the glory of God.' Notice that the Scripture says *all*. And Romans 6:23 makes it clear that because of this sin, the wages, or the price we must pay, is death.

But the verse goes on to say that the *gift* of God is eternal life." He passed around a small sheet with the letters on them.

Oh, the gift. That was the verse I was trying to recall from my Gideon Bible. Leah glanced at the paper. She'd have a reference to go to now if she was careful about not leaving it for *Maem* or *Daet* to find. They wouldn't want her reading Scripture on her own.

"In the second step, the letter *B* stands for believe. We must next believe that Jesus is God's Son and accept God's gift of forgiveness from sin. John 3:16 says 'God so loved the world, that he gave his only begotten Son, that whosoever believes in him, should not perish, but have everlasting life.'

"In the third step, the letter *C* stands for confess. This means we must confess our new faith in Jesus Christ as our Lord and Savior. Romans 10:9–10 says 'if you will confess with your mouth the Lord Jesus, and believe in your heart that God raised Jesus from the dead, then you will be saved.' It's a simple plan, really, and we can pray a prayer tonight with anyone who needs this plan of salvation."

Matthew spoke a little more about Christ, but Leah was barely listening. Instead she was wrapped in the words Matthew had read. Salvation was as simple as that? No rules to follow? No lifelong promise to obey the bishop and the church? No pressure to conform to the community and what was expected?

Leah glanced around the room, noting the relaxed faces and eager discussion. In her church, gatherings were often tense, especially for women. It wasn't easy to speak out in a group when she knew her words would be weighed by the bishop and others. It all added up to exacting measures in order to be good enough to earn heaven. But these verses, stating so simply that Jesus Christ had already paid the price for her sins, were like honey to her, feeding her soul with sweet meaning and freedom.

The hour passed quickly before she was suddenly aware of headlights flashing against the window. A horn blared twice, bringing Leah back to the real world. She realized her ride had arrived and rushed to gather her things.

"Leah, who's picking you up?" Matthew asked.

"Martha Mast's boyfriend, Abe Troyer. I didn't know how long this lasted, so I told them to come back in an hour. I'm sorry for interrupting."

"No problem. I hope you can make it again next week."

The group members told Leah good night and also encouraged her to come back.

As Leah hopped into the truck, Martha grinned. "So how was it? Feel pretty holy now?"

Leah laughed. "No. But it was good."

"Did they feed you anything?"

"Brownies and coffee. Good goopy brownies with frosting."

"Ahh . . . so the *Englishers* can bake?"

"I think Naomi made the brownies—"

"Oh yeah—I forgot, she's Amish."

Abe squealed tires as he maneuvered a corner. "That better not be no Amish house—with all those cars in the driveway." He spat out a rough chuckle. "I can stir up trouble with a bishop, if it is."

Martha punched Abe's side. "You dummy! They aren't Amish anymore." She turned back to Leah. "Were they nice?"

Leah nodded. "Yes, very, and so were all the others there."

Martha gazed out the windshield, saying nothing, but Leah saw the haunted look in her eyes. Her friend shook herself and waved a hand. "Not for me, though. I'm not getting mixed up with more religious fanatics. Dealing with Amish nuts is more than I can handle."

Abe snorted. "You can say that again. Glad we're getting away from them, babe."

Martha kissed his cheek and turned challenging eyes to Leah. "Don't go spreading that around, okay?"

"I won't." But as Leah met Martha's gaze, she couldn't keep a frown from creasing her brow. Martha broke the stare and flipped the radio on. Country music bounced from the speakers, causing Leah's heart to thump in time with the beat. She was glad to see her lane ahead and was ready to get out of the truck cab as soon as Abe pulled to a stop under the shadow of an ash tree near the drive.

"Hey, don't look so sour. Everything's going to be A-okay. I'll see you tomorrow if I can," Martha promised.

Leah nodded. "Thanks for taking me tonight. I really appreciate it."

"You're welcome. Good night!"

Abe pulled out, and as he sped away, the roar of the truck echoed through the silent countryside. She took a deep breath of the crisp night air and started home. Hoping that the evening wouldn't be spoiled somehow, she couldn't wait to get to her room and pull out the little New Testament so she could reread what Matthew had presented tonight.

The lights were off in the downstairs rooms, so her parents were probably in bed. She breathed a sigh of relief. As she climbed the stairs and passed her parents' bedroom door, *Maem* called, "Is that you, Leah?"

She paused outside the door. "Yes, *Maem*."

"Good. Have a nice time?"

"*Ja*. It was fun." She wasn't lying at all about that.

"Have a good rest. See you in the morning."

"G'night, *Maem*."

"Good night."

She went to her room, got into her soft flannel gown, and lay down. She dug her head deep into her feather pillow, finding the perfect spot as she closed her eyes.

The room was quiet and still, and as the pale light from a buttery moon streamed in over the foot of her bed, she thought of how she had gone against *Maem* and *Daet*. The stress of sneaking out and lying to her folks had worn her out. *What a day. I'll have to come up with an honest way to do all this.*

She yawned. Just before drifting off to sleep, she remembered the reading materials Naomi had handed her as she went out the door. Getting up, she crossed to the corner where her apron hung and rummaged through the pockets until she felt the papers.

Better hide these. She crept to her dresser, pulled back a stack of underclothes, and laid the study pages neatly under the pile. *Maem* rarely washed Leah's laundry anymore, so it was unlikely she would find the study materials in the dresser.

In spite of her fatigue, Leah lay awake a bit longer, thinking over the evening.

How could she be happy to do something that the bishop, *Ordnung*, church, and her parents considered sinful? Was Satan taking over her mind, as many of the preachers often warned when other members had strayed from the Amish church? Surely it was so, if she had to lie her way to get there . . .

Yet all those people at Bible study seemed so joyful. What was missing from her life that they had?

⁂

At breakfast the next morning, Leah's sister and parents were extra-absorbed in their scrambled eggs when she came to the table. No one lifted their eyes to greet her. Something was wrong. She tried to catch Ada's eyes, but she uncharacteristically kept her gaze averted.

"Good morning, *Maem* and *Daet*."

Maem looked up, and the pain Leah saw on her face made her stomach drop. Something was definitely going on, but *Maem* said nothing beyond "*Gut morgen*."

Leah ate her breakfast in silence, and for once, Ada was anxious to be off to school. She hurried through her breakfast and left. By the time Ada was gone and Benny had wiped the last of the jelly toast from his chin, grabbed his books, and dashed out the door, Leah was a nervous wreck. Neither of her parents said anything to her, and she wondered if someone had told them about her visit to the Bible study.

Once the three were alone in the kitchen, Leah stood to wash the dishes but *Daet* motioned for her to sit back down. Her parents' expressions were grim and serious.

Daet fiddled with his beard and sighed. He shook his head. "Leah, I'm not going to beat around the bush. The bishop came by this morning and told me someone saw you getting into Abe Troyer's truck last night. He said Martha was in there, too. I'll not waste time asking you if this is true. What I *am* going to ask you is why and where did you go?" *Daet*'s eyes never wavered from his daughter's face, and his expression warned her not to even try denying it. She dropped her eyes, acknowledging the truth.

"I'm sorry, *Daet*, *Maem*. I went to the Schrocks' Bible study, and well, Martha said she would give me a ride with Abe, so—"

"So you rode in the truck to an *Englisher* Bible study, and you lied and told your *Maem* you were going to Sara's place. Is that right?" *Daet's* voice was steely.

"*Ja*, and I'm sorry that I didn't tell you, *Daet*—and you, *Maem*—but I did try to ask. I wanted to do it with your permission."

"You wanted to go to an *Englisher's* place—especially *that* man's house—and you thought *Maem* and I should allow it? And since we didn't, you lied and went anyway?" *Daet* reiterated, his anger growing.

"It isn't that I wanted to disobey, but I do want to learn more about the Bible, and it is the only Bible study I can go to. None of the Amish have one."

Daet stood, pushing back his chair with force. "And may I remind *you*, young lady, that our church *Ordnung* does not encourage group Bible studies. You know that, Leah. We prefer to teach our own families in our own homes. And nowhere is there something that allows for you to be in a group of *Englishers* studying the Bible. It is forbidden for you to have that kind of connection. Forbidden! And to go to the Schrocks, of all people—the very people the bishop warned us about. You heard him yourself. That Matthew Schrock helps the youth leave their families and disobey their parents. He is a very bad influence, no matter how nice he seems." *Daet* was pacing back and forth, his face puffed with anger.

"*Daet*, he and Naomi are *good* people, and all they've ever tried to do is to help me. I promise that's all."

He rushed to her, raising the flat of his hand as though to strike her. Leah flinched just as *Daet* caught himself and stopped. He swallowed a couple of times, obviously trying to control his rage at her disobedience and her defense of the Schrocks.

"I can guarantee that if you're with them for long, you'll want to leave, too. No!" He shook his head vigorously. "I have to be strong with you and forbid you to go to any more of these . . . these . . . Bible study things. No more, Leah. Furthermore, Bishop Miller will be watching you to make sure the Schrocks and Martha don't influence you again."

He towered over her. His wrath, spurred by disappointment, scared her in its intensity. "This is your last chance to do the right thing, Leah. The last warning."

She lowered her chin, trying not to notice the slow burn that was growing inside her. Equal parts fear and resentment scalded her throat, forcing words to her lips she tried hard not to speak. She *knew* the *Ordnung* was wrong this time—the bishop was wrong. Even her parents were wrong. It was wrong to keep her from a Bible study. It was.

She clamped her mouth shut until *Daet* finally calmed down.

He walked to the back door, pausing before he went out. "Okay. I've said enough. I'll need your help in the shop today, so go and get your chores finished. This is the last time we'll discuss any of this."

His tone was dismissive, as though he spoke to a child and not a young lady. She clenched her fists at her sides, pressing them against her skirt, knowing this wasn't the time to fight back.

She glanced at *Maem* as she left the kitchen, but her mother kept her head down, refusing to look at her.

Leah hurried to her bedroom and set about her mundane tasks. She wanted to do as she was told with no back talk or sass, but the burgeoning feeling grew: she had to find freedom. Freedom to learn about what the Bible really said.

Leah sensed she would soon be forced to make a decision about her faith, something she'd never imagined she'd have to do. And considering leaving *Maem*, *Daet*, Benny, Daniel, and Ada was hard to imagine; her heart ached at the thought. Surely, she wouldn't have to go away like the others who were at the Schrocks' Bible study. Her parents were more reasonable than that. More concerned about the truth. She prayed the choice would never come.

<hr/>

When she came downstairs, Leah overheard her parents talking in the kitchen. She knew she shouldn't, but she slipped quietly to the door so she could hear what they were saying, certain the discussion centered on her.

"I'm nearly finished with the Schrock bedroom suite; I'll tell him today that I can't do any more work for him." *Daet*'s deep voice sounded frustrated.

"I hate to see you take such a strong stand against an *Englisher*, especially Matthew Schrock, but I know it should be done," *Maem* answered. "I'm disappointed Leah snuck off to the Bible study. What do you suppose has gotten into her, John?"

"She's going through the years of rebellion, Rachel. With Daniel being so eager to join the church, I didn't think we'd have trouble with our daughters; it's usually the sons who are the ones trying and testing and sowing wild oats. I just didn't expect this from Leah. And Martha sure doesn't help."

"I'm still hoping she'll be fine, John. We'll have to pray for her all the harder yet."

Leah heard her father sigh as he pushed the kitchen chair out from the table. "I'd best get back to work. Schrock is coming at 10:30 to pick up the first part of his furniture order. Tell Leah to come on out as soon as she can."

The back door creaked open and then slammed shut, while *Maem*'s steps approached the living room. Leah hurried to the bottom of the staircase, her heavy shoes making extra-loud thumps down the wooden treads.

"Oh, there you are, Leah. *Daet*'s ready for you in the shop if you have your chores finished."

"I do, *Maem*. I'll go now."

As she passed her, *Maem* put out her hand. "Try not to test your *Daet* anymore today. Please?"

Leah nodded, then forged ahead with what she knew must be said. "I am sorry I lied to you."

Maem patted her on the arm. "And about the Bible study?"

Leah dropped her gaze and hurried to the pegs behind the door where her shawl was hanging, afraid to look back at her *maem*'s face, afraid the disappointment would make her determination crumble.

Heading quickly out into the morning sunshine, she adjusted the shawl to completely cover her shoulders and arms—the days were getting nippy. Today would be a tough day, but she resolved to keep her thoughts to herself no matter how she felt.

As Leah entered the shop, her father was walking from the pallets of lumber to his workbench. His shoulders slumped, and she was sorry to be the cause of his worry. *Daet* gave a polite nod, and she nodded back, trying to keep her thoughts on the orders and the paperwork stacked on the desk. She spent the morning writing out orders and bills, and before Leah knew it, it was time for Matthew Schrock to come by.

As he entered the door, Matthew shook hands with *Daet* and walked with him to the back of the building to help load the finished pieces.

After the gleaming headboard and footboard were loaded and wrapped with blankets, the two men approached the desk to settle the bill.

"Matthew, I hate to tell you this," *Daet* said, "but I think you know the Amish community around here is pretty close. The youth pay a lot of attention to what we adults do and what the other kids do. Because of your association with those who have left the Amish, Bishop Miller thinks it would be best if we limit the amount of contact we have with you. For that reason, I will find someone to deliver the rest of your bedroom set to you when it's finished. Then I think we will have to end our business relationship. I'm sorry." *Daet* glanced at Leah. "And my daughter won't be coming to any more Bible studies. This is not a good idea for her, as you should know."

Matthew Schrock looked down at the invoice. He shook his head a little and then looked *Daet* in the eyes.

"I don't want to be the cause of trouble, John. Not at all. But I think you should know the Lord guides my steps, and I do His bidding when He calls me to do it. I hope you understand, and Bishop Miller, too, that sometimes my calling from the Lord is not what the Amish church would call right, but I see it is right in the Lord's eyes." He shrugged. "I don't want to be a problem between your daughter and you, though."

He turned to Leah, and her eyes filled with unshed tears. She felt the heat fill her cheeks as embarrassment and disappointment flowed over her.

"It's important for you to do what's right, Leah. Time spent praying is never a wrong thing to do, as I'm sure your *daet* would agree." He glanced at *Daet*, who nodded. "You're always welcome at our Bible studies, but please consider your *Daet*'s request first. Okay?"

He gave her a warm smile and said he'd be praying for everyone. Then he left.

The atmosphere in the shop was heavy with sadness and censure. Leah kept her eyes on the figures of the paperwork piled on the desk and didn't try to speak. She was too upset and afraid that if her father tried to talk to her about any of this she'd end up shouting. She might even feel like leaving home.

Daet kept silent, too. He puttered from one end of the shop to the other without comment. They worked in uncomfortable silence the rest of the morning, and after lunch, Leah returned to her duties just as quietly. Later in the afternoon, the bell rang over the door, and Jacob Yoder came through with a box of hardware.

"Hi, Leah." His grin was genuine and open. Maybe he hadn't heard what she had done.

"Hello, Jacob." *Daet* clenched his teeth, and Leah could feel her cheeks flush with heat.

Jacob handed the box to *Daet*. "I checked the contents' list, and it appears everything is in there, John."

"I have a chest ready for these knobs, so I thank you for bringing this box, but I'd better get back to work."

Daet glanced at Leah with a look that said, *Here is your future—not with the English.*

After John left the room, Jacob walked to the desk and leaned on the counter. He held Leah's gaze, winking at her when her cheeks flushed once more.

"Don't you know you shouldn't be hanging out with a sinner like me?" Her chin wavered, tears gathering at the corners of her eyes.

He raised his eyebrows. "I guess I'm attracted to spunky girls."

In spite of her emotions, she laughed. "You've come to the right place then. I'm in real trouble this time, I'm afraid."

"I heard."

"You did?"

"Yes, and you shouldn't be at all surprised the gossip mills are running full-tilt with talk of your sinful ways, Leah." Though he was teasing, there was undoubtedly an undercurrent of truth in what he said.

She grew serious. "Jacob, why are my parents and the bishop so set against me going to a Bible study? You'd think they'd love it when one of the youth wants to study Scriptures."

"I don't think it's that you want to study the Bible so much as it is you going to the English and reading an English Bible—that's why they're upset with you. They can't have you getting ideas about the ordinance letter or finding your own path of religion. Our people are all about what our forefathers did. We aren't supposed to question any authority over us or even look as though we are."

Leah walked to the window and scanned the yellowing fields. "But I don't understand the German Bible, and right now, I feel I *have* to read more and study more, Jacob. I don't know why. I can't seem to fight this feeling that I need more freedom. That somehow all the rules aren't quite right. Maybe if I can see for myself where God asks us to follow these rules, maybe I can make myself obey. I can't help but wonder if the *Ordnung* and everyone else are wrong about this."

Jacob ambled to her side. "I don't always think the church is right about everything, either, Leah, but I don't know any other life, and I'm not so sure the *Englisher* world is any better or any smarter for knowing more."

"I guess you're right." She sighed. "I really don't want to go away from my family. I'd much rather stay here, but I just wish—" She broke off, knowing it was hard to make herself understood. "Do you know anyone who has been under the miting before?"

Jacob walked back to the desk. He shrugged. "Yes. A fellow I knew a year or so ago when I went to Indiana to work one summer. Andy Zook. He was questioning everything, and he was a wild one—drinking, partying, drugs. Then he went to a revival at one of the English churches, and he said he got saved—born again. He quit drinking and smoking and running around. He tried to go back to his Amish church, and they were glad to have him until he started talking to everyone about being saved the way he was. After a while, they went to him and told him he had to stop."

"But why? What did he do? Did he stop?"

"Well, he tried, he really did. But he couldn't keep it inside. He kept telling people about his 'personal relationship' with Christ. He talked to me about it all the time. Though I didn't agree with him, I'll admit that his certainty and his excitement made me think. Then he started asking the elders and the preachers and the bishop questions. They finally had enough, and they put the ban on him."

"What happened to him?"

"He wanted to stay around, but he told me after our boss let him go that he missed his family so much he couldn't stay in the area." Jacob shook his head. "He was crying, and his shoulders were shaking, he was so upset. It made me feel real sorry for him, and I kept letting him talk to me. Then the bishop told my boss he'd have to fire me if I kept talking to Andy Zook. I had to tell him to stop talking to me at work. He eventually left. I don't know what happened to him after that."

The pain in her heart grew as she wondered if this could be her someday. "I don't want that to be me, Jacob. I don't. But what can I do to stop this feeling that I need more freedom? I don't know how it happened, but I'm thinking all the time about being free, and when *Daet* or the bishop or *Maem*, even, tells me what I *should* be doing or feeling, I get this churned-up feeling. I'm angry enough to think I could pack my things and leave right there."

Jacob smacked his hat against his thighs a few times, a frown furrowing his brow. "Don't think like that then. Just tell yourself it won't work and think of other things. You know what I think of when I'm upset?"

Leah shook her head.

"I think of my future and what I'll have someday: a family, a sweet wife, and a farm—all the things that make life good." He grinned. "It's a simple dream, but it works for me. It makes me think of other things besides what's happening to me at the moment."

Leah knew he meant well, but his method wouldn't work for her. It hurt that Jacob didn't understand what she was talking about, but she couldn't blame him. All Amish *jungen* were supposed to think like him. She was supposed to want those same things, and maybe she did. But not now. Right now, she simply wanted more. She yearned to learn and grow, and she couldn't understand what was so bad about that.

She strolled to the desk and picked up the invoices. "Thanks for letting me spout off, Jacob. I promise to consider what I *should* want and not what I think I want."

Jacob held up his hand in a pledge. "I'll keep your secrets, Leah, and I'll pray *Gott* helps you make the right decision when the time comes. Tell your *Daet* I'll be back on Thursday to bring in the shipment of hardware he ordered last week."

"I will. Thanks, Jacob." She walked him to the door and waved him off, then turned back to the shop and the work that waited for her on the desk. She hoped Jacob really would be praying for her—she didn't know how she'd decide anything if *Gott* didn't help her.

CHAPTER EIGHT

Leah dressed quickly the Sunday morning Sara and Daniel's wedding banns were to be published in church. She was excited to be a part of his important day and had just found out that Sara and Daniel were planning to pair Leah with Jacob as helpers at the wedding.

The church service seemed to take even longer than ever, but soon, one of the preachers stood and read the banns of those who were going to be married that month.

"Sara Wengerd and Daniel Raber will be married on the first Thursday of November. The service will be at Nate and Susan Gingriches' place, next door to the Wengerds'. Lunch and dinner will be at the Wengerds' place after the service. They have chosen Paul Yoder, John Wengerd, and Eric Hochstetler as *hoslers*. The *navohugga* includes Lydia Wengerd, Sarah Yoder, and Leah and Ada Raber, Aaron and William Miller, Jacob Yoder, and Levi Schlabach."

Sara and Daniel smiled at one another across the room; the future bride blushing shyly from the attention she was receiving.

As the reality of their marriage hit Leah, she felt a flutter inside and wondered what her own wedding would be like. Sneaking a peak at Jacob, she just as quickly looked away for fear he'd guess her thoughts.

⁓

The next few days were busy assisting Sara and Daniel as much as possible. Though it was customary for the bride and groom to live with the bride's family after their marriage, Daniel and Sara were blessed with a little house of their own. The old *dadihaus,* the house Leah's grandparents had moved into when they deeded the farm to her parents before they passed away, would be Daniel and Sara's new home.

Daniel took Leah with him to the house one day so she could help him add a few things as a welcome for Sara. He had finished updating the kitchen and wanted to put final touches on the rest of the house.

Leah had made a set of embroidered pillowcases—nothing too fancy—to put on their bed; the cheerful vines and flowers were very inviting. She had carefully pressed rows of pleating into a flat sheet so it could be spread under the mattress crosswise to act as a lovely bed ruffle. The pillowcases under the embroidered ones were also ironed into intricate pleats, their creases crisp and neat. She turned to view the small bedroom with a critical eye. The pure white bed coverings appeared a bit stark to her, so she went in search of something to warm up the space.

She found Daniel in the kitchen unpacking boxes he and Sara had brought over the day before. He was unwrapping and stacking white pottery plates and cups from their new set into the sink so they could be washed and put away clean.

"Hey, *Bruder,* I can wash those up for you. But first, I'd like to know if you and Sara have a nice throw or comforter that I can put on the foot of your bed. It needs something else to brighten the room."

Daniel thought for a minute and then led her to a box in the corner of the living room. He rooted through the carton until he pulled out a soft throw that had the colors of a grape arbor on it: creams and greens and purples. The fringes rippled as he tossed it to her. She spread the beautiful throw at the foot of the bed. *Wish I could find some fresh flowers, but at least the throw brings a bit of color and warmth to the room.*

Back in the kitchen, she helped Daniel continue unpacking and stacking the pottery dishes. Once they had them all out of the box, she primed the sink pump until cool clear water filled a large kettle. She lit the woodstove and put the pot on to boil water for the washing up. While she waited for the water to heat, Leah helped Daniel move boxes into the right rooms so Sara could unpack more quickly once they moved in permanently.

Back in the kitchen, Leah poured hot water over the dishes and began washing. She mused about her and Jacob being paired off for the wedding. It was the first time the two of them would be together in public. She smiled when she remembered the fleeting look of embarrassment that flashed across Jacob's cheeks when Daniel asked him to help make food the day before the wedding. But then he'd glanced her way and grinned as she nodded, so it was all set.

"What are you and Sara planning to have Jacob and me do for the wedding meal, Daniel?"

"Sara thinks we should make you guys clean the chickens," her brother teased. "I figure after hanging out with you all morning and then being exposed to the smell of a chicken coop, Jacob will change his mind and take off for the hills."

She laughed and flicked sudsy water his way. Daniel ducked the attack and grinned back. When she was happy like this, feeling helpful and like a girl who was about to fall in love with a good Amish boy, she could almost believe her months of troubling questions and rebellious attitude were a thing of the past. She finished the dishes and wiped her hands on a clean towel.

Daniel grew thoughtful and motioned for his sister to sit down in a chair at the kitchen table. He rubbed his hand over the brightly colored oilcloth she'd unpacked and pressed over the round surface earlier that day.

"Leah," he began. "I look at you now and I have trouble thinking you're the same girl who lied to her parents, rode in a sinful man's truck, and went to an *Englisher* Bible study."

She was shocked at Daniel's blunt record of her recent sins; she had no idea he was aware of all she had done. She pulled the kerchief off her head, readjusting the loosening pins in her hair before positioning the kerchief back in place. "Daniel, I just have these feelings—"

"Still?" he interrupted.

"Yes. *Still.* Though I don't want to give up my family and the good times like this, I can't keep ignoring this fight for freedom in my heart."

As she admitted her inner thought, she was embarrassed. It was difficult to tell her brother her doubts. He was not going to like how rebelliously she was thinking.

"But what about Jacob Yoder? He seems to care about you very much, and I haven't seen you turn him down on anything yet, so do you plan to make him follow you into the English world or something?" Leah's head snapped up in alarm.

"No, of course not! I haven't said anything about leaving. So don't go running home to tell *Daet* a thing like that."

Daniel watched her and slowly shook his head. "I wouldn't, and you know it. I just can't figure you out. One minute you're in here all rosy cheeked and happy, helping me get the house together, and the next minute, you're telling me you need this freedom or you'll be sad forever."

She sniffed and turned away. "I can't explain it, Daniel, I just can't, but I know that *Gott* is trying to tell me something—"

"Leah," Daniel warned again, "it's prideful to think we hear *Gott* speaking to mortals. Our parents wouldn't like to hear you talking that way, and neither do I."

"I didn't mean it like that," she said impatiently. "I just meant . . . well, I think *Gott* is in the questions I'm asking, maybe prompting me to ask them because I think there's something not right with the *Ordnung*."

"Leah Raber, you are standing on slippery ground. You've allowed yourself to ask too many questions and to focus on too many problems instead of on the good things about our life. It isn't right to get too big of a head, Leah, and start thinking you know so much."

"I'm not saying I know so much. It's that I don't know enough, and I *feel* a lot, and it makes me so frustrated sometimes." She pushed up from the table and got the bread and peanut butter spread out for lunch. She made him a sandwich first, set a glass of cold water in front of him, then made herself a sandwich and a drink.

They ate in silence for a time before Daniel finally asked her, "Aren't you ever afraid of the consequences of thinking like this?"

"What? Why? I'm only asking questions. I'm not drinking or smoking or anything truly sinful."

"Sister, *Daet* gave me this letter to carry in my pocket a long time ago. Let me read it to you."

She grimaced when she realized which letter he meant. It was the angel letter: an ancient warning that whoever ignored this "new" missive from the hand of Jesus would suffer terrible maladies. Though *Daet* professed he was not the sort who believed in magic, he did think this particular letter was a good thing to have on hand. Leah was never sure why the letter was accepted as a kind of protection against harm, but many of the church members carried it and truly believed in its power.

Daniel laid the much-folded missive on the table between them and read it aloud:

A Wonderful Letter from God:
Printed in letters of gold and dropped by an Angel near the city of Madgesburg in Europe, where it was found. Whosoever desires to copy it is permitted to do so and whosoever despises it from him, we shall withdraw ourselves.

Whosoever labors on the Lord's Day or Sunday is accursed for this reason. I command that ye do not labor on Sunday, but reverently go to church and do not adorn your faces. Ye shall not wear false hair and practice pride and vanity of your treasure. Ye shall give to the poor. Give abundantly and have faith and believe that this letter was written with my own hand and sent out from Christ himself. And that ye do not as the unconscious Brutes.

Ye have six days in the week, and in these ye shall do your work. But the seventh day, namely Sunday, ye shall keep holy. If ye will not do this, then I will send wars, hunger, pestilence, and famine amongst you. And I will punish you with many plagues. I also command you all; whosoever ye may be, young or old, great or small, that ye do not at any time work late on Saturday. But ye shall mourn over your sins that be forgiven you.

Do not count silver or gold. Do not give way to lust of the flesh or to your carnal desires. Remember that I created you and that I can again destroy you.

Do not rejoice in poverty of your neighbors, but much more have compassion on him, and it shall be well with you.

Children, obey Father and Mother that it will be well with you upon earth. Whosoever does not believe and do this is condemned and lost.

I, Jesus, have written this with my own hand. Whosoever shall oppose and despise it, that same person may not expect any help from me. And whosoever has this letter and who does not reveal or publish it to others shall be accursed by the Christian Church. If your sins be ever so great, they shall nevertheless be forgiven you, if ye sincerely mourn over them and repent of them. He that does not believe this shall die and be punished in Hell at the judgment day. I will ask you about your sins and you will have to answer me.

The person who shall carry this letter with him or keep it in his house shall not be harmed by thunder or lightning, shall be secured from fire or floods, and he that shall make it known among the children of men shall have his reward and shall have a blessed and peaceful departure from this world. Keep my commandments, which I have sent by my Angel.

The True God from Heaven's Throne,

The Son of God and Mary

Daniel took his time refolding the letter and then tucked it back into his pocket. He looked long and hard at his sister. "It says right there the child who disobeys her parents is condemned and lost, Leah." He sat back in his chair and crossed one leg over the other, his chin tilted down and his eyes on the floor. He looked confident and sure that what he had just read to her was enough to scare her into submission. What he didn't realize was the superstitious letter had only made the flame in her chest suddenly and ferociously leap to life and begin burning its way to her mouth.

Why did Daniel think this old letter had any power over his life? Or hers? It did not make sense to Leah and demonstrated another confusing idea about her Amish church: believing in something like a letter to protect a person or to condemn a person. Was this biblical? Her gut feeling told her it wasn't. And why use a letter like this to attempt to control her? She clenched her hands together in frustration.

She had to leave the *dadihaus* or she would end up speaking her mind, and then Daniel would have no choice but to report to *Daet* that she did not believe in the letter and, by extension, their Amish tradition.

Leah stood. "I think I'd better be getting home. I'm sure *Maem* has plenty for me to help her with, what with the wedding being only a few days off. Besides, I haven't completely finished my own dress. I need to get that together as soon as I can."

He looked momentarily irritated at her lack of response but then pushed himself away from the table and began to help clean up. They spent a few minutes more gathering things and putting a few items away, then they headed to the buggy for the short ride home.

She kept her mouth tightly shut until her mind and heart calmed down. Daniel turned into the drive, and she leapt from the buggy like a shot as soon as he halted the horse.

"Leah," he called after her, "don't forget, obedience equals a good life. Remember that!"

She ran up the stairs and down the hallway to her room. Inside, she felt safe and protected. She lay down on the bed and looked at the ceiling. *What can I do? I can't leave—I can't—but stuff like that letter . . . how can I go through my whole life ignoring that?*

She waited until she heard her brother's buggy leave the drive and then made her way slowly and quietly down the stairs. She wanted to find a place to sit and think. She wanted to figure out what to do next, if anything.

Leah walked out to the fields surrounding the farm and found a quiet rise near their neighbor's corn field. The corn was shocked and the field was stubbly. She spread out her skirt, positioning herself in a soft, grassy area. The ground smelled damp and musty, its moisture settling into her skin. She looked up and saw a group of crows flying in busy circles, cawing out their complaints. They suited her mood.

She spent time praying, asking the Lord to show her the path to take. More than confused, she was desperate to understand how the Amish church could coexist peacefully with her muddled thoughts.

"Why?" she asked the crows. "Why can't I be like all the others and just be quiet, join the church, and do what they want me to do? Why do I get frustrated with the things the church says and does?"

She stared across the field, watching her Amish neighbors going about their business. A horse trotted down the road, a black buggy rolling

merrily behind it . . . an Amish woman pedaled her bike toward home
. . . a straw-hatted farmer carried the seed pail to feed his chickens.
So normal—yet none of it had meaning anymore. It was like she was
already on the outside, looking in, and what she saw didn't seem to have
anything to do with her real life.

Her eyes caught sight of *Maem* coming out the back door. She saw her
pause and search the yard. *Uh oh, she's looking for me.*

Leah got up, brushed the broken and dried grass from her skirt, and
started walking slowly home. She had no idea what to do next but knew
she couldn't keep going on like this.

Maem and Leah worked in the kitchen side by side for the rest of the
afternoon, and then she hemmed the skirt of her wedding-day dress.

"How much do you still have to do, Leah?" asked Ada as she poked
her head into the room.

"I'm on the skirt—need to hem it and then press the seams, and it
should be almost finished."

"Do you want help?"

"Sure."

Handing Ada the needle to continue hemming where she'd left off,
Leah began laying out her new apron. She measured the yard goods
carefully and placed the pattern on the fabric, traced it, and began to
cut it out.

"Daniel told me he was planning to talk to you when you went with
him to the house today. Did he?" Ada asked curiously.

Leah rolled her eyes and frowned. "You should have warned me."

"I'm trying to stay out of this, remember?"

Leah sighed. "I know. He pulled out the letter."

Ada put down the needle and looked at her sister. "The letter of
warning?"

"Yes, the one that tells the bad things about the sinners and the good
luck to those who carry it and believe in it."

Ada shook her head and returned to her work. "Don't you believe that
letter?"

"I don't know, but it made me so angry that I couldn't say anything—
couldn't even question it. The problem is everything makes me mad if it

means I have to keep quiet about it. Having to stifle my questions makes me want to scream."

"*Daet* thinks that the letter will keep Daniel safe from lightning strikes while he's in the fields."

"I know, but I don't think I believe that anymore." Leah sighed again and continued carefully cutting the fabric.

"What was the Bible study like? You never got the chance to tell me."

"It was good. The people were nice, and the Bible lesson was very interesting." She looked around and then whispered, "I brought some materials home for reading—a little more Scripture work and a lesson about salvation."

"Will you let me read it, too?"

"I want to read it first, and then I'll see if you should, okay?"

"What are you afraid that I'll read?"

"*Maem* is making me feel guilty about leading you astray. I don't want you to read things she may blame me for later."

Ada laughed. "Heaven forbid I should read something in a Bible lesson!"

They spent the rest of the afternoon sewing and pressing Leah's dress. It was wonderful to giggle and talk with her sister without fearing judgment from *Daet* or the bishop. Once they hung the finished dress in the closet, she breathed a sigh of relief. "I'm glad that's done. I won't have to worry about getting it finished once we get busy before the wedding day."

As she lay in bed that night, she took the papers from the Bible study and started to read the Scriptures by the light of the moon. As she read, Leah's eyes filled with tears. The verses all made sense to her. It was as if God had written them just for her. When it was too dark to read any longer, Leah snuggled down into her bed and drifted off into a peaceful sleep, happily surrendering thoughts of her talk with Daniel and all the unsettling questions floating around in her head.

❧

Two days before the wedding, *Maem*, Ada, and Leah went to Sara's parents' house to help the women set up the tables and chairs. Leah brushed off the chair seats and washed the tabletops until they shone, but halfway through the work, she noticed a couple of the other ladies whispering, looking at her, and then whispering again. When she caught their eyes, they dropped their gazes, their demeanor stiff and aloof. She wanted so much to know what they were saying to one another but was too afraid to ask.

Martha came by on her bike, and as she leaned it against a bench under a huge oak tree, Leah noticed the whispering and behind-the-hand talking increased. She even caught *Maem* watching as Martha approached.

Her friend, seemingly oblivious to the gossipers, smiled as she walked over. Leah pointed to a group of teen girls who were staring intently.

"Our fan club is watching us, Martha."

Martha giggled. She boldly waved with a flourish to the group of girls. They immediately turned their heads and scurried off, still massed together in a clump, but their giggles and laughter floated back long after they were out of sight.

"Martha," Leah admonished, "you're already in a lot of trouble; why would you tease them that way?"

"If I'm going to be kicked out soon anyway, why stop having fun with them? They're just being *nahsich*, and nosy is as nosy does." Martha shrugged her shoulders indifferently.

The two friends started their work, going from table to table, cleaning and dusting and straightening the rows. Leah asked Martha how things were at home.

"Abner stares a hole right through me every time we're in the same room. *Maem* sees him and looks worried, but she won't interfere. I think she'll be glad if I get the miting."

"Oh, Martha, you can't think like that! No *Maem* wants her child shunned by the church."

"It will solve a lot of problems for them all, except for my sisters. I'd be gone right now if it weren't for them."

"You wouldn't be afraid to get kicked out?"

"Abe and I plan to get married anyway. He's looking for an apartment for both of us, and he wants me to come and live with him as soon as I can, but he understands why I'm staying."

Leah dropped the rag she was using to wash tables into the bucket of bleach water. "You mean you'll live with him without being married, Martha?"

"We *can't* get married. Not until I'm eighteen, unless my *maem* signs for me—and that isn't going to happen."

"You really will be in trouble if you move in with Abe before you get married."

Martha tossed her head. "I don't care anymore. If I move out from home and don't join the church, I'll be doomed anyway."

Lunchtime came, and their chance to talk privately after the meal was interrupted by *Maem* requesting Leah to come peel apples for the applesauce that would be made later in the day. As she walked off with *Maem*, she looked back in time to see Martha making a face at a group of little girls who were darting around her and sticking their tongues out at her.

She felt sorry for Martha, and resentment sprang to life at the mean behavior of the children. Some of the mothers rushed over to shoo the girls away, but no one apologized to Martha.

"Come on, Leah, don't dally. We have a lot to do." *Maem* tugged her daughter along.

When she saw the look in *Maem*'s eyes, she knew she had pulled her away from Martha on purpose. The women they joined in the kitchen kept their distance in a polite manner.

Is this how it would be to be shunned?

If her pink cheeks were any indication, poor *Maem* was aware of what was going on, so Leah tried hard to be friendly and polite while she worked with the women for the rest of the afternoon. *I don't want Maem suffering for my troubles.*

A few of the ladies kept their distance all day, but most became friendlier as the day wore on.

Just as the women were finishing up, Martha came to the kitchen door, looking for Leah. Tension filled the room, and the ladies stopped their friendly bantering. All eyes turned to the two friends as they stood at the back door. Leah's spine crawled with unease.

Martha whispered, "Leah, here's my cell number, just in case you ever need to call me." She slipped a small piece of crumpled paper into Leah's hand, and then smiled as she boldly pronounced, "Yes, this has been a good day, but now it's time for me to go back home so I can see what my stepbrother Abner needs me to do for him yet."

The women murmured, heads down, eyes averted at the bald statement. Martha's bitter expression told Leah what was behind her provoking words. And of course the women understood the unspoken message: they had let Martha down in their dealings with Abner. They had let him remain in the home with the person he was abusing, and as if that wasn't enough, the women's behavior and attitude toward Martha made it clear whom they blamed for Abner's difficulties.

Impulsively Leah reached out, hugging Martha just before she turned to leave. She watched as Martha marched across the yard and retrieved her bike. Her friend pedaled furiously away from the Amish women and their judgment.

Leah spun to meet a sea of eyes regarding her reproachfully. She experienced a momentary lack of courage, but when she thought of the tears she'd seen on Martha's face as she'd related her story about Abner that summer day, fierce strength returned, and she coolly met the women's gazes. *Maem* cleared her throat, busying herself with finishing the cleanup of the tools they'd used to make the applesauce.

The face-off ended moments later when Sara's *maem* hurried over with a hug for Leah and a cheerful thank-you to her and Martha for being so helpful. She guided her to the back porch.

Once they were out of earshot from the others, Miriam Wengerd regarded her. Her face held sympathy. "Don't worry. They'll gossip for a while, and then something else will come along to get their attention."

Leah looked at Miriam through the tears swimming on her eyelashes. "Thank you, Miriam, for being so openly gracious to Martha and me."

Lowering her voice, Miriam continued. "I have reason to feel sorry for Martha and the position the church has put her in. I had a similar experience as a child. No one was there to protect me, and I'm very sorry it is still happening in the church." She sighed. "We are not a perfect people by any stretch of the imagination, Leah."

The younger woman absorbed this news and wondered how many others also hid secrets. The back door screeched open. *Maem* stood there, glancing from her daughter to her future in-law. Her expression was guarded, but she told Miriam she would be available to help out any time during the next couple of days.

Miriam smiled. Turning to Leah, she explained, "From here on out, Sara has her friends paired up very well and has assigned most of the remaining chores to them. You and Jacob, for instance, are going to be in charge of plucking chickens, I hear," she teased.

Leah laughed. "I sure hope not. I'm not very good at plucking chickens."

They exchanged good-byes. *Maem* and Leah went in search of Ada, and by the time they rounded her up, dusk had settled in. As the three Raber women walked the lane toward their house, Leah was thankful Miriam had broken the tension between *Maem* and her. She could enjoy having a pleasant chat with her mother for a change, rather than enduring the misery of silence all the way home.

⸎

The morning before the wedding, Leah dressed and waited for Jacob to come by to pick her up. This was the day all the paired-up couples would put the finishing touches on the food, the tables, and the decorations. She and Jacob were assigned to clean the celery and then cut each stalk into several pieces. Several stalks were kept whole with their bright green leaves attached at the top, washed, and placed in vases to decorate the tables at the wedding meal. Some of the celery was cut into chunks so it could be cooked into creamed celery for the dinner.

Leah examined a stalk of celery for a moment and wondered idly why it was used at every wedding. No one ever seemed to know why the Amish did many of the things they did. It was what their forefathers had done, and that was supposed to be a good enough answer. But this kind of obedience to a tradition not completely understood, and even a bit silly, was an example of why she was often confused about her people and their ways. She took a chomp out of the celery, wishing she could just as easily swallow her questions.

After the celery prep was finished, she and Jacob were assigned to mapping the placement of the benches and tables. Jacob had a good eye for how to fit all the benches in the barn, and of course the bride and groom had decided where the *eck* would be placed.

This was the corner where two tables and benches met and the bride and groom sat. To their left and right, the attendants assembled, boys across from girls down each side of the corner.

"Aren't you glad we're already considered a couple, Leah?" Jacob grinned.

"*Ja.* I would hate to be waiting to see who Sara was going to pair me up with like I did last year at Katie Weaver's wedding. It was so embarrassing having both Miller brothers tell me they didn't want to walk in with me. Talk about a red face!"

"Ah, those guys didn't know a good thing when they saw it, Leah. You know they were both trying to get Red John Yoder's sister."

"I knew that, but it didn't make me feel any better when I was among the last waiting to be placed with someone. Awful."

"This time, you'll be with me, and you won't have to worry about being alone."

Leah smiled and bent to wipe down the table in front of her. Her thoughts drifted to the day when she would be making these same marriage preparations. Would she be sitting at the *eck* with Jacob? She glanced his way and felt her cheeks flame. His long eyelashes fanned down and lifted, fanned down and lifted as his gaze shifted in his work. She'd never noticed before how long and dark his lashes were. He glanced up, caught her scrutiny, and gave a quick wink in return. She blushed. One thing was sure: working with Jacob made the whole event more fun.

After the two finished setting up the tables, they wandered back to the kitchen and found Sara and her sisters, along with most of the wedding party, working hard.

"What can Leah and I do next?" Jacob asked.

Sara turned to him, her cheeks flushed pink against her ivory skin. The wedding preparations were tedious and hard, but Sara was surprisingly resilient. "Oh! I know! Can you and Leah go to Henry Miller's and get some platters that my aunt is loaning us? And also, Matthew Bontrager's—they said they can loan some of their flatware."

Sara continued with a smile. "And thanks, Leah, for helping Daniel wash our new dishes. That's one less thing I have to do today. I'm going to place them on the *eck* table, and it was such a pleasant surprise to see them already washed and ready to be used."

Leah acknowledged the thanks with a grin. "I'm glad I could do it for you, Sara."

Jacob and Leah climbed in his buggy and rode off to the neighbors to get the borrowed items. Daniel and Sara's wedding would be relatively small compared to some Old Order weddings, but they still had to feed more than 175 people, and that would take a lot of silverware and dishes. It was customary to borrow enough from family and friends to fill out the tables. Some helpers were already lined up for sink duty in case the dishes had to be washed and reused throughout the day.

On the way to the Millers', Leah told Jacob more about the Bible study she'd attended the previous week. He listened and then asked what her parents thought of it.

Leah made a face. "You know that already. *Daet* is dead-set against me going, and he has already told the Schrocks that he will not accept any more of their orders and that my going to their Bible study is out of the question."

"I know how much you'd like to study Scripture, but maybe if you just stopped all this talk about it for a while, your parents would be more open to letting you go again someday."

She snorted, shaking her head. "As long as *Daet* is thinking about Martha Mast and what Bishop Miller said about Matthew Schrock, he isn't likely to change his mind. He's bound and determined to keep me from being like Martha, and he wants to protect and control my every move."

"Try being patient with him. He just wants to keep you safe. Any man would."

Leah swallowed hard at the implication.

"Soon, he'll realize you aren't going down the same road as Martha. Which reminds me: how much do you know about the new ex-Amish friends Abe Troyer has linked up with?"

Leah glanced at Jacob, noting how he eyed her steadily. "Not very good people, I'm afraid. She told me a little bit about them. They have some bad habits I wish Martha wouldn't get involved in."

"Did she say anything about drugs?" he asked carefully.

"Yes. She said Abe is smoking pot now. I wish that weren't true."

"It's more than pot, Leah."

"No! You mean, like cocaine or something?" Leah was alarmed by this news. Martha seemed to be jumping from the frying pan right into the fire with her decision to leave her family and move in with Abe.

"Oxycontin, crack—that's what I'm hearing from the boys who are hanging around with Abe."

"Jacob, I never dreamed Martha could get messed up in such things. That Abe—what in the world is wrong with him?"

"He's going wild right now. No other explanation for it."

They rode back to the Wengerd home in silence, and she prayed Martha would not cause herself even more sorrow with this latest direction she was taking. If Leah's parents knew even a little of what Martha and her friends were caught up in, it was no wonder they were being overly strict with her.

The rest of the long day of work was nearing an end, and Ada and Leah said good-bye to their friends. It was time to head home. Jacob drove them, chatting amiably with Ada all the way. Leah appreciated his kindness to her sister. It also distracted Ada enough not to tease Jacob and her. There would be enough teasing going on at the wedding.

⁂

Leah fell into bed that night, exhausted and weary, but right before she went to sleep, she opened up the little New Testament and looked for the first chapter of John. Different verses leapt out at her as she read.

"But as many as received him, to them gave he power to become the sons of God, even to them that believe on his name."

She thought about that and then continued reading, until she came to one that she remembered from the Shrocks' Bible study: *"For God so loved the world, that he gave his only begotten Son, that whosoever believeth in him should not perish, but have everlasting life. For God sent not his Son into the world to condemn the world; but that the world through him might be saved.*"

Further into John, she read, *"If the Son therefore shall make you free, ye shall be free indeed.*"

Leah sat up straighter as she read that last verse. She read it again and again and yet again. Her heart raced as the meaning sank in. Tears fell. She was learning something she'd never given any thought to before: through Christ alone, she could be set free.

Chapter Nine

Morning chores started early on this important day, and Leah was up with the rest of the bustling household. The service would start at 9:00 a.m. and last until noon, so she had to be sure to get a good breakfast. She pulled the new dress out, carefully smoothed it, pulled it over her head, and then put on the apron. She fastened all the pins and fastened her *kapp* securely, making sure her bangs were neatly tucked behind her ears.

Breakfast was a hurried and harried affair. Daniel was understandably nervous, and *Maem* was a mixture of sadness and excitement. The Raber family was small in number by Amish standards, and Daniel was *Maem*'s firstborn. Leah knew her *maem* must be thinking of how fast they were all growing up, and by the end of the day Daniel would be on his own with his new bride.

Leah caught a glimpse of *Maem* wiping her eyes as she turned to the stove. Most Amish didn't think it good to show too much emotion, especially on such an auspicious and holy day for Sara and Daniel, but she supposed that all *maem*s felt the fleeting years at the marriage of their first child.

When breakfast was finished, they divided the family into two buggies: Daniel and Benny in one buggy, and everyone else in the other. Daniel looked handsome in his black suit and bow tie—the only day a tie was not considered too high and mighty.

The Wengerds' neighbors had offered their barn for the wedding service because it would be challenging for Sara's family to ready their own barn for the service and convert the place for the lunch and dinner, too.

The service started with singing from the *Ausbund*. Leah watched as Daniel and Sara quietly made their way to the group of preachers and the bishop at the front of the room. The couple followed the leaders out of the barn for their counseling or *abroth* session while the guests sang the first of many songs.

The congregation neared the end of the *Lobleid*, the last song of the service, when Daniel and Sara reappeared along with the preachers and Bishop Miller. The bride and groom sat facing one another with their attendants on either side of them.

Then the preaching began, and Leah yawned discreetly, giving a little shake of her head. The droning on of the preaching combined with a late night and hard work was making it difficult for her to keep her eyes open. She inched forward on the bench to steal a glance in Jacob's direction. He was also stifling a yawn. Leah smiled.

The next preacher started his sermon in the Old Testament and gave examples of godly marriages, beginning with Adam and Eve. By the time the congregation had sung more songs, prayed, and then waited through another long sermon about New Testament marriages, Leah thought she would surely disgrace herself by falling asleep right on the bench in front of the whole church. Finally, the bishop finished his sermon and addressed the bride and groom directly for the first time that morning.

"Here we have two of one faith, Daniel L. Raber and Sara M. Miller. If there is anyone present who knows any scriptural reason why these two may not be married, let yourself be heard now." Bishop Miller paused for a full thirty seconds while Daniel and Sara sat tensely in the silence.

The bishop turned to Daniel and Sara and stated, "If it is yet your desire to be married, you may, in the name of the Lord, come forward." Daniel and Sara stood, joined hands, and approached the bishop.

"Daniel, do you believe and confess that it is scriptural order for one man and one woman to become one, and state that you have been led thus far?"

"I do."

"Sara, do you believe and confess that is it scriptural order for one man and one woman to become one, and state that you have been led thus far?"

Sara answered softly, "I do."

Turning back to Daniel, Bishop Miller asked, "Can you, brother, state that the Lord directs you to take your sister as your wife?"

"I can."

The bishop asked Sara if she could state that the Lord had directed her to take Daniel as her husband, and having received her positive answer, he went to the next question.

"Daniel, do you promise to support your wife when she is in weakness, sickness, what trials may befall you, and stand as a Christian husband?"

Daniel promised he would and Sara promised to support Daniel, too.

The bishop turned again to Daniel to ask the last question: "Can you vow to remain together and have love, compassion, and patience for one another and not to part from one another until the beloved God shall part you in death?"

With their answers of "I will," the wedding service neared completion.

After a special prayer, the bishop said to Daniel and Sara, "Go forth in the name of the Lord. You are now man and wife."

The bishop finished his sermon, the congregation knelt for prayer, and after singing a final wedding hymn, the ceremony was over. The congregation filed out, older men first, followed by younger, then the women in the same order. As the families broke line, they began to make their way to the Wengerd farm next door.

Jacob and Leah climbed into a buggy with Sara's sister and Daniel's friend, and the *hoslers* whisked them, along with the bride and groom, back to the Wengerd place so the celebration could began.

The wonderful smells of roast chicken, mashed potatoes, noodles, dressing, corn, and creamed celery greeted the wedding party as they filed into the room and made their way to the *eck*. The table held an assortment of *eck sachs*. These decorated candy dishes were gifts from aunts and uncles, sisters, brothers, and cousins and were filled with brightly wrapped candies. Already, the little ones were hanging out near the *eck*, hoping to receive a sweet treat from the bride or groom.

Once Sara and Daniel were seated, the wedding party followed and the *ecktenders* came to serve the food. Leah was nervous being in the spotlight for the first time with Jacob across from her. Her parents knew, of course, they were a couple, but now that the other wedding guests were watching and gossiping about who was sitting across from whom, she dropped her eyes to the table, smoothing a wrinkle near her plate. She could still hear whispers and snatches of conversation in the crowded room. "Look, Leah and Jacob are together!" "I hope he knows the girl well." "Do you think they'll get married?"

As she raised her eyes, Jacob grinned. "*Gut* dinner, right? Let's enjoy the day. Ignore the talk."

She smiled back at him. "Why not?"

Once the wedding party finished with lunch, Daniel and Sara went off to open a few gifts and to rest before coming back for the evening meal.

Jacob and Leah wandered out to the area where chairs and blankets had been spread under a giant oak. It was quiet and a little chilly outside, but she was happy to have a few minutes out of the public eye. They sat down on a brightly patterned quilt, and she rested her head against the tree. Jacob barely spoke, but she felt his gaze on her from time to time. She was tired, but she still had the dinner and singing to attend.

"Sara and Daniel are truly married now, Jacob. It's hard for me to imagine he'll be living on his own."

"They're lucky to have a house to go to right away. Not so many have that luxury."

"Yes. The empty *dadihaus* turned out to be a good thing for my brother."

"They'll do fine, Leah." He took her hand. "Maybe we'll have that kind of luck someday."

Leah smiled, the feeling of his hand on hers causing her mind to speed forward—seeing the future—their church membership—their wedding day—their family. Suddenly, the thought of all those years stretching ahead, being Amish for the rest of her life—always *doing*, never questioning—dimmed her smile. Could she ever again think of living and dying Amish without panic rising to choke her dreams? She moved back slightly from Jacob, and eased her hand from his. The look of puzzlement she glimpsed in his eyes tugged at her heart.

I'm not being fair to him. He doesn't understand that my worries are not about him, but about the church. About being Amish.

Just as she was wondering how to explain, a small group of women approached the tree from behind them, not seeing the two under the canopy of branches. Before Jacob or Leah could greet them, they heard the ladies' laughter. Leah caught Martha's name, followed quickly by her own.

"And that Martha Mast, she's going to be banned for sure, if she ever decides to join church. I've never seen such willful disobedience from a girl. And Leah! If that were *my* daughter . . ."

"It makes me wonder why the bishop hasn't already warned Martha she's in deep trouble if she keeps this up. She's an *awful* influence on the young people."

"She hasn't joined the church yet. He can't really put the ban on her, but he could ask her parents to show her how it will feel to be shunned. That might get her attention."

"And what *about* Leah Raber? She's almost as bad, though some would say that going to an *Englisher* Bible study isn't nearly so wild, but getting involved with those Schrocks! It's like she's trying to be English. When I asked her *maem*, she shook her head and said no, like I was making that up, or something."

"*Ja.* It's best to nip that kind of behavior in the bud while you can. Her parents are good people; it's a shame—"

At this point, Jacob cleared his throat and the ladies became aware of Jacob and Leah's presence. They stopped talking mid-sentence but were sensitive enough to turn red at their blunder.

"Good afternoon." Jacob nodded to the ladies. They nodded back, glanced at Leah, and hurried back to the house.

Leah stood, her heart beating wildly and her cheeks flaming at what she'd heard. She had to get away from the talk and the scrutiny. Her feet turned automatically toward home.

"Leah," Jacob called softly. She stopped, waiting for him to come near.

"Don't pay attention to those ladies. They don't know the real you or what you're going through."

Her eyes filled with tears. "That's just the problem. No one understands what I'm going through. No one."

Jacob tilted his head, pushing his hat back. He studied her, a sudden
longing covering his face. "I'd like to understand, Leah. You could help
me understand." He reached out and wiped a tear from her cheek. His
touch was gentle and kind—everything Jacob did for her was gentle and
kind.

She swallowed. *Why can't I just give in and stop worrying?*

Just then she spied the women hovering near the back porch, eyeing
her and Jacob like a group of black-winged ravens hungry for juicy gossip. Their ebony bonnets hid their faces, but she knew how much they
would love to watch her for life: waiting for the moment when she would
fail. And she knew she *would* fail. There was no way she could ever lead
a perfect Amish life.

"I'm very tired, Jacob. What do you suppose would happen if we just
left and you took me home?"

"Some will wonder where we are—but I could come back and tell
them you have a headache or something."

She considered his offer. It didn't seem right to let him make excuses
for her, but the increasing pounding in her head would not be a lie. The
thought of home and quiet and her soft clean pillow drew her.

"Honestly, my head *is* on fire with pain, so if it's okay with you, I
would like to go home."

He nodded, obviously trying to mask the disappointment of not
spending the rest of the day with her. "Okay. Let's go."

She followed Jacob to the throng of black buggies lined up by the barn
and climbed up into his. The two-mile drive was quiet for both of them,
and when he pulled into the lane in front of her house, she breathed a
sigh of relief.

"Thank you, Jacob. You took good care of me today. I do appreciate
you."

"I'm glad to, Leah. Go in and get some sleep now. You'll feel so much
better once you rest, and I'll be sure and tell your *maem* about your
headache. Maybe, if you feel better later on, you could get someone to
bring you back out."

She shook her head. "There won't be any cleanup tonight, so I'll just skip the dinner and singing. I don't think people will care if I miss tonight or not since I'm such a bad influence on all the kids. They might even be relieved."

Her complaint sounded petty, even to her ears, but Jacob leaned in, and barely brushed her lips with a kiss.

"Don't let the gossip hurt you. They just don't know you. *I* know you, and you're not a troublemaker. Maybe a little feisty . . ." He grinned.

Leah's cheeks warmed at the touch of Jacob's lips on hers. She leaned away slightly, to gauge his expression. His brown eyes sparkled as he lifted a hand to her face.

"Your cheeks are rosy. Is there a reason for that?"

She pulled back more, and his hand fell to his side. A puzzled frown slipped over his face. "Are you upset because I kissed you?"

Leah shook her head, and a slow smile grew as she fastened her eyes on his. "No. I'm not upset. But I am wondering how your *daet* and *maem* will feel about you and me . . . being together." She felt the flush deepen as she pondered the kiss. Did he truly have serious plans for their future?

A relieved sigh escaped his lips. "Whew. You had me worried there, you know. As for my parents and their feelings about you, neither one has ever said anything bad about you. My parents don't gossip, but even if they're worried over hearsay concerning your connections to Martha, they would make up their own minds and not judge you by that alone. They've seen you in church. *Maem* considers your *maem* her friend. They've been around your family and you for years and years. They aren't worried."

"But maybe they don't know about us." Leah tilted her head, curious for his reply. Had he talked about her at home?

Jacob chuckled. "Oh, I get it! You're fishing for information, eh? No, seriously. They like you, Leah. *Daet* even teased me once about going after a wife with such spark."

Leah lifted her brows. "Wife?" She pursed her lips in mock disapproval. "Taking my approval of you as husband material for granted, aren't you?"

He grinned.

"But you may be biting off more than you can chew with me, Jacob Yoder. I'm feistier than you know, I'm afraid." She frowned, thinking of her growing desire to let go of *everything* Amish.

Jacob shook his head. "I don't believe that. Go rest and try not to fret. I'll come by in the morning to take you back over to the Wengerds' for cleanup."

"Thanks, but *Maem* already said we were going to walk over together to help with the cleanup, so if you need to do something else, it's okay."

"I'll still try to get over there. They may need someone to run the dishes and borrowed things back."

"Jacob, thanks again," she said sincerely.

"Bye, Leah. See you tomorrow."

She hopped down from the buggy and watched him pull away. In spite of Jacob's unexpected kiss and the talk of their future together, her head felt like it could explode from the stress of overhearing the gossip about her. She couldn't wait to get in her bedroom and lie down.

Even on a wonderful day like this, gossips have managed to spoil it. Why?

❦

The day after the wedding, Leah got up early and went down to breakfast. The Raber women would be going back to the Wengerds' to finish redding up, and some of the other church members would be there, too. She was hoping to see Martha, who hadn't come to the wedding. Leah was worried something had happened to her.

At the table, *Maem* didn't say anything about her being absent from most of the wedding celebration after lunch, and she hoped her parents wouldn't think she'd been with Martha.

Benny suddenly spoke up. "Why did you go away from the wedding, Leah?" His quizzical look made her smile, and she reached out and rubbed his towhead.

"I had a bad pain in my head, and I wanted to come home and take a nap for a little while."

"You *wanted* to take a nap?" he asked incredulously.

They laughed at his expression, and *Maem* said, "Sometimes grownups need to rest, too, Benny." She looked at her daughter with a tiny smile, and the word *grownup* was not lost on Leah.

After a few more minutes in the kitchen, breakfast was finished, and *Maem* sent Benny out to help *Daet* in the shop while the girls walked back to the Wengerds' place.

Leah entered the already steamy hot kitchen, seeing that the big job of cleaning the dishes used at the marriage dinner was underway. The bride and groom were already awake and busily washing the china, silverware, and borrowed dishes. In deference to the bride and groom's privacy on this first morning after their wedding, only the bridal party worked with them.

Leah didn't see Jacob anywhere, and since she didn't really want to be a fifth wheel with the couples helping the newlyweds, she wandered out to the barn to see if the workers out there wanted her to wipe off the benches and tables before they were put away. Three bench wagons were parked near the barn doors, and young men and boys were diligently pulling the cleaned benches out of the barn to stack them back into the wagons.

Church was coming up Sunday, and the wagons needed to be at the proper homes in preparation for the services. Since the Wengerds had hired two extra wagons from other church districts, there was even more work to do. The older boys and men were back at their jobs or in the fields, so she went into the barn to lend a hand with the tables and benches.

The barn was cooler than the kitchen, but it was still warm enough to break a sweat with the bending and scrubbing she was doing to the tables. She used her apron to fan herself several times. While she was working, she saw Martha talking to Miriam at the door of the house. Anna Mast was with her and joined the other ladies in the kitchen. Soon Martha hurried to the barn.

"Martha! There you are! Where were you yesterday?"

Martha pulled her friend to the side, out of earshot. "I had to go to town to sign a rental lease with Abe."

"You're kidding!"

"No. It's a very cute apartment downtown." She giggled. "Abe told me to pick out a kitten—we're allowed to have a pet." Her eyes were lit up with happiness. Leah tried to think back to when she'd last seen Martha so excited.

"I'm going to miss you, Martha."

"I'll still be around. Don't worry. Let me help you with the tables."

While they worked, the two friends whispered about Martha's plans to leave the Amish by the end of the next week. Leah, her brain buzzing with the news that Martha seriously meant to leave home soon, tried to focus on the conversation. Her stomach churned when she realized she would soon have to say good-bye to her friend. Leah tried to talk Martha into not going—at least, not so soon.

"When I think of not being able to see you at church, Martha, my heart breaks, and you'll be shunned, too—not officially, but they still won't like me seeing you."

"I know, but when has anything the church or the elders or the bishop have done made me not speak to you or come find you? I'll be out here, calling your name and sneaking you into my car. Just you wait."

She laughed, but Leah did not join in. Somehow, Martha's rebellion seemed hardened and bitter. *I hope I'm not going down that path. I don't feel as carefree about leaving as she seems to feel. Does dabbling in the English world lead to that?*

Martha sobered. "My only fear is that Abner will soon go back to looking for another victim, and that means maybe my little sisters will suffer what I have."

Leah shuddered. "Isn't there something we can do?"

"Abe thinks I should go to Child Protection Services once I'm out of here, but I don't know."

"Don't you think that will make everything even worse for them?" Leah exclaimed. "The bishop and the church wouldn't like that at all."

Martha chewed her lip. "I wish I knew what might happen. I have no idea what the law would say or do if I go to them."

"If you leave next week, will your *maem* and *stepdaet* call the sheriff to have you brought back?"

"I'm not of age, so they could if they wanted to, but I have a feeling they'll just go along with shunning me and leave it be. They've had enough of me this past year."

Even though Martha said this with a flippant attitude, Leah sensed her friend was truly hurt.

"Do you have a job lined up or anything like that?"

"Abe says he'll help me find work. I'm pretty sure I could get a job at a fast-food place or even clean houses and factories if I have to, and I want to get my driver's license soon, too."

"Have you thought any more about contacting the Schrocks?"

"Abe said he knows a few of the former Amish who have gotten help from the Mission to Amish People ministry the Schrocks started. He said we might be able to get some clothing or household items if we need it." She made a face. "But he isn't into the church stuff they want people to do, so I don't think we'll ask them for too much."

They continued cleaning in silence, but then Leah hesitantly asked the question that had been troubling her. "Martha, are you afraid you'll die and go to hell if you leave?"

Martha sat down on a hay bale stacked in the corner out of the way. "This past year has been so bad, Leah, I think I'd rather die as a heathen *Englisher* than live the rest of my life as an Amish person going to heaven."

Leah sputtered. "Martha! You don't mean that!" She wanted to tell Martha not to be so hasty, but she held back, knowing she was thinking some of the same things about the Amish life. *But would I ever want to be shunned or know I was going to hell?*

"Honestly, I just don't care much anymore if I'm breaking the *Ordnung*. It makes no difference to me whether I live like a heathen or not. Abe has taken me to some parties the ex-Amish have at their places, and it's fun to have a beer or two and loosen up a little. It doesn't hurt me, and I feel like I'm in control of my life for the first time."

"You mean you've been drunk?"

Martha laughed. "Not really, silly! I just feel a little bit good. I don't use the drugs that can be there, but some of the kids do."

Leah shook her head. The rumors were true then. She worried Martha was going to get hurt or get in big trouble if she kept up with these practices.

"Leah, you just don't understand. If you ever decide to leave, you'll find out there's way more to life than being stuck out here on farms."

Martha regarded Leah for a moment. Then she stood and shook the dust and hay bits off of her skirt. "In case you don't know, some of the Amish kids are coming to these parties, too. You'd be surprised how many of them hide cell phones in their pockets." Martha laughed. "They like to be called and told where the next big party is going to be."

Leah walked with Martha to the doorway of the barn, thinking about how naive she was in comparison to her friend. In her heart, Leah knew if she ever decided to leave their Amish life, it wouldn't be for parties or drugs or alcohol. Those things held no attraction for her. But having freedom—the freedom to learn more about *Gott*, and the ability to live a modern and less burdened life—to be able to live without constantly being worried about the *Ordnung*—those were the things that made her secretly dream about the English world.

"Leah . . ." Martha hesitated. "By this time next week, you may not be able to spend time talking with me like this anymore. If I leave, remember you have my cell number. You can call me anytime, and I'll be sure to answer. If you want to leave, too, call. Okay?"

Tears came to Leah's eyes as she realized her friendship with Martha was likely never going to be the same. "Be careful."

"You know it! Life is going to get much more exciting for me!" Her friend waved and darted off.

"I'll miss you," she whispered.

Martha got on her bike, turning to wave as she pedaled out of the driveway. Leah had a feeling this was the last time she would see her friend in Amish clothes.

She sighed and went to look for Ada. She had to talk to someone about what Martha was planning to do—this kind of news she couldn't keep to herself.

Chapter Ten

The family slept a little later the Saturday morning after the final cleanup day at the Wengerds'. When Leah came down for breakfast, everyone was gone except for Ada. She was slumped at the table, her hair a mess, and her yawns coming one after another as she tried to eat her oatmeal.

"Where's *Maem?*" Leah asked as she poured a cup of coffee.

"She went out to the shop to see if *Daet* needs her to get anything for him at Home Hardware today. We're going into Ashfield to shop." Ada glanced out the window. "At least the sun is shining. I'd hate to go into town as cold as it's gotten overnight without sunshine to warm us up." She took another bite of oatmeal and glanced at her sister. "You coming along?"

"Sure. I don't mind getting away from this house today. With all the work we've been doing for the wedding, we haven't had time to buy groceries or anything for a couple of weeks."

"Did you really have a headache on the wedding day?"

"I did, but I was also upset."

"About what?"

"I overheard some of the church ladies talking about Martha Mast. They said she was a bad influence . . . and then they started talking about me."

"What?" Ada's eyes grew wide and she frowned. "What were they saying?"

"That I'm also a bad influence and hooked up with the awful Schrocks."

"Those women and their *nahsich* noses!" Ada exclaimed, but Leah didn't miss the worry creasing her sister's brow.

The back door opened, and *Maem* called into the kitchen, "Are you girls ready to go?"

They exchanged looks and quickly rose to get ready. Ada called back, "I have to get my hair put up, *Maem*. We'll be out in about fifteen minutes."

Leah whispered, "Ada, don't let *Maem* know about the gossipers at the wedding, okay?"

"I won't, and they should be ashamed of themselves, but please, Leah, don't give them anymore cause to talk—I'd hate for people to talk about us the way they prattle on about the Masts!" Ada stomped up the stairs.

"I'd hoped *somebody* would be on my side," Leah muttered as she went to the hooks by the back door and pulled down her shawl. "I guess Jacob is on my side." She smiled when she remembered how kind he had been the day of the wedding. She would have to be sure to thank him again.

Maem drove the buggy to the hitching post behind the hardware store, and Leah helped Benny water the horse before they left him. It might be a longer shopping day than normal, so she also gave the horse a feedbag. Benny pranced and twisted his way through the parking lot until *Maem* told him to mind himself.

They went into the hardware store first. Leah told *Maem* she'd like to look through the kitchenwares, just for the fun of it, and started up the aisle. Right in front of her was Naomi Schrock. It seemed she ran into one of the Schrocks each time she went to town. Was God trying to tell her something?

Naomi stopped to greet her, then greeted *Maem* too, but *Maem* gave a short nod and kept walking. Leah blushed and tried to make up for *Maem*'s curt behavior by returning Naomi's greeting with a broad smile.

"*Wie gehts*, Naomi?" Leah asked politely.

"*Gut.* How are you and your family, Leah?"

"Doing well."

"Your brother just got married, didn't he?"

"Yes. Just this week, to Sara Wengerd."

Naomi nodded her head toward *Maem*'s retreating back. "Is your *Maem* adjusting to his being out of the house yet?"

"Not so much. But we're happy for him and Sara."

Benny ran up, grabbing Leah's hand and trying to drag her away. "*Maem* says to hurry along 'cause she has a lot of shopping to do."

"Benny! Don't be rude. You interrupted our conversation."

"But *Maem said*, Leah," Benny whined and stamped his feet as Ada came up behind him.

Turning to Ada, Leah asked, "Do you mind taking him back to *Maem*? As wild as he is today, he's liable to break something."

Ada nodded and grabbed Benny's hand, which he promptly tried to pull away. She gripped him all the harder and marched off with their ornery brother in tow, warning, "Wait until *Maem* hears about your behavior."

"I'm sorry, Naomi. He's full of wild oats today because we've had to do so much for the wedding the last few weeks. I'm afraid he's been overlooked and overworked."

Naomi chuckled. "No problem. I've got two sons so I know how much energy they can build up."

Leah glanced around to see if *Maem* was lingering at the corner, but noticing she was out of earshot, she leaned closer to Naomi. "I enjoyed the Bible study. I sure wish I could come to another one, but I'd have to go against my *daet* to do it. I was wondering if you have more worksheets—or study sheets—to loan to me. I've been trying to read my Bible at night, but sometimes it's hard to understand what the words mean. A study sheet would help a lot."

"We have special Bible lessons you can sign up to receive through the mail, Leah. Would your parents object to you studying the Bible if you didn't actually attend the Bible study?"

"I don't know for sure, but I think it will be okay." She caught a glimpse of her mother peeking around the aisle. "I'll ask my parents. Thanks, Naomi. I'd better get going now since I can see *Maem*'s waiting for me."

"Sure. Just let me know when you're ready to begin lessons."

Leah rounded the corner and saw *Maem* had moved to the checkout counter, her lips a tight line, her shoulders rigid. She met Leah's gaze and shook her head. Leah glanced away, gathered the bags, and went ahead. She climbed into the back of the buggy to place the hardware items in a box under the seat. *Daet* wanted them to lock the box once they placed something in it if they planned to go to another store, so she snapped the lock tight. When she climbed down from the back, *Maem* was waiting.

"Leah, your *daet* and I have made it clear to you that you can't be friendly with the Schrocks."

"But *Maem*, I can't walk past Naomi without greeting her, can I?"

"A polite nod is all that's necessary, Leah. *Daet* told Matthew Schrock straight out that we didn't think you should be going to their house or associating with them anymore. But there you stand—talking to Naomi for several minutes and right in front of me yet."

Leah glanced at Ada who was trying to keep Benny occupied nearby. Her sister rolled her eyes.

Maem continued, "I'd be careful with the Schrocks from now on."

This wasn't the time to ask about the Bible study through the mail, so she followed *Maem*, Benny, and Ada across the street to the grocery store.

When Benny became restless again, Leah took him by the hand and told him he could pick out a cookie at the bakery. Benny hopped along beside his big sister, his cute, shining smile drawing attention as they walked. Suddenly, a lady came toward them, pausing as she brought her cell phone to her face. Before Leah could react, the stranger took their picture. As they hurried past the woman, Leah heard her talking excitedly to someone on her cell phone. "Did you see that? It's real-life Amish people! Really! I can hardly believe my eyes. I thought all the Amish people were in Holmes County. Yes! A little boy . . ."

Her cheeks flushed, but Leah kept her head down. The *Ordnung* forbade photographs, and the local people rarely took pictures.

Leah helped Benny choose a cookie, and then they went to find *Maem* and Ada. The shopping was nearly finished when the same lady snapped another picture of them at the door to the store. She followed their family across the street and through the parking lot, taking pictures and talking as if they couldn't hear her. She snapped picture after picture as they loaded the groceries and snapped more while Ada untied Sparky. They left the lady trying to keep up behind the buggy, still talking and taking pictures with her cell phone.

"Well," sighed *Maem*, "that was a fitting end to a day filled with frustrations, I would say." She kept her shoulders tense and her lips tight all the way home. Leah guessed *Daet* was not going to be very happy once he found out about her conversation with Naomi, but she also thought about the Bible studies she might get through the mail. No matter what, she was determined to find a way to learn more.

Ada and Benny helped *Maem* unload the groceries while Leah took the hardware items from the locked box to *Daet*'s workshop. He was busy at the back, sanding a table, and glanced up long enough to acknowledge she'd brought what he needed.

As she was going back to the house, she passed *Maem* heading to the shop. Leah sat down on the edge of the well house. She knew what *Maem* was going to tell *Daet*—better to just wait for his call.

The November breeze was getting increasingly chilly, foreshadowing the frost that could descend any night now. She stared at the back porch and its serviceable white siding. No window curtains framed the windows, and if any had been needed, the *Ordnung* allowed only dark purple, to be drawn at night.

Leah remembered seeing Amish houses in Holmes County when she traveled to visit some of *Maem*'s relatives. Their houses and yards were cheerful and colorful, with beautiful and well-tended flower gardens and lush vegetable gardens. Dainty and clean starched white curtains fluttered at the windows, and at a cousin's place, a phone booth stood in the driveway for the use of the family and their neighbors. Leah had marveled at the indoor plumbing and the kitchen appliances that ran on propane. Even the lights, sewing machines, and mixer ran on propane.

In her own yard, all she saw was dirt and drabness. The *Ordnung* forbade them to plant flowers for decoration—that was considered prideful. Though many of the gardens could be outlined with marigolds to help keep the deer away, flowers as ornaments were frowned upon. Simplicity and plainness were all the group could focus on with their Old Order homes. Consequently, the paint colors allowed were white on the outside and white on the inside. The wooden floors and trim inside the house were painted dark gray. They had outdoor plumbing with well water that came into the kitchens through a hand pump. The water had to be heated on wood-burning stoves, and no luxury was allowed to make lives easier.

Leah often wondered why it was not sinful for her New Order Amish cousins to use propane stoves and refrigerators, but for her group, it *was* sinful. Everything they did was spelled out according to the local bishop. It made no sense. She had heard that her cousins in Holmes County did not practice shunning and did not ostracize their family members who left the Amish. It seemed it would be easier to be Amish if she'd only been born fifty miles farther south. She sighed and thought again of the Schrocks.

They'd left the Old Order, too, and they seemed happier. They were kind and loving and didn't have as many hang-ups about *Gott* as people in Leah's church did. They didn't worry in the least whether they would die and go to hell just because they weren't living the Plain life anymore. The Schrocks told Leah they had peace knowing Christ made all the provision for their sins—nothing they could do, or not do, took that sin away, and once they gave their hearts over to Jesus, their sins were forgiven. They said they were *sure* they were going to heaven.

She thought back over the plan of salvation Matthew had shared. It was full of love and grace. And forgiveness: *"If we confess our sins, he is faithful and just to forgive us our sins, and to cleanse us from all unrighteousness,"* Matthew had said. Could living a Christian life really be that simple?

"Leah," *Daet* called from the shop door. "Please come here for a minute."

She groaned and decided tonight she was going to tell *Daet* she wanted peace—no matter how she had to get it, even if that meant studying the Bible. She had to have time to think about the Amish way of living. She didn't want to be like Martha—but Leah just couldn't stand not being allowed to find out about grace and forgiveness through Christ alone.

Leah stood and squared her shoulders. She knew she'd be causing a division in her family that might never heal, but she went into the workshop trying to appear confident.

Daet started in immediately. "Your *maem* tells me you spoke to Naomi Schrock in Home Hardware today."

"Yes, *Daet*, but—"

"No," he interrupted. "We are done talking about this. After tonight, if I see you speaking to the Schrocks or going with them or having *anything* to do with them, I'll ask the bishop to speak with you for willfully disobeying your parents. Is that clear to you? I'm trying to keep Satan's grip off of you, Daughter, and your disobedience shows me you've already succumbed to his evil ways."

"Evil ways?" Leah gasped, tears in her eyes. "*Daet!* I've done nothing for you to be so upset with me. Martha has disobeyed her parents over and over—she wants to live with her boyfriend—others have smoked and drunk and hidden their cars—gone into town to party—told their parents they were *rumspringen* . . . and me? What have I done that's so terrible? I've gotten to know a wonderful and loving family. I've been to *one* Bible study. I still go to church, still help out around here, and still do everything I'm supposed to do as a Plain person, but all you and *Maem* have done is find fault with me!" She stormed to the door and turned to face her parents. "I want peace!"

Daet stalked toward her. "You will *not* find this peace you want so much by going with *Englishers* who help Amish *jungen* leave their families and, more importantly, their church." Her father's hands were clenched at his side, and his face was crimson with fury and frustration.

Leah stood her ground, but her whole body was trembling. She'd never talked back to either of her parents before. "I came in here to tell you I plan to continue studying the Bible. I'm either going to get a Bible study from the Schrocks through the mail, or I'm going to go to their house for one. I've made up my mind."

Daet's quiet tone belied his deep anger. "If you do this, whether by mail or in person, I will talk to the bishop."

At that moment, Jacob Yoder came to the door. His gaze went from her to her father and back to Leah again.

She continued to look *Daet* in the eye but was able to calm herself enough to say, "All right. You do that, *Daet*. In the meantime, I'll do what I have to do to learn more about *Gott* and the Bible. For that, you can punish me if you feel you have to."

Jacob opened the door and whispered to Leah to wait for him on the front porch of the house. Now that the confrontation was finally over, she felt a wave of relief.

Leah walked to the porch and sat down on the swing. The breeze blew through her hair and across her hot cheeks. The coolness of the silent wind calmed her spirit.

She gazed out over the darkening fields and watched a flock of late-flying geese, neatly formed in a V, making their way south. After what seemed like ages, she heard the approaching footsteps of Jacob as he came around the corner and up onto the porch. He sat down on the swing, his broad shoulders barely touching her chilly arm. They pushed the swing back and forth silently for a time before he finally paused.

"It took some coaxing, but I've talked your *Daet* into letting me take you to the Bible study next Tuesday."

Leah looked at him, eyebrows arched in amazement. "You have? What about your parents? Will they agree to let you go along?"

"I had already mentioned the idea to them. My *daet* is not worried, but *Maem* pressed me not to get too involved." Jacob gave a short nod. "Yeah—they were a little concerned, but they know I plan to join the church, so they weren't as upset as your parents. I thought if I convinced your *daet* to let me take you, maybe he'd feel you wouldn't be so easily influenced. It appears I came by at just the right moment." Jacob smiled softly, then began to gently push the swing again. "I can tell he feels bad, Leah. He knows you're not doing anything that is really sinful, but he's worried this ex-Amish couple will influence you to leave. He worries you're not happy with the family and the church anymore."

She thought about that statement. "He's right about that, but he's wrong that it's because of the Schrocks. Something is not right inside of *me* anymore. The *Ordnung* rules create hard lives for us but seem to make no real difference in getting us to heaven."

Jacob nodded but kept still.

She sighed, long and deep. "I appreciate your offering to take me next Tuesday. I'm glad."

"It's going to be a long drive, but I think we'll get home before too late." Jacob stood and stretched. "Now, you need to go in and get some sleep. Oh, and it might be good to let your *maem* know you're not mad anymore," he suggested with a wink.

Leah rose with a sigh. "Yes, you're right. I'll see her before I go upstairs." She touched his arm and smiled. "Thanks, Jacob. I don't know what I'd do without you." She opened the door, its hinges protesting loudly in the quiet as Leah reluctantly went to look for *Maem*.

❧

The weekend passed with Leah working hard to stay out of *Daet*'s way. She tried to do whatever *Maem* asked of her. And she didn't say anything more about the Bible study, though she was anxious for Tuesday to come.

At the dinner table Tuesday evening, even Benny was quiet and subdued. *Daet* was clearly uncomfortable, and Leah feared he'd change his mind and order her to stay home. He hadn't said much over the weekend, only glancing at Leah once in a while with a sad, questioning look on his face. She thought back to the times when *Daet* teased her as they worked in the shop. Leah had been his helper since she was old enough to take care of the bills. She missed the tranquil moments in the shop where even her *daet* would sometimes break out in laughter.

The time came for her to get ready. Jacob would be along soon, so she went outside on the front porch to watch for him coming down the lane. To her surprise, *Maem* came out and sat with her.

"Leah, just remember, *Daet* may have given you permission to go tonight, but he didn't mean you can go again."

"I know, *Maem*."

"He's doing this so you can see there's nothing you're missing in our way of life."

She didn't answer but leapt up at the sound of Jacob's buggy.

"See you later, *Maem*."

She ran off the porch and down the steps before *Maem* could call out any more advice. Leah met Jacob at the yard's edge just as he was turning the buggy toward the house.

"Whoa, Bingo—whoa." Jacob pulled the reins back on his horse. "Leah, you scared Bingo—don't run at him like that again!"

She was out of breath, winded by her own exuberance. She crawled up into the buggy, apologizing for her rash actions.

"I was in such a hurry to get going, I guess I didn't watch what I was doing." She glanced in the back and saw his younger brother. "Hi, Erb."

"Hi." He looked bored.

"I brought Erb so he can take the buggy back," Jacob explained.

"What do you mean?"

"I got someone to call Matthew Schrock today and he agreed to meet us at Raysburg General Store. He'll give us a ride from there."

"How will we get back home?"

"I'll be back to the store around nine," said Erb.

"Oh, that's a good idea—we won't have to go as far in the dark. It makes me nervous that we can't have anything but a lantern on the back of the buggy, especially when it gets dark so early."

"*Ja.* That's a pretty dangerous thing to do nowadays."

As they started down the road, Leah wondered aloud, "Jacob, does it ever bother you that some bishops think a triangle sign is a sin, but other bishops don't? Or why one thinks a skirt that is six inches from the floor is modest, but another bishop thinks eight inches from the floor is modest?"

"I must say I have wondered about some of those things, but I try not to dwell on it, Leah." He glanced back at Erb. "The *Ordnung* mostly makes sense to me—the parts that don't, I just don't think about."

"But see, that's what I get in trouble over, Jacob. I can't figure out why each church is so different. If they all think *Gott* is talking to their bishop, why would *Gott* give them all different rules?"

Jacob shook his head. He glanced back to Erb again, and Leah got the hint. Not good to talk of these things in front of his brother.

She watched Jacob's face as he drove the buggy. His eyes roamed over the fields, and she realized there were probably many things he didn't understand, either. For him, questions about the *Ordnung* would be tempered by the draw of farm life and the peaceful way of Amish living. Leah thought it was harder on the women. Much of the *Ordnung* was written about what women wore and how they should dress, how their houses should be run. *Maybe he'd be more concerned if he had to obey all the rules women had to obey.*

The store parking lot was busy for such a little place so far in the country, and Jacob guided Bingo to a spot out of the way where they could wait for Matthew. As she hopped down from the buggy, Matthew Schrock pulled into the parking lot. Jacob waved to Erb, and the pair walked to the car. She went around to the back door and got in while Jacob settled into the front seat next to Matthew.

It was a pleasant ride to the Schrocks' place, and Matthew made sure they were not uncomfortable, asking after their families and making small talk on the short ride. When they pulled into the Schrock drive, several cars were already parked, and a few former Amish were going in the house. Jacob appeared sure of himself, not nervous at all. In contrast, Leah struggled with butterflies in her stomach and was glad to have Jacob along.

The young people gathered in the living room greeted them, and she took a seat next to Jacob. He already knew a few of the young men so they struck up a conversation.

Matthew asked them each to give a short account of how their week had been, and by the time it came around to Leah, she was relaxed and glad to share with the others. Leah was touched at their concern and care over her disagreement with her parents. How was it that near strangers seemed more concerned for her well-being than her own parents?

The meeting moved on to the Bible study, and she was happy to hear Matthew lead the group toward the Scriptures she'd read that week about salvation.

An hour later, Jacob and Leah were still talking to Matthew in a corner of the living room. The others had drifted off to chat and eat snacks in the kitchen, but her hunger was directed at knowing more about this salvation plan that didn't require her to bend herself under a heavy yoke of rules and regulations.

"It's what I yearn for, Matthew," Leah said. "To know I'm truly saved and to no longer live in fear of breaking rules." With Matthew's help, Leah finally understood the free gift of grace offered to her by Jesus' death on the cross and accepted it with joy. Something truly miraculous happened. She was like a new person—born again into a relationship with Jesus Christ. She was clean and blameless for the first time and felt loved beyond measure.

Matthew shared the good news with the others. Leah had accepted Christ and now she was ready to start her walk with Christ. She received many hugs as the ex-Amish prepared to leave and head home.

While Leah and Jacob stood by the door waiting for Matthew to take them back to the store, Naomi approached and gave her a hug.

"Leah, welcome to the family of God. I'm so glad you've accepted this wonderful gift from the Lord. Did Matthew give you some literature to read?"

"Yes, it's here in my apron pocket. Thank you, Naomi."

"Good. Now, let me know if there is anything we can do for you this week. I know it's sometimes hard to adjust to this new way of thinking."

"Thank you. I feel very hopeful my parents will understand once they hear what I've learned and experienced tonight." She turned to Jacob. His smile was genuine, but there was a hint of worry in his eyes.

The ride back to Raysburg General Store was peaceful. Leah couldn't wait to get home and share with her parents what had happened. As they approached the store, Matthew cleared his throat.

"Leah, I'm very proud of you tonight, and I know you have a calm feeling in your spirit, but I need to warn you that your parents may not be happy with your decision. Be prepared for them to confront you and not like what you tell them."

"But I can't think what would upset them. I've done nothing but have my soul filled with peace and assurance—"

"That's the very thing they may get upset about. This group of Old Order Amish doesn't believe in that kind of assurance. They won't like hearing you say you know you're going to heaven, especially since you haven't yet been baptized or joined the church."

Leah looked to Jacob, but he unexpectedly turned his face to the window and watched the parking lot approach. She was a little disappointed that both Matthew and Jacob dampened her joy about her telling her parents. "I'll keep that in mind, Matthew."

Just before he left, Matthew reminded Leah again that he and his wife were available anytime she needed to talk or if she wanted help of any kind. They would try to be there for her. He gave her his cell phone number, and Leah tucked it into the papers he'd given her at the Bible study.

When they got to the store, Erb was waiting, so they hurried to the buggy. Leah waved to Matthew as he remained standing by his car, watching as they drove into the night. A small frown creased his face. She felt a tiny flutter of anxiety start to grow. Still, Leah knew no matter how much opposition she encountered, she'd met the Savior, and there was no going back.

⚬⚬⚬

Jacob was quiet as the horse pulled the buggy back toward Leah's house, but joy flowed in her heart and mind, easing the jitters she felt when thinking of her discussion with her parents.

"Jacob, I can't believe how much better I feel! I wish you could know this feeling, too. Did you think about giving your heart to the Lord tonight?"

Jacob shuffled his feet uncomfortably and glanced at Erb. Keeping his voice low, he told Leah he was worried about what her parents would say. "They might think I didn't keep my promise to look after you, Leah. Your *daet* might not even let me see you again."

"I don't think it will be that much of a problem. My parents want what's best for me, you know."

Jacob shook his head slightly and looked away from Leah, but she decided to leave whatever happened in *Gott*'s hands.

Except for a dim glow through the purple window coverings, no lights shone through the dark night from the neighbors' houses. It was pretty late for Amish folk. As they pulled into the lane, she glanced at the windows. No light could be detected from inside. The front windows were dark, but she wondered if someone was still in the kitchen. Jacob helped her down and then waved as she opened the front door to the dark living room.

❦

Maem was sitting at the kitchen table, a glass of milk in her hand and a worried expression on her face. When she saw Leah walking toward her, she breathed a sigh of relief and smiled. "You're not too late. That's good. I think *Daet* was thinking you'd be out long after dark."

Leah poured herself a glass of milk and sat down opposite *Maem*. She was relaxed and happy, a fuzzy warmth settling over her shoulders like a cozy quilt. *Maem* watched closely as she pulled a cookie from the jar on the table.

"*Maem*, tonight I made a decision, and it's the best decision I've *ever* made."

"You have?" *Maem* sounded surprised.

"Yes. I accepted Jesus Christ as my Savior and now I *know* I'm going to heaven. You just can't believe what a difference this has made to me already." She munched the cookie happily, oblivious to her mother's sudden stillness.

Maem's voice held a sharp tone. "What do you mean? You haven't even been baptized or joined the church. How can you say you *know* you're going to heaven? No one knows that for sure."

"I found out by reading the Scriptures I don't *have* to be baptized to be save—"

"Leah! You know that isn't true!" Shock filled her mother's face. Her hands shook as she set her glass of milk down forcefully.

"*Maem*, please, let me finish." Leah could see Matthew was going to be right about this. Already *Maem* was looking back at her in disbelief. She stammered on anyway.

"I mean—once I accept Christ, it's the ABC plan of salvation: accept I'm a sinner, believe in Christ as my savior, confess my sins so He can forgive them—"

Maem jumped up from the table, her eyes confused and filled with fear. "Oh, Leah! You *can't* mean this—you can't mean what you're saying!" She broke off, pacing as she wrung her hands in distress. "I can't lose one of my children," she whispered.

"*Maem!* I'm not going anywhere—"

"You'll be as good as shunned. You'll be talked about and won't be as free as you once were to be with us! Can't you *see* that?"

Maem's tears were running freely down her face. "Your *daet*—he'll blame himself, and he'll have to go to the bishop and tell him what you said, and then, well, the whole church will know, and they'll be against you, too. You must not say *anything* about this to anyone else! Do you understand?"

Leah stood up and wrapped her arms around her mother's shoulders to comfort her. Her hands trembled as she felt *Maem's* shoulders shaking with emotion.

"Don't worry. You'll see, *Maem*. I haven't done anything wrong. *Daet* and Bishop Miller will understand once they hear me out. It's all in the Bible. Please, don't cry."

Maem shook her head as she pulled from Leah's embrace. "Daughter, I've been trying to keep this from happening! Don't you see how *Daet* and I have done everything we could to keep you out of trouble?" She slapped her hand on the tabletop. "Why did you have to go to that meeting tonight? Why? Now we'll have to tell what you've done, Leah!"

"But *Maem*, what have I done?"

"You're saying things that are heresy! They aren't true, and you've let Satan get ahold of your mind! Don't you *know* that?"

The door to the kitchen opened, and *Daet* stepped into the dimly lit room. "What's wrong? What's going on in here?"

Maem turned to him and wiped her eyes with a corner of her apron. "John, ask Leah what she just told me."

Daet turned, raised an eyebrow, and waited for Leah to explain.

"It's just that . . . I think *Maem* doesn't understand what I was saying."

"I understood *exactly* what you were saying," *Maem* interrupted.

Daet looked from *Maem* to Leah and back to *Maem* again. He was confused.

"I told her I'm born again now, *Daet*. I accepted Christ as my Savior tonight. I know I'll go to heaven—"

"What? Born again! You know you're going to heaven?"

"Yes, you see, it's not like we've been thinking all along, *Daet*. Being a Christian isn't just doing good or following the *Ordnung* exactly. It isn't about obeying the bishop or our parents. *Daet, none* of that will get me to heaven. The Bible says that only the blood of Jesus will get me to heaven. Nothing *I* can do will change my sinful heart—"

"Stop!" *Daet* squared his shoulders, and she heard him take a deep breath. "You will stop talking like this now! It's prideful and sinful to say you're going to heaven in such a way. No one can say they are going to heaven—it's not the way we believe, and you're going against the *Ordnung*. You were born Amish—for you, there is no other way to heaven but to stay Amish and follow the *Ordnung*. If you're good enough at the end of your life, maybe you will go to heaven. There is no other way!"

Daet waved his arms, his cheeks bright red from anger. "Going outside of the church is a sure way to hell for an Amish person!"

Like *Maem*, he paced back and forth, shaking his head and muttering under his breath. "I knew it was a mistake to let you go to that meeting. You have come back a different girl!" He stopped and looked at her, hands fisted on his hips.

"Yes, *Daet*, I *am* different. That's what I'm trying to tell you and *Maem*. It's the happiness and freedom I feel now—"

"I told you to stop talking like that, and I mean it!" *Daet* rubbed his beard and began pacing again. "You have given me *no* choice. In order to save your soul, which is being influenced by the Devil, I'll have to go to the bishop tomorrow."

He stopped, pointing his finger to the door. "You go upstairs to bed and think this over carefully. If you repent of what you've said by morning, then I won't go to him; but if you don't repent, then we'll let him and the elders know that you are talking crazy and are outside the will of the church and the *Ordnung*. Now go!"

Leah tried to say something, but *Daet* held up his hand and pointed again to the stairs.

She glanced at *Maem*, but her back was already turned away, stiff and unyielding. Tears clouding her way, Leah left the room and stumbled up to her bedroom.

Falling across her bed with a sob, she thought about the way things had changed in her heart. Leah knew she'd done the right thing—the peace in her soul confirmed that—but hearing her parents and knowing now that there would be no acceptance of her decision, she slowly realized living her faith here at home was not going to be easy.

She got down on her knees beside her bed to pray.

"Lord, show me what to do. I want to hear Your clear voice telling me what to do now. I don't want to have to choose between my family and You. Don't make me choose, Lord. How could I do that? Oh, Lord, what began so sweetly tonight is ending in fear. Help me overcome that fear. Lead me to You."

She got up and stretched out on her bed. Tears ran as she buried her face in her pillow and poured her heart out to the Lord. "Tomorrow, *Gott*, I'll have to figure out a way to please both You and *Daet*. How can I do that? Please give me wisdom and strength. Please help me. In Jesus' name, Amen."

She pulled the covers over her shivering body. *I guess Matthew was right. I am in a heap of trouble.*

CHAPTER ELEVEN

The next morning, breakfast was tense. Ada kept a steady gaze on her oatmeal, and Benny looked at Leah with big blue eyes, not understanding what but knowing she had done something wrong. She guessed her siblings had been told they shouldn't speak to her. *Daet* was already in his shop, and *Maem* was busying herself at the cook stove, with not even a glance at her.

Leah said a silent prayer and ate breakfast without trying to talk to anyone. She hadn't realized how hard it would be to be ostracized. She swallowed a lump in her throat and tried to eat as fast as possible. For the first time, she didn't have a list of chores to accomplish or time to spend in the shop helping *Daet*. It was as though she'd been erased from the family.

"Ada and Benny, it's time to get ready for school now," *Maem* said. Leah's siblings got up obediently and left the room. *Maem* took their dishes to the sink and washed them, then pulled her cape from the pegs by the back door and hurried outside without speaking a word.

It cut Leah to the heart not to have a kind "good morning" or a smile from *Maem*, and she felt the shame spread over her neck and face.

"So this is the way it feels, and this is how it will be."

She wiped her tears, finished breakfast, then walked to the sink to wash and dry her dishes. She knew she should put them aside—away from the rest of the family's utensils, so she neatly stacked them at the end of the shelf and left the kitchen with a heavy heart.

After a long morning and afternoon spent sequestered in her room, Leah crept quietly down the stairs, made herself a quick sandwich, then walked through the house and out the front door. Grabbing her cape as she left, Leah decided to take a walk up the lane to think.

She turned onto the main road just as Abe Troyer's truck approached. He slowed down, pulling the beat-up machine to the edge of the dusty road. Leah walked to the passenger side, leaning in the window so they could talk.

"I was hoping to see you somewhere today. Martha wanted to let you know she's leaving the house tonight. I plan to pick her up at the end of the driveway. She's been taking some things out of the house slowly, and she's ready to leave."

"Tonight? Everything's changing so fast, Abe. You should know unless I repent of saying I'm a born-again Christian, I'm in trouble with my parents and I'm sure the church, too, by now. I don't know what will happen, because I don't plan to repent."

Abe raised his brows. "Why get yourself into trouble over something like that?" he muttered. He shifted in his seat, waved away the topic, and gave his advice. "Be sure you know what you're doing. With me and Martha, we'll be together, but you won't have Jacob if you keep on this way. You'll be alone, Leah."

She stared at him, then smiled softly. "But that's just it, Abe. With Jesus in my heart, I'll never be alone again, no matter what happens to me."

He grunted and placed his hands back on the steering wheel. "Suit yourself. I'm just saying—well, never mind. You know what you want, I guess. Listen, I got to go. I have a job lined up for tomorrow, and I need to get things squared away before I come back for Martha." He pointed a finger down the road toward her friend's house. "Maybe you could go by and let her know what's going on."

She nodded and waved as Abe drove off. Leah watched his truck grow smaller and smaller on the lonely road until the sound of horse hoofs behind her shifted her attention to who was coming. It was *Daet*. As he neared, Leah lifted her hand in greeting, but he kept his eyes straight ahead on the road and passed by without a glance.

She lowered her hand, her gaze turning toward the road. Her parents' rejection was almost more than she could take, and as she set out on her walk to Martha's house, she came close to changing her mind about her salvation. She nearly ran home to repent and recant her testimony, but as she scanned the bright November sky and watched the crows fighting for the last of the corn in the fields, an odd strength entered her spirit. Leah knew she could never deny the truth.

She'd changed—she'd found peace, and no amount of shunning was going to take that knowledge away from her. Her eyes were opened, and there was no going back, no matter what it cost.

⸎

The late afternoon sunshine had warmed the air by the time she came to the lane that led to the Masts' home. Leah saw Martha in the side yard, gathering clothes off the line. She was filling a handmade basket with the shirts and pants of the men in her household, and as Leah drew nearer, she saw tears running down her friend's cheeks.

"Martha!"

She dropped the shirt she was unpegging and turned to see who had called her name. "Leah! I'm so glad you came by today. Did you see Abe?"

"Yes, that's one of the reasons why I'm here. He said you're leaving tonight, and I wanted to come to say good-bye."

She nodded. "It won't be like a real good-bye, you know. You can come and visit me whenever you want." She pulled her apron up and wiped her eyes. "Sorry you caught me crying; getting sentimental about my sisters. I'll worry about them."

"I know. I'm sorry you have to leave them. It'll seem different without you here. Do your parents know about your plans?"

"I think *Maem* suspects, but my *stepdaet* just tries to ignore anything in the household he doesn't want to know about."

They walked to a bench near the barn door and sat down. "What about your sisters?"

"Believe it or not, I told Abner that if I ever hear of him touching one of them, I'll go to the Ashfield County sheriff. Now that I'll be on the outside, he looked a little more worried about whether I'm a real threat. I hope he thinks twice, because I meant what I told him." She stared out over the barnyard for a time, her face hard and emotionless. She turned to Leah finally and asked, "How are you getting along with your parents?"

Leah dropped her chin, afraid she might cry if she tried to speak. After a moment, she told Martha about going to the Bible study and getting saved. Martha looked surprised.

"How'd that go over with your parents?"

"Not very well. *Daet* has made up his mind to tell the bishop that he and *Maem* consider me to be in the hands of Satan—really rebellious against them and the church. I don't know what the bishop will say. I know he won't think too much of me saying I'm a born-again Christian."

Martha shook her head. "He isn't going to like it, Leah. If you were older or a member of the church already, I'm sure you'd get the ban."

"*Daet* and *Maem* are already treating me like I'm under the miting."

"They are?"

She nodded. "They see my confession of faith as full-out rebellion against the church. *Daet* thinks by saying I know I'll go to heaven when I die, I'm under Satan's influence. He thinks the only way to bring me to my senses is to shun me back into the fold."

"He really means business, doesn't he?" Martha was surprised.

"*Ja.* His biggest worry is that I might go to hell. And I have to admit, it still worries me sometimes, after hearing over and over that if we don't stay Amish, we can't go to heaven."

Her friend shrugged. "I don't know and I don't care. Like I told you, I don't care if I go straight to hell as long as I don't have to live Amish the rest of my life."

"But, Martha, you have to think about where you're going to end up. Don't you think about the end of your life?"

"Ha! No way, Leah. I've had nothing but Abner and the church and *Maem* and my sisters to think about, but hell or heaven? Nope." Martha stood suddenly and pointed to the back porch. "You'd better go. I see my *stepdaet* looking for me, and when he bothers to look for me, it's usually not a good thing. Hurry! Let me walk you down the lane, and then maybe by the time I get back, he'll have forgotten what he wanted me for."

Leah stood and walked quickly with Martha to the road, listening as she chattered about the new apartment Abe had found for them. She was excited to be leaving, she insisted, and would never miss the clothes or the life or the church, and especially not the *Ordnung*.

As they neared the end of the lane, Martha stopped, grabbing her arm. "You'll not let them boss you too much, will you, Leah?"

"I hope I can please *Daet* and *Maem* without getting banned. But I also know this: I can't give up what I believe now, this freedom, this joy."

"What about Jacob Yoder?"

"He went with me to the Bible study, Martha. He watched me accept Christ, and on the way home he was really quiet. Sometimes I think the Lord's working in his heart, too."

Martha laughed. "Looks like I'm leaving you right at the best time if you're going to get all religious, Leah."

She reached over and gave Martha another hug. "I'll be praying for you. Stay safe, Martha. Be careful out there with those *Englishers*."

"I will. Hey, my guy says things will be fine, and I believe him. It's been a long time coming, and I'm ready to move out of here."

"Okay. Just don't try to do everything all at once. I wish you didn't have to live with Abe. Have you asked the Schrocks if they have space for you in their downstairs apartment?"

"You think like the Amish. You worry too much about what other people will say about you." She tossed her head. "I told you before. I don't care about what people think of me."

"I know, but—"

"I just want to be happy, Leah. For once—just once, I want to be happy and free of those dumb rules."

"I'll still pray for that, Martha. I'll pray for *Gott* to help you be happy. And"—she fished around in her apron pocket until she found the pamphlet the Schrocks had given her about Mission to Amish People—"here's a number where you can reach the Schrocks, in case you need to call them to help you. I know they will."

Martha took the paper and put it in her pocket. "Thanks, Leah. I won't need to call them, I'm sure, but thanks anyway. And go ahead and pray for me; I guess I could always use the extra help."

They said final good-byes, and as Martha walked back down the lane, Leah stopped to watch her. She saw the determined set of her friend's shoulders and wondered if Martha was truly as carefree and happy as her words tried to convey.

⁕

For the first time in her life, Leah realized she was not looking forward to going home. As she approached the house, *Maem*'s silhouette was visible, moving from the kitchen to the living room, lighting the lamp by the door as she went. She prayed *Maem* would come to understand her desire to follow Jesus.

She went in the front door just as *Maem* was going up the stairs to bed. *Maem* glanced down at her but slowly turned and went up the steps without a word or a smile.

"Good night, *Maem*."

Maem's only reply was the gentle closing of her bedroom door.

Leah blew out the lamp and went up to bed, too. As she passed her parents' room, she heard *Maem* crying. Leah stopped, placed her hand on the doorknob, and started to go in, but when she heard *Maem* talking to *Daet*, she changed her mind. She'd only be an unwelcome interruption.

She went quietly to her room, lit the lamp, and snuggled into her flannel gown. Reaching into the drawer for the New Testament, she unfolded the papers the Schrocks had given her and began to read some verses they'd listed, first in the book of Hebrews, and then a verse in the book of 1 Peter. It's as if they knew exactly what struggles she was going to face.

"Wherefore seeing we also are compassed about with so great a cloud of witnesses, let us lay aside every weight, and the sin which doth so easily beset us, and let us run with patience the race that is set before us, looking unto Jesus the author and finisher of our faith; who for the joy that was set before him endured the cross, despising the shame, and is set down at the right hand of the throne of God. For consider him that endured such contradiction of sinners against himself, lest ye be wearied and faint in your minds.

"That the trial of your faith, being much more precious than of gold that perisheth, though it be tried with fire, might be found unto praise and honor and glory at the appearing of Jesus Christ. . . ."

She turned down the lamp and lay in the dark for a time. Leah didn't want to lose heart, but the way things had been going the last few days, it was difficult not to feel tired and weary of it all.

"Lord, help me to put my trust in You. Help me not to mind the sorrow of being shunned by my parents but to remember all the ways You sorrowed to love me and accept me. Keep Martha close to You so she one day knows You can help her, too. In Jesus' name, Amen."

⚜

By the next day, the news that Martha was gone was spreading through the community. Leah waited until *Maem* and *Daet* finished eating their lunch before she went in to fix herself a ham and cheese sandwich. She sat at the table and listened to her parents talking in the hallway.

"She was warned, of course, but her parents found a note from her on the table this morning."

"Oh, John, I hate to hear that news, though we've known it was coming for some time."

"She's moved into an apartment with Abe Troyer."

"Did the Schrocks help her?"

"It doesn't look like it—seems she did it on her own."

"I know she had a hard time at home, but leaving is no way to fix things, and living with her boyfriend, well, I suppose it's no worse than running away."

They moved off, and Leah continued eating lunch. It was depressing to know Martha was truly gone.

That afternoon, the bishop came to call on the family and asked to have a word with Leah about Martha. *Maem* asked her to come into the living room.

She followed *Maem* to the room where the bishop sat with his hat on his knee. *Daet* sat stiffly in a chair by the hallway door. His demeanor showed how highly embarrassed he was to be having this conversation with the bishop.

She took a chair across from them and waited politely for Bishop Miller to speak.

"Leah, your parents let me know what has happened to you since last week—this born-again thing you claim you experienced. I need to warn you before it's too late that you're playing with fire. The more you listen to this kind of teaching, the more likely it is that you will get burned. Now, Martha is an example of what can happen once you decide to let Satan take hold of your thoughts. I'd like to know where she has gone. Do you have an address for her?"

"I'm sorry, Bishop Miller, but I don't have an address for her." Leah shifted in her chair, her cheeks warm from the lecture he'd just delivered.

"Then do you have a way to get in touch with her? Her parents are very concerned for her and might like to call the sheriff. She is under-age," he continued gravely.

Leah sat up straight. "Did they say they'd do that?"

"I think they see how I view this thing, and they know I encourage families to call the authorities when their underage children run away." He frowned slightly and continued. "Not that we like to get the law involved—it's not our way—but we can't just hand our youth over to Satan. So I feel the families need to do whatever they can to get their children back into the fold."

He regarded her a few minutes longer and then stood to leave. "One last thing, Leah: your *daet* and *maem* have every right to correct you in your rebellion if you continue to go to these *Englisher* Bible studies. Of course, if—or should I say when—you make the rightful decision to join the church, your public repentance will be required, too."

Leah made no comment and stayed seated while her parents led the bishop to the door. *Maem* came back in, looked at her pleadingly, and then followed *Daet* out the back door to the shop. *Daet* hadn't spoken one word to her. She sighed and climbed the stairs feeling more and more like her bedroom was both a solace and a prison. Jacob should know what the bishop said, in case he wanted to stop seeing her. It wouldn't be fair to get him into trouble, too.

✦

Dear Jacob,

I wanted to let you know that Bishop Miller has been to see
me about Martha. He also asked me to repent of my born-again
beliefs, but I just can't do that—it is what I now know to be true,
and just like it says in the Bible, it has set me free. *Daet* thinks I'm
just being rebellious, but I don't think I am. Bishop Miller will
make me confess and repent if I decide to join the church.

Jacob, you should know that I'm not certain I can stay here.
It breaks my heart to even write it. If only the church and my
parents would let me stay and follow my Savior, then I would
gladly remain here and join the church. But that doesn't look like
it will happen.

If you decide you can't be with me anymore, I will understand.
I know the trouble I have had by being a friend to Martha, and I
expect the community will do the same thing to you if you stay
with me.

I've been told I can't go to the Bible studies anymore, but I
plan to do it anyway, somehow. I'm so hungry to learn more of
what *Gott* says in His Word! Thank you, Jacob, for taking me to
the Schrocks. I have peace even though I'm sad and not sure what
will happen next. If I decide to leave, I will contact the Schrocks
to help me. You should not be involved in any way, so the church
will not blame you or punish you.

Take care, Jacob. You have been kind and thoughtful to me
over and over these last few months and I appreciate you very
much.

Your friend, Leah

With tears streaming down her face, Leah folded the letter and put it
in an envelope, then found a stamp and decided to mail the letter that
afternoon. No sense in giving *Maem* or *Daet* the chance to intercept it.

✦

Another day of solitude passed, with Leah feeling increasingly like an unwelcome, invisible guest in her own home. Ada's eyes filled with tears every time Leah entered the kitchen, and Benny's clear confusion over their new family rule nearly broke Leah's heart. Obviously, her *daet* hoped to give Leah a taste of what a real *meidning* would be like. She took to eating her meals after the others had left and keeping to her room as much as possible to avoid the painful silence that greeted her.

Finally, she could bear the isolation no more, and she ducked outside to get the bike from the shed when the others were busy with lunch.

The air was turning colder, and the sky looked gray; snow was not far away, but she was only going to ride to the general store and back, just to stretch her legs and feel the wind on her face again. Deep in her heart, she also hoped to hear back from Jacob.

Many of Leah's Amish neighbors passed her on the way to the store, but only one or two waved or nodded a greeting. Already the word was getting around she was in trouble. Her neighbors might not know why, but they would not want to be on the wrong side of the bishop or the church if she was shunned in the future.

Leah was tired by the time she got to the store, so she decided to rest at the picnic tables that were clustered outside under the trees. The sun was setting quickly, and she knew better than to linger or it would be dark and too dangerous to be on the road with her unmarked bicycle. *Daet* and the rest of the men in the community had removed all the bike reflectors just last year after Bishop Miller had decided they were too showy. As she was about to gather her bike and head for home, a familiar buggy pulled into the lot. Jacob waved. Relief washed over her; at least he was still acknowledging her.

"*Wie gehts*, Leah?"

"*Gut.* I wasn't sure you'd talk with me, Jacob."

"Silly, Leah. After I got your letter this morning, I was hoping for a chance to speak with you face-to-face." Jacob grinned sheepishly. "My brother spotted you on the road, so I headed out, figuring you might end up here."

Leah, suddenly overwhelmed with emotion, looked away to gather her thoughts. "Jacob, I don't know what to say. Between Martha's leaving

and the bishop's accusations, I thought you'd be done with me, and I just
. . . I just don't want you to feel obliged. Or get into trouble because of
me. That's all."

He steered her bike to the side of the building. She followed, watching
as he carefully leaned it against the wall. He turned to her, his expression
calm and sure.

"I don't want to talk about that, and I don't want you to think about
it anymore, either. Whatever happens, I'll stick by you; if you want me
to, that is."

"Even if I have to leave?" she asked suddenly.

He searched her face, finally shaking his head. "I'd like to say you won't
make that decision, but the way your folks and the bishop are talking . . .
you may not have a choice if they won't let you be the Christian you want
to be. I'd understand that, Leah, but I'd be hurt."

He paused. "You're the only girl for me." He smiled sadly. "And I
can't imagine not having you in my life, but truthfully, I also can't see
myself living life outside the Amish community. The life is hard, but I
like the farm and the community atmosphere. I don't always agree with
the things the *Ordnung* requires, but I accept it. If you aren't there, Leah,
it would all be different."

He shuffled his feet. "I don't know if I could stand being around folks
if they were shunning you. The thought of you being hurt—"

He swallowed, then looked out at the blackening sky. "It's getting late,
and you shouldn't be biking on the roads after dark. I've got my buggy;
let me put your bike in the back and take you home." He whispered, "I
have a reflector I can put on the back."

Leah was surprised. "Jacob Yoder, you're going against the *Ordnung*
by using a reflector?"

Jacob tapped her nose with his finger. "Looks like we may be more
alike than we thought—both stubborn and rebellious."

She laughed, relief and gratitude coursing through her—and another
emotion too, that left her a little breathless. Climbing into his buggy, she
gave him a quick kiss on the cheek, ever so grateful for Jacob Yoder and
praying that somehow things would work out.

Almost the entire ride home, Jacob talked about plans for the farm, the new shed he was helping construct, and the silly antics of his younger siblings. It felt so good to think about something other than her troubles, to laugh and enjoy the company of such a special friend. Before long, she was safely home.

Jacob lifted her bike down from the back, and she gripped the handlebars, suddenly feeling awkward. Just as she was about to blurt out a good-bye, Jacob put his hand over hers. "Leah, I'll go with you to the Bible study on Tuesday, if you're still determined to go."

"Oh, Jacob. That would be great. Should I call for a ride?"

"Better. It's too dark now for us to take the horse and buggy."

"Okay. If you come by tomorrow, I'll let you know if I get in touch with the Schrocks."

"See you then. Good night, Leah." A quick kiss on her lips and he was gone.

Chapter Twelve

When she got up on Saturday morning, Leah found the bishop was not ready to let her be. *Maem* had left a note on the breakfast table saying that Bishop Miller was waiting for her in her father's shop. With no appetite for breakfast, Leah gulped down a few sips of coffee, took a deep breath, and walked outside with as much confidence as she could muster. When she went in the shop, Leah discovered a grim bishop along with two stone-faced church preachers.

Bishop Miller started right in. "Leah, the preachers would like to counsel you about your sinful ways. You know Preacher Andy Weaver here is someone whose daughter left the church, and he wants to warn you about what can happen to you."

Andy Weaver was one of the long-winded preachers in the church who tended to preach on everything considered sinful, from rubber tires to riding in cars.

He cleared his throat and stepped forward. Leah glanced at *Daet*, standing in the shadows, his arms folded and his eyes cast downward. His shame made her heart ache, but a surge of irritation swept over her that her parents were being humiliated for nothing important. If only these men would listen to her testimony, then they might not feel she was doing anything bad after all.

From somewhere within herself, she summoned the courage to speak before Preacher Weaver started on his diatribe.

"Excuse me. I need to ask something of you three men. If I listen patiently to your views, would you then agree to hear me out about what I've learned from the Bible?"

Daet's eyes swung to her, and he stiffened at her boldness. Bishop Miller took note of *Daet*'s frown and sighed. He reluctantly nodded agreement and then asked Preacher Weaver to proceed.

"Leah Raber, I have a word of warning for you." The man took out a folded piece of paper from his pocket and smoothed it between his hands.

Leah barely stifled an exasperated sigh as she recognized the paper as one he had used several times in church while he was preaching. He cleared his throat importantly and began to read the often-quoted letter:

> Dear Father and Mother,
>
> It has been in my mind to write to you for a while, but after leaving, I was afraid of what you'd say to me. I know I have sinned against God, and I wonder how He will ever be able to forgive me. Now that I am married, I fear there is nothing left to do but to beg you to forgive me. I wonder if God will forgive me.
>
> My sins bother me every day, and every night I think of what I have done wrong. I will probably never escape the feeling that I have sinned. I am afraid sometimes that my wrongs against you both will eventually kill you. I am so sorry.
>
> Even though you taught me right and wrong, it is my fault that I decided to do the wrong thing.
>
> I am writing this letter through my tears. I pray every night God will hear my prayers. When I think of how much you must miss me and how hard you tried to raise me right, I feel just terrible. Please do not forget to pray for me, and please, please forgive me.

Andy refolded the letter and tucked it carefully in his pocket. He studied her. "Do you know who wrote that?"

Leah nodded.

He ignored her nod and went on with his message. "It is from a girl like you who thought she knew what was best. She thought the church was too old-fashioned or too strict, but now, as you have heard, she is heartbroken that she left and knows her sinful ways have doomed her. You would do well to listen to her words of sorrow and turn from this path you're on. It is the path of destruction, the same path Martha Mast has chosen."

Weaver closed his mouth tightly and stepped back behind the bishop.

Bishop Miller then nodded to the other man, and Preacher Earl Plank rocked on his heels a bit before launching himself forward. He steadied himself inches from Leah's face. He, too, pulled out a much-folded piece of paper and started on his mini-sermon.

"First of all, this letter is to a man who left, and I think you need to hear what kind of pain his friends felt after he turned away from his Amish community. Listen closely, Leah, so you can hear the truth."

He rocked back and forth from toes to heels as he read, his deep, slow voice emphasizing each word of admonishment.

> Dear David,
>
> Greetings from on High. Out of deep concern for you and your dear family, I tell you to stop and think what you are doing. You know better. This is far from what your parents taught you, and you know it.
>
> Satan has a hold of you. You say the Lord shows you to do this and that. David, how can you say it's the Lord when you know that is not what you were taught? You say we don't understand. I think it's time you realize who doesn't understand. Satan has you where he wants you. It is sad and sad indeed to see your dear children being so misled. You can turn the Scriptures around as you like, but you cannot change what's right and wrong . . .

Leah's mind began to drift as Preacher Plank's voice droned on, and she couldn't help allowing a sigh escape. How could she make these men—and her parents—understand what she'd experienced that night and accept what she now knew to be true? Would these men let her live peacefully among them and still hold tight to her newfound faith? And what of Jacob . . . would all this be too much for him to bear? Leah sighed again, barely hearing as the preacher continued.

. . . How can you sit in a worldly vehicle and dress like the world, and drive around like the world, and say the Lord shows you to do these things? It's unthinkable and terrible, how can you go to sleep at night? Only because Satan has you in his grip!

This is written to you out of deep Christian love and concern for you and your dear family.

Concerned friends,

The Lapps

Earl Plank added a note of warning that she not follow Martha into the pit of hell, then pulled back and let the bishop finish the meeting.

"Again, your parents are heartbroken you are considering the same kinds of things the people in these letters did and the same path as Martha Mast," Bishop Miller began, his voice growing louder with each word. "Heed the word of the Lord: set yourself apart and don't let pride turn your eyes away from the truth. Cast off this lie of Satan and don't let him get hold of you anymore. Repent and come back to believing the things the *Ordnung* and our traditions have always upheld as truth."

He turned to the two men who accompanied him and ended with, "Our forefathers never for a minute doubted we have been blessed by knowing the truth—to having the *Ordnung* to guide us and our church to help us make the decisions all of us need in order to live a humble and helpful life in our community. Don't turn away now from all you've been taught. Don't walk the path Martha has chosen to walk."

The repeated references to Martha burned Leah's heart. This was not fair to her or to Martha. She waited until he was finished. The group of men stood silently, their imposing wall of rebuke intimidating Leah. She steeled herself and spoke.

"All my life I've obeyed my parents and followed the rules laid down for me, but last week, I experienced Jesus' grace for my soul—" Leah was so filled with emotion that her voice nearly betrayed her. Before the men could interrupt, she hurried on. "I came to the understanding He paid the price for my sins on the cross. I can't do *anything* to deserve or to earn this salvation. I've looked at the Scriptures myself, and I finally understand them. I now know that my works and my good deeds can't begin to cover up the sins and troubles I am born into. But God, through His Son, has offered me hope. I don't have to do anything but accept this gift—not works, or following the *Ordnung* perfectly—nothing but saying 'I accept this gift, Lord, and I confess and repent of my sins. Cover them all with your blood.'

"And as for Martha"—Leah paused, looking each of them in the eye—"you three surely know what drove her from us—the abuse from her stepbrother Abner and then having to live in the same house with him, with no help from the church, no support for her sorrow. Nothing was done to make him feel his own shame, but for Martha, there was no mercy, no love, just guilt heaped upon guilt—"

"Leah! You have no right to discuss that with these men; they have done their duty for that girl!"

She fell silent at her father's interruption, focusing on the men, trying to judge their reactions.

Bishop Miller spoke. "Martha Mast accused her stepbrother, and he accepted our judgment. When he is allowed back to church, his confession and repentance will be accepted. Martha has offered no recent confession nor shown any sign of repentance."

"But she's hurt, and no one offered to help her!" Leah exclaimed.

Bishop Miller put up a hand. "This matter is not yours and has been taken care of by the church. I'll not discuss it with you." His expression shut down further argument.

She hesitated, waiting for the rest of the men to say something, but it appeared they were finished speaking. Leah sighed. At least she'd had a chance to speak. In spite of the turmoil in the room, they knew just where she stood.

Bishop Miller shook his head sadly and motioned for the men who were with him to leave. One last time, he turned to her and warned that she was terribly confused and listening to Satan. "You must *want* to come back to the church, Leah, and confess you have fallen prey to the deceiver before we can do anything more for you. Until you do this, I agree with your parents that they should have limited contact with you. They do this out of love and not hate, Leah—as do we all—with the hope it will set you to thinking and cause you to change your mind.

"I have the unfortunate task of asking you not to come to church until you're ready to repent and leave this rebellion. We can't have the other youth thinking you're being encouraged in your sin. May *Gott* help you, sister."

He nodded his good-bye to *Daet*. The trio trouped out, their task fulfilled.

Limited contact . . . not come to church . . . Leah was momentarily stunned to finally hear the words but not surprised.

She eyed *Daet*, but he ignored her and walked away to the back of the shop to start work. His stooped shoulders stabbed her heart. Again, deep regret filled her that he and *Maem* were made to suffer over her decision.

She left the shop and stumbled back to her room, feeling numb. There she slipped to the floor and prayed again that the Lord would help her make the right decisions. She didn't want to abandon her faith. "Lord, help me understand. Give me wisdom."

She wiped the tears that covered her face and got up, not sure what was next for her. Moving to the window, she stared at the tranquil fields and hills so dear and familiar to her.

She wondered if Jacob would be coming to the shop. If so, he'd be told what had happened. *Daet* would, no doubt, let Jacob know there would be no hard feelings if he decided not to pursue his relationship with Leah.

Why does it have to be this way, God? Will I be forced to choose between my Savior and my family?

The world around her seemed threatening and dark. Her room, once a sanctuary, had become ominous and stifling. Far worse than feeling like a stranger in a foreign land, she was now branded an enemy. A sinner who'd finally found forgiveness, only to have the bishop label her rebellious, caught in the grip of the Devil. *Dear Gott, help me cling to Your truth . . .*

"Leah . . . Leah . . ." A soft knock interrupted her thoughts. It was Ada. She hurried to the door. Her sister stood in the hallway, looking cautiously over her shoulder before whispering to Leah, "Can I come in?"

"Yes, surely." Leah swung the door wide. "Please, sneak in any time you want. I've missed talking to you."

She gave Ada an impetuous hug, but her sister received the overture of affection coldly. This was not like Ada, and it broke Leah's heart. Ada stepped around her to sit on the window seat.

"I've only come to tell you to do the right thing. You're turning our family upside down, and you're causing *Maem* and *Daet* embarrassment. You have to stop this right now." Ada's face radiated anger and recrimination.

"Ada, I'm not doing this on purpose. I'm only—"

Ada stood. "I'm not here to argue with you. At first, I found your interest in the Bible to be kind of exciting, but now, I think your selfish behavior is awful. Have you seen the suffering on *Maem*'s face? You have to stop and consider the rest of us. If you don't care what people think of you, you should at least think about what people are saying about *Maem*, *Daet*, Benny, and me. You've been at the quiltings—you know how the ladies will be talking us up and down. They'll find fault with *Maem* and *Daet*. They'll snicker behind their hands when *Maem* and I show up. How *could* you do this to your own family? I don't understand you at all. I thought it was like a joke in the beginning, but now—"

"It's not a joke, Ada. I've found true peace, and I know that Jesus has forgiven me my sins. Please, let me explain—"

Ada gave Leah a dismissive wave of her hand and walked out the door, leaving her sister rooted to the floor, sorrow washing over her.

❧

Maem raised her eyebrows in surprise as she saw Leah approach the laundry shed later that day. She glanced away, breaking eye contact.

"*Maem?*"

She glanced up, pursing her lips.

"Um, I've been thinking, and I . . . I just wanted you to know . . ." Leah's voice trailed off nervously.

Maem glanced toward her shaking hands, and Leah noticed the lines in her face soften, but still she turned away.

"Since you and *Daet* already believe I'm sinning, I've decided I may as well go to the Bible studies." She paused, but the relief that she'd finally revealed her plans was immense. "I love you both very much"—she faltered, emotion choking her voice—"but I want to know more about *Gott* and His Word."

Maem continued to hold her lips in a tight grimace, as though it was hard for her to not respond to Leah.

Leah paused, waiting for some tiny sign that her mother understood. When nothing came, she continued speaking. "I just wanted you to know so you wouldn't worry about where I am Tuesday night."

She hesitated. "And *Maem* . . ." Again *Maem*'s set shoulders and tight mouth revealed nothing but censure. "I . . . I am truly sorry you've been hurt by this."

Leah stifled a sob and turned away. Nothing more could be done. Her beloved parents had shut her out.

Chapter Thirteen

With the bishop's visit and the preachers' warnings piled up inside her, Leah burrowed down into her covers the next morning, listening with an aching heart as her family left for the Sunday service. She couldn't remember ever missing church, and wondered what would be said of her absence. Brushing away tears, she dressed and went to the kitchen, pulling her cape off the hook as she headed out. Not sure where to go, Leah started down the lane, desperate to get away from her sorrow-filled house. She walked for twenty minutes before realizing she'd gone half-way to the general store.

The frustration and humiliation of the last few days tumbled in her head, and she knew the decision facing her would change her life forever. Would she live like an outcast among her family or deny her faith and become a "good" Amish girl again? Both options made her stomach twist in agony. After what seemed like hours of thinking, walking, and praying, she knew she was not going back home again. Others had done it. Others had walked away with nothing but the clothes on their backs, but Leah had never dreamed she'd come to the same decision.

She pulled the heavy glass door open and looked around. The bell on the door of the store had a cheerful ring, mocking her somber mood. On the counter by the register was a phone, and Leah timidly asked the manager if she could use it. He pushed it toward her without a word while she dug the phone number out of her pocket. With shaking hands, she carefully dialed the numbers from the wadded and wrinkled piece of paper and waited for the connection to go through. After several rings, Matthew Schrock answered the phone.

"Hello, Matthew. This is Leah Raber."

"Leah, I'm happy to hear from you. How are you?"

"The truth is, you were right. It hasn't gone well."

Her chin trembled, and she turned her face away from the curious manager, though he tried to pretend he wasn't listening to her end of the conversation.

She swallowed hard and continued. "I'm afraid I'm not welcome at home anymore, and need to find another place . . . a place to . . . um . . . stay for a while."

There was a pause. "Oh, I see. I'm very sorry that you've had some difficulty, Leah. I'm very sorry to hear that. I always pray that, somehow, it will one day change—this tension between the Amish ways and the born-again Christians, but—" Matthew sighed.

She heard him shuffling through papers. "Leah, I have about an hour before I can leave church—I've got a quick meeting to attend. Are you someplace where you'll be safe and warm?"

"Yes. I walked to Raysburg General Store."

"Okay. Good. Have you had lunch or anything to eat?"

She shook her head, then realized Matthew couldn't see her. Her cheeks flamed as she glanced at the store manager, who was smiling. "No, I haven't had anything to eat. I'm sorry to be such trouble to you, Matthew."

Matthew answered in a calm voice. "Leah, are you sure this is what you want to do?"

Leah thought for a minute. The truth was she wasn't *totally* sure, but she knew there was nothing else she could do now. Her home was a battle zone. She needed to get away and think. "Yes, I think so. As much as I can be sure, I guess."

"Okay. I understand. I have to ask you, though, if you're of age?"

"Do you mean am I eighteen? No. I'm seventeen. Does that matter?"

"Hmmm. We usually don't take in anyone under eighteen, but if you've already made up your mind, then we'll make an exception. Is there a chance your parents will call the sheriff to have you taken back home?"

"I don't know. No one in my family has ever done this before. I guess I didn't think this through very well, did I? If you say I should go back . . ." She left the sentence unfinished. She was confused. If she was going to cause the Schrocks trouble, she didn't want to go there.

Matthew said nothing for a second or two and Leah looked around for the manager. He was cleaning the ice-cream case, but his face showed concern.

"Leah?" Matthew asked.

"Yes—I'm sorry, I'm still here."

"I'll talk to Naomi, okay? She should be able to get to you in about twenty minutes. Will you be all right until then?"

"Yes—sure."

"Good. Why don't you wait for her at the tables by the ice-cream counter. She'll be driving a silver pickup."

"Okay. Thanks, Matthew. I really appreciate it."

She hung up, and the manager strolled over to place the phone back where it belonged. He eyed her, and she gave him a weak smile. "I'm going to be meeting someone here in about twenty minutes. Is it all right if I wait over there at the tables?" She nodded toward a corner where three tables and sets of chairs stood empty.

"There's no one in here for ice cream while it's this cold, so go ahead. If I get a few customers in for lunch, though, you'll have to make room for them."

"Thank you."

Leah walked to the table closest to the window and farthest from the manager. She pulled her cape closer and gazed out. Two or three neighbors rode past in their buggies, but they didn't even glance toward the store. *The church service must be over.* She checked the clock hanging above the door: one o'clock. *No wonder I'm hungry.*

She could feel rumblings and grumblings in her stomach. *I never want to be dependent on anyone else for food or shelter. I will find a job and work.*

The manager of the store went about his business, but he appeared to be keeping an eye on her. Leah glanced his way a couple of times and saw curiosity in his eyes, but he didn't ask anything. About fifteen minutes into her wait, he suddenly appeared at the table and slid a small dish of ice cream across to her. Leah looked up, surprised.

He shrugged, "I had to empty a container. It was getting low. No point in wasting this little bit left in the bottom. If you like butter pecan, you're welcome to it."

She thanked him. The first taste of the creamy treat was wonderful. Maybe because she was starving, his kindness added to the pleasure. She savored every bite, and by the time Naomi arrived, she had finished eating it.

Naomi spied her and walked straight over. "Leah, it's good to see you. How have you been doing?"

"The last week has been hard, but I'm okay."

"Matthew said you want to leave home today. Is that so?"

"Yes, I have a feeling if I don't leave, things will only get worse for my family."

"Is the bishop involved?"

Leah nodded, dropping her eyes in embarrassment.

Naomi gave a reassuring smile. "Don't be embarrassed. I know how it is. I had troubles similar to yours when I left. It hurts a lot, but in the long run you'll find that you're happier and healthier as you grow in your faith. I know it's not easy and often very hard to start over. In the meantime, we'll add your family to our prayer list." She paused. "I'm very sorry you've had to make this decision. I was really hoping your parents would accept your new faith."

Leah couldn't say another word for fear of crying.

"If you're ready, we might as well go."

Leah stood but before she left the shop, she thanked the manager for allowing her to wait in the store and for the ice cream.

He waved away the thanks. "No problem. Glad you liked it."

Once they were on the road, she sighed and sat back in the seat, wanting to think things through. Naomi had soft music playing on the radio and Leah closed her eyes for a minute and listened. It was a beautiful song with peaceful words and a haunting melody that soothed her troubled heart. Naomi seemed to sense Leah needed time to herself and didn't try to talk.

Leah opened her eyes and watched the scenery fly past. It always amazed her how cars were so readily available and yet her people never took advantage of the speed, convenience, and comfort. The ride to the Schrocks' didn't take long.

"Have you had lunch, Leah?" Naomi asked as they entered her home.

"No, I'm sorry. I was taking a little walk when I suddenly realized I didn't want to go home. But the store manager gave me some ice cream."

Naomi got out a loaf of bread and deli ham for a sandwich. She placed an apple and a slice of cheddar cheese on a plate with the ham sandwich, went to another cupboard, took out juice, and served lunch.

Naomi's kindness touched Leah's heart. The simple sandwich looked so good, and her stomach rumbled impatiently. As Leah ate, she glanced at the clock and saw it was now nearly two thirty. *Has my family even realized I've gone?* A wave of fear at what she was doing flowed over her, followed by a wave of desire for the familiar. What would *Daet* do when they discovered her missing? She closed her mind against her own imagination. Tears threatened to overflow if she didn't stop thinking about what was likely happening at home right now. She was glad when Naomi interrupted her tortured thinking.

"I don't mean to pry, Leah, but have your church leaders decided to ban you from church yet unless you repent of your born-again experience?"

Leah nodded, wiping her mouth with the paper napkin Naomi placed in front of her, the stiffness of the paper a sharp contrast to the cotton napkins she'd washed so many times at home. She had a feeling there would be a lot more than just napkins to learn about in the English world. "They came yesterday and told me I'm going down the same path as my friend, Martha. 'In the grip of Satan,' they said. It was hard to listen to their words when I knew it was me they were talking about. I've never been in trouble before." She smoothed out the napkin, trying to blink back tears before they fell.

Naomi described how things had been for her when she left. It helped Leah to know she wasn't the only one struggling with the decision to leave.

"I know you'll need some clothing. Do you have something in mind you'd like to wear? Some girls want to stay in dresses, while others would like to wear jeans."

"Really, I haven't given much thought to what the *Englisher* girls wore, though I tried on a pair of Martha's jeans once." Leah shuddered at the unhappy memory.

Naomi chuckled. "I expect that to change soon. It's been my experience most ex-Amish want to fit in with the English. It's part of their desire to leave old ways behind and begin anew. For teens, especially, it's hard to dress in Amish clothes once they leave home. Even English teens have a need to fit in. The former Amish are no different."

Leah was filled with relief and grateful Naomi was able to understand.

Naomi raised her eyebrows. "Unfortunately, many English think we former Amish lived in a perfect world. Our clothing is a symbol to them of this simple life, but they fail to understand how difficult the Amish life really is. Nothing is simple in the Amish community." She glanced at Leah. "Many of the English I first met couldn't understand how much I wanted to leave the rule-laden life behind. I expect you might face some of those people, too. But don't worry. It will work out."

She swept crumbs into a little pile by her coffee cup. "Now, let's move on. We have used and new clothing donated for the ex-Amish. Tomorrow, we can let you look through some of those donations to see if you can find something to wear. You can take your time choosing a few outfits. But first, I think you've had a stressful and tiring day, so I'm going to take you down to the apartment we have in the basement. We have one girl staying there now, but she's with friends from our Mission to Amish People group for the afternoon. You'll have a chance to settle in and rest before you meet your new roommate."

Naomi stood and led her down the basement stairs to a door on the right. She unlocked the door and handed Leah the key.

"We like the girls to have privacy and a place they feel is theirs." Naomi reached around the wall to the right and flipped on the light switch.

Entering the apartment, Leah saw they were standing in a kitchen area with full appliances against the left wall. To the right was a large open living room with two open bedroom doors toward the back of the room. Naomi led her across the living space to the room on the left and flipped on the light.

"Leah, this is your room. Here's the closet," Naomi explained as she opened a sliding door to the right. "The bathroom is in here."

She went to the door next to the closet and showed Leah a small bathroom.

Naomi led her back into the common room. "Your new roommate will be home around five thirty, so you'll have an hour or two to rest and adjust. I'll bring down a gown and clean underwear and things like a toothbrush, comb, and soap. Okay?"

Leah nodded, a little embarrassed she needed to accept charity from her hosts and had not thought to get those things from home—hadn't thought through anything, really. She promised herself she'd find a job soon and repay the Schrocks for their generosity.

Naomi started toward the door. "If you want, you're more than welcome to come up and have dinner with the family tonight. We leave it completely up to you. Some girls want to meet the rest of us, and some need a little time to settle in. I'm fixing spaghetti tonight."

"I'd like to come up for dinner, thanks. And, if you need my help, I'd be more than happy to help prepare the meal," Leah added eagerly.

"If you're sure—I never turn down a helping hand! Thanks, Leah. We eat around six."

After a minute or two, Leah could hear Naomi treading lightly in the kitchen above. She looked around and decided to explore her bedroom and bath first.

The room was small, but cheerful, with a mossy green and soft yellow decor. The bath was also small, but it had a sparkling clean sink and shower. Soft, moss-green rugs warmed the tile floor. She felt welcome and safe in this space. She wandered out to the living room to explore.

A television sat in the corner. Fascinated with the electronic gadgets, she tentatively turned on the television. It took her some time to figure out how to use the buttons on the remote control, and then she flipped through the channels. Many of the scenes appeared to be dark and unhappy, but Leah couldn't turn it off until she'd explored each and every channel. The realization hit that she was *watching* television, and on a Sunday, too. She looked around guiltily, expecting *Maem* or *Daet* to be right beside her, frowning in dismay. It was interesting to her that remotes were needed when the television was mere steps away. But when she looked the TV over carefully, she realized there were no control buttons on it.

She shut off the television and went to get a drink of water. A small table, cheerily covered by a light blue cloth, sat just inside the entrance door. A Bible, along with two pens and a yellow marker, lay neatly atop the table.

She opened and shut cupboards until she found a set of clear glasses. Turning on the faucet, Leah marveled at the clean, cool water she didn't have to pump into the sink. She filled the glass and drank thirstily.

Leah went back to her new bedroom and lay down on the bed. A glance at a clock on the bedside table told her she still had some time before meeting her new roommate. The stress of the day overwhelmed her, and her eyes slipped shut.

⚜

A soft rustling woke Leah. She was disoriented for several seconds as she tried to figure out where she was. The unfamiliar walls and bed felt strange and somehow lonely, and Leah sat up quickly. She listened to sounds coming from the sitting room as her eyes turned to the clock beside the bed.

"What? It's past six thirty!" She'd slept right through dinner. She rose and opened her bedroom door slowly. A thin, dark-eyed girl with long brown hair turned from the sink and smiled at her.

"Hi. I'm Hannah."

Her thick Amish accent made Leah relax. "I'm Leah."

"Yes, Naomi told me about you when I stopped in upstairs."

"I'm embarrassed to say I've overslept and missed dinner."

"It's okay. Naomi sent a dish down for you to reheat when you woke up. I slept for hours my first day here, too. It's the stress of leaving."

"How long have you been here?"

Hannah walked to the couch and sat down. Leah took a seat on a nearby chair and propped her chin in her hand as she listened to her new roommate. Her brain still was a bit fuzzy from the long nap.

"About eight months, I guess."

"Naomi said you have a job. Was it hard to find? I really want to work as soon as I can."

"I worked for the last seven months cleaning houses because I didn't have my GED—"

"What's that?" Leah interrupted.

"It's a General Education Degree, a way to get your diploma from the state of Ohio. Many places want you to have one before they hire you. I studied a lot but failed my first test. I had to wait to take it again, and I passed it the second time last month. I started my new job in a factory the next week."

Leah hadn't thought about the lack of education she had. She was nervous to think of starting over in the *Englishers'* world with little or no experience or education. Hannah sensed her apprehension.

"Don't worry. You can get a job cleaning, too, and one lady will even pick you up to take you into town to work. One thing about us former Amish girls: we know how to clean and work hard, so people are usually happy to hire us." Hannah laughed, and Leah smiled, but sudden worry overcame the humor in the remark.

"You'd better get your dinner heated up. You must be hungry." Her new friend went to the fridge and took out a dish.

Leah took the food and turned to the stove. She looked at it helplessly for a minute: all those knobs and buttons, she didn't know which one to turn.

Hannah giggled. She pointed to a small microwave oven above the stove. "Use this. It will heat it quicker and better than in the oven."

Hannah showed her how to place the food inside and set the microwave to heat. In just over a minute, the spaghetti was hot and ready.

"That's fast!" Leah took the dish to the table and used the glass she'd had earlier to get a drink of water.

"There's milk in the fridge, or soda if you want it."

Leah thanked her but decided water was fine for now. She sat at the table and said a silent prayer. She was nervous but also excited about the new life she was beginning. She ate dinner while Hannah kept her company with happy chatter.

After her dinner, they watched television until nine o'clock. At first, the sound disturbed Leah's ears. The volume of the commercials and the music in every scene she watched assaulted her. She blinked a few times at the quickly changing scenes. But soon, she grew accustomed to the imagery and became engrossed in the stories.

At last, Hannah got up to get ready for bed since she had to be at work early in the morning. Leah's eyes had grown heavy long before that, but she didn't want to be rude and leave her roommate sitting alone the first night. After Hannah got up and went to change into her pajamas, Leah must have dozed off because she was awakened by a soft knock on the apartment door. She struggled up and hurried over to open it. Naomi was there.

"Hope I'm not interrupting you two, but I wanted to check in on you before I go to bed. And here is a gown, change of underwear, and toothbrush and toothpaste for you to use."

"Thanks, Naomi. Hannah and I have been getting acquainted."

"Good. I won't keep you up. I also wanted to let you know I'll be driving to town tomorrow. There's a lady who has some clothing to donate. I thought you might be able to wear some of it. Would you like to go along?"

"Yes, please, that would be nice. Thanks. I'm sorry I missed dinner. I slept right through the time. Please tell Matthew I'm grateful to you both."

"He was glad to hear you got some rest. It's very traumatic, leaving for the first time, and you needed to recharge after all the stress. I'll see you in the morning. You can come up for breakfast about eight thirty."

"I will. Thanks again, Naomi."

Leah closed the door and headed for her bedroom. She couldn't stay awake any longer. It had been a very long, hard day. After a quick shower, she changed into the gown Naomi loaned her and went out to say good night to Hannah. She was sitting at the table reading her Bible, but she glanced up as Leah came over. "I hope you sleep well, Leah."

"Thanks. I'm so tired, I can barely hold my eyes open, even after that long nap." A yawn escaped to prove it.

"I was like that, too, the first night. Try not to think too much about everything. I'll pray you get a good night's sleep so you can be refreshed in the morning. There's time to start changing your world soon enough."

"Thanks. I'll try to sleep—I really think I will sleep *gut*, for tonight, at least."

Leah padded to her bedroom and climbed in the soft bed. As she drew the fresh smelling sheets to her chin, she lay blinking in the dark and remembered she'd left home without her little Gideon Bible.

Lord, maybe I can go back to get some of my things. Let it work out so Maem *and* Daet *will allow me to.* She sighed as a tear slipped down her cheek. *And don't let them worry about me too much. I hope they guess where I am. Lord, I think I should let them know, somehow, that I'm all right. Help them, please, to accept what I want to do. And help me to somehow show them who You really are. Give me strength and courage to change my life, Lord. I'm scared and homesick already, but I want to serve You, Lord. And Jacob . . . What about Jacob?*

She drifted off and didn't remember anything waking her until morning. Leah opened sleepy eyes, rubbed them to see more clearly, and glanced at the clock, surprised to note it was seven thirty already. At home, she was always up by five.

She scurried into the bathroom. Cleaning up was so much easier than on the farm, with hot running water that needed no woodstove to heat it. The warmth felt heavenly as she rubbed the washcloth across her face.

As Leah started to pull her hair back to ready it for the *kapp*, it dawned on her she didn't have to do that anymore. She let her long hair fall loose. Looking in the mirror still made her uncomfortable, but she turned this way and that to get a better view of the long brown hair resting on her neck and shoulders. Then she brushed it until it shone. As she felt the waist-length strands swing from side to side, a huge weight lifted off her heart. She was free.

Leah smiled to her new self in the mirror. It was considered prideful to look in mirrors, and they were forbidden at home, but today, she wanted to study her features.

The overhead lights above the sink showed her skin plainly. It was as if everything around her was brighter and more vibrant than what she'd been used to in the dull and dim oil lighting at home. Her skin looked brown from the sun, and her cheeks were cherry red. Her deep amber eyes looked back solemnly.

Do I really look so serious all the time? She stuck out her tongue, then giggled, tilting her previously serious lips upward. She'd never noticed a tiny scar on her eyebrow before. She leaned in closer to examine it.

It came to her that she'd gotten it years ago when the handle of the wagon she was pulling flew back as she'd bent to arrange baby Benny in the blankets. It had been a cold morning, and they were on their way to church at the neighbor's farm. Instead of hitching up the horse, they'd decided to walk. The air had been crisp and fresh, and Benny was a sweet little *bobli*. They had all laughed at his little baby noises, and the sisters had teased each other about the day when they'd have their own little ones. A perfect morning spoiled only by the rush back to the house for bandages. Leah was surprised by the size of the scar—her little-girl memory of the event held it much smaller in size.

The mirror pulled her deeper into those long-ago years—memories of happier times with *Daet, Maem,* Daniel, Ada, and baby Benny. But it was the memory of *Daet*'s smile that broke the spell. A smile that was rare, but something Leah would have cherished seeing more often.

Leah shook her head and looked away from the past. She wiped tears, squaring her shoulders and drawing her chin up.

After today, I will put away the dress and the apron. After today, I will try not to look back but will look forward. After today, I will dress in jeans and T-shirts, or whatever else I can find that fits me. Leah paused at the thought of that. *Jeans! What will it be like to wear jeans all the time?*

Again, the image of the last time she had worn jeans—the day Abner had attacked her friend—flooded in. Shudders rippled through her. "Too many memories, Lord," she whispered. "Help me to trust You."

When she left her bedroom, she noticed her roommate had already gone to work. A note was propped on the table against the Bible.

Leah,

Please use my Bible if you want to. I've learned it's the best way to start my morning—without it, I'd be lost!

Enjoy finding your English self today. Hannah

She smiled at her roommate's generosity and sat down to open the Bible. Several verses were underlined throughout the book, and one whole passage on love jumped out at her right away: *"Dear friends, let us love one another, for love comes from God. Everyone who loves has been born of God and knows God . . ."*

She read the passage out loud again, focusing on this thought: *"There is no fear in love. But perfect love drives out fear, because fear has to do with punishment. The one who fears is not made perfect in love. We love because he first loved us."*

No fear. She let the words sink in. She need not fear for herself or her parents. She continued reading, and her smile grew. The words made so much sense. This Bible was written in English and was much more understandable than the German Bible her family read and even the Gideon Bible she'd left at home. Since Leah's whole family had lived their lives in fear of breaking the *Ordnung*, could they possibly have been going against the Bible all these years? She'd never before thought the *Ordnung* could be wrong. She'd felt some things made no sense, but could it be because they had been written by men? Maybe the men were troubled, and they didn't fully understand the Scripture. A new world of ideas opened to her. Some of it left her feeling better, but other thoughts made her uneasy.

Naomi met her at the top of the stairs and welcomed Leah to the kitchen.

"I've made morning glory muffins today. Help yourself, and there's coffee in the pot over there, if you like it."

Leah poured a cup of coffee, liberally doctoring it with sugar and cream. She noticed Naomi suppress a smile as she watched the coffee process. Leah's amateur coffee drinking was evident.

"Did you sleep well?"

She stirred the milky brown liquid and brought the cup to the table, took a couple of muffins from the plate, and munched on one slowly. "I did. In fact, I couldn't believe I woke up so late! It was seven thirty before even one eye popped open."

"I'm sure you needed the sleep."

"I think so, too. I had no idea how tired everything made me yesterday. Naomi, I have a question. Do you mind if I ask you something?"

"No, go right ahead."

"I was reading in Hannah's Bible—she left a note saying it was okay—and the words made more sense to me than the German Bible at home. And even more than the Gideon New Testament I found and have been reading. Why is that? What's different about her Bible?"

"She's got a different translation called the New International Version." Naomi reached for her own Bible on the table. "It doesn't use the old-fashioned language we're used to reading in the Bibles the Gideons gave us."

Leah thought about this. "So if I can find a Bible like that, will it be all right to read it?"

"Sure. In fact . . ." Naomi stood and went to a desk in the corner of the living room. She rummaged through a couple of drawers until she found a small blue Bible and brought it to Leah. "Here's a little take-along version of the NIV my son had before he moved out. He's away at college right now. He has several more Bibles, so go ahead and take this one."

She opened the small book and read through the first few verses in Genesis. Though the thoughts were similar, the words conveying them stuck in her mind readily. "I don't know how to thank you and Matthew enough."

"It's okay. We needed a lot of help getting started, too, Leah—all of us former Amish had someone to take us under their wing. It's how we manage to move on." She glanced at the clock. "And speaking of moving on, we need to get going soon. It's time to find you some new clothes."

Leah hurried downstairs to get her cape. She was excited to have new clothes. It would be nice to wear a coat for one thing—she'd always wished she could have one again, but the current bishop had decided the black wool capes were more in the right tradition for Amish people and had made the women stop wearing coats. She'd shivered through winters since that time.

She washed her hands and brushed her teeth. By the time she went to the door leading to the garage, the car was out in the driveway, and Naomi had the engine heating up. Leah closed the passenger door against the wind and cold, and snuggled into the warmth of the car. She smiled at Naomi. "Oh, so many nice things to be thankful for, aren't there?"

Naomi chuckled as they pulled out of the drive.

The trip to town didn't take long, and they turned off the main road into a short driveway. A woman came to the door of her quaint little house and ushered them inside.

"Good morning, ladies! How are you, dear?" she said to Naomi.

Naomi hugged the diminutive lady, seemingly careful of her fragile shoulders. "Fine, Miss Emma. How are you doing?"

The elderly woman waved her hand as she led them to the living room. "Oh, you know we old folks have our complaints, but I'm still happy to be servin' the Lord!" She laughed and pointed to the sofa. "Have a seat, why don't you? I'll go get the bags of clothes."

Leah sat down, but Naomi interrupted Miss Emma. "No, no. You go ahead and visit with Leah. I'll get the clothes. Do you have them stored in the second bedroom yet?"

"Yes. There are two bags on the floor by the bed. Thank you, kindly. I don't mind if I do sit here a bit and talk to this pretty young miss."

She turned to Leah, her wrinkled face soft and rosy. She had the kindest eyes Leah had ever seen. "Now, what's your name again, dear?"

"Leah Raber, ma'am."

"Leah. That's a pretty name. A good Bible name, too."

"Thank you."

"I dare say you'll be wanting to look at some of those clothes I've got in the bags. Yes?" Her head tilted, and her expression reminded Leah of a curious little bird.

She nodded. "I think so."

"Just now leaving the Amish?"

Leah nodded again, her cheeks flushed. The gentle lady's curiosity didn't offend her, but it sure made her nervous to talk about herself to a stranger, even one as nice as this one.

Miss Emma regarded Leah a moment and then reached across and patted her knee. "Don't mind me. I get nosey and I ask too many questions. But just in case you're interested, I think there are a couple of pairs of blue jeans and some tops that would fit you perfectly in those bags. And . . ." She put a finger to her chin and tapped once or twice. "I think there might even be a nice winter coat in your size, too. When I bought those things at garage sales this past summer, I was able to get the coats for a song." She giggled. "Nobody wants to buy coats when it's ninety degrees outside. But I got to thinking of how many of you girls leave home with no coat at all, so I bought however many I could find."

She sat back in her chair, a pleased and happy expression on her face.

"That's very nice of you to think of others. It will certainly help me out to have clothes and a coat. I won't be able to buy anything until I get a job."

Miss Emma nodded her head, her blue-gray curls bobbing merrily. "I understand, and I haven't met a one of you girls yet that don't work real hard to get on your feet. It's a pleasure to help out in this little way."

Naomi came back from the hallway with two large garbage bags, filled to bulging. Leah jumped up. "Let me help you."

After they placed them near the door, Naomi turned and walked back to Miss Emma.

"Thank you again, Miss Emma. I can't tell you how nice it is to be able to give these girls some good clothes to wear until they get a job and can buy their own things. I know they appreciate the help."

"It *is* thoughtful of you," Leah repeated.

The older lady laughed and stood up. "Now, don't go overboard with the praise, ladies. I don't need to get a big head at my age. Would you two like a glass of sweet tea?"

"That sounds lovely. We'll sit with you at the table and chat a bit, if it's okay with Leah." Naomi glanced at her.

"Yes. Sure."

Naomi winked at her as Miss Emma scurried around her neat-as-a-pin little kitchen. She got three glasses and filled them with ice and then poured the sugary, caramel-colored tea to the brim of each. They sat at the table and chatted with Miss Emma for an hour. Then Naomi nodded toward the clock.

"I hate to say it, but it's time for us to get going. Thanks so much for the clothes and the tea. A nice little chat is just the thing for a chilly Monday like this."

She gave Miss Emma a hug and Leah stood to do so, too. The woman's frail bones felt light as a feather when Leah hugged her, like a stiff wind could blow her away. It was awkward for Leah to show affection this way to strangers. In the Amish world, they were taught not to show feelings or to touch others. But warm physical touch was one of the many things Leah was beginning to appreciate about the English world.

Miss Emma squeezed back fiercely. "Now, Leah, you be strong. Before you know it, you'll be on your own and helping others like I've helped you. I have no doubt of that." She patted her arm. "Take care, and trust the Lord always."

"I will. Thank you."

On the way home, Naomi explained that Emma had been buying clothing and household items for the former Amish for more than five years. It gave her something to do, and she enjoyed knowing she was helping young people. "She used to be a teacher, and she misses her students."

Leah went with Naomi to the grocery, and then they stopped for a bite of lunch at a fast-food place. It was a treat for her, since *Maem* and *Daet* rarely went to a restaurant with the family.

All in all, her first day among the English was turning out to be a hectic, yet happy day. When they got back home, she helped carry in and put away the groceries, and then went out to bring in the clothing bags.

"You might as well look through these first, Leah. Miss Emma is good at trying to find modern clothes, and she usually buys several sizes. I pick the clothes up from her house about three times a year. Why don't you take those bags down to your apartment and try on as many clothes as you want."

"Okay. Thanks. And thank you so much for lunch. That was a nice treat."

"It's fun to have someone to go with me once in a while."

Downstairs in the apartment, Leah took a bag and turned it upside down. A number of pairs of jeans and some T-shirts tumbled onto the floor. She had no idea what size to try on first, so she sorted several pairs of jeans and a couple of shirts into a pile. She gathered the pile and went to the bedroom to try them on.

The first pair of jeans was too big, and the second, too small. She found a perfect pair after several tries and a shirt to match, too. Then she tried on more jeans from the other bag in the living room until she had three pairs of jeans and three shirts. There was a nice dress that was just a bit big in the waist, but she could sew it to fit.

But the best find of all was a down parka. It was dark blue and knee-length with soft fur around the cuffs and hood. When she snuggled into it, she sighed with delight; it was so cozy. She almost couldn't wait for the first snow so she could test its ability to keep her toasty warm.

She hummed a happy tune as she carried her new things to the closet. She wiggled into a pair of jeans and a heather-colored long-sleeved T-shirt. Miss Emma hadn't neglected shoes, either. A pair of flats fit her well, so she put those on, too.

She stood at the mirror over the sink in the bathroom and took a long look. The change was dramatic and amazing. She hardly recognized herself. A confident, young lady stared back at Leah, cheeks rosy with excitement. What a difference!

Chapter Fourteen

The next few days, Leah woke in time to have breakfast with Hannah and then went upstairs to help Naomi around the house. She enjoyed working with her, but as the days passed, Leah noticed how her home-sickness grew as the dark of night came and she didn't have anything else to keep her busy. She wasn't homesick for the rules or the clothes or the hard way of life, but she so missed her family and friends.

She tried not to think of Benny because it made her cry. His cute little face and rambunctious ways were precious to her. She longed to talk to Ada again. She missed helping *Maem* with breakfast and lunch and being with *Daet* in the shop. Leah found herself both relieved and saddened that her family had made no effort to track her down.

And she missed Jacob more than she thought she would. In fact, the first Tuesday night Bible study at the Schrocks after she moved in, she half expected him to show up. When the hours came and went with no sign of him, her heart broke. Had he decided not to see her again? Was he choosing his Amish life over her? Leah couldn't blame him; after all, it was she who had left—and without a word to him. She knew he didn't fully understand her questions about the Amish lifestyle, but somehow, she still hoped he would come to see her at the Bible study. She pondered writing him a letter, but maybe that wouldn't be fair to him . . . he should have time to make up his mind about her, in light of what she had done.

More than anything, Leah wished with all her heart her family and Jacob could feel this freedom—this desire to serve God in a way that made a person happy and not filled with fear and guilt. *Grace* had become a beautiful word to Leah, and she savored the Scriptures where grace was spoken of regularly. She lived in this new world the best way she could, but the aching and longing for family and for Jacob never ended.

❦

Three weeks passed quickly, and in that time Leah had applied for a social security card, filed for a copy of her birth certificate, and written her parents. She broke down, too, and sent a letter to Jacob. She wanted to explain her sudden decision, though not hearing from him made her hesitate as she placed the stamp on the envelope. Maybe he had decided she was not worth thinking about after all. One morning she asked Hannah if she minded taking her out to her folks' place to try to get some of her belongings.

"Are you sure you want to do that, Leah?"

"I wrote *Maem* and *Daet* a letter to ask if it would be okay."

"Did they answer you?"

"Well, no." Leah shook her head, sadness filling her as she admitted they ignored the letter.

"Do you think they'll let you come anyway?"

She sighed. "I really don't know, but I sure would like to get my personal things, and it would be nice to see them again."

Hannah's gaze scanned Leah's while she pondered. "Okay. We might as well see what happens."

The drive to her parents' place took longer than Leah remembered, giving her time to imagine the family's reactions. Her stomach churned as she thought of the ways they could still hurt her with their rejection. Would *Daet* yell? Would *Maem* cry? She felt sure Benny would welcome her, but how about Ada? She'd been so cold in the days leading up to Leah's departure; she couldn't believe her sister may have changed her attitude since she'd left.

They pulled into the drive as Leah's eyes swept the yard and barn area.

She saw no sign of activity, but nothing was out of place, either. In fact, the familiar scene startled her with its sameness. After all she'd been through, it was hard to believe life had gone on here as it always had. Her absence hadn't seemed to matter.

Hannah braked and shut the motor off. Leah heard a few chickens squawking and a cow lowing in the pasture. The stillness settled over her like a shroud. It felt heavy and thick, stifling her ability to breathe freely. She got out and crunched her way through the gravel to the porch. She knocked, feeling silly to be standing like a visitor at the front door of her own home. Soon she heard footsteps approaching from within. *Maem* opened the door. Her eyes reflected surprise, but she stood back, silently, to let Leah inside, though not before a quick, disapproving glance at her daughter's *Englisher* jeans and coat. *Maem* backed into the living room, wiping her hands on a kitchen towel. She still said nothing.

"Uh—*Maem*, I'm glad you let me in. How are you and *Daet*?"

Maem looked down at her shoes, not answering and not moving.

Leah swallowed. This was going to be as hard as she imagined it would be. "Did you get my letter?"

Maem nodded.

"Do you think it's okay for me to go up and get some of my things?"

Again, her mother nodded, but immediately turned away and hurried back to the kitchen. Leah trudged up the stairs, her gaze resting on each polished step as she ascended. Nothing had changed.

Her old bedroom door was shut tight. She turned the knob and heard it squeak the way it always had. No covers were on her bed. The room was barren and swept clean. The dresser top was stripped of her brush and comb, the stack of books she'd been reading, and the stationery set she'd kept there. It was as if she had never lived here.

In a daze, she roamed the room, pulling open drawers and gathering underwear, socks, and gowns. At least they hadn't gotten rid of those. She'd imagined everything being tossed onto a burning heap. She couldn't find her books or the stationery set, but she did find the comb and brush placed neatly in a drawer.

Her meager belongings made a small pile on the bed, but she couldn't find the Gideon Bible. It was one object sure to be destroyed, and its loss brought a deep sadness.

She collected her things into a plastic grocery sack she'd wadded in her pocket before they left the apartment. One bag fit it all.

Leah made her way carefully down the steep stairs and went quietly to the kitchen door to say good-bye to *Maem*. She was sorry neither Ada nor Benny was around.

"Is *Daet* in his shop?" she asked *Maem* with a nod toward the back yard.

Maem stopped stirring what looked to be jam in a huge pot, but remained mute. She was frozen to her spot, unable or unwilling to do more than breathe while Leah was in the room. Her arm was suspended over the pot, stiff and unnatural in its pose. Her shoulders were tight but her face was hidden from Leah's line of vision. *Maem's* body trembled, but still she didn't speak.

Leah couldn't help herself. *Maem's* pain over seeing her again broke her heart, and Leah moved softly over to touch *Maem's* back. "Please, can't we chat a minute or two before I have to leave? I've missed you all so much."

Leah's voice broke the spell, and *Maem* whirled, throwing the long-handled ladle into the pot of boiling jam. She glared as she pushed away from Leah and slammed out the back door. The screen door bumped against the frame a few times, *Maem's* fury giving it energy to spare.

In the stillness that followed, Leah heard the clock ticking and the jam roiling, but it was her turn to stand frozen to the spot. She couldn't believe how far her family was prepared to go to let her know of their disapproval. Slowly she gathered her wits and the sack of belongings and turned to leave.

Just before Leah shut the front door, she whispered a prayer into the room. "Lord, keep my family safe, and work in their hearts to want to know You. Help them forgive me and help them to know how much I still love them."

Hannah didn't press her when Leah returned to the car minutes later. Leah kept her eyes on the floor of the car as they pulled away from the home place. She couldn't say good-bye a second time.

More days passed, and Leah tried hard to fit in and keep busy. She attended church with the Schrocks, but in spite of the newfound freedom she was enjoying, she grew increasingly depressed. She struggled to sleep, lying awake in the early hours thinking of home and family.

Though she was growing in her knowledge of God and His grace, Leah still felt overwhelmed with adult responsibility and being completely alone. She teetered between feeling gratitude to the Schrocks and her roommate, Hannah, and all they were doing for her, and feeling that she had no one. Panic rose every time she stopped to think about navigating her future without the structure she had always known.

At night she thought of the letters that she'd heard in the Amish church services, read as warnings to those who were tempted to leave the Amish faith. She wondered if the contents in those letters lingered in other former Amish minds the way they lingered in hers. Was she being punished? Should she go back?

Eventually, the endless questions and homesickness began to take their toll. She lost weight and even more sleep. She read the little blue Bible every day, but still, the peace she started with began to fade slowly away. What should she do?

Leah was washing dishes one Sunday afternoon in mid-December when she heard the doorbell ring upstairs. Naomi and Matthew were in New York for a presentation of the MAP ministry at a church there, so she dried her hands and climbed the steps to answer the door.

A young girl, younger even than Leah, stood on the porch, a ragged suitcase in one hand, and a plastic grocery bag in the other. She wore an old winter coat that hung unevenly to the top of her ankles. "Can I help you?"

"Is this the Schrock house?"

Leah took in the faded jeans and scrubbed face and knew this was a runaway Amish girl.

"Yes, it's the Schrocks' home," she answered softly in Pennsylvania Dutch. The girl's eyes widened.

"You speak PA-Dutch?"

"*Ja*, I'm from the Old Order Amish around here. Where are you from?"

The girl shifted her belongings uncomfortably and shrugged. "I'm from down around Mt. Vernon."

Leah held the door open for the girl and invited her in.

"My cousin gave me this address. She said this is a safe place to go . . . is that true?" The girl's chin trembled slightly.

"First, my name's Leah." She motioned for the girl to have a seat in the living room.

"I'm Rebekah."

"Rebekah? Good to know you. Second, this is a safe place, but the Schrocks aren't here this weekend. They've gone to a ministry meeting in New York. Is this something you've discussed with them?"

Rebekah tossed her head and laughed nervously. "I left without discussing it with anyone. So, no, they don't know me at all."

"Oh. I don't exactly know what to tell you. I have a phone number for them if you'd like me to call."

Rebekah thought for a second. "Okay. I need a place to stay until I can get a job. I can't go back home." She stared at her feet, shifting the dirty toes of her shoes under the couch.

"I'll be right back, then. Do you want something to drink?"

Rebekah shook her head.

Leah called Naomi, and explained the situation.

"I'd better let you speak to Matthew," Naomi said, and Leah heard her talking to Matthew before his friendly voice came on the phone. She explained a second time, and then Matthew asked her to find out how old the girl was.

"Rebekah, Matthew wants to know how old you are."

She looked away and kept her head turned as she mumbled, "Fifteen."

"She's fifteen, Matthew."

"Ah. That's a problem. Could I speak with her, please?"

Leah handed the phone to Rebekah and left the room while Rebekah talked to Matthew. She straightened the kitchen and waited for the phone call to end. Soon, Rebekah handed the phone back to Leah. "He wants to talk with you."

"Hello?"

"Leah, I told Rebekah she could stay just for a few days, but I'm worried that with both of you underage, this could be a problem for MAP. We try to not interfere with parental rights, but she says she'll sleep on the streets if we turn her away, and she refuses to let me send her home. I agreed to let her stay for a few days. If it's okay with you and Hannah, Rebekah can sleep on the couch in your living room. I hate to ask you to take her in while we're gone, but it's too cold to let her leave. We should be home in a few hours. Can you help her settle in?"

"Yes. I'll do what I can."

"Thank you, Leah. I appreciate that. We're leaving now and should be home by eight or nine."

"Okay. Drive safely."

"Thanks, Leah."

Leah led Rebekah down to the apartment and settled her in while she made some hot cocoa in the microwave. As she placed the cup of steaming chocolate in front of her on the table, Leah asked, "Are you hungry? I have leftovers from lunch."

She nodded and sipped her cocoa. "If it's no trouble. I didn't have breakfast before I left home."

"How far away from home are you?" Leah asked as she took chicken and noodles from the refrigerator. Leah put a large helping of the casserole on a plate, added green beans, and popped the plate in the microwave. Rebekah seemed to be watching her every move, her eyes showing her hunger.

"I think about fifty miles or so. I'm not sure. But I hitched a ride with my *Englisher* neighbors. They were coming to Richland, and I rode with them that far; then I walked until I got a couple of rides here and there. It's been a long day." She sighed.

Leah took out a couple slices of bread and smeared one with thick, sweet Amish peanut butter spread. "Would you like some?"

Rebekah nodded. "Mmmm." She ate quickly.

The microwave dinged and Leah got the plate out and placed it in front of Rebekah, with a glass of cold water, then sat down across from her. Leah sat quietly as the girl ate.

Finally, Rebekah put down her fork and looked across at Leah. "So, why did you leave home?"

Leah thought about the question. "I accepted Christ—became a born-again believer." Leah glanced at her. "My church and bishop were going to shun me, even though they couldn't do it officially since I hadn't yet joined the church. They wanted me to repent of my new belief. I didn't want them to do that, and I couldn't give up my new faith." She shrugged. "So I left . . . How about you? Why did you leave?"

Rebekah laughed. "It wasn't something as good as why you left." She looked up, the smile still on her lips. "I got tired of being Amish, is all." She tossed her head. "You know how it is—those *rules*. Do this—don't do that—act like this—don't act like that. I just couldn't stand it anymore."

Leah nodded. Many young people left for the same reasons. But they usually went back—some of them, anyway.

The two girls spent the rest of the afternoon chatting, and when Rebekah decided she needed a nap, Leah went to her room and read her Bible so she wouldn't disturb her.

After Hannah came home, they ordered a pizza and watched a movie. By the time Matthew and Naomi got back from New York, the girls were sleepy. Naomi came down and asked Rebekah to join her upstairs.

Leah took the opportunity to say good night to everyone. Her eyes were heavy, and exhaustion pulled her to bed. Chatting with Rebekah and playing host all day had worn her out. Just before she went to sleep, Hannah tapped at her door and asked if she could talk a minute.

Leah sat up. "Sure."

Hannah settled on the side of the bed. "I think there might be an opening for a full-time cleaner with this lady I used to work for when I first came out of the Amish. I was wondering if you might be interested in talking to her about the job."

"Oh, yes. That would be great!"

Hannah handed her a piece of paper. "This has her number on it. Her name is Sally and she's really nice. She likes to hire the former Amish girls whenever she can."

"I'll call her tomorrow. Thanks for telling me about it."

She stood. "You're welcome. Get a good night's sleep."

"Good night, Hannah."

Leah's eyes closed before Hannah even shut the door, and she smiled to herself when she thought of getting a job. It was just what she needed. "Thank You, Lord."

The next morning, Hannah and Leah were eating breakfast as quietly as they could so they wouldn't wake Rebekah. She was out like a light on the sofa, and Leah wondered how long she'd stayed upstairs to talk with the Schrocks last night.

They heard the doorbell upstairs ring. Leah and Hannah exchanged glances. "Someone is out early," Hannah commented.

They went on with breakfast, but soon they heard footsteps coming down the stairs, and shortly after, a knock sounded on their door. Leah got up to answer it. Naomi and a police officer were standing in the doorway.

"Leah, I'm sorry to disturb you two, but the sheriff is here to take Rebekah back to her parents."

Leah glanced at the sheriff as he shuffled his feet, looking apologetic but resigned to doing his job. He cleared his throat. "Her mother called and asked us to bring her home since she's underage."

Leah pointed to the couch. "She's still sleeping. I'll wake her."

Leah moved to the couch and gently shook Rebekah awake. She sat up, her eyes bleary and unfocused. "Rebekah, you need to get up. Your *maem* called the sheriff to bring you back home."

Rebekah stared wide-eyed at the officer. "Am I—in trouble?"

"No, no. I just have to drive you back to your house."

Rebekah stood and tried to straighten her clothes. Evidently, she'd fallen asleep in them. Leah felt sorry for her. She looked scared and sad.

"I'll pray for you," Leah told her.

Rebekah nodded as she gathered her things in the beat-up suitcase and plastic bag. Naomi came to help her, patting her tenderly on the back. "It'll be all right, Rebekah. We'll *all* be praying for you."

The sheriff turned just before he led Rebekah out the door and up the stairs. "We don't always know what these kids are going back to, but we have to adhere to the law. The Amish used to never get the law involved, but lately"—he shrugged—"the bishops are starting to tell the parents to call the authorities when the kids are underage. I can't blame them, you know? The world is filled with terrible things, and I would worry, too, if it were my kid."

Leah, Hannah, and Naomi followed them to the front door and said good-bye to Rebekah. After they left, Naomi sighed. "I wish that hadn't happened, though I know she has no right to run away at her age. She told us last night there's trouble in her home." She leveled a worried look at Leah. "If it was like Martha's trouble, we might have been able to stop her from going back home, but she wouldn't agree to talk to anyone about it." She sighed again. "We can't do anything for her if she doesn't want to tell us what's happening."

Leah stared out into the semidarkness. "I sure hope she'll be okay when she gets home." She went back to the apartment, and Hannah went to work. What happened with Rebekah put a damper on the day, but after praying for Rebekah as she said she would, she got the phone number and called Sally.

Leah was disappointed to learn Sally had already filled the full-time spot, but she thanked her, asking if she'd keep her in mind if another full-time job opened.

⁂

Christmas came. It was a quiet day because she just didn't feel like celebrating. Leah thought of her family and all the fun Benny would be having—and the food—and her parents and sister. She wondered, too, whether Jacob ever thought of her anymore, or if he'd moved his attentions to another Amish girl.

She ate dinner with the Schrocks and then went back to the apartment. Since Hannah had spent the day with her boyfriend's family, Leah had the place to herself. She watched a couple of Christmas movies and went to bed early.

Leah couldn't wait for warmer weather with its longer daylight. She sighed as she closed her eyes. She'd read the Christmas story from Luke with the Schrock family earlier in the day. What must Jesus' mother have thought? Did she know what would happen to her little baby?

Just before Leah went to sleep, she whispered to Jesus, "Thank You for coming to earth. Thank You for saving me from my sins."

Though she missed her family terribly, she couldn't imagine giving up her newfound salvation to go back to the Amish. Her heart hurt, but Leah knew Christ would help in the coming year.

Chapter Fifteen

Leah heard the phone ringing in the living room as she woke one early spring morning. Hannah answered and the low murmur of her voice lulled Leah back toward sleep, but not before the ache for her family settled over her. The long winter was over, and she was now busier with a couple housecleaning jobs and schoolwork to get her GED, but the frozen loneliness in her heart when she thought of her family never thawed. They seemed so very far away.

In the beginning, some of the ways of the English confused Leah. She couldn't understand why it was so important to call people before she dropped by to visit, but Naomi Schrock had given her a booklet about being polite, calling ahead to arrange visits, and especially about being clean. Leah had to admit some of the Amish boys weren't that keen to wash up every day. She knew a few *buves* who went to bed with their feet still caked with manure from the barns. When spring came, the Amish children stopped wearing shoes, so in families where cleanliness was not stressed, washing off the day's dust and grime wasn't a priority. On the other hand, it seemed the English were obsessed with getting rid of any dirt or odor possible.

One product Leah bought for the first time a few months back was deodorant—something *Maem* had never purchased. It was stressed in her strict Amish church that primping by the females was a prideful and sinful thing to do. Feeding the human nature by beautifying the outer body instead of the inner spirit was frowned upon.

Leah thought back to the first time she shaved her legs. She had feared she would shave the skin right off. The stinging nicks and cuts happened less often as she practiced, but it was still a foreign custom. She had to fight the feeling of sinful pride when she smoothed a hand over her gleaming, clean-shaved legs.

She sat up in bed as her roommate knocked on the door.

"Leah?"

"Yes?"

"Are you awake?"

"Yes, but I'm still in bed."

"I have a message for you."

Jumping out of bed, Leah grabbed her robe and opened the door. "Who was the message from?"

"A girl who says she knows your friend, Martha. Martha asked her to call and let you know you're invited to a party this weekend."

"A party?" Leah was still puzzled.

Hannah paused. "Some of the kids go to different fields or apartments to party. I don't go, and I'd suggest you don't go, either. They can get pretty wild."

Leah frowned. Why would Martha ask her to come to something like that and how did Martha even know where she was living? Since leaving home, Leah had heard nothing from her—until now. But she was so lonely, the thought of seeing her friend again, no matter what the circumstances, led Leah to consider going.

"How do I find out more?" she asked.

Hannah shook her head slightly but gave Leah a small slip of paper.

She glanced at an address downtown on Second Street. "I wonder whose place this is."

"The girl said the party was either going to be at that address on the paper or another apartment. She said she'd tell you for sure when you call back."

Leah thanked Hannah and quickly phoned the number on the paper. "Hello? This is Leah."

"Hi, Leah. I'm a friend of Martha's. She wants you to come to a party this weekend. She asked me to call 'cause her cell phone is dead right now. Can you come?"

Leah hesitated. "I'm wondering how you got this number for me."

"She told me she ran into Jacob. He told her where you were."

So Jacob did get her letter. The realization that he had chosen not to answer stung her. He had apparently moved forward with his life. She swallowed. Time for her to move forward, too.

"Is it going to be at her place—or where?"

"She lives on Second Street, but it might be at someone else's place. If it changes, I'll call you back."

When she still hesitated, the friend of Martha wheedled. "Please say yes. Martha really misses you."

Leah chewed her lip. Partying wasn't something that appealed to her at all, but maybe this once would be okay. Just to see Martha and get a taste of home. "Okay. I'd like to see her, too."

After she hung up, Hannah was quiet.

"Do you think I did the right thing, Hannah?"

Her roommate shrugged, but her eyes were worried.

"Where is Second Street? Do you know? Will I be able to get a ride? I'm not a partier, Hannah, but I am lonely for my friends—"

Hannah put her breakfast dishes in the sink and turned the water on. "Just be careful. I guess we can drop you off when my boyfriend picks me up for the movies on Saturday."

"Okay. I promise I'll be careful. Can you also pick me up from the party on your way back from the theater?"

"Sure. We're going to the seven o'clock show, so by the time the movie's over and we get a bite to eat, it will probably be about eleven. Does that sound all right?"

"Yes. And thank you."

⚜

The day of the party came and Leah was both apprehensive and excited to be going. She couldn't wait to see Martha to catch up on all that happened to both of them in the last few months. When Hannah's boyfriend arrived, she and Hannah climbed into the cab of his truck, and Leah smoothed down her new top and jeans, then fiddled with her hair. Hannah had taught her how to braid it while it was wet, giving her long soft waves when she brushed it out. Still, Leah was nervous about fitting in with a crowd she knew little about. Before long, the truck stopped in front of a dismal-looking gray house. It was two stories tall and had a set of outside stairs that rose steeply and precariously against the left wall of the house. Gray asphalt shingles hung askew here and there, with more than a few cracked windowpanes.

As Leah opened the truck door, Hannah reminded her again to be careful.

"I will," she promised. She turned and looked at the house. "I wonder which apartment the party's at?"

"There's a lot of light in the upstairs windows. I'd think that might be the place." Hannah pointed upward.

"Uh-huh. I guess I'll head up there."

"We'll wait until you wave."

"Thanks, Hannah."

Leah made her way to the rickety stairs and started up. As she neared the battered apartment door, she heard loud music coming from inside. She knocked, but no one could hear over the thumping beat. Leah turned and shrugged toward Hannah, then gave them a wave as she opened the apartment door.

The music rolled over her like a tidal wave, causing her to pull her shoulders up instinctively to protect her ears. A grubby, metal-trimmed Formica table stood in the center of the kitchen; its chairs dragged to the living room, visible just beyond an arched doorway.

Blue smoke from many cigarettes, and another, sweeter smell, filled her nose. She coughed a couple of times and wondered if she would recognize anyone . . . or if they would know her. A few girls swayed their way through the living room, meeting Leah at the arched doorway. They pushed past her as though she weren't there, seemingly not surprised that a stranger was in the apartment. As they went by, their breath held the strong, soured smell of alcohol, and their eyes were unfocused. They giggled as they rummaged through the refrigerator.

Leah walked through the arch and encountered a room full of bodies in similar condition to those of the girls she'd just seen. Everywhere she looked, young people swayed and drank while they laughed and smoked. None of them seemed coherent, and a few of them were stumbling. She recognized the bowl cuts of Amish young men and could see some of the girls had their hair pinned back, but not severely. Though they wore jeans and T-shirts, their thick-soled black Amish shoes hadn't been replaced yet. Some were obviously Amish kids who were out to party for the night.

Leah searched for Martha, but the press of people kept her from finding her friend right away. She wandered through the room and then down a short, narrow hallway. At the end of the hall was a tiny, pink-tiled bathroom. The stench of vomit filled the air, and she pulled back as a girl with heavy black eyeliner stumbled out of the bathroom, wiping her mouth on her gray hoodie sleeve. The girl moaned and leaned against a door to the right, pushing it open with the weight of her body. Leah watched as she fell into the room, landing against the edge of a messy bed.

"Get outta here, Anna! My gosh, what is *wrong* with you? Get up! You stink. Go in there and tell Abe to give you some coffee. Go! Whew. You can't handle any kind of alcohol, you Amish geek."

Leah could see a pair of hands tugging at the girl, who she supposed was Anna, and she thought she recognized the voice now cursing at the nearly passed-out teen. Could that be Martha?

Leah walked toward the bedroom and peered in. There was her friend trying to make Anna stand on her own two feet.

Leah was shocked, not only by Martha's pale and puffy face, but at the sight of her bulging belly! Martha was obviously pregnant and not long from delivering her baby. She hadn't heard a word of this news from any of the former Amish—or *Englishers*, for that matter—in the months since Martha had left home.

The anger coming from Martha was as fierce as the music pounding Leah's brain. "Martha!" Her friend did not hear her above the din, and Leah called several times before Martha finally turned her way.

"Leah!" Martha squealed. She let the drunken girl fall back onto the bed and ran to hug her. "You came! I was hoping you got the word I wanted to see you. Here, help me get this girl out of here, and then we can close the door and talk."

Leah was too shaken to do anything but nod. The two managed to push Anna up and onto her feet. They half dragged her into the living room and plopped her down in a beat-up recliner in the corner. Leah was a little concerned about Martha doing so much heavy lifting at her late stage of pregnancy.

Martha motioned Leah back to the hallway and then led the way into the disheveled bedroom. Coats of every kind were flung on the bed, but Martha unceremoniously swept them onto the floor. She lay down on the bed, her legs splayed out uncomfortably before her. She patted the bed for Leah to sit. "I bet you're shocked, huh?" she laughed. She rubbed her stomach and giggled.

"I am a little. I had heard about you living with Abe, but—"

"Gossip? Yeah. I just bet I was talked about by all the old women and the girls at the last quilting, right?" Martha scowled.

Leah shook her head. "I wouldn't know. I've been gone a while now."

"I heard that, but I could hardly believe it. Why'd you go?"

Leah pulled her feet up under her and told Martha her story.

Martha snorted. "I can't believe you want to live there! They have a reputation of being strict. Why go from the frying pan into the fire, Leah?"

"It isn't like that at all. I have as much freedom as I need, and I'm working to get my GED. I'm also practicing to get my driver's license, and I have some work. It's not bad."

Martha regarded her friend skeptically, shaking her head. "Too much religion for me."

"They do like us to go to church, but you know I'm born again, so I like going to church anyway."

Leah's enthusiasm seemed naive and childish even to her own ears as loud music and the noise of the drunken partygoers filtered through the shut door. Martha cackled and adjusted herself into a more comfortable position. "Good for you, but I like the life I have here."

Leah looked at her. "When's your baby due?"

"Two months, they say. I don't know. Seems like he might come at any time." She nodded toward the door. "Abe's in seventh heaven now that we know it's a boy."

"Are you—do you—have the right things for the baby?"

Martha shrugged. "We'll be ready, I guess. I have a lot of stuff I've been buying at garage sales, and there's this place called Catholic Charities where we can get vouchers to buy stuff, too." She hung her head. "I'm trying to find a job, though. Abe thinks he might get laid off from the factory. It makes him grumpy sometimes. He worries too much."

She glanced toward Leah. "You hear of anything coming open anywhere? I was thinking of waitressing or maybe cleaning, fast food, whatever. I can do just about anything."

"No. I'm sorry. I don't know of anything. Are you sure you'd feel like working, though?"

"Sure."

Leah could not imagine being in Martha's shoes. She was really worried about her, but it was none of her business, so she changed the subject.

"You should have Abe bring you over sometime. I have my own apartment—almost my own. I share it with another former Amish girl. She's really nice."

Martha seemed suddenly depressed. "Maybe I will." Martha picked at some fuzz on her bedspread and Leah grew uncomfortable when she stopped talking altogether.

Finally, Leah stood and gave Martha a tight hug. "I should get going. Is there a phone I can use to call someone to come pick me up? It's earlier than I'd arranged."

"Here. I got my phone fixed." She leaned to her right side and pulled the red cell phone out of her pocket. It was the one she'd shown Leah months ago, the day of the summer frolic, when she'd told about her stepbrother Abner. It seemed a long time ago now, and while Leah felt a longing for the simple days that had existed for her back then, she remembered none of those days had been simple or safe for Martha.

She glanced at Martha's sad eyes and wished she could make everything right for her.

Leah sighed, took the phone, and punched in the Schrocks' number, but then she snapped the phone shut. What was she doing? She couldn't call the Schrocks—they were gone for the evening, and she'd have to wait another two hours, at least, for Hannah and her boyfriend to be ready to pick her up after their movie. How would she get home? Leah surely didn't want to stay here any longer.

"What's the matter?" asked Martha as she handed the phone back.

"I forgot, the Schrocks aren't home, and my ride won't be picking me up until after eleven."

Martha laboriously pulled herself from the bed and motioned for her to follow. "What's wrong with staying until eleven?"

Leah tried not to sigh, but her heart grew heavy thinking about being in this place any longer. It was sad seeing her friend this way, and Leah was caught off guard by the noise and drinking. The whole situation made her anxious to leave.

Martha grinned. "Oh, I get it. Not your favorite kind of party, eh? I'll get Abe to drive you back."

Leah hesitated as she imagined the shape Abe might be in. Martha saw her concern and laughed again. "Don't worry. He takes turns staying sober with the other guys so he can drive everybody home. He's dry as a haymow tonight."

They pressed their way back through the crowd until Martha found Abe in the corner of the living room, shouting about a movie he and Martha had watched the night before. The thud of the bass made Leah's head pound, and a time or two, she felt her heart beating in time with the music. A strange, lonely wave rolled over her. Though she was surrounded by former Amish kids just like her, she did not fit in. Would there ever be a place in the world for her again?

Martha balanced her swollen body on the arm of the chair Abe was sitting in and leaned over to rest her head against his. She looked tired.

The smoke that fills this room can't be good for the baby. Then Leah was shocked to see Martha take a drag from Abe's burning cigarette. On a closer look, she realized the smoking white stick wasn't just a normal cigarette. She frowned. Leah would have never guessed Martha would put her own child at risk by smoking pot.

Martha caught her disapproving look and grinned. She nudged Abe and said in a loud voice, "My goody-two-shoes friend here is not happy with us, Abe."

Abe glanced up for the first time and nodded dully to Leah. He went back to his conversation, but Martha wasn't through needling her friend. She grabbed the arm of one of the girls swaying nearby and yelled, "This is my *Christian* friend. Her name's Leah. She doesn't approve of our party, ladies."

One of the girls turned her head and stared with an angry scowl. "What's she doing here then?" she asked sharply.

Martha giggled. "She thought she was coming to a singing."

The gang of girls howled and giggled as they broke out singing a song from the old hymnal. They linked arms with Martha, substituting silly and filthy words for the old Amish ones. They burst into new fits of giggles.

Leah's face grew warm from embarrassment and anger. Though she didn't want to be a part of the Amish anymore, she didn't like the way these girls were making *sputz* of the sacred hymns they had so often sung together on Sunday nights. Leah retreated to a chair in the corner and sat with her head down. *Why did I come here?*

One of Abe's friends stumbled over to squeeze into the chair with her. She tried to push him off, but he perched precariously on the arm, waving his cigarette around her face. His breath was as foul with alcohol as everyone else's in the room, and his aftershave was strong and cloying. She gagged at the sickening combination of odors. Her head continued to pound with the music.

"You friends of Abe an' Martha?" the man slurred. He spit on her hand as he talked.

"*Ja.*" She wiped the moisture from the back of her hand.

"Me, too. I come from Hartville way. You from around here?"

"Yes."

He stopped talking but continued to stare. Then his eyes traveled up and down her body, and Leah cowered further into the chair, trying to ignore him.

"You want a *real* man to take you home—show you a good night?" he blurted out suddenly.

Leah glared sharply at the man. His leering smile and drunken eyes sickened her. She shook her head and tried to stand up, but he grabbed at her clothes and wrestled her back to the chair. He tried to slide under her just as she lost her balance and fell into the seat. Leah fought to jump up and away from his smelly body. She was amazed a person so drunk could still be this strong. He would not let her stand. Panic flew through her at his touch, and she struggled harder. "Stop! Please! I have to go home—let me up!"

Leah looked around for help, but Martha was still joking and singing with her friends, and no one else seemed to realize what was happening. She continued to fight his groping until finally she was able to wiggle away from the man's sweaty grip.

She fell to the floor and hurriedly crawled away from his grasp. He leaned back in the chair, hooting and jeering at her. "What a *dumbkopf*," he sneered. "Go on home, you ugly *Englisher*." He waved Leah off and began to chuckle at nothing.

Leah stood on trembling legs as she forced her way through the crowd of partiers to Martha.

"Martha, I'd like to go home *now*. Could you ask Abe again?" Leah had to yell for her to hear.

Martha glanced her way, stopping her swaying as she regarded Leah's frantic expression. She turned to Abe and asked him to go get the car to take Leah back to her Christian family. She emphasized the word *Christian* again with a smirk.

One of the young people standing near Martha turned and asked Leah what she was bothering with religion for. "You got out, right? So why go back to all those rules?" The girl slurred her speech and leaned toward her, sloshing beer on Leah's sleeve. Now she reeked of alcohol, too.

Leah was past talking about her Christianity. All she could think about was getting out of the smelly room and back to her peaceful apartment. Martha wasn't in any condition to argue with or reason with, either. In her heart, Leah knew Jesus made all the difference in her life but saying that now seemed like a waste of breath. Most of the former Amish at this party wouldn't care or listen. It hit her that they were trying everything else but God to fill the holes in their hearts.

Tears of compassion flooded her eyes, and Martha noted them. Something melted in her. She reached out, grabbed Leah, and hugged her close. "I'm sorry."

"Martha, I really want to go, *please*," Leah whispered. She couldn't understand how Martha could take this noise and chaos night after night, especially with a baby on the way.

Martha looked around and saw Abe by the door. She gave Leah another hug and pushed her through the crowd. Leah took one more look at Martha.

"I'll be praying for you, Martha. Please let me know if you need anything and call when the baby is born. Okay?"

Martha nodded, staggering back to her friends and her party life, giggling.

The deep notes thumped through the air and wrapped around Leah as she descended the shaky stairs. Abe was waiting in the truck and sighed loudly when she climbed in.

"Sorry to take you away from the party, Abe."

He nodded as he tuned his radio to a loud station. *So much for trying to talk.*

She stared out the window and watched the quiet houses as they passed by in the night. Leah was unsettled and lonely. The face of Jacob Yoder came to mind, his smile something she sorely missed. She was disconnected out here in this *Englisher* world. Sometimes, it was very tempting to give up and go back. If only she could do both: live under grace and be with her family and community. There was no way she could go back on the Lord, but was there still hope the bishop would give in about her going against the *Ordnung*?

The moon was large and bright, its yellow glow mellowed by clouds that sailed over its surface. It reminded Leah of happier times with her family when they had lazily watched the moon on hot summer nights after dinner. She yearned for reconciliation. She missed *Maem* and *Daet*. She missed Ada, Benny, Daniel, and Sara. No one could take the place of family, but Leah knew she couldn't stand to live under the religious laws and rules of man anymore. There didn't seem to be a way to do both.

Abe made the few miles to the Schrocks' house a quick trip, and before she knew it, he was pulling into the driveway. No lights showed in the house, though it wasn't that late. What would they think of her if they knew where she'd been?

What in the world got into me that I had to go to this party?

"Thanks, Abe, for bringing me back." Leah paused. "I'll be praying for you and Martha—and the baby."

Abe snorted, a look of disgust crossing his face when she mentioned the baby. His reaction startled her.

"Whatever," he replied shortly.

Even Abe seemed less than happy with their new life, and Leah wondered how things could have so quickly turned out wrong for both him and Martha.

She let herself in the door to the downstairs apartment and lightly descended the concrete stairs. With a sigh, she shut the door and turned on the light. Her bedroom seemed more like a refuge than ever after the loudness of the party. She hurriedly peeled off her stinking clothes. They smelled like cigarettes and beer. She took them to the washer and dropped them in. She turned on hot water and poured a capful of detergent over the smelly fabric.

Leah scurried to the bathroom, pulling a clean washcloth from the shelf. Warm water sluiced away the feelings of disappointment and disgust. The fresh scent of soap was soothing. She pulled a soft gown over her head, breathing in the unsullied smell of clean cloth. Padding barefoot to the bed, she pulled back the crisp sheets and blankets and picked up the phone to let her roommate know that she was already home.

As the pillow wrapped its spotless scent around her, she sighed. Never had Leah felt such thankfulness for this bed or for this room or for this house. She said a simple prayer of thanks for the Schrocks and for God's protection over her during the party. She was exhausted and closed her eyes soon after she turned off the light. Just before she slipped into sleep, Leah imagined she heard *Maem's* voice wishing her good night, and a deep sadness filled her heart.

❧

Leah worked hard all spring, cleaning houses and studying for her GED. She was learning to drive and was trying to save as much money as she could toward a car. As the months had passed, she'd hoped to feel more at home in the English world, but with summer approaching, the

familiar weight of loneliness and longing for her family settled on her
shoulders. She added volunteering in the MAP offices once a week to
fill her schedule, but she still had too much time to think about home.

To her surprise, a letter came for her a few weeks later. Her heart beat
faster when she noted the return address from Jacob Yoder. He wrote! He
finally wrote. Eagerly she tore open the envelope, dropping the torn edge
to the floor in her haste to read.

> Dear Leah,
>
> I hope this letter finds you happy. I'm sorry it took me so long
> to answer your letter. I've had to do some thinking. I don't have
> much time to write, and I'm not a writer anyway, but I want to
> let you know how much I miss you. Things are about the same
> here. Except you are gone. And that's a world of difference. I hope
> to run into you sometime when I'm in town—and I sure wish I
> could drive out to see you. It seems especially hard since you're
> not far away, but I don't want to upset your new life. (I also know
> it may be too hard for me to leave you and drive back home. Ha!)
>
> I ran into Martha in town after I got your letter. I told her
> where you were. I hope that was okay. She sure has a lot on her
> plate, but I'm guessing you know that by now.
>
> Your *daet* and *maem* have not said much about you, but that's
> not a surprise, is it? It seems to be how things are done when
> someone leaves. Ada is missing you, and so is little Benny. He
> doesn't understand why you're not at home anymore, and I'm not
> sure your parents have told him why you're gone.
>
> I also want you to know I read the gospel of John in an
> English Bible that was given to my little sister by the Gideons. If I
> can be trusted to understand what I read, I might see why you are
> thinking the way you are thinking. (Ignore my poor grammar! A
> country farmer is what I am, I guess, and what I'll always be—
> not a *gut* writer.) Anyway, I have to go. I don't want my parents
> catching me putting this in the mailbox. Take care of yourself,
> and I hope you think of me from time to time.
>
> Jacob

Leah wiped tears as she read. The letter—so simple, yet so poignant—tore at her heartstrings. "Oh, Jacob! Why does it have to be this way?" She secured the precious letter in her dresser box and hurried to get ready for work. All day she wondered about Jacob. Would he think about joining her in the English world? Could there ever be a future for her with him? She tried to put the letter from her mind, choosing to focus on the here and now. If God had a plan for Jacob to be in her life, she prayed to be patient and open to the possibility.

⚜

One morning, Naomi drove Leah to the library to get a few books for her GED class.

"Okay, now that's done, let's go get some lunch," said Naomi. "How about the Lynway? Ever been there?"

"No. I've seen it a time or two and heard about their famous pies."

"Sounds good, doesn't it?"

Leah grinned as they walked back to the car. She raised her face to catch a cool breeze. The sun was shining brightly, and she felt a lift in her heart for the first time in days.

Leah opened the door to slide in when she heard the familiar clopping of horse hooves. She glanced around in time to see a black buggy coming toward the library. Her hand froze on the handle of Naomi's car as she recognized the caramel coloring and mannerisms of Sparky. Her gaze flew to the faces of those in the buggy: *Maem*, Ada, and Benny. Leah's heart turned over. Before she realized what she was doing, she ran to the edge of the street and lifted her hand in a wild and happy wave.

At first, her family didn't see her, but as they passed by, Leah saw Benny excitedly pointing to her. His eyes lit up, and he lifted his hand to wave back, but *Maem* quickly stopped him, pulling his hand down to his lap. She showed no recognition of her daughter whatsoever but kept her eyes straight ahead on Sparky's haunches. Benny gave *Maem* a bewildered look and then dropped his head in shame. Ada glanced Leah's way but made no further sign of acknowledgment—no wave, no smile, no anything.

Leah's heart plummeted, and she burst into sobs. She watched the buggy roll on down the busy street as tears fell on her T-shirt. She hungrily kept sight of the black buggy until it was lost in traffic and no longer visible. By the time Naomi reached Leah, she was a mess. Naomi hugged her tightly, leading her back to the car.

Naomi turned the key and flipped the AC switch to send cool air through the car. She waited for Leah to regain her composure before she spoke.

"Leah, I had this same type of thing happen to me. It hurt so much and made me ache for my family. It also made me mad they were willing to leave me behind—like they'd totally forgotten me. That's what it felt like anyway."

Leah sniffed.

"But what I had to remember was they weren't trying to hurt me. They were really concerned I was going to go to hell, and they believed it with all their hearts. In their minds, being cruel to me through shunning was worth it if it brought me back—kept my soul from going to hell, made me come home. Rejoin the Amish church. Live my life Amish and then die and go to heaven. You know?"

"I know," Leah replied. "But it hurts to see my little brother and sister and *Maem*—" she shook her head. "She always loved me—*always*. I can't imagine doing that to my daughter."

"It does hurt, and, in some ways, it never stops hurting."

Leah tried to imagine Naomi being young and lost without her family. She wondered how she lived with the *meidning* all these years. "Do you still miss your family, Naomi?"

"Yes. It's been twenty years, and my parents have passed on now, but my sisters have figured out a way to see me without getting in too much trouble with their bishop. They let me come to visit now that *Daet* and *Maem* are gone."

"It's been that long since you left?"

Naomi nodded. "Yes. My family has missed so much of my life. I think I was most hurt that my parents were never grandparents to my children. They didn't watch them grow up. That made me angry once in a while, but we did have a family from our church who 'adopted' us.

They were there for us right from the beginning. That helped. They took us in and made us a part of *their* family."

Leah stared out the window. "Did you ever think about going back?"

"Sure. Often. And as you've heard, Matthew and I tried to go back—but it just didn't work. As time went on, I grew more adjusted to being English, and above that, I just couldn't go back to living under the *Ordnung*. I knew I couldn't give up on God."

Again, Leah nodded, fully understanding the mix of emotions.

"Are you okay?" Naomi asked gently.

Leah gave her a watery smile, but in her heart, the pain was still so strong she felt as though she must be bleeding. The sharp sadness of rejection stabbed more than she could have possibly guessed, and for the first time in a long while, that old familiar anger started to burn again.

Leah was mad at the bishop, mad at the church, and even mad at *Maem* and *Daet*. After all, if they loved her, they would stand up for her. Wouldn't they? How could parents turn against their own child? She shook her head in confusion as Naomi put the car in gear.

Then Naomi added an insight that struck Leah deeply. "One thing: don't let bitterness and anger toward your family or even toward the Amish church take root in your heart. I know for a fact it isn't worth the trouble and pain it can cause you." She glanced at Leah. "From this day on, ask the Lord to help you release it and let it go."

She was silent. Leah wasn't sure she could do that yet.

Naomi continued, "Leah, take my advice to heart as from one who knows what it can do to bottle up those feelings and feed that anger. Ask God to take it from you. He cares. He wants you to live in peace. He didn't call you out to live for Him in grace and mercy, and at the same time, to carry anger and bitterness in your heart. It will steal your peace and your joy."

"But how can I get over this? My *own* mother has turned her back on me!"

"I know. It hurts, but Jesus can help you as He has helped me. We'll start to pray He'll do just that, okay?"

Leah nodded and leaned back in the seat. She shut her eyes, immediately praying for peace. Peace that suddenly seemed elusive and far away.

The ache in her heart kept hurting, and all the way home, silent tears squeezed out and ran down her cheeks.

It was harder now, more than ever, to think of a future without her family in it. She could not picture herself being happy again without them. She'd imagined that as time passed her family would come around, but now Leah knew just how strongly they felt and how difficult it would be for them to accept her new life. *God, help me learn to live with this—please.*

Chapter Sixteen

The sunny hot days of summer moved in, and on top of her worry over Martha, Leah was thinking more and more about her family. She couldn't get out of her mind the image of little Benny as *Maem* jerked his hand to his lap. The look on his face, his disappointment and shame, made Leah sad every time she thought of it. Anger toward *Maem* increased; anger toward all of them. And then came a letter from home. As Leah opened it, her hands trembled. She recognized *Daet*'s handwriting.

> Daughter Leah,
>
> Many times I thought to write this, but every time I tried, I could not find the words. Bishop Miller thinks it is good to send this to you. We want to tell you that it is not too late to shake off Satan's deceptive hand from your shoulder. Come home. Your *Maem* cries for you. Your brothers and sister also would like you to be back in the family fold. Don't stay on this path too long, or you may find yourself dragged to the depth of Satan's den and then, if your soul is required of you before you have the chance to return to the Amish, you will be lost for all eternity. Heed your wise Daet's warning before it is too late. Until you come home for good, it is best for you to not come home at all.

Leah dropped the letter, the pain it carried burning her fingers like fire. The words only intensified her deep loneliness. To bear *Daet*'s censure, his order to not come home until she wore the *kapp* and dress of the Amish, broke her spirit as well as her heart. Despair wrapped its heavy mantle over her shoulders. It was nearly impossible to shake off its weight—even when she reminded herself that Jesus promised a light burden to those who followed Him.

She tried hard to study instead, but some of the English words made no sense. Every test, every lesson took more concentration than she could give. She was grumpy and short with her roommate and with the Schrocks. Naomi wisely kept quiet and offered no more advice, but Leah was building a wall, and distance was mounting between her host family and herself. She thought seriously about going back home.

At breakfast one morning, she was eating with the family when Matthew said a prayer for the food. He then asked the Lord to bless Leah with peace, calm, and acceptance of her family's actions. Leah's cheeks warmed as a slow burn grew.

How can he say that? How could I ever accept that kind of thing?

After the prayer, she made her disapproval known when she took a drink of coffee and set down the cup forcefully.

Matthew glanced at her. "Is there something you want to say?"

She pressed her lips together firmly, trying to keep from speaking, but bitterness couldn't be suppressed.

"Yes!" she blurted through tears. "You have *no* business praying that kind of prayer for me. It makes me feel like you think my family's rejection is a minor problem. It *isn't!* It hurts, and you've forgotten that feeling or you wouldn't say such a thing."

Matthew quietly regarded her. Finally, he spoke. "Leah, my *daet*'s rejection of me still has the power to make me feel small—even after all these years. There's no way I can forget the pain, but I *know* what a waste it is to let the anger and sting of it control my life."

Leah shook her head, tired of listening to this same message, first from Naomi and now from Matthew.

"Is it worth it?" she asked Matthew. "Is it? Shouldn't I go back and try to get them to see the Lord *through* me instead of abandoning everything they know and respect?"

Leah was trembling with guilt and loneliness.

Matthew let her express her feelings, but Leah could tell he didn't agree with her position. She continued, unable to stop the emotion pouring from her. "You know, I used to think there was no living with my family after I was born again," she persisted. "But I haven't even tried to be back with them since I started on this road. Maybe if I join the church and settle in, they'll have more respect for my faith. Maybe they'll see the new way I'm thinking and the happiness the Lord has brought me."

Matthew glanced away and blew out his breath. "Leah, this is the *same* thing I thought when I asked my wife to move back into our Amish community after we left. And you know what? It just didn't work. We wanted it to; we *really* did, but the bishops and the *Ordnung* didn't have room for us and our faith. I wish I could say things have changed, but you know change is not something the Old Order or Swartzentruber Amish embrace. Not at all."

"But—"

Matthew put up his hand. "I don't want you to think I'm insisting you stay out, but I want you to be aware of what it will be like if you return. Obeying the forefathers, the bishop, and the *Ordnung* were the top priorities when we went back all those years ago, and they still are today."

"I know." She sighed, quiet for a minute or two while she thought about what Matthew said. Still, Leah couldn't help but wonder if she might be missing the chance to lead her family to true salvation and grace. Maybe change *was* possible, and she was the one to help. The guilt over disobeying her parents and deserting her sister and brothers was overwhelming, and Leah wasn't sure if she'd last another week.

"You've made a life-changing decision, and we can't sit here and tell you that you must do this or you must do that," Naomi said, glancing at Matthew. "We couldn't do it at first, either, Leah. Youthful desires to belong and be part of a loving family are powerful emotions. Knowing you've lost your parents' love is so painful, it can't even be explained or anticipated. You just have to feel it and experience it and then do what you can to stand."

She made a circular motion between herself and Matthew. "We still have times when we wish we could go back, but the burden of following the *Ordnung* is too heavy to carry, Leah. We'll be praying that you will discover what God wants for you because He wants only the best. He is the only Father who will love you purely and without selfish thought."

Leah put her head down and sat still. She knew the Schrocks were right.

"I have work to do, so I'd better get to it," Matthew said. He rose and walked to the door. He paused, looking back with an understanding expression. "I'll be praying for you, Leah."

⁂

Leah woke on Sunday morning in the middle of a dream. She stretched lazily and lay still, remembering the feel of Sparky's leather reins in her hands. In the dream, she drove her brother and sister to town, all of them laughing the way they used to before she left. It was so real she felt she could *see* Benny and Ada beside her.

"Leah?" called Hannah through the door. "I'm leaving for church soon. Do you want to go this morning?"

She decided it wouldn't hurt to go and pray about her situation with fellow believers. "I'll ride with the Schrocks, Hannah."

She hopped out of bed and grabbed a dress from the closet. It took twenty minutes to shower and dry her hair. She was ready to go just as the Schrocks were walking out the door.

The ride to church seemed longer than usual. Leah zoned out and didn't listen to the conversation going on around her. The heavy feeling in her chest weighed her down as she stared at the passing scenery. They were getting close to the area where her parents lived. She kept her eyes glued to the lanes and roads as they crossed each one, but she didn't see Sparky prancing along as she'd hoped.

I don't even know if this is the off-week from church. I'm so out of touch with everything I used to know. Realizing this added to her misery.

For the first time since starting at the little community church the Schrocks attended, Leah couldn't wait for the singing and the preaching to be over. She was restless and wanted a chance to kneel at her seat to pray. She tried praying silently, but she couldn't concentrate and couldn't block the sound of the music and the pastor's voice.

Guilt pursued her. Guilt about thinking of leaving the Schrocks after all they'd done for her. Guilt for trying to ignore the service, and most of all guilt that she had abandoned her family in the first place.

At the invitation to pray, she knelt at the pew, dropping her head on her arms. She poured out her feelings to God, but by the end of the prayer, Leah still felt miserable and lonely.

Sunday dinner was tense. Hannah kept her distance and quietly went about her business. Leah watched an old movie for an hour, but the restless feelings grew.

At home, she would be relaxing with the family by now. If it was a church day, she'd be getting ready to go to the Sunday night singing. The desire to see Jacob Yoder rose in her heart, and she fought a longing to run home. She almost couldn't stop herself from packing her things and walking out the door.

Hannah wandered in. She sat on the chair across from Leah. "It's hard, isn't it?"

She nodded.

"I still miss my family, and it seems Sunday is the worst day for that."

Again Leah nodded mutely.

The silence in the room deepened. Suddenly, Hannah stood. "Let's go get some ice cream. Doesn't that sound good?"

Her smile was open and inviting. Leah responded as best she could. "Sure."

She couldn't wait to get out of the house.

Once in town, Hannah drove past the turn off to the Dairy Queen located on Main Street. "Aren't we going to the ice-cream stand?"

"It's such a nice day, I thought it'd be good to take a drive in the country and get our ice cream at Raysburg General Store."

Leah's heart raced, knowing they'd be traveling close to her family's farm.

Maybe I'll see someone I know.

The winding roads following the hills and curves of the farmland north of Ashfield lulled her into a peaceful trance. She viewed the passing landscapes and remembered the feel of the asphalt roads under the roll of the buggy wheels. She could almost imagine the pull of Sparky against his reins and the sound of his clopping hooves striking the hard surface of the blacktop.

Soon they were pulling into the store parking lot, and she suddenly thought of her English clothes. What if she saw Jacob? Or worse yet *Daet*? *Maem* and her brother and sister had already seen Leah in her *Englisher* jeans and T-shirt, but the thought of *Daet* seeing her—it was harder to imagine his reaction.

She glanced nervously around as she got out of the car and shut the door. The store was surprisingly busy for a late Sunday afternoon, but many of the people shuffling in and out of the store were tourists or locals who came in to get a snack or rent a movie.

The wooden floors creaked as they wandered down the aisle past the cash register and over to the ice-cream counter perched atop a freezer that held many icy confections. She leaned against the cold glass as she made her selection of ice cream. The man who waited on them was the one who had helped her the day she left the Amish. She wondered if he recognized her in her new garb.

The two friends paid for the cones and settled into the very booth Leah had sat in while waiting for Naomi to pick her up months ago. The outside air was hot and sticky, and a patch of moisture trickled down the inside pane of the air-conditioned window. She looked across the table at her roommate, and a feeling of warmth and affection for Hannah's thoughtfulness spread over her sore heart.

"Thank you, Hannah."

"For what?"

"For this." Leah gestured to the store. "For bringing me to see the place again and for understanding I needed to be out here for a while."

"You're welcome." Hannah's rosy cheeks glowed as she grinned at Leah.

Leah rolled an icy cold drop of sweet frozen cream over her tongue. "Being here reminds me of the day I left. The urge to somehow find out more about myself and God. I'd . . . forgotten."

Leah gazed out the window to the surrounding fields, houses, and passing cars. When she'd left her Amish home, the ways of the English had been a mystery. Now she knew that along with the freedom to choose a path for herself came much responsibility. She had no family to help her. And her role in life, while open for God's plans, was complicated by not really having a clear identity. Among the Amish, she had been Leah Raber, good Amish girl and future wife and mother.

Out here, the prospects seemed endless, scary, and exhilarating at the same time. There were no hard-and-fast rules of who she could be, what she could accomplish, and how she would choose to live her life. The Amish way, though very hard, was straightforward. The path of her life was already decided, long before she'd even been born. In that, she supposed, people could say it was a "simple" life. But the freedom to choose was strong in her heart and something she didn't know how to squelch. There was good in her upbringing, and there was support, but there was also frustration for someone like her who grasped for an independence that didn't fit the Amish way.

She mulled these ideas around and came to the conclusion that, for her, life in the English world was worth the sacrifice. She fanned the spark of contentment. Just for today, she would think of the good things she'd accomplished and gained and put the losses aside for another time. She was young. The day was beautiful. The sun glowed over the warmed earth, and her friend was by her side. Yes. Today, it was enough.

The two friends chatted amiably while finishing their ice cream. Just as they were throwing the napkins away in the big trash bin outside the general store's double doors, Leah heard the unmistakable sound of a buggy coming down the road.

She stepped away from the building and watched as the buggy drew closer. It was not Sparky, but she did recognize the neighbor's black horse. His huge size and large head set him apart from all the other horses.

As the buggy drew nearer, the Amish man seated on the front seat threw up his hand in a friendly wave. The Amish commonly offered a greeting to the *Englisher* tourists—Leah had done it herself many times without even paying attention to who the people were, but as they passed Hannah and Leah, the Amish wife's eyes grew large as she recognized their neighbor's wayward daughter in her English clothing.

Leah felt an ornery tug and smiled as she called, *"Wie bisht du, Ruth und Erb?"*

Hannah raised her hand in a friendly greeting, too. Ruth nearly twisted her neck getting a backward look at Leah as the horse pulled their buggy through the intersection and away from the store.

Hannah shook her head and giggled. "You know how the gossip mill is, Leah. It's going to get around to everybody by morning that you were seen at the general store in your *Englisher* clothes, and had the nerve to ask Ruth and Erb how they were."

Leah joined her in laughter as they walked slowly to the car. She stopped to take a long look around. The sun was starting to set, and the rosy hues of its dying rays spread over the summer fields like a thick blanket. She breathed deeply of the humid air and let out a sigh.

"This is nice. Thanks, again, Hannah."

"Ready to go?"

"Yep. I am."

Later that night, something seemed more settled in her soul. She read the Bible and asked the Lord to help her make it through. This time, she felt like she was reaching God. Leah felt His Spirit breathe on her and asked Him to send His peace deep into her heart.

As she turned out the white hobnailed lamp by the bed, she whispered another thankful prayer. Determined to shake off her blues and quit feeling sorry for herself, Leah decided it was time to nurture a little bit of hope. It felt awfully good to fall asleep with a smile on her face.

❧

The next morning, before she went to volunteer at the Mission to Amish People offices, Leah decided to write her parents another letter. She wanted to tell them what she'd been doing since she left. Being seen by their neighbors the night before prompted her to write. She knew gossip would reach her family soon enough, and she wanted to have her letter in their hands not long afterward.

She'd just finished the letter and was putting a stamp in the corner when Naomi called down to ask if she was ready to go. Leah ran up the steps to join her and placed the letter in the mailbox at the end of the driveway.

The drive to MAP was similar to the drive with Hannah the day before, along the same roads and viewing the same rolling hillsides and lovely farmsteads. The MAP office building sat at the back of the church the Schrocks and Leah attended. The large room housed offices and long tables for volunteers to sit and grade papers or fold newsletters. The group needed many volunteers to hold the weekly children's club and respond to the mail.

In one part of the building, shelves held gift bags of needed supplies to give to those who had just left the Amish—often with nothing but the clothes on their backs. The bags held deodorant, shampoo, and other toiletries, as well as material about MAP help.

A few ladies sat at desks, marking papers. Levi, who helped Matthew with MAP business, greeted her with a smile. It felt right, knowing she was doing something positive to help other former Amish as well as spreading the gospel message.

The day passed quickly as Leah moved from station to station doing whatever was needed. She prayed that God would always call volunteers to be willing to aid the ministry. She had seen for herself how much they helped her.

⚜

Later that evening, just after Leah finished helping with the dinner dishes, the phone rang. It was Sally Burns, wanting to know if she was still interested in a full-time cleaning job she had available in the evenings. A lady who'd been cleaning for Sally had quit that very day.

Leah hesitated because she wasn't sure how to get herself there. Though she'd been saving, she still didn't have quite enough money for a car of her own, not to mention she didn't have her driver's license yet.

"Don't worry about a ride," Sally offered. "I can pick you up on my way into town, and since we'll be working together, you'll always have a ride."

"Then, yes! I've been hoping I could get a full-time job."

"You'll need to go into town and get a work permit since you're still under eighteen, but that shouldn't be a problem at all. Or do you have one for the houses you're cleaning?"

"No. I didn't know I needed one, but I can get it this week."

"Okay. Call me when you have that, and we'll plan to start as soon as that's taken care of."

"All right. And thank you, Sally." Leah put down the phone and scampered into the living room to share the good news with the Schrocks.

"God is good!" exclaimed Matthew.

"Yes, He is!" agreed Naomi with a broad smile. Leah smiled back at them and felt a piece of the puzzle coming together for the first time since she'd left home.

Maybe I really can make it on my own here in this Englisher *world.*

"Why don't I take you into Ashfield tomorrow morning?" Matthew suggested. "Then before you go clean Mrs. Lewis's house, you can get your worker's permit."

"Great! Thanks, Matthew."

Leah was relieved she would finally be able to help contribute more to her living expenses. What a gracious couple to let her move in and wait patiently for her to find a full-time job. She was glad God had blessed her with these friends.

⚜

Leah drummed her fingers on the door frame as she waited for Sally Burns to pick her up on her first night of the new job. The shift started at six because they were cleaning the offices of a science facility that closed at five thirty. She watched as Sally's car pulled in the drive. Sally had red hair piled high on her head and long, dangling earrings. Her fingernails were painted bright pink. Leah wondered how she kept them in such good condition, considering she cleaned alongside her hired workers.

Leah got in the car and introduced herself. Though they'd chatted the night before on the phone, she hadn't imagined the fun-loving lady who sat beside her now. Leah sensed working with Sally would be an experience she would not soon forget. Sally chattered a mile a minute, laughed often, and called Leah "honey girl" and "girlfriend." How could a person not like Sally? Leah was enthralled and couldn't help smiling.

Before the two ladies started work at the facility, they sat in the parking lot while Sally showed Leah how to fill in the forms she needed to file for taxes.

The job site was overwhelming with its many buildings, but Sally quickly explained their responsibility to clean only pertained to the office building. Now inside, she carried a set of keys that unlocked a large storage room, where a utility sink and all the cleaning provisions were located. Sally got out the buckets and mops and showed Leah where to find gloves to protect her hands from the harsh chemicals they used to disinfect the floors and surfaces.

Aha! So that's how she keeps her nails so neatly polished.

Leah glimpsed a light spilling from an office down the hallway.

"Do we clean around the people who are still working?"

Sally glanced toward the back area. "Ah, that's Mr. Sedak's office. He works late every night. He'll go down to the cafeteria to take a break and get some coffee when he sees us. You'll hardly ever run into anyone else in here after six."

She explained how to clean swiftly, yet thoroughly, and they passed the time together chatting about families, popular TV shows, and recipes. Leah was enjoying her new employer and thanking God He had helped her to get this job. Sally was not at all uncomfortable or bossy.

⚜

The summer days passed quickly and autumn showed itself in the cooler temperatures each evening and the changing leaves each morning. Leah continued studying for her GED, volunteering in the MAP offices when she could, and working her evening cleaning job. She also continued cleaning two houses during the day. It wasn't that she was never homesick anymore, but keeping busy helped her handle moments of homesickness better. She also loved the Tuesday night Bible studies and enjoyed the new friendships she'd established there. But if she let herself dwell on thoughts of Bishop Miller or the *Ordnung*, a burst of anger and bitterness about the changes they had forced on her life shot through her. Best not to linger on those thoughts.

⚘

One sunny, crisp day, she rode into Ashfield with Naomi. It was an important milestone for Leah: she was going to take her written test to get her driver's license permit. Though she had studied, she was still afraid of failure, and in the back of her mind, she had to admit her Amish teachings against cars were playing games with her mind. In her Amish church, driving a car was one of the worst sins she could commit.

There was no doubt *Maem, Daet*, and her Amish friends and neighbors would consider what she was planning to do an act of utter rebellion and rejection of the *Ordnung*. Leah's parents would be convinced she was headed straight to hell by even considering driving a car.

An unwanted melancholy settled over Leah's spirit as she reflected on their disapproval if they knew what was happening to her. Dressing like an *Englisher* was one thing, but no one in her family had ever driven a car. Maybe some families had wayward *rumspringen* teens who drove and then hid their cars and trucks on their dad's property, but it wasn't like that in Leah's family. Neither *Daet* nor *Maem* nor her grandparents had been as wild as all that in their youth.

Leah shook off the negative thoughts and picked up the exam practice book to cram a bit more information into her head before they reached the DMV office. As Naomi pulled into the parking lot, Leah felt a flutter of indecision.

Should I be doing this? What if the Ordnung *is right? What if driving a car really is a mortal sin?*

She pushed the thoughts from her mind as she climbed out of the car and walked into the building.

Thirty minutes later, Naomi congratulated her on passing the test. Leah was on her way to even more freedom. She agreed when Naomi suggested a celebration ice cream at the Dairy Queen.

"But first, I have to get a roll or two of duct tape for a project. Let's go to the hardware store on the way, okay?"

"Sure. I'd like to pick up a small box of thumb tacks and a bulletin board while we're in there. I want to put it above my desk so I can post my work hours."

Home Hardware was a busy, crowded place when they went in, so it took a few minutes to find the selection of bulletin boards. Leah spied a cheerful one with bright daisies around the frame and decided it was just what she needed to perk up the wall above her desk. As she wandered the aisles looking at the beginnings of Christmas displays, a prickly sensation went up her spine.

Is someone watching me?

She glanced up. Jacob Yoder was smiling down at her. Her knees wobbled and hands trembled. His eyes seemed to drink her in.

He looked so familiar and yet unfamiliar. His Amish dress appeared foreign to her now, and she realized for the first time what English people saw when they looked at the Amish. Leah had grown accustomed to the short hair and T-shirts of the English men. The uniform colors and style of the Amish seemed to hide Jacob's individuality. He looked like a clone of so many other Amish men.

Is this how I looked when I was Amish? No wonder the English say we all look alike!

Jacob grinned as he ambled over. "Leah! I'm so glad to see you. *Wie bisht'd?*" Hearing the Pennsylvania-Dutch words spoken to her again brought a familiar sense of homesickness to Leah's heart. She fought to maintain her composure.

"*Gut. Und du?*"

"*Gut.* I've been wondering how you were doing."

"I'm doing fine. I'm working and still living at the Schrocks' place. They've been very supportive of me."

"I'm glad of that."

Jacob's familiar grin held a hint of melancholy. His eyes held hers, and all the things they'd been to one another flooded back to Leah's mind. She swallowed a growing lump in her throat. Now was not the time to fall apart. Now was the time to show Jacob she was, indeed, doing okay.

She hesitated before finally asking, "How's my family?"

Jacob played with his hat brim. "They're doing all right. They don't say much." He held her gaze. "You know they don't want to talk about you, but I think they miss you."

Leah glanced around quickly. "Are you by yourself? I just thought if anyone sees you talking to me . . ."

"It's okay. I *am* here by myself." The rules of the *Ordnung* didn't necessarily forbid him from talking with her since she had not yet joined the church, but the unspoken community rules frowned on Amish having contact or conversations with those who had left their teachings.

They stood in silence until Jacob asked, "Do you ever miss us—I mean . . . your family?"

She nodded. "I get homesick often."

"You do?" Jacob raised his brows. Was he surprised by her admission? Did he think she could walk away and *not* think of her parents, siblings, and especially him? Leah glanced at his hands. They clutched his hat, turning the brim around and around. Her heart lurched when she noticed his left hand trembling. She longed to reach out to him, to reassure him of how much he still meant to her. She longed to meet with him. Talk with him. Share her day, her job, her new friends with him.

She sighed. That would be foolish. It would only bring him more pain and maybe even trouble if the bishop discovered they were together. She could not keep her eyes off his hands. How they betrayed what was going on inside. She lifted her eyes to his, and for an instant, he let her see the desire to be with her. Quickly though, he shuttered his soul and broke the gaze.

She swallowed again. She would let him know she was moving forward. In the end, it would be kinder to let him know that.

"*Ja.* Lately I'm too busy and too tired to think about things much, but I have moments when I really miss *Maem* and *Daet* . . . and, all of you, really."

If her reply stung him, it didn't show on his face. Jacob hesitated before asking, "Do you ever think you might come home someday?"

All that had been between them was in his question. She glanced away. "I'd come home tomorrow if they'd let me be a born-again Christian."

"I know you think your new religion is better for you—"

She searched his eyes, holding his gaze as she asserted her point. "It isn't a religion, Jacob. It's real, and it means the world to me."

Jacob flushed and swallowed. "*Ja*, that's what I meant, but do you think it's any better than what we already have in the Amish?"

"What I had with my family was wonderful, but the *Ordnung* and the church and the bishops, they're not allowing me to follow Jesus and do what the Bible says. I can't go back to that, Jacob. It isn't me that has left; they've made me leave because they won't accept me anymore. And Martha didn't have *anything* nice in her Amish life, and still the church let her down. No one cared enough to make her stepbrother stop or take him to the law." She shook her head again. "I don't understand that kind of thinking. It's not right."

Jacob glanced up suddenly as an Amish family approached the doors of the hardware store. Their time was up.

Hurriedly, he took her hand and squeezed it gently before turning to go. He looked at Leah over his shoulder and whispered, "If you ever change your mind, I'm waiting for you. And if you ever want to come home, just get word to me." Then he walked casually to the doors and greeted the family coming in with a nod.

"*Tag*, Elam *und* Velma."

"Good day, Jacob."

Their manner turned stone cold when they spied Leah. Both the good man and his wife put their heads down and totally ignored her. She blushed but felt little anger at the miting they practiced toward her. It was what they had to do.

She went to find Naomi. As they checked out, Leah told Naomi she had seen Jacob.

"Oh yes? And how was that?"

"He was . . . nice."

"Good." Naomi didn't pry, but Leah was sure she understood the pain of what had just happened.

"But Elam and Velma Miller came in and they ignored me."

"Ah."

Leah shrugged, squaring her shoulders to hide the rejection. No matter how often it happened, she couldn't dismiss the sting of her people's censure. "I guess that's their problem, though. I'm still happy I got my permit today." Leah met Naomi's eyes and smiled, trying with all her heart to bring back the triumphant joy of her achievement.

Naomi returned the smile. "Yes, you have accomplished something very important, Leah. Be proud of that."

They had a good afternoon celebrating Leah's success and went home satisfied, but she was still thinking of Jacob. He looked so wonderful. She realized the feelings she had for him before she left the Amish had not diminished. Leah missed him more than ever. She missed his smile, his gentle teasing, and the way he glanced at her from time to time from under those thick, long lashes. She missed the smile crinkles that showed his good nature, and she missed how he understood her moods and her desire to know more about God. She missed knowing she was special to someone in this world in a way no one else shared.

She spent a lot of time trying not to think about his offer to come and take her back to the Amish.

It's too hard to go back now—isn't it? I've come so far—haven't I? I'm working. I have my permit. I have so many plans for my future. I have the freedom to worship God in the way He calls me. I am learning to know myself as Leah, apart from my Amish heritage. That's meager to some Englishers, but it's an entire world I've gained for my life. That's worth staying here . . . isn't it?

It had been a long day. All night Leah dreamed of the sound of horse's hooves and the rolling buggy wheels on the roads around her farm home. In the dreams, she sat on the front porch with *Maem* and *Daet*, Ada and Benny. And Jacob turned into the long lane with his buggy clean and shining, ready to keep her company.

CHAPTER SEVENTEEN

Leah slowly guided the car into the Walmart parking lot and carefully pulled into an empty spot. She turned the key off with a sigh.

"That was good!" exclaimed Hannah.

"I don't know. It makes me so nervous! I don't think I like driving." She slumped in the driver's seat.

Hannah laughed. "It took me a long time to get used to it, too. Don't worry; in no time at all, you'll be driving like you've done it all your life."

Leah wiped her sweating forehead with a tissue and shook her head. "I don't think so. It makes me almost sick to my stomach to do this."

"I won't make you drive home, but let's go on in and get our things and head back."

"I'm good with that idea!"

The girls hurried to shop, and Leah was more than a little relieved when Hannah hopped into the driver's seat for the trip home.

"I can't believe how easy I thought driving was, Hannah—until now. I guess I'll have to force myself to keep at it, though."

Hannah laughed at her friend's dejected tone. "I understand, Leah, but you're doing great. I would never guess you're a novice driver."

Later that night, Leah sat on her bed, knees pulled to her chest, as she studied her GED lessons. It seemed impossible to grasp all the ideas in this section. Math especially was not Leah's strength. Trying to cram four years' worth of learning into her brain, from ninth grade to twelfth grade, was nearly driving her crazy. She'd barely passed the last test in science. She wished, not for the first time, that she had the sharp mind of her sister, Ada.

She put down the book. Being fully English was taking its toll on her ego. There seemed to be so much to learn and do. And what seemed easy to the English girls was incredibly challenging to Leah.

Will I ever fit in here? I don't fit into the Amish world anymore and am barely fitting into the Englisher world. Why, Lord?

With a sigh, she worked on. After another futile twenty minutes wrestling with the math lesson, she gave up. It was Sunday night, and tomorrow would be another busy day at MAP. Then she'd have to get home before Sally arrived to pick her up for work. Maybe it would be better to get some sleep and try the math again tomorrow.

Leah placed the books in a neat pile on the floor beside her bed and lay down. She opened her Bible and turned it to where she was reading in the gospel of Mark.

She came upon the scene where Jesus healed the man on the Sabbath. Leah was amazed at the power and fearless actions of Christ. While she was with the Amish, she'd never considered a Christ who was anything other than a meek man who walked around doing good. That is, if she thought of Him at all. But in this passage, He showed Himself to be a confronter of men who were thinking evil things. He even healed a man right in front of his enemies!

Leah put down the Bible and turned off the light. It was not the way of her people to be confrontational, nor would she ever think that even one of the Amish she knew would do something that the church would deem wrong. Yet Jesus cared more for the reasons *why* people did the things they did, and not just the practice of doing things for tradition's sake.

Leah yearned to have Christ's strength, but in all honesty, the *Englisher* world was increasingly complicated. And as each challenge grew more difficult, she thought often of Jacob's invitation to take her back to the Amish.

Home. It would be so easy to go back.

In the MAP office one day while Leah was busy grading Children's Club lessons, one of the volunteers told her she had a phone call. Leah hurried to answer it, curious as to who would be calling her.

"Leah, this is Sally."

"Oh! Hi, Sally. I didn't expect to hear from you."

"Did I catch you at a bad time? Your roommate told me you were at MAP today. I have a question for you about Thanksgiving."

"Okay. I have time to chat a bit."

As the ladies in the office had talked earlier about holiday plans, Leah had been very aware she had no family to go to for Thanksgiving. She'd thought of the dinner *Maem* usually made: turkey, mashed potatoes, noodles with the turkey gizzards, and pan gravy. Leah and her sister had been helping *Maem* cook the dinner since they were little girls. Her heart had grown heavy with the thought she wouldn't be with them this year, but now her pulse quickened. Perhaps Sally had a plan in mind. Maybe she wouldn't be alone after all.

"I was wondering what your plans are," Sally said.

"I . . . don't know, I guess. I used to help *Maem* cook the dinner, but . . ."

Sally forged ahead while Leah forced the tears from her voice.

"Honey girl, I wish I could replace your family. I know you'll miss them, but we always have enough to feed an army, and it will be just my husband and me this year. Our kids are with their in-laws. We'd love to have you join us, if you want to. You could come early and help me cook a turkey dinner. I know how good you are in the kitchen. How about it? It would be fun. We'd consider it a blessing to have you with us!"

Leah was surprised by the invitation, but somehow it was hard to accept. Could she get through the dinner without breaking down when thoughts of home intruded? Leah contemplated saying no and staying at the Schrocks', but when she thought of Sally's fun nature, she realized the day could be a wonderful time of getting to know her friend better.

"Sure. That sounds lovely. Thank you, Sally. It's so nice of you to ask."

"Sugar, you don't need to thank me. With my kids gone, this old house will feel mighty lonely without a young person in it. I'll pick you up, okay?"

"Okay." Leah hung up the phone and smiled. Already her spirits were lifting as she considered spending the day cooking and eating with her employer. Sally had a heart for others, and her joy was contagious.

⁂

Thanksgiving Day dawned bright and chilly. A few snowflakes darted and danced in the air as Leah rummaged through her meager supply of clothes for a sweater and slacks that were warm. By the time she finished dressing, she heard a knock on the side door leading to the garage. That would be Sally. She'd promised to pick Leah up around ten so they would have plenty of time to prepare dinner together. She went to open the door just as Hannah was making a dash from her bedroom.

"Leah! Let me give you a hug before you go," she called.

Leah laughed and returned her friend's heartfelt hug. "Where're you going for Thanksgiving, Hannah?"

"My boyfriend's family. They're ex-Amish, too."

"Have a good day, Hannah."

"You, too."

⁂

Leah found herself basking in the warmth of Sally and Len's home that Thanksgiving, grateful for the laughter, the noise and cheers of the football game, and the new foods—all so different from her own traditions but good all the same. Even cleaning up was fun, with Leah and Sally chattering about the upcoming holiday season. For Leah, the warmth of her growing friendship with Sally was a balm to her lonely soul. Sally knew no strangers, and her infectious laugh and boundless energy never failed to encourage Leah.

Driving home later that evening, Sally asked if Leah wanted to come to her place on Saturday to help prepare for a catering job for a local cancer fund-raiser.

"Catering? You do that, too?"

"It's more a side job. I do some fund-raisers and donate the food. I usually have a few nephews and nieces to help me, but this Saturday, they're all on vacation with their families. It isn't a big job, but I sure could use some help getting the food prepped and then serving. I'll pay the same as your hourly rate for the cleaning, if that's okay. What do you think?"

Leah thought about the chance at extra income, knowing it would put her that much closer to getting her own car. Naomi had helped her open a checking account, and she had also gone back on her own and opened a savings account. Leah was setting aside a portion of every check for the day when she would be able to move into her own apartment and buy a car.

"I'd love to help. I'm trying to save for my own apartment and car so any extra work will be appreciated."

"Good. I'll pick you up about three—it will take us almost three hours to prep the food and then about four hours after that to serve and clean up. Sound all right to you?"

"Sounds good. I'll see you Saturday afternoon."

When she entered the apartment, Leah realized Hannah hadn't returned yet, so she had the apartment to herself. She put the plate of Thanksgiving leftovers in the refrigerator, kicked off her shoes, and stretched out on the sofa. It had been a good day after all.

Just before she dozed off, she thought of her family. She thought of Jacob. His smile and kindness to her. How he made her feel safe. She fought to stave off the familiar sadness that crept in, but she whispered a prayer for all of them—especially Jacob.

❧

The following Thursday, Hannah drove Leah to take her final driver's test. She had passed the written exam with flying colors, but she was nervous again when it came time to take the road test. The examiner asked all kinds of questions and then indicated for her to get in the car to demonstrate her driving skills.

Leah did well at the four-way stop, kept the speed limits, and even aced the parallel parking, but when it came time to turn left onto a small road near the exam office, the examiner spoke up, "Don't show me your bad habits. That corner was sloppy and you drove too far into the other lane. Keep your cool."

Of course, keeping her cool was the last thing Leah thought she could manage, but she concentrated on the road, and when she finally turned into the parking lot of the DMV, she turned off the ignition with a sigh.

The examiner scribbled on the clipboard in his lap. At last, he turned to Leah, his face serious.

"If you keep driving like that"—he paused dramatically, a frown covering his face—"you'll be a very good driver." He offered a broad smile. "Congratulations—you passed!"

Leah exhaled loudly. "Thanks!"

She couldn't wait to tell Hannah. She followed the examiner into the building and filled out all the appropriate paperwork. Finally, the clerk handed Leah her first official driver's license. She couldn't help herself: a huge grin spread over her face as she hurried to the lobby. She waved the license in the air as Hannah stood to congratulate her with a hug.

"Woo hooo! Let's go celebrate, Leah! Here"—she tossed her the car keys—"you drive."

They spent the afternoon treating themselves to lunch and running errands—and Leah had to admit, doing all the driving gave her quite a sense of confidence. Now she couldn't wait to save enough money for a car.

That evening the Schrocks invited Hannah and Leah up for dinner to celebrate reaching her goal. Afterward, she thought of how she'd love to share her happy news with her family, but the sober reality of how they would condemn Leah for the success hit her. No way would *Maem* and *Daet* be happy or proud of her tonight. Instead, the bishop and everyone in the church and community would claim Satan had a grip on her soul for sure.

Leah settled in front of the movie Hannah had switched to, but her thoughts were not focused on the story unfolding on the screen. Instead, her heart sadly recognized the things she was accomplishing in the English world were further distancing her from Amish family and friends.

Even Jacob would have trouble defending me now.

Chapter Eighteen

Saturday morning, Leah drove into Ashfield alone for the first time. A few snow flurries drifted around the car, and though she was nervous, she experienced a sense of freedom and independence she'd never realized could mean so much.

The mega store was busy, and as she cruised up and down the rows looking for a parking spot, she noticed the line of horses and buggies tied to a rail. Because the air was nippy, the horses were covered in blankets. She slowed down to see if she recognized any of them, her heart beating with the hope of catching a glimpse of her family or Jacob Yoder. but she didn't see Sparky or Jacob's horse, Bingo.

Leah found a spot and parked.

The wind was picking up, and as she hugged the warm parka to herself, she remembered how cold she'd been in her black wool cape. Though the wraps did an adequate job, the wind easily came under the hem, blowing frigid air from bottom to top.

Brrr . . . I don't miss that at all.

Inside, the cheerfully decorated store brought joy to Leah's heart. She hummed a carol as she shopped. An Amish Christmas wasn't as decorative, but it still was a happy and festive time for the family. Special cookies and foods were prepared, and Leah especially loved the secret gifts they made for each other the last weeks before Christmas. Longing for *Maem*'s special holiday pies, Ada's silly jokes, Benny's excited cries, and even *Daet*'s readings from the German Bible crept in. She'd been gone for just over a year.

"Leah!"

She turned to the voice interrupting her thoughts and caught a glimpse of Martha wheeling a shopping cart between the bustling crowds. In the cart, she could see an infant car seat, a little baby just visible beneath the canopy. Leah heard his whimpers and saw tiny fists waving in protest. Martha rushed to her side and hugged Leah tightly.

"Martha, you had your baby!" Leah exclaimed as she moved to the cart and grasped one soft, little hand. "How old is he and what's his name?"

"He's four months old and his name is Johnny." Martha proudly smoothed the soft chestnut hair of her son as she smiled. Though her happy expression seemed genuine, Leah could see dark circles and worry lines framing her eyes.

"Are you still in your apartment downtown?" Leah asked.

Martha frowned and shook her head. She picked at the fuzzy blue yarn of the baby's blanket, and then forced a tight smile. "Actually, we're staying with friends right now."

"Oh. Is Abe still working at the factory? I know he was worried last summer he might get laid off."

"He did get laid off. And then he moved out of town."

"What? Are you going to join him?"

"No." Martha shook her head sadly. "He left me and Johnny. He was stressed over not having a job, and one day, about a month ago, he came home, told me he had a job offer in Florida, and packed up and left."

"Oh, Martha! I'm so sorry. I don't know what to say!"

Martha looked embarrassed. Johnny began to cry, and she lifted him from the seat to give him his bottle. "Leah, I hate to say this, but we've got to go back home."

"You mean home to your family?"

"Yes. *Maem* wrote me after I sent a note home with one of the Miller girls, and she told me I could move back in if I confessed and joined the church. The bishop okayed it, too." She shrugged. "I don't have a choice, do I? I can't get a job with Johnny so young, and none of my friends are willing to let us stay with them for free."

Leah was speechless as she contemplated Martha's news.

"It isn't the end of the world. At least Johnny will have food."

"I guess so. I mean—you have to do what you need to for Johnny."

Silence filled the space between them. Finally, Martha put her hand on Leah's arm, her eyes bright. "Leah! I've just had an idea. Why don't you go home, too?"

"What? No . . . I mean . . . I don't want to go back. Not yet anyway."

"But Leah, it's Christmas! Think of how much your family will love having you back."

"Yes, but—"

"And especially think of Jacob. You still like him, right?" Martha jabbed Leah's shoulder and winked. "I bet he really misses you after all this time."

"Well . . ."

"And you said yourself last summer that you're homesick. You still are, aren't you?"

"Sometimes, but I don't want to give up my Bible and my church—"

Martha smirked. "Is that all? Why can't you take your Bible with you? And won't there be enough church to suit you once you're back in the fold again?" Martha grabbed Leah's hand. "I don't want to go back without you. You know what it's like at my house. You're the only one who understands. The only one who cares enough to check on me and Johnny. Please? Think about it. Don't say no right off. Just think of the fun we could have again. We'd see each other more, and we'd be at church together . . . please? "

Leah gently pulled her hand back, thoughts swirling in her mind. Could this be the Lord's timing? His will for her life? Was He telling her that it was time to go home? She thought of Martha and how much she'd need her support now that Johnny was in the picture. And perhaps Leah had learned enough about God that she could help *Daet* and *Maem* gain their own spiritual freedom. There were many reasons she should go home when she considered it carefully.

Though Leah found herself shaking her head, the notion had taken hold in her imagination. She could see herself being accepted back into the family. She could feel the warmth of Benny's skinny-armed hugs and Ada's infectious laugh. And there was *Maem* and *Daet* . . . and of course,

Jacob. The more she thought of all of them, the more the idea appealed to her. Leah noticed Martha's eager gaze.

"I'll think about it," she promised.

"Okay, but don't think too long. I plan to send for a ride home no later than two weeks from now. If I have to go back, I want to go before Christmas. It's the only time my family is any fun to be around."

Leah remembered Martha's stepbrother. "What about Abner?"

Martha laughed. "Can you believe it? He was bed courting, in this day and age, and ended up having to marry Lena Swarzentruber! She's one of the oldest old maids around. Her *daet* couldn't wait to get rid of her—told her to put her lantern in the window, and it only took two weeks before she attracted my insect of a stepbrother with that light." A dark look came over Martha's face. "Serves him right."

Leah had an image of Lena—pale and weak and very unsure of herself—and felt a pang of pity for what the woman was probably putting up with from Abner. And the crass way Martha was talking about Lena's situation added more sorrow to the story.

"Poor Lena," Leah muttered.

Martha frowned. "Yeah. I can't help but feel sorry for her, too. Her *bobli* is due in the spring." Martha shook off her thoughts. "But anyway, Abner won't be a problem for me anymore. And good thing, too—I'll have enough to handle with *Maem* and Johnny in the same house."

The turmoil likely to come from Martha's homecoming made Leah cringe for innocent little Johnny. She shook off doubts about Martha's wisdom in the decision and tried to refocus on the errand at hand. Besides, she needed time and quiet to think about her future. "I'd better get going with my list. I'm borrowing Hannah's car for this morning. I just got my license this week," she added proudly.

"Maybe you won't need that after all, eh?" Martha's eyes twinkled.

Leah lost her smile and turned away. So many things she'd worked to achieve would have to be forgotten if she went back. *Am I ready to do that?*

"I'll keep in touch, Martha. Even when you go home, I can send word to you, okay?"

"Send word? I'm not planning to give *this* up." Martha flipped open her red cell phone. "You still have my number?"

"I think so. Somewhere."

"Okay then. You can call me if you decide to come with me. In the meantime, think about it, please? It wouldn't be the same to go home without my best friend there. *Please?*" she begged.

"I promise to think about it."

Johnny's fists waved, and he wailed his unhappiness. Martha gave Leah a quick hug and hurried her baby and the cart to the checkout.

Leah stood, dazed, thinking of the possibility of going home.

Maybe it would be different. Surely Maem *and* Daet *have missed me enough to want to compromise on spiritual things.*

After she checked out, Leah dashed to the car with her purchases. She spied a small, red-cheeked Amish boy as he streaked past her, giggling as he outran his older sister. His blond hair flew out around his face like Benny's used to do. She smiled as she watched him evade his sibling. He ran around the horse and buggy before his *maem* finally called *"Schtope!"* The small family teased each other merrily as they loaded their packages in the buggy before getting in and backing the horse carefully away from the hitching post.

As the horse clopped past Leah, her heart longed for home. Maybe this would be the perfect time . . . a Christmas homecoming.

❧

Leah had to hurry once she got back to the apartment in order to be ready in time for Sally's catering job. She had no idea what she'd end up doing, but she trusted Sally.

Sally asked Leah to wear a white shirt and black slacks. The simple outfit looked elegant. Leah was pleased at her reflection.

She decided to go festive with a silvery barrette for her hair. She added a pair of simple silver earrings that dangled delicately at the curve of her face. Leah smiled when she thought of how these colors weren't far removed from her Amish palette, but what a difference it made to wear slacks and a few sparkly baubles.

Sally came right on time. She explained that serving and keeping up with the demands of the party guests would be hard, but it was worth it in the end. "I always feel so much better after it's over when I think of how much help will be provided for the charity by the money that's raised tonight. They make sure people who are diagnosed with cancer can afford to pay for some of their medical needs—like nutrition supplements and other medications."

"That's wonderful! My people are used to taking care of each other this way, too. We often have no insurance, so we have to help each other out when medical problems arise."

Sally glanced at Leah. "You're saying 'my people' and 'we have no insurance.' That's the first time I remember you talking like you're still Amish. What gives?"

She was used to Sally's blunt questions, but Leah was surprised at how quickly the woman had noticed her reconnection to the Amish culture. Leah hadn't really thought of what she was saying herself.

"Hmm. I guess I didn't even notice I was doing that, Sally, but I have to be honest with you—I'm having thoughts about going back home before Christmas."

"What? But you're doing so well, Leah! Why do you want to go back now?"

"Some of it is my friend Martha. She has to go back, and she really wants me to go when she does. I've also been very homesick for a long time. With Christmas coming up . . ." Leah's voice trailed off as she thought of all she'd missed last December from not being home.

"I can't pretend to understand what it's like for you to leave your home and all your family and friends, but I do know you've grown and blossomed into a wonderful, independent young lady. I'd hate to see you go backward in life. So much potential is lying dormant in you, Leah. Just make sure you think hard about this decision. Promise?"

Leah nodded, but she was taken aback by Sally's passion for her remaining out of the Amish.

They worked side by side the remainder of the evening, and by the time they had the pots and pans and serving dishes washed, the leftover food tucked away in boxes, and the kitchen spotless, Leah was dog tired.

They rode home together in silence. Snowflakes shimmered in the headlights, and Christmas carols filled the car. Leah savored the peaceful moment.

Tonight had been a special time. Working with Sally to help raise money for a worthy cause had given her a wonderful sense of belonging and satisfaction. Tears misted her eyes when she thought of how much she'd miss Sally if she went back home.

There's such irony in life. I miss my Amish family and my friends, but I've also made many good friends in the Englisher *world. Why does everything have to be black and white? Why do my people make me choose?* Leah sighed.

"Are you tired?" Sally asked.

"Yes, but it's a good tired." Leah smiled. "I really want to thank you, Sally, for asking me to help. It was fun, and I felt like I did something important."

She glanced at Leah. "You did. We have community in our world, too, you know."

Leah chuckled. "I get the message."

Leah turned to watch the Christmas light displays that adorned the houses they passed. Though it wasn't part of her Amish heritage to decorate with lights and displays, she took childish delight in the twinkling lights and shimmering glow spread over the rooftops and dripping from tree branches. This part of her English experience was enjoyable. She drank in the happy feeling the lights created. There was so much for both worlds to offer her. Wasn't there a way to have both?

"You know, Sally, I don't always want to go back—only when I feel homesick. If I could have my family and the English world, too, that would be perfect."

"I get it, kiddo. It has to be hard to be away from them—especially during this time of year."

"To tell you the truth, if I could stay out of the Amish community but still see my family—that would suit me the best."

"Are you sure you can't? I always thought the Amish were very forgiving."

"It's hard to explain. Even though forgiveness of others who have personally wronged you is stressed, this is different. Leaving the Amish is leaving my only hope for heaven. That's how it looks in my church. If you're born Amish, you must stay Amish to have a chance of reaching heaven. Maybe in the New Order churches there's more leeway, but no, not in my strict Old Order church. There's no forgiveness for me as long as I stay outside the church."

"I guess I don't know as much as I thought about the Amish, huh?"

"Don't feel bad. Even we Amish have trouble understanding all the rules."

They rode the rest of the way back to the Schrocks' in silence, and when Leah got out of the car, Sally handed her a Christmas card.

"Consider this a bonus for work well done."

Leah thanked her and gave her a hug. "You're one of the best people I've ever known, Sally. Thanks for taking a chance on me."

"Aww, go on in and warm up now, honey girl."

Leah closed the car door but turned to wave, knowing Sally would wait until she was safely inside.

The house was quiet this late at night, but when she went into the apartment, Leah was delighted to see a little Christmas tree shining and twinkling in the corner by the TV. She sat down on the couch facing the tree as she undid her coat buttons and removed her gloves. The lights blinked off and on in cheerful greeting.

Hannah's bedroom door opened slowly and she appeared, yawning, a groggy smile across her face. She sat on the chair opposite Leah and both watched the tree for a while in silence.

"I love it, Hannah," said Leah finally.

"I thought about it last week when I saw the little tree on my way home from work. Tonight I thought, 'Why not?'"

"It's so pretty! Thanks for doing this. Did you get the lights, too?"

"Yes, and Naomi had a few extra ornaments she brought down."

Hannah stood up and shuffled into the kitchen, her slippers slapping the cold floor softly. "How about some hot cocoa since we're both awake?"

"Sure."

Leah leaned her head against the sofa, closing her eyes. She hummed one of the carols she'd heard in the car.

If only I could have my family and this world, too. If only . . .

"Hey! Are you sleeping now that I have the cocoa ready?"

"Sorry. I wore myself out, I guess, at the party." Leah sat up and took the mug of cocoa. "Thanks, Hannah."

"You're welcome. How did it go, by the way?"

"It was fun. It was hard work, but I felt good doing something nice for others." She faced her friend. "It reminded me of what our families do. Helping others."

"The difference is we get to do it because we want to now, and not to please our parents or a bishop, right?"

Leah didn't answer.

"Oh, by the way, a Christmas postcard came for you today. Here it is." Her eyes twinkled as she handed the card to Leah.

Leah stared at the wintery scene on the front: a horse and buggy surrounded by a snowy wonderland. She flipped to the back. *Merry Christmas, Sister! Love from Ada*

Leah sighed and held the card to her chest. Tears wet her lashes. Hannah broke the silence.

"Are you thinking of going back, Leah?" she asked suddenly.

"I don't know. Sometimes, I miss my family so much, I just can't stand it."

"I miss my *maem*, too, but not enough to live that hard life anymore."

"I know, but . . ." Leah leaned back into the cushions again as she stared at the tree. "I ran into Martha Mast, my Amish friend. Remember me telling you about her?"

"You mean the one who left? Married Abe?"

"I wonder now if they really did get married, but either way, she's had her baby, and Abe has left her."

"No!" Hannah sat up, her face a mix of surprise and anger. "What will she do?"

"She's going home." Leah fingered the napkin under her cup of cocoa. "And she asked me to go back with her before Christmas comes."

Hannah jerked the cocoa away from her mouth, sloshing steamy chocolate over the rim of the cup. "What did you tell her?'

"I didn't know what to tell her. She reminded me how it is to be home

at Christmas—she made me think about Jacob and all that I'm missing."
Leah paused and wiped up the spilled cocoa. "Haven't you been tempted
to go back, Hannah?"

"Once, at first, but not in a while. I had too hard a life back there." She
waved her hand. "No way do I want to live like that again. *Ever.* Besides,
I've made a good life for myself here, and you can too."

Leah stood and stretched slowly. It had been a long day, and her
thoughts were whirling. "I just need to get to bed." She leaned over to
give Hannah a hug. "Thanks for the tree. It's beautiful."

"You're welcome. Get some sleep—and don't make your decision
until you've had time to think and pray about it, Leah."

"I won't."

"You know they'll watch you even more if you go back. Right?"

"Yes. I guessed that."

Leah headed to her room, slipped off the satiny black slacks and the
pretty top, pulled the barrette from her hair, and washed her face.

So many changes had happened in the last year or so. What would
it be like to go back? She pulled her hair up into the tight bun she
used to know so well, stared at her pale, cleanly washed face, but even
so, it didn't seem like she was the same Amish girl anymore. Leah had
changed.

⁂

At breakfast on Monday morning, Naomi came downstairs and
knocked on the door.

"Leah? Do you have time to run into Ashfield with me for some
last-minute Christmas shopping?"

"Sure. I have a few things to buy, too. And I'd like to talk to you about
something."

"Perfect. I'll get the car warmed up."

The snow covered the dead grass beneath it, but the roads were clean
and dry. The sun reflected blindingly off the white fields. Leah put on
sunglasses, grateful to have them shading her eyes as she brought up the
subject of going home.

"Naomi, I talked to one of my old friends. I saw her at Walmart a few days ago."

"Really?"

"Yes, it was Martha. Remember the one I went to see at her house? She was going to have a baby."

Naomi nodded.

"She decided to go back home. Her boyfriend left her, and she's had her baby. She can't work right now, and her family said she could come back if she joins the church."

"Oh?"

"She asked if I'd go back, too."

Naomi didn't say anything. She kept her eyes on the road, but a sigh escaped her.

"What do you think about that?" Leah asked.

"What do you think?"

Leah chewed her lip. "I don't know. I'm not sure. Sometimes I wonder if I should go back with her."

"Why is that?"

"I . . . I'm just homesick all the time."

"Do you think it's because of Christmas?"

She shrugged. "Maybe."

"Leah, let me tell you something: we went back. And it was harder going back. I felt suffocated, and more than that, it was like turning away from Christ. Even though the church said it was all right for us to read our Bibles, they watched us in everything. We had to obey every rule, or they were on us to not go back to our English ways. Every time I did something just the least bit different, I had someone telling me to conform."

"But maybe my family has had a change of heart by now."

Naomi nodded, but Leah could tell she was doubtful. "You know what? I'm not going to think about that for now. Let's go have fun. I really enjoy seeing the Christmas lights and hearing the music."

Naomi took the cue and let the subject drop, but Leah knew many prayers would be said before a final decision was made.

Later that evening Leah prayed she wouldn't be led by feelings of homesickness but out of obedience to the Lord. Somehow, she had to convince her parents that salvation was real. It wasn't simply about what the forefathers or the bishop or her parents thought was right. It had to come from the soul. Following Christ was much more than tradition.

She wondered if the Schrocks thought she was being naive in her hopes for her parents. But if God could reach Leah's heart, why not theirs? She remembered what someone had said the first time she attended Bible study at the Schrocks'—*the Lord can do miracles with our families if we just let Him.*

Leah turned off the lights. Outside, the snow was falling thick and fast, and she was at peace. It was good to think about going home. She wanted to dream of her family . . . and a kind young man named Jacob.

⚜

The next Friday, as Leah was doing laundry, her cell phone rang. Caller ID showed it was Martha.

"Hello?"

"Leah! I'm going home in just a few hours! Are you coming?"

"What do you mean? I thought you weren't going for at least a week yet!"

"Things are bad for me and Johnny. My friends are kicking us out, so I have to go now. After he gets off work, my friend's dad is driving me out to the farm. If you're going with me, Leah, it has to be today."

"Oh no, I just—I haven't had time to think about it, Martha!"

"It's been a week since I told you. I think if you really want to go home, you'd know by now. Don't let me push you, though. I have to go now." She paused. "I'll be sure to tell your family how you're doing, and Jacob, too, of course."

Leah knew she was trying to convince her—and it was working.

"No—I mean—wait. Don't hang up!"

A wave of anxiety rolled through her stomach. She'd toyed with the decision, but now that the time had arrived, she didn't know what she wanted to do. "Martha, can I call you back in about an hour?"

"An hour? Sure, but how can an hour help you decide?"

"I want to pray."

Martha laughed. "Oh, Leah! Call me back soon. I have to make arrangements to come get you, you know."

Leah ended the call, confusion tearing at her heart and mind. How could she decide so suddenly? She had a job, and she'd have to tell the Schrocks. There was the thought of her family, too. How could she get word to them she was coming? It just didn't seem possible to leave this quickly.

Leah sat down on the stool by the dryer and said a hurried prayer.

"Lord, help me! I don't know what to do. I want to see my parents and family, but I have responsibilities here. How can I just walk away—all in one day?"

Then the phone rang again, and of course, it was Martha. Leah answered with a sigh.

"Leah? I just wanted to tell you I can get word to Jacob and your family, if you want me to. I have a friend who's going right past the Yoders; they can let Jacob know, and he can go tell your parents. Okay?"

Leah didn't answer.

"Leah? Are you there?"

"Yes, I'm just—I don't know."

Martha took charge. "Now here's what you do: go to your room, pack a few things—you can always send for the rest of your stuff later—get in the car with me and go home. What's so hard about that?"

"I know, but I have a job. How can I walk out on Sally?"

"She'll understand. You can call her with my cell later."

"Oh, I don't know . . ." She moaned.

"Leah! Don't think. Just *do*, girl. We'll be home for Christmas this year. Pies and cakes and candies galore. It'll be fun. C'mon!"

"Well . . ." She took a deep breath and sighed. "Okay."

"Really?" Martha squealed.

"Yes." As Leah thought of the possibilities back at home, she grew more assured. "Yes, I really want to go home."

"Great! I'm going to call and send word before you have a chance to change your mind. See you in a couple of hours!"

Once Leah hung up, the thought crossed her mind that she was making a big mistake, but the promise and hope she had for her family squelched her uneasiness. She ran to her room and gathered her things in the middle of the bed.

Leah went upstairs to get something to hold her belongings, but no one answered the door. She felt funny walking into the kitchen when the Schrocks weren't there, but she couldn't wait for them. She grabbed some grocery bags from a stash, and looked for something to write on.

A note pad sat on the counter, so she scrawled a brief message, sharing her excitement at being home for Christmas and thanking the Schrocks for all they had done to help her over the last year. As she propped the note up on the island where someone was sure to see it, Leah felt she was betraying the Schrocks' trust in her. She paused to glance around. Lots of good memories had been created in this kitchen, and she felt an unexpected rise of tears. She wiped her eyes hastily before hurrying back to the apartment.

She stuffed her belongings into the bags, but as she carried everything into the living room, it occurred to her that she wouldn't be allowed to use most of her things at home.

"What was I thinking?"

The energy of the last few moments drained away as she sat heavily on the arm of the sofa. The plastic bags slipped to the floor when she realized she was going back to something she'd worked very hard to leave.

"Am I doing the right thing?" she whispered.

If only someone was home—Hannah or Naomi, Matthew, or anyone she could run her tumbling, jumbled thoughts and feelings past.

"Lord, I need Your wisdom. I want to go home so badly, but I don't really want to deal with everything else. What should I do?"

Leah waited for some kind of answer, but the Lord was silent.

She sighed and dumped her things back on the bed. When she finished sorting through everything, the only things she could take home were some toiletries, a few nightgowns, and her NIV Bible. Its bright blue cover brought the most pain to her heart. She loved it so much and had been happy to see it at the end of many tiring days, its cheerful cover always bringing a smile. If she'd only had the foresight to buy a somber black cover, she might be able to sneak it into the Amish world, but this—this bright blue cover? Never.

Leah picked up the Bible and held it close to her face. The smell of the leather and the feel of the silky pages brought a rush of tears.

No! I won't leave this, she vowed. *I'll have to find a way to keep it hidden.*

In that second of disobedience to the *Ordnung,* Leah knew what she was doing was not right for her. Her hands shook as she wrapped the Bible carefully in one of her nightgowns. She stuffed it into the bottom of a bag and glanced around, as though spying eyes were watching her every move. Was this the right way to begin her homecoming?

She went to the closet, reached way to the back, and pulled out the dress, apron, and stockings she'd worn when she left home. She wondered if they still fit. Leah glanced up and saw the *kapp* sitting on a shelf behind black, thick-soled shoes. She gathered them all and went into the bathroom.

Surprisingly, it took some time for her to relearn how to fasten her dress with straight pins. And her hair seemed to rebel against going back in hiding under the gauzy *kapp.* The stockings and shoes felt heavy and dreary, and when she finally finished dressing, she galumphed her way to the long mirror hanging at the end of the hallway. Looking back at her stood an Amish *maed.* It startled Leah.

A sad smile contoured her lips, but confusion reigned in her heart. Her cheeks appeared rosier, and her face, devoid of makeup, looked young and scared.

Leah sighed. She couldn't believe she was actually going to go home. Then the thrill of seeing her family and Jacob hit her. She smiled, glanced at the clock above the stove, and realized she'd have to hurry. Martha's ride would be pulling in to pick her up in less than five minutes.

She brushed a strand back under the *kapp* and picked up the two bags stuffed with her things. Leah looked around the apartment. Everything was neat and tidy. Her bed was made, the sheets freshly washed this morning.

When I did that chore, I had no inkling I wouldn't be sleeping under those sheets tonight.

As she went to the door and opened it, she was aware of the heavy and oppressive feeling of her clothing. It was as though the weight of the fabric mimicked the weight of the *Ordnung*. She hesitated. Leah heard a car crunching into the driveway and a horn beeped impatiently. She turned the lock in the doorknob and shut the door firmly behind her.

As Leah approached the pickup truck, she saw Martha waving from the small backseat. She could just see the top of Johnny's fuzzy head.

The driver leaned across and opened the passenger door. Leah climbed inside the cab and turned to look at Martha. She was still in her jeans and T-shirt, with a warm winter coat covering her body. Leah was shivering already since the one Amish item she'd gotten rid of was the hated black wool cape she'd escaped in last fall. Thankfully, the driver saw her shaking and cranked up the heater a notch.

"Thank you," she said shyly. "I don't have my cape."

Martha laughed and slapped her arm. "I can't believe you still have all that stuff, silly. I plan on hiding my jeans and T-shirts for when I go to town. Did you bring yours?"

Leah shook her head.

"Why in the world not?" she asked incredulously.

"I don't know. It didn't seem right trying to sneak those clothes in now. I mean, I'm going back, right?"

Martha laughed again. "Oh, Leah, you are such a Goody Two-shoes, y'know? I, for one, plan to keep my *Englisher* stuff and go to town as much as I can."

"But the church—you said you have to join—"

"So? Let them catch me. Mr. Brown, could you wait while Leah goes in to get her other clothes?"

"I guess, but I don't have all the time in the world."

"No. I really don't plan to bring my clothes, Martha. You don't have to wait, Mr. Brown. I'm ready."

He gave her one long look and then nodded. They left the Schrocks' driveway, and Leah watched through the side mirror as the house receded into the background. She was fighting the urge to ask Mr. Brown to stop. Thoughts and feelings seemed to slow down to a crawl. She had trouble thinking about anything except the mantra, "I'm going back . . . going back . . . going back."

Twenty minutes later, Mr. Brown pulled into her family's lane. It was just after six o'clock, and Leah knew supper would be almost finished. The yellow-orange glow from the kerosene lamps faintly lit a couple of the front windows, but the rest of the house loomed dark and cold. It was very stark sitting there in its colorless jacket, the winter wind beating against its windows and corners.

She shivered once again in apprehension of going through the front door. She debated going in the kitchen door at the back, but thought of how much more time it would give her to think of a greeting to the family if she went in the front and down the hall to the kitchen.

She turned and gave Martha a trembling smile. "Here I am. I'll talk to you soon, okay?"

Martha nodded, her face a ghostly glow in the near dark of twilight.

Leah turned to Mr. Brown. "Thank you for the ride. I can give you some money for gas—"

He waved her off. "Good luck."

She could tell he wanted to get Martha home, so she slid out of the cab, grasping the plastic bags in both hands, and hurried to the porch. The wind knifed her in the back as she rushed toward the shelter of the front door. She ended up barely glancing at the truck as it pulled out of the driveway. Leah had the feeling that with it went her last chance at freedom.

She tried the doorknob and, as she knew it would, it opened with a squeak. Fighting back rising panic, Leah stepped back in time and shut the door on modern life.

CHAPTER NINETEEN

The wooden floor of the living room squeaked as Leah stepped across it. She could hear the low murmur of voices in the kitchen, and the scent of apple pie, fresh from the oven, drifted through the air. Did *Maem* bake a pie for her homecoming? The thought warmed her and hurried her steps. Leah smiled as she walked into the kitchen.

There was the family. *Maem* was standing at the stove, her hands still in the pot holders, clutching the steaming pie. As Leah came in, *Maem*'s teasing expression turned to shock, then just as quickly to stern.

Daet sat in his usual place at the table with his back to Leah, but he twisted his head slightly, saying nothing. Only Benny ran to her, but just as he reached her outstretched arms, he stopped and shyly looked to *Maem* for permission to greet his long lost sister. She nodded—once. He jumped into Leah's arms and laughingly teased her about her cold, red cheeks.

Leah couldn't believe how solid and tall he had grown in a year!

"Hey, you have to jump down! You're nearly as big as me now." She smiled and ruffled his blond hair as she gently placed him on his feet. He giggled, leading her by the hand to the table.

"Look! Leah is home again!"

His voice was excited and loud. *Daet* gave Leah a short glance, taking in her Amish clothing, but still didn't speak. She looked across the table to Ada, but her sister had her head dipped low over her supper plate, not even a glance in Leah's direction. *Maem* carried the hot pie to the table and slipped into her chair, her gaze locked on the tops of Leah's black shoes. Leah noticed *Maem*'s lips twitch, and a small puzzled frown dipped her eyebrows lower.

Other than Benny, no one uttered a single word. If he noticed the snub, it didn't stop him from chattering on and on about all the things that had happened to him since she'd been gone. Leah listened, but her heart was breaking. This was not the welcome she'd envisioned.

Finally, after she stood five minutes awkwardly, Leah slid into the empty chair marking her old spot at the table. Benny's chattering sputtered to a stop and he looked around the room. His face reddened as he noticed the heads bowed low over the dinner table and no one speaking but him.

All right, then it was up to her to start the mending. She cleared her throat. "How have all of you been? I've missed you—very much."

Maem said nothing. Ada said nothing. Benny didn't answer either, but his eyes regarded everyone with wide-eyed curiosity. Leah faltered, but went ahead with her apology.

"I, uh . . . I'm very sorry for the trouble I've been to you this past year or so. I've had a lot of time to think—" She stopped. Why didn't they act like they knew she was coming? Could it be they hadn't gotten word? "Martha told me Jacob was going to stop by and tell you I was coming. Did he?"

Maem, her eyes averted, shook her head.

Ahh, so the pie wasn't for me, after all.

They were stunned, it was clear, that she'd come home. Silence ruled the room for several more seconds. Benny squirmed in his chair as Leah's blush deepened.

What should she do now? Just as Leah started to say something again, *Daet* turned to face her. He cleared his throat.

"You need to speak to the bishop in the morning," he said tersely. "Once we've talked with him, then we can discuss your plans to join the church. Until then, please do not behave as you did before you left. This is not settled between us until you have confessed and made things right before the church. And after tonight, you must eat at the small table *Maem* will put in the corner over there. Once you have confessed and joined the church, we'll have you back with the family." He stroked his beard. His face was set. "There'll be no more talking tonight."

He stood, and *Maem* and Ada joined him. They moved toward the door, Benny pushed along by *Maem*. He turned back for a last glance at his sister, his lips formed in an O, curiosity and confusion flickering in his eyes. One by one they left the room, leaving her sitting alone at the table.

Leah glanced around the familiar kitchen, tears of shame filling her eyes. Never in her life had she felt more alone than at this moment, here in her home. After a few minutes of listening to the clock in the hall tick its lonely message, she pushed the chair back, brushed away her tears, and quietly started up to her room. She glanced toward the table. Even the pie was abandoned in her family's hurry to get away from her.

As she climbed the stairs, she thought of what the rest of her time would be like here at home. She had not imagined they would still be nursing the old wound. She had not imagined time could only have deepened the break and filled it with pain and bitterness. This was not the homecoming Leah wanted, but she thought back to Naomi's counsel: things got worse for her and Matthew once they'd gone back. Would it be the same for Leah? Where was the love her parents had for her?

Her sister, too. They had been so close, and she had sent her a Christmas postcard! How had the past year erased all the time they'd shared growing up? It was as though her family's love had been washed away with the rulings of the church. True, Leah had no idea what had been said about her in the months past. For all she knew, her family hadn't expected to see her again.

Leah opened the door to her old bedroom, knowing she'd find it stripped bare of all but the bed and the chest. She carried her measly possessions and unpacked them carefully into two drawers of the chest. Leah went across the room to the window and lifted the purple curtain. No light from the moon illuminated the outside and, not having been offered so much as a candle, her dark room brought shadows down on her head like a shroud. She leaned against the cold frosty glass.

"Lord, have I done the wrong thing? How can I witness to my family of Your grace and mercy when they won't even speak to me?"

A tear slid down her cheek, and she wiped it away. She went back to the bed and sat on the edge—still as a statue.

Would Jacob bother to come and see her? She had no idea who would befriend her or who would still shun her. She hadn't yet joined the church and look at the treatment she was getting! If she joined and then disappointed them all, would she be put under the ban?

Shuddering at the thought of meeting Bishop Miller again, Leah went to the chest and searched the dark drawers for the flannel fabric of her nightgowns. She took off her *kapp* and apron and carefully removed each pin before pulling the dress off over her head. She shook out the soft folds of the flannel and pulled the comforting fabric over her body. Leah hung her clothes on pegs in the empty closet.

She crawled beneath the chilly covers, grateful her *Maem* had at least kept bedding in the room. She'd forgotten how cold this upper room was in the winter, despite the banked fire in the stove below.

Leah couldn't sleep. Though her body ached with fatigue, her mind churned with questions and fear. She'd never felt such worry. Not even when she sat in the general store those many months ago and waited for Naomi to pick her up. She'd known nothing of the *Englisher* ways then, but the fear had been mixed with anticipation of what her future might hold in the English world. She felt none of that anticipation now.

She snuggled deeper into her blankets and wished she'd thought to get her Bible out of the dresser, too.

Never mind—it's too dark to read anyway, and I am so very tired. Lord, please don't leave my side. If I've made the wrong decision, please help me know what to do.

Her last thoughts before she fell asleep were about the bishop— what would he say to Leah tomorrow?

⊱─⊰

Leah woke with a knock at the door, and as she opened her eyes, she could see the sun's rosy hues beginning to spread over the sky. Again a soft knock. Ada's voice carried through the door.

"Leah? *Maem* and *Daet* are waiting in the kitchen. The bishop will be here soon. They want you to come down quickly."

Leah jumped out of bed and hurried to open the door, eager to talk with Ada, but Ada made a hasty retreat to her bedroom, casting a fearful glance at Leah before she quickly shut the door. Leah walked across the hallway.

"Why won't you speak to me, Ada?"

When no response came, Leah said softly, "Thank you for the wintery postcard. I loved it and still carry it with me."

Inside her sister's room, she heard a muffled sound—a sob?

"I'm back, aren't I? And willing to talk with the bishop and do everything the church and *Maem* and *Daet* want me to do. Can we talk?"

Silence.

Leah went back to her room and prepared for the bishop. She made sure her hair was tucked under the *kapp* as cleanly as possible and tried very hard to get the dress and apron on straight and wrinkle free, though she couldn't keep her hands from trembling. She wanted the bishop and her parents to know how seriously she planned to take her homecoming.

Butterflies danced in Leah's stomach, and she fought panic as she descended the steep steps. She breathed a silent prayer to God, and then thought she should have read some Scripture before going in for the interview. Just thinking about the blue Bible resting in her bottom drawer—hidden though it was—brought more churning to her stomach. She was already disobeying one of the rules.

As Leah entered the kitchen, the smell of freshly brewed coffee greeted her, and she was suddenly hungry. She hesitated at the doorway when she spied a small round table pushed into the corner of the kitchen. The bishop pointed to it and motioned for her to be seated there. Though she really wanted to help herself to a cup of coffee first, she sat where he indicated and quietly folded her hands on the tabletop. Leah waited for the bishop to begin the interview.

Maem brought the men their coffee and seated herself carefully at the far end of the table, leaving several chairs between herself, *Daet*, and Bishop Miller. She didn't glance at her daughter once and didn't offer her a cup of coffee, either. A long-subdued, familiar ribbon of anger uncurled itself inside Leah's heart.

Will I ever learn to control this resentment after every little snub or offense?

Leah watched *Maem* pour a thin milky stream into her coffee—watched her stir it slowly with the spoon—watched as she accidentally made eye contact with Leah when she raised the cup to her lips. Her hands shook, and she glanced away, then down at the table again.

The silence in the room grew heavy. The bishop finally cleared his throat as he took a last sip.

Leah checked the mounting feelings of bitterness and tried to keep her mind open to his message. She didn't know how in the world she would be able to stay home for any length of time if she couldn't get rid of the emotions that surfaced when she faced the bishop. Even the offense aimed at her parents was something she knew she needed to contain. Their snubs and slights wounded her tender heart more than she ever thought they could. And the wounds seemed to quickly turn sour.

Lord, help me be humble before the man who is here to advise me today.

"Leah, you've done a grave and serious harm to your family over this past year. Are you aware of that?"

She nodded, not trusting herself to speak.

"*Ja,* and you've made some terrible choices that have moved you from the safety of your family and church to the world and all its sinful and harmful ways. *Ja?*"

Again Leah nodded.

"We need to see where this worldly and sinful living has left your soul. We have to figure out if you're homecoming is genuine and if you're truly ready to ask forgiveness from your family, your church, and your community."

Bishop Miller's eyes bored a hole into her as she squirmed under his searing gaze. Sensing he was waiting for a verbal response, she lifted her head and cleared her throat before offering any response.

"Yes. I mean, I'm ready to say I renounce the world and its ways."

He nodded, but his eyes held distrust.

Why did I think this would be easy?

"And I want to hear the things you did while you were out there. Your *Maem* and *Daet* tell me they saw you driving a car. Is this true?"

"Yes."

"And you attended an *Englisher* church regularly?"

"Yes."

"And I heard from Martha you have an *Englisher* Bible."

Leah didn't answer him, too shocked that Martha had revealed this to the bishop. She forced herself to look Bishop Miller in the eyes, but she did not answer his question.

"Answer him, Leah!" demanded *Daet*.

She maintained her silence. *I can't lie, but I can't give up my Bible.*

Daet and the bishop exchanged a long look, and out of the corner of her eye, Leah saw *Maem* wringing her hands as her eyes swung from the men to Leah and back again.

Finally, Bishop Miller stood. He sighed and ran his hands through his scraggly beard. "I can see there's still some stubbornness in this daughter, John. Let her think about her answer for a few days, and then we'll talk again."

He glanced at the table in the corner. "In the meantime, I think we'd best let her sit to herself a few meals to think over the way she wants things around here."

He turned to Leah. "You and I will talk before the next church service. I suggest you think long and hard about what you want and what your confession will be."

He nodded his good-byes to her parents and left.

Leah sat motionless, waiting for *Daet* or *Maem* to say something, but they both went about their breakfast preparations as though she was not in the room.

So it was going to be like this again? How did I ever think this would be a joyous reunion?

Leah got up and walked out of the kitchen, through the living room, and to the front door. She turned the knob and stepped onto the porch, the brisk December air biting her lungs and the winter wind chasing her skirt, chilling her inside and out. She needed a few minutes to herself—she needed to think.

She suddenly realized this must be an off Sunday, since the bishop expected to see her again before the next service. She stared across the road. The frost-laden fields were silent, though she spotted a timid rabbit making its way toward the shelter of the fence line where the tall grasses clumped together. The Amish farmers left the grass standing to encourage the animals to winter over. The mice and other critters ate the insects that came out in the spring and gave the crops a little extra help to get started.

My Amish family and friends are so wise, Lord, in so many ways, but they know little about the freedom You offer in Christ.

She breathed a prayer for her family. Leah wanted to be a part of them again, but the way things were going, she had little hope they'd ever forgive her or forget her past sins. Could they learn to treat her as they once had?

Tears slipped down her face, but she wiped them away, frustrated at the pain they represented. She had to be strong. She had to make this work. She had to think of a way to get herself right with the church and her family . . . without sacrificing her faith.

Leah went back in the house and gathered eggs, bacon, and bread to make her own breakfast. Her sister and brother were at the table with *Maem* and *Daet*, and on the little round table in the corner, *Maem* had placed a cup, plate, and silverware.

Leah glanced at the family, but they kept their eyes on their breakfast. Humiliation burned her cheeks.

Pride. It's a matter of controlling my pride, Lord. Help me be humble. Help me accept this punishment with grace.

She prepared her breakfast quickly and in silence, then took the food to the little table in the corner. She sat down, bowed to pray, and then ate. From time to time she glanced at her family, painfully aware of being left out.

But I chose to come back. I chose to be here, knowing it would most likely be this way. Now I have to endure it. She squared her shoulders and soldiered on. *It's only a matter of time. I can do this. I will do this.*

The isolation was broken for her when Benny leaned his head around Ada's body and grinned. He gave a quick wink. Leah's heart melted, and she winked back at him.

Her world felt a little lighter. Oh, how she wished all of them could be as forgiving as Benny!

By Monday morning, Leah had decided she had to do something with her time. Ada and *Maem* discussed the Christmas cookies they planned to bake later in the afternoon. Of course, no invitation was offered to Leah.

"*Daet*, I wondered if I could go to the shop and sweep for you this morning."

The back of his neck turned red, but he nodded slightly. At least she'd be able to help out, and she might get to see Jacob today, too. She was more than curious how he would greet her.

"Benny, time to go to school," reminded *Maem*. "Hurry and finish your breakfast. Your lunch is on the counter. Now, go on."

Benny jumped up, rushing around to grab books, coat, and hat. Leah smiled at the one thing that hadn't changed in the morning routine. Before he ran out the door, Benny skittered to her table in the corner and, to her delighted surprise, gave her a sloppy kiss and a little-boy hug.

"Thanks, Benny," she whispered against his floppy blond hair. "Have a good day at school."

Soon only Leah and Ada were left in the kitchen. *Maem* had asked Ada to finish drying the last of the dishes, while Leah waited for the sink to be free in order to wash hers. *Daet* went to the shop to start work for the day, and *Maem* took herself off to her housework.

Ada refused to look at her sister, and finally, not able to stand her silence anymore, Leah started talking.

"Ada, I wish I knew why you won't speak to me. I mean, I can understand *Maem* and *Daet* have to listen to the bishop, but you and I . . . can't we go back to the way it was between us?"

Ada remained silent, but a tiny shake of her head made Leah's frustration grow.

"You act like I'm the only Amish girl in the world who's ever moved away for a time. Remember the fun we used to have at Christmas? The cooking and baking and all the secret presents we made for each other? Remember?"

A smile flitted across Ada's face, betraying her feelings. *Maybe a tiny smile is enough for the day.*

Forging ahead, Leah said softly, "Ada, I'm still your sister. And maybe—when I've made things right with the bishop—maybe then you'll forgive me."

Leah watched her younger sister finish her task silently. Ada wiped her hands on a linen towel, then quickly left the kitchen.

After Leah washed and dried her own breakfast dishes, she hurried to her room to get her bed made. To have a job and a way to pass the time was a great relief, but Leah couldn't say she was looking forward to being in the shop with her reticent *Daet* all day.

Inside, no one was stirring and no sounds of work were heard. She moved to the desk and found a note propped on the account book stacked there.

> Leah, I've gone to deliver an order in the next town. Sweep and
> mop out the shop and see if you can straighten the accounts. *Daet.*

Okay. At least this would keep her busy the whole day and maybe into tomorrow, too. *Maybe if I work hard, Daet will thaw toward me, just a little.*

She went to the storage closet and got out the big broom and mop with bucket.

"Might as well get to it right away," she murmured.

She filled the bucket with water and swept up the curls of wood and soft shavings littering the length of the building. It felt good to be useful.

As she swept, Leah was reminded of her job with Sally. She made a mental note to send her a letter as soon as she could today, explaining she'd gone home. Leah hadn't been scheduled to work until Saturday. When Sally unexpectedly offered her a few evenings off, she had no idea that she'd be spending them at home. Hopefully, Sally would have her letter in time to get someone else to fill her position.

❧

Leah spent that week working with *Daet* in the shop. Though he never talked to her directly, his attitude improved each day. He knew Leah had a good work ethic and still appreciated that. He even smiled at her a couple of times but then turned quickly away. Sometimes, Leah caught the pain in his eyes. This was her only indication that he, too, felt some sorrow over having to shun his eldest daughter.

Leah knew that her parents and the bishop thought not only of her past behavior but how she might influence her brother and sister in the future. In the eyes of the church, Leah had been rebellious—and this rebellion could have dire consequences if it led her siblings down the same path. And that path would lead to hell. She tried very hard to see this whole situation from their point of view.

Maybe if I can understand their motivation, I can better endure this season of punishment.

But deep in her heart, she wondered how anyone could be so harsh to someone they loved.

On Saturday afternoon, Jacob finally came in the shop. From her experiences with others who had come to the house over the past few days, she knew better than to rush to greet him, but it didn't stop her from smiling at him when *Daet* wasn't looking. When Jacob retuned her smile, Leah's heart soared. He chatted with her as though nothing had changed. *Daet* watched them, and Leah sent sidelong glimpses at *Daet*, too. She couldn't decide if he was happy to see Jacob's acceptance of her or worried that their relationship had not changed.

Finally, *Daet*'s lips tilted ever so slightly upward and he hurried to the door. "I'm heading in for lunch. You two keep each other company."

Leah broke off her conversation with Jacob, a slow grin spreading over her face. Eyebrows raised, she turned astonished eyes to Jacob.

Jacob came to sit on the tall stool by the counter with his lunch bag. He snorted when she told him she was surprised *Daet* left them alone together.

"Your *Daet*'s hoping I can convince you to renounce your new faith during the church service tomorrow."

Her smile froze. "What?"

Jacob shrugged. "I don't have a problem with your faith, Leah, but I know what the bishop wants and what your parents and the elders want. They hope your, um . . . attraction for me will convince you to give up your sinful notions about being born again."

"Who's saying these things to you?" she demanded.

"Oh, everybody, I guess." Jacob's brown eyes were soft and free of any kind of judgment. It was emotional for Leah to hear what was expected of him.

"I'm sorry, Jacob." She shook her head in confusion and shame. "I never thought things would get this bad."

"I know. It's our church. They're pretty strict. When you left, I snuck away a few times to other churches."

Leah's eyebrows rose. "You did?"

"Yep. I found out not all Amish are this strict. If we switch to New Order Amish, we can even have Bible studies and visit with *Englishers*. It's a better way to live and still be Amish."

"You said 'we'—you mean you and me?"

He grinned. "I was always hoping you thought pretty *gut* of me, you know, Leah." He watched her face closely. She couldn't keep the look of surprise and love from her eyes. He chuckled. "I was hoping you'd look this happy."

Feeling hope bloom for the first time in days, Leah couldn't keep the joy from her voice. "Jacob, after all that's happened, I never thought we'd still—well—that you'd still want to be with me."

"I think you know how I feel about you, Leah. It's been no secret to anyone else. Love doesn't stop because someone has new ideas."

She got up and walked to his side. She touched his sleeve gently. "Jacob, I think I'll never find anyone more understanding than you, but I want you to be sure."

He gave her a hurried hug. It was quick and not very tight, but his reaction spoke volumes to her heart.

"I don't care where we have to move in order for you to be able to keep your new salvation, Leah, but I do know I can't live my life without you in it." He shook his head. "I learned that the hard way."

A weight that had bowed her low for months lifted from Leah's heart. "Jacob, I hope you'll never be sorry you chose me."

"Never." His voice was sincere and sure.

Leah wanted so much to kiss him then and there, and she thought he felt the same way, but they both knew it would be a risk if *Daet* caught them. So they put some space between themselves and sat down to eat lunch.

The twinkle in Jacob's eyes as they chatted and laughed, catching up on each other's lives, warmed her weary soul. It made all the difference to know she had someone who loved her and trusted her.

Jacob gave her tips on what to say in order to be convincing to the congregation, elders, and bishop with her confession the next day. Knowing when Jacob and she married, he planned to move to a less strict church district gave Leah the push she needed to try harder to please the bishop and her parents. She hoped her and Jacob's time in this church wouldn't last long.

When Leah went to bed that night, she could hardly sleep for delight over plans Jacob and she had made that day. But when she thought of the next morning, in spite of her pledge to be strong, her stomach twisted. Leah wasn't sure what questions the bishop and elders might ask before the service, though Jacob had given her a pretty good idea of what was to come. *Father, help me to answer the men honestly, without jeopardizing my future or denying my faith.*

Leah was disappointed to learn the next morning the bishop wanted her to wait two weeks before sharing her confession with the church. He wasn't convinced she was truly repentant. Maybe he was right, but she suffered tense hours over the next few days and wished she could just end it by getting on with joining the church.

Leah had a hard time living with her family under the restrictions applied. Breakfast, lunch, and dinner were eaten in silence. A couple of times, Jacob brought his lunch to eat with her in the shop, and when he came, *Daet* always left them alone together. She sighed when Jacob would come and sit on the stool, swinging his legs, chatting comfortably, as though there was nothing in the world wrong in their lives. Leah would feel her muscles unwind, her shoulders loosen in ease.

He was so good for her. He always came with a funny story to share or simply a willingness to let her vent her frustrations. As they bowed to pray over their lunch, his hand would search out hers. The first time it happened, Leah opened her eyes, surprised to discover he went right on with his silent prayer, as though holding her hand in prayer was something he had always done. And though it wasn't typical for Amish couples to do that, it felt right. And good. And special. And Leah needed his affirmation and support now more than ever. Most of the Amish from their church group still did not fully accept her.

In town, when other Amish families met her, they still avoided eye contact. In the shop, at the grocery, anywhere she went, she faced rejection. The worst moment came when she was with *Maem* in town. They turned a corner, and Leah saw Matthew Schrock coming toward them on the sidewalk. As soon as he spied them, his broad smile lit up his face, but Leah, conscious of her precarious status within her Amish community, dropped her eyes and kept her head down as they passed him.

She had glanced back once they were safely out of speaking range and saw him standing immobile, his expression frozen in sad disbelief, his shoulders slumped. She faced forward, hurrying onward, but her mind preserved the picture of his dejected stance.

She knew how that must have hurt him. She knew because she had experienced the same thing when she was out among the English. And still knew it when her Amish neighbors turned away from greeting her even now—the gut-wrenching dismissal of someone withholding a simple, friendly smile.

It began to wear on Leah. The shunning was doing its job; turning her back to being Amish. Back to surrendering her individuality, if for no other reason than to feel like a human being again.

The Saturday when the bishop and the preachers arranged to talk with Leah again finally arrived. It was sunny and warm for a late-December day, and her spirits lifted. The house was filled with the good smells of the coming Christmas season, and all in all, she was ready to answer the bishop's questions the way he wanted her to.

Leah knew she could never be the same unquestioning Amish girl she used to be, but maybe there would be a way to keep her own private beliefs and live the Amish life, too. And since she had passed her eighteenth birthday, she was sure there would be no trouble with her parents if Jacob and she wanted to marry soon. Maybe they would be planting celery this spring!

Those thoughts were in her mind as she sat in the chair facing the bishop and the elders.

Bishop Miller opened the meeting with prayer, and she noted his tone was softer than the last time he spoke with her. The preachers, Andy Weaver and Earl Plank, still regarded her skeptically, and she knew it would be hard to convince them her confession was genuine.

"Now, Leah," began Bishop Miller seriously, "you've stated you'd like to confess before the church tomorrow and then be accepted for becoming a member. Is that right?"

"Yes, Bishop Miller."

"You also have renounced your living in the world and all the things we deem wrong and harmful to our Amish beliefs. Is that also right?"

"Yes. It is."

"Now. We have heard you have an *Englisher* Bible, and when asked about this the last time, you wouldn't answer the question. We need to know: do you still have this Bible?"

This was the question Leah had dreaded, and it had worried her considerably. Suddenly, she understood.

Just yesterday, in the shop at lunch, Jacob had abruptly asked her to give him the Bible. She'd looked at him as though he was out of his mind, but he'd insisted he wanted to keep it. She'd felt silly sneaking the bright blue Bible down from her room and out to the shop, but he'd only winked as he tucked it into his shirt before going home.

She had to suppress a smile now. "No sir. I don't have the *Englisher* Bible anymore," she answered honestly.

Thank you, Jacob, for being so wise. Later, she might feel remorse for deceiving these men, but for the moment, Leah was too worried about the rest of the questions to think about anything else.

The questioning went on for another hour, but to her surprise, most of the inquiries were fair. The last one, however, left Leah speechless for a minute.

"And now, Leah," said Preacher Weaver, "we're very worried about this born-again experience you told us about the last time we spoke to you—before you left."

All eyes were fixed on her. She swallowed nervously.

"Yes. We need to be sure you have renounced this as a heresy to our religion and to the church," Preacher Plank added.

Leah had a moment when she imagined herself rising up and defending her faith—of never betraying her Savior, Jesus Christ. Under their scrutiny she wavered, feeling the pressure to conform and the overwhelming desire to be included again, and then she buckled, and nodded her agreement. Leah, like Peter, betrayed the Christ she knew so personally.

Tears sprang to Leah's eyes, but the church leaders misinterpreted them as signs of remorse. Yes, they *were* tears of remorse, but not for the reasons the bishop and preachers and *Maem* and *Daet* thought. Once the tears started, she couldn't stop them.

The men gathered and prayed one last time, and, satisfied her heart was now true again to the Amish faith, they left with assurances Leah would be welcomed in the church when she was ready to join. She could safely be called upon in the morning during the Sunday service to ask for forgiveness and give her confession.

After the men left, for the first time in more than a year, *Maem* gathered her in a hug and let her prodigal daughter cry on her shoulder.

Daet called Leah's brother and sister into the living room and told them the happy news. Laughter and smiling faces surrounded her again, but Leah's tears never stopped flowing.

Her heart was broken. She had betrayed her Christ.

Never had her feet felt heavier than as she ascended the stairs to bed that night. And in the morning, she would make it official: no more grace for Leah, no more freedom, and no more lightened yoke. She was *theirs* again.

⚬❧⚬

The service the next morning followed its usual pattern. The preachers offered sermons, but this time used Leah as an example of why one should never leave the church. Each one read lengthy and dire letters from those who had left, and once in a while, they threw in a verse or two about obedience to parents and to the church. But through the entire service, no mention was made of Christ's sacrifice on the cross and the grace so freely given for all sins.

As she waited for the time in the service where she would be called forward, Leah prayed God would forgive her for her betrayal. She struggled to keep her tears at bay. The happiness shining on her family's faces didn't, in any way, penetrate her heart, and she was left feeling cold.

Leah glanced across the room to where Jacob sat, and though she hadn't had the chance to speak with him about yesterday, he seemed to realize what this day meant to her. He gave her a grave look, but then lifted his eyes to heaven—willing her to know God was still there for her. She closed her eyes and nodded.

After Bishop Miller gave his sermon, Leah was finally called forward and asked to kneel. Before she could even take in what she was saying, the confession was over and the forgiveness by the church pronounced. Soon, they would encourage her to be baptized and join the church, and if Jacob and she wanted to be married, the classes to join would have to take place soon. No one could marry before joining. That was one way to get the youth to stay in the church. It was a long-standing and useful tradition.

After the service, Leah stood at the front while the ladies came and gave her a holy kiss on each cheek, and the right hand of fellowship was given to her by the men. She was welcomed back, and many took the opportunity to whisper in her ear the sooner she joined and was baptized, the better it would be for all.

Leah nodded over and over again.

Finally, the service ended and she walked unsteadily to the porch for fresh air before the meal began. She took a deep breath and slowly let it out, watching the nippy air turn her warm breath into a visible white mist.

Jacob managed to slip out behind her to give her a pat on the back. "You did fine. Don't worry. It will all work out in the end." He glanced around before he slipped his hand in hers. "One day, we'll have more freedom to decide what to believe, Leah. I know this."

She nodded, giving him a watery smile. She didn't want to spend this day crying, so she distracted herself by gazing over the frosted field that bowed its head under winter's icy clasp.

Like me in the grip of the Ordnung, *nature has no choice but to accept the cold stranglehold of December's bitter power.*

She silently thanked Jesus for showing her soul the warm spring of grace and forgiveness, instead of winter's frozen law of justice. He gave her sinful soul what she didn't deserve.

"Jesus loves me, Jacob. I know this."

He nodded, and they stepped back inside together.

The rest of the afternoon was spent talking and chatting with her church family. They opened their hearts to her again, but for some members, her sin was too much. They stayed at their tables and avoided her.

Once dinner was over, she was relieved to go home with the family. They chattered happily as the buggy rolled behind Sparky over the snowy roads. Evidence of Christmas was seen in the windows of the English neighbors around their farm, and Leah remembered how happy the carols made her as she had listened to them on Sally's car radio.

She had the singing to look forward to tonight. Popcorn balls and taffy were planned for the *jungen* to make, and of course, Leah would be with Jacob on the long ride home. She was as happy as she could be, for now.

Chapter Twenty

The morning after the confession, Leah was sitting down to breakfast when her thoughts turned automatically to her Bible. Reading Scripture each morning had become such a habit that she could hardly bear to miss it. But Jacob still had her little blue Bible. Leah wondered if she could go to town and buy herself another one, maybe one more discreet. With a black cover.

As *Maem* came in to get a drink, Leah asked her if she needed to go into town yet before Christmas.

"Yes, I could use a bit more flour if we're going to make the *pfeffernusse* cookies."

Leah's mouth watered at the thought of these traditional cookies with nuts and a mixture of pepper and spices.

Maem glanced at Leah. "Would you feel comfortable handling Sparky? Ada can go along. And I think we could use more candy for the dishes and for Benny on Christmas morning."

"Sure, *Maem*." Leah paused and decided to tell her the truth. "*Maem*, I'd like to find a King James Bible, you know, one old fashioned in translation. Just so I can read a verse or two in the mornings."

Maem turned to look at Leah, her eyes wide and worried.

"It will be okay, right?" she rushed on. "I will only be reading it to myself and not to anyone else."

Maem shook her head. "This is not what our people do, Leah. You know we leave the interpretation of Scriptures to the man God has chosen to guide us. We only read the German Bible. I worry you'll get yourself into trouble again by reading on your own and misinterpreting it."

"I promise, *Maem*, I'll only read and not think too much about what I'm reading. It comforts me to read the Scriptures every day."

Maem didn't say anything else, but the look on her face was clear. She didn't want Leah to have a Bible.

As she left the kitchen, she said, "I'll ask *Daet* what he thinks, but this soon after coming home, it doesn't look good to be doing this, Leah. Why you have to be so headstrong I don't know—always trying too hard." She went out muttering under her breath.

Leah stood for a time in the kitchen and wondered what in the world she had just done. She shouldn't have asked for a Bible of her own. Maybe, though, *Daet* would consent to read to the family after supper every night. He used to do that sometimes when they were all younger.

Leah would ask him, but she already knew why he wouldn't want to. He had struggled with the German words and, of course, knew very little of the actual meaning.

She decided to get Ada and take the buggy into town, anyway. It would be fun to buy Christmas candy for Benny and the rest of them.

When they got home later that day, *Daet* came into her room and threw a couple of books down on her desk.

"*Maem* told me, right in front of Jacob, mind you, about you wanting to buy another Bible. That is out of the question. I found some good Amish books to read. You need to read something in the morning? You read these and leave the Scriptures to the bishop and the preachers. No more questions like that, you hear me?" He frowned as he held her gaze.

Leah was surprised by *Daet*'s anger. She picked up the books: novels about obedient Amish girls, how they got married, had children, and lived a *gut* life.

Okay, Daet. Message received.

Leah fingered the books with a disheartened nod. She'd have to get used to being told what to read again. She stacked the books on her dresser, their presence an obvious reminder of *Daet*'s rebuke.

A day before Christmas, Jacob came to the house and asked *Daet* if
he could take her for a quick buggy ride. Leah knew what that meant;
he wanted to give her a Christmas gift. In their family, it was traditional
for them to make or buy one thing so each family member had a gift on
Christmas morning, but they usually didn't share gifts too much with
others.

Daet glanced Leah's way. "Go ahead, but don't stay out too long. It's
freezing out there." He looked at *Maem* and grinned. In his look was
hope for his daughter—hope his rebellious Leah just might be a *gut*
Amish girl after all—if she got married soon.

"When you come back, be sure to come in, Jacob, and have a cup of
chocolate and some cookies, too," *Maem* added.

Outside, Jacob's horse snorted a puff of warm air into the frigid atmosphere and stamped his hooves. Jacob helped Leah into the sleigh he had
hooked up to Bingo and drew a thick lap robe over her. He climbed in,
gave Bingo's reins a slap, and they took off over the ice with a whoosh.

The bells on Bingo's halters jingled merrily, and peace and contentment covered her like the warm robe. She hadn't felt this way since coming home. Jacob guided Bingo down a side lane, where the overhanging
trees had been coated with shimmery ice diamonds and then frosted
with white snow. It was breathtaking.

"Ahh, Jacob. This is so pretty. Thank you for bringing me here."

Jacob, his cheeks, red-chapped from the wind, broke into a boyish
grin. "You're welcome."

Bingo pulled the sleigh toward a small area under one of the decorated
trees, and Jacob halted him. He searched on the seat behind and took a
brown-paper-wrapped package from a bag.

"I hope you like this, Leah."

"Jacob, thank you! I have your gift at home. When you come in, I'll
give it to you."

"Go ahead and open this now, Leah."

He seemed more excited than she was, so Leah tore the paper off, and
what she saw made her cry. In her lap lay a black, soft leather Bible. The

cover even had her name on it: Leah Raber. "Jacob! Oh my—this is the best gift ever!"

"I knew you wanted one, Leah, and I thought, 'Why can't she have a Bible? What is so wrong about that?' So I ordered it and asked them to put your name on it. They had to rush the order." He laughed.

"Jacob, I don't know how to thank you."

Leah turned to him, and he wiped the tears off her frozen cheeks. Impulsively, she gave him a kiss. He smiled and pulled her into a hug.

"Now," he reached behind him again and brought out a lovely woven basket. "I got this so your parents wouldn't wonder what you got from me. You can use this to take things with you back and forth to the house and the shop. There's a cover for your Bible in the bottom of the basket. It stretches over the book so it won't show the title."

"Jacob, this is wonderful! I'll get to read my Bible in the mornings after all."

"*Ja,* just don't lay it out right on the kitchen table, okay?"

"No, I'll keep it in my room. It's so lovely. Thank you ever so much!"

Jacob slapped the reins, and Bingo began to trot. "We'd better get back. You're getting cold. Let's go get some cookies and hot cocoa."

As they passed by the mailbox at the end of the lane, Leah asked if they could stop. Jacob jumped down and brought a handful of cards and letters back to her. She shuffled through the stack as they drove up the lane to home.

"Oh! Here are cards from Sally and the Schrocks. I'd better read these later."

"*Ja,* I don't think cards from your English friends would go over well with your parents right now. Best to keep them hidden."

She tucked the cards in her apron pocket, and when they got back inside, she showed the rest of the mail to *Daet* and *Maem.*

They spent the evening playing games and singing carols. The last thing the family did before Jacob went home was string some popcorn to hang over the stairwell. The Amish decorations consisted of fresh pine boughs and berries and a few festive popcorn strings, but no tree and no commercial decorations.

Leah walked Jacob to the back door. There, away from prying eyes, she gave Jacob his Christmas gift—a pair of wool-lined leather gloves. "Peek inside, Jacob," Leah said softly, suddenly nervous about her surprise.

Reaching into one glove, Jacob pulled out a blue vinyl-covered bankbook. Confusion creased his brow, so Leah jumped in quickly, "It isn't much, but it's all I managed to save this past year." She smiled up at him, then laughed. "Thought I'd be buying a car with it. Now, I'd like it to go toward our future together. The start of something *gut*."

Jacob looked down at the bankbook, then brought his hand up to her chin, tipping her face up to meet his. "Leah," he whispered, "you are *gut*."

In the quiet of the candlelit kitchen, with the happy sounds of family sprinkling in from the other room, Jacob said a quiet and special goodbye to her.

All eyes were on Leah when she returned to the living room. Ada ran over to her and threw a handful of pine needles over her sister's head.

"Blessed Christmas, Leah!" she laughed.

Benny giggled and ran circles around her until Leah chased him.

After the others had gone to their rooms, she lay on her bed and carefully took the cards from her pocket. She opened Sally's first:

> Dear Leah,
>
> I hope this card finds you happy and healthy. I got your letter, and though I was sorry to know you had gone back (because you're my best worker!), I don't blame you for wanting to be with your family again.
>
> Anyway, I'll be praying for you and thinking of you. If you ever want a job again in the future, just call me up.
>
> Merry Christmas,
> Sally
> P.S. Here is your last paycheck.

The next card from the Schrocks was also a lovely and forgiving one. They wished Leah well and reminded her they would be praying for her every day. They also said they fully understood why she went back, but if Leah ever wanted to leave again, to let them know.

She carefully folded the cards and placed them inside the Bible, tucking the check in there, too, happy to have something more toward the future . . . *their* future. She felt only a tiny pang as she recalled plans for a car, a place of her own, a future to pursue. It seemed as if it'd all been a dream.

Shaking off her melancholy, Leah snuggled into bed and opened her new Bible to read the story of Christ's birth by the lantern's glow.

Once Leah finished the passage, she turned down the lamp and watched the snow fall softly against the window.

Thank You, Lord, for the best Gift of all—Your Son.

⁂

A few days after Old Christmas, Leah asked *Daet* to let the bishop know she wanted to begin classes to join the church. Jacob made the decision, too. They wanted to have the six months of classes finished before midsummer so they could plan an early October wedding. They would have liked to get married sooner, but Jacob had committed to helping his brothers with their harvests. Even October was still pretty busy, but it was the soonest he thought he could be ready.

Of course, they kept all thoughts and plans to themselves. In the Amish way, Leah and Jacob wouldn't announce they were getting married until the banns were read at church.

Things settled down at home, and Leah fell into a pattern of helping *Daet* in the shop, *Maem* at home, and Ada with any work she had to do. The winter months passed slowly as Leah and Jacob pressed onward with the every-two-week classes.

One Sunday night in March on their way back from a singing, Jacob allowed Bingo to mosey along toward Leah's house. The moon was bright, and the air held a weak promise of spring.

"Leah, I've been meaning to tell you something for a while now, but I've been worried about what you might think."

She looked at him, eyebrows raised. "What?"

"I took your blue Bible and put it away in the drawer at the bottom of my dresser. But one night when I couldn't sleep, I went and got the Bible and read it." He paused and glanced at her.

Leah waited for him to continue, but her heart was starting to speed up when she guessed where the conversation might lead.

"Anyway, I really began to understand some of the stories and sermons I think the bishop has been trying to tell us for years. His readings in German, though, just didn't stick with me like the English Bible. Before, I didn't understand why you wanted to pray for salvation that night at the Schrocks' Bible study. But after reading a few verses, I made my mind up to find out. When I was in town last week, I called Matthew Schrock."

"Oh, Jacob! Did you?"

He nodded. "Matthew plans to meet with me sometime this week. He's excited to talk to me, too." Jacob looked shy and a little uncomfortable with his news. Leah was proud of him.

But right then she felt that denouncing her born-again faith in Christ was the worst decision of her life. And though she'd been doing everything the bishop, the church, and her parents had wanted, she was ashamed, ashamed of sneaking in her room to read the Bible. Her sadness reflected in her eyes. Jacob took her hand.

Leah loved him for his openness in sharing with her, but she couldn't help wondering how his family would take the news if he announced he was a born-again believer. Would they react the way *Daet* had? Would they make him renounce his newfound belief?

Though Jacob's parents were known as gentle, kind people who were more open-minded than many in the community, they would always be Amish. Jacob's ancestors included many bishops and lay preachers. Their kin were deeply respected, and no one in their family had ever left the Amish community.

Would his decision to serve Christ wholly lead him to be the first in his family to be brought under serious discipline? Leah didn't know if she wanted him to experience the same hurts she had.

She met his gaze, and for a brief moment, she saw uncertainty fill his eyes. But with a deep swallow that lifted his Adam's apple, his expression fixed in resolute determination.

"It's all going to work out right in the end, Leah. Don't worry. We'll figure it out."

He brushed a stray tendril back under her *kapp*. His compassion brought tears to her eyes. He turned away and slapped the reins lightly on Bingo's back. "Get along, Bingo."

Later, she prayed for Jacob's new curiosity and hoped this would truly be the beginning of an entirely new life for him. Leah prayed God would give her courage to do what was right. If He meant for her to stay, then she would. She also wanted to read the Bible in the open again. Hiding felt like lying. Leah just couldn't believe *Maem* or *Daet* could really be upset about Bible reading.

⁂

A few days after Leah talked to Jacob, Martha came by the house. Her baby was crying pitifully in the buggy seat beside her, and she looked flustered and hot. Leah walked out to greet her, glad she'd come by. She had only seen Martha once or twice since they came home. Martha had been skipping membership classes and not going very often to church services. Though it was only a rumor, Leah heard Martha was close to being reprimanded by the bishop again.

Leah went around to the side of the buggy where baby Johnny was howling his displeasure and took him in her arms. His little face was red with anger, and his hands flailed. She tucked him close to her chin and rocked him gently. "Aww, little *bobli*, shhh shhh . . . it's okay."

Martha gave Leah a dry look, her eyes weary. "He's teething, and he's majorly grumpy." She led the horse to the hitching post and gave him a portion of oats.

"A long visit, is it?" Leah asked, observing her.

Martha sighed. "I hope you don't mind. I need to get away from *Maem* for a while. Gosh, she's a mess sometimes! And Johnny gets on her nerves when he's having a crying jag."

Leah led her into the living room and settled Johnny on his blanket. He was content when she brought him a cold washcloth to chew on. He actually gave Leah a timid smile once or twice.

Martha claimed the rocker so Leah sat on the sofa and watched the little boy play.

"How old is he now?"

"Um, let me think: eight months, or near to that, anyway." Martha leaned back into the chair and yawned. "I never get enough sleep anymore."

"I wanted to ask you something, Martha."

"Yeah? What is it?"

"When we first came home, I had to talk with the bishop."

Martha rolled her eyes.

"Anyway, he asked me if I still had my Bible. He told me you said I had one."

Martha laughed. She waved away the question. "Oh that. He asked me all kinds of questions, mostly about myself. But when he asked if I knew anything about your life out there in that bad old *Englisher* world, I told him you were too busy being a Goody Two-shoes to do anything bad. I said you were probably holed up in your room from dawn to dusk reading your Bible." Her eyes grew big. "Oops! I think I probably shouldn't have said that. But honestly, how can they be worried about you being too good?"

Leah frowned. "It's water under the bridge now anyway, but I was surprised when he told me you were the source of his information."

"Don't let that worry you. If they only knew half the stuff I'm doing, well . . ." She laughed and leaned closer to her friend. "Did the old Amish grapevine tell you I have a new boyfriend?"

"You don't!"

"I do. And get this: he's English." Her grin stretched from ear to ear, but Leah didn't understand what was so funny.

"Martha, I don't know why you even bothered to come home."

"Oh, you know why I did *that*. But if I'd met Randall before I came home, you can bet your horse's teeth I wouldn't have done it. It's been nothing but yelling about everything I do. If it isn't my *stepdaet*, it's *Maem*, and if not her, then the bishop."

"You came home knowing they expected you to join the church and be a good Amish girl."

"Yeah, they don't know me very well, do they?" She smirked. "I met Randall when he saw me walking toward town one day, pulling a wagon with Johnny in it. He stopped to give me a ride. He's a good guy. We go to the movies together, and he takes me to nice places to eat in Richland. That's where he lives."

"Martha, you're going to get caught. Then you'll be in trouble, and they may even ban you. Believe me, that is no fun."

Martha shrugged. "It's no big deal, Leah. I have a plan with Randall." Her eyes lit up, and Leah guessed her friend was about to get herself into more hot water.

"You're going to have nothing but grief if you keep this up."

She gave a brittle laugh. "Grief is *all* I've known. Now I'm looking for some happiness!"

Leah glanced at Johnny and saw he was asleep. "Who's keeping an eye on Johnny when you're out with Randall?"

"Nobody, silly. I take him along. That's the only way *Maem* will keep her mouth shut. If I tried to leave him with her, she'd have a hissy fit. We just take him with us, and I give him lots of bottles to keep him happy."

Leah watched poor little Johnny as he busily chewed the washcloth and wondered what kind of life he was going to have. She prayed for him right then and there.

Martha stayed through Johnny's nap, but Leah was relieved she moved to another topic. By the time she left, Leah's head was splitting. She determined if the bishop ever came asking about Martha again, she would only tell him one thing: pray for her.

⚜

A pouring rain woke Leah the next morning. The gloomy light through the window let her down. Rain was needed for the new crops being put in, but for her, the dreary day was the start of something else. She felt sad and sorry. She wanted to stop hiding who she was. The classes with Jacob and the preachers, along with Bishop Miller, were getting pretty serious.

Leah could not possibly obey all of the rules in the *Ordnung,* but she also couldn't figure out any other way to not be Amish and still have her family.

She thought about what Jacob had said when she first came home:

there were Amish who preached the gospel; they didn't shun their family members who left. A church like that was where Jacob and she hoped to move someday, but Leah had a hard time believing it was true. She often wished she could see this church with her own eyes. Still, she wouldn't be near her family, and even if Jacob and Leah stayed Amish, she wasn't sure her family would be able to associate with her since Bishop Miller wouldn't allow their members to mingle with more liberal churches.

Leah sighed. *All this thinking is getting me nowhere.*

She got out of bed and rummaged through her drawer for the Bible. She curled up in the warmth of the covers and started to read.

Leah left the Bible face-up on the bed while she got dressed. As she passed the bed on her way downstairs, she picked up the Bible and held it.

It would be more honest if I took this downstairs to read it like I used to at the Schrocks' apartment.

Before she could change her mind, Leah tucked it under her arm and headed downstairs. Her palms were sweaty as she walked into the kitchen. *Maem* wasn't there, and Leah could see Ada outside checking on the newly planted garden. She poured a cup of coffee and took an apple from the fruit bowl on the counter, bit into its juicy middle, and seated herself in the chair facing the window.

Dim light fell across the pages of the Bible, as she carefully turned to the last passage she'd been reading. In the cozy warmth of the kitchen, she quickly became engrossed in the comfort of the Psalms.

"Leah. What are you reading?"

Leah jumped. "I'm . . . I'm reading my Bible."

Maem sat down. "Leah," she breathed. "Leah."

"Yes, *Maem?*"

"You know you can't do that! Why . . . how . . . you have to stop right away! *Daet* will be back soon, and he'll . . . you know he'll have a terrible fit about this!"

"*Maem*, please. It's just my Bible. I have to read it, *Maem*. Please try to understand. Please?"

Maem stood and crossed to the window with her back to Leah. "You *have* to put that away. You have to get that Bible out of this kitchen!"

Leah shook her head. When *Maem* heard no answer, she turned to face Leah.

Leah shook her head again. "I'm not going to stop reading it, *Maem*."

"Is this starting over?"

Leah said nothing.

"Is it?" *Maem* demanded.

Leah closed the Bible. She stood and went to *Maem*. "I'm not starting anything, *Maem*. I'm just reading my Bible," she said quietly.

She walked out and went upstairs to put the Bible away. She stayed out of the kitchen and away from *Maem* for the rest of the day.

The next morning Leah went downstairs, again with her Bible. She fixed her usual cup of coffee. She made an egg and toast, and then sat down and opened the Bible to read.

This time, *Daet* came into the kitchen. He stood still in the doorway, and *Maem* hovered behind him. Their presence spread over her like a gathering storm. She hunched her shoulders against the coming wrath and kept reading.

Suddenly, *Daet* slammed his hand flat on the table and yelled, "You will stop this right now!"

"No, *Daet*." Leah's throat was dry.

"You will! You know the *Ordnung* says you must obey your parents, no matter how old you are. You must listen to me as the authority in your life. You have to stop reading that book."

She stood, gathered the Bible and her breakfast, and said to *Daet*, "I have to read my Bible every morning, *Daet*. It's my lifeline. That's all I'm trying to do, just read. I'm not trying to interpret Scripture or write a sermon."

As she left the room, he grabbed her arm. He pulled her around to face him. Leah had never seen *Daet* so angry, but in his eyes, she saw something else: fear.

"If you continue this rebellion, I will tell the bishop, shout it from the rooftops if I have to, in order to save your soul!"

Leah hated giving him this trouble, but she couldn't live a lie.

"I'm sorry, *Daet*. I really am," she continued softly. "This is doing nothing to hurt you or the church or the bishop. Other Amish, like those in Holmes County, read their own Bibles. Nothing is wrong with it, *Daet.*"

"Don't talk to me about other churches. Around here, we leave the Holy Scriptures to the bishop. He's God's man and the only one fully able to interpret the verses right. It's wrong for you to take this on yourself."

"*Daet*, again, I'm just reading God's Word, written to you and me. What's wrong with that?"

"Don't question me. Get in your room while *Maem* and I discuss this—now!" He pointed to the stairs, and Leah could see there was no sense in trying to convince him otherwise.

She ran up the stairs and fell on her bed. Her heart pounded, and her head raced with a thousand thoughts.

Why was simply reading the Bible a wrong thing, a thing worthy of shunning and ostracism? Why?

Leah remembered to hide her Bible. She had no doubt if anyone saw it, it would disappear. She stashed it carefully under some extra quilts in the bottom drawer.

What will happen to me? Will they tell the bishop this time? What will he do?

❧

The next two days were very tense. Everyone walked on eggshells with each other, even Benny. Leah wasn't happy to be the cause of family discord. Again. She fluctuated between feeling guilty about reading the Bible and feeling puzzled about why it was such an issue.

Daniel came over one day while *Maem* and Ada were shopping and Benny was in school. He asked if she would have lunch with him. Leah made them sandwiches and coffee.

He ate in silence for a minute or two, but she knew something else was on his mind, and it didn't take a smart person to figure out what that would be.

Leah swallowed a bite. "Daniel, you should come right out and say what you've come to say."

His eyebrows lowered, shading his eyes from her gaze. "Okay. I'm your brother, and I worry about you."

"*Ja,* I know."

"Um, *Maem* and *Daet* are really worried. Worried about this Bible reading you're doing."

"I know that. I know the *Ordnung* says we can't do that, but I want to know why."

Daniel shook his head, sighing as he put down his coffee cup. "This again. I think I told you before that you have to stop asking questions, Leah. It isn't the Amish way. You know that. We were born Amish. The good Lord wanted you to be Amish, or He wouldn't have put you in this family. It's your job to be the best Amish woman you can be—to obey your parents always—to look for ways to serve others always—to obey the *Ordnung* and the servants of the church always—to keep yourself separate from the world *always.* So, what is hard about that, Leah?"

His face was earnest and puzzled. To her brother, questioning the Amish church was never right or justified. Sometimes, when trouble swirled around her, Leah wished she were more like him, but then she wouldn't have met Christ and His grace, and that was not something Leah would choose to undo. Once spiritual eyes were opened, was it ever possible to go back to blindness?

With a sigh, Leah met his gaze. "Daniel, I can't promise you I won't read my Bible anymore, but I will promise you I'll try my best not to upset the applecart any more than is necessary for me to live honestly and right before my Lord." Leah put out her hands. "That's all I can promise."

He probably wasn't satisfied, but he had done his duty. Leah was sure he had other things in his heart and head more worrisome to him than his rebellious sister. Sara was expecting their first child, and he was struggling to get his crops in through the rainy spring.

They spent the rest of lunch talking about Sara and their excitement over the coming birth, and of his farm and what he needed to do to make it all work.

Leah was certain that this wasn't the last confrontation she would have to endure.

CHAPTER TWENTY-ONE

Spring led to summer, and the heat came on like a furnace. Jacob and Leah finished classes early since they went to the bishop for more instruction between services. The celery *Maem* had planted, hidden in the far rows of the garden behind the pole beans, was growing tall and hardy. And Leah had kept up her Bible reading in the mornings. *Daet* refused to look at her, and *Maem* left the kitchen as soon as she came down, but they didn't shun her, and they didn't tell the bishop. Leah wondered if they hoped she would grow out of the morning Bible reading with the passing of time, especially since she was joining the church and getting married soon.

After Jacob and Leah started to formally plan their wedding, Leah stepped up the pace at home to help as much as possible. She knew *Maem* was trying to keep things on an even keel long enough to get her married off. After that, they could more easily distance themselves from her reckless decisions. She tried to help by being a kind family member to all of her siblings and responsible and hard working with her parents. As Leah's remaining time at home grew shorter, an increased sadness enveloped her. Even though the last two years had been hard, she'd had a good childhood and would miss her family once she moved into her own home.

The tradition to live with her parents for a year after the wedding was, in Leah's case, not even being discussed. She imagined her parents were happily relieved when Jacob came to them one Saturday and told them he had found a small farm he hoped they could buy soon after the wedding. That way, they wouldn't have to stay with them for long before they'd saved enough to purchase the farm. Leah's parents didn't ask him where it was. They asked nothing.

She knew it was not in the area, and it seemed best not to tell them. It would only upset things more.

Today, Jacob was coming early to drive her to town. While she was still reading her Bible, a knock came at the back door, even earlier than she expected. Leah called out for him to come in, and she glanced up, a smile curving her lips.

There stood Bishop Miller. He greeted her, and his gaze fell on the book she was reading. He had no trouble recognizing what it was.

He blew out his cheeks, an expression of disbelief on his face at her blatant disobedience. Just as he opened his mouth to speak, *Maem* came in the kitchen. Could things get any worse?

"Uh, good morning, Bishop Miller," *Maem* stuttered. She didn't have to look Leah's way to know what she was reading, and her pink cheeks told the bishop all he needed to know. Clearly, *Maem* and *Daet* knew what Leah was doing and had not stopped her or told him.

"*Gut morgen*, Rachel." He gestured to the Bible. "I know we should talk about this, but I think it will be best if I get control of my feelings before we do. So just let me say I'll stop in the shop and let John know we will be talking. *Soon.*"

With that, he turned on his heels and slammed his way out the door. The two women could hear his heavy footfalls marching angrily toward *Daet's* unsuspecting haven.

For a moment, Leah thought *Maem* would simply leave the kitchen. Suddenly, she whirled toward the table, snatched the Bible out from under Leah's hands, and ran to the stove. Quickly opening the oven door, she angrily thrust the Bible into the fire.

She turned to Leah, her face pale except for two red spots highlighting her cheeks. "There! It's over. Now let there be no more rebellion from you until you wed and leave this house forever."

She hurried out of the kitchen, crying as she ran up the stairs.

Leah got up slowly and walked to the open oven door. The flames eagerly licked at the pages of the precious Bible. The sight made Leah's stomach turn. She couldn't watch it burn.

She banged the iron door shut and dashed out of the kitchen and down the steps to the driveway. As she waited for Jacob to come, she found a spot behind the corner shrubs out of sight. She sank to the cool grass and let the tears wash her face.

Around the back at *Daet*'s shop, she heard the door thud as Bishop Miller left. His buggy wheels threw pebbles in its hurried wake as he passed her. A few minutes later, *Daet* left the shop. His rapid, heavy footsteps announced his irritation.

Not only was Leah in trouble, but her parents were, too. They had never before been in any kind of noncompliance with the church; it would be a difficult burden for them to bear.

Jacob came for Leah, and she scurried from her hiding place to meet him. Before he could help her in the buggy, she was on the step and seated beside him. Her tear-streaked face let him know something was very wrong.

"Leah?" he began, concern marking his features.

"Jacob, let's go quickly. I'll tell you what happened on the way. Hurry! Before *Daet* stops us."

Jacob slapped the reins to hasten Bingo's pace. Once they were out on the road, she told him what had happened.

"She burned it, Jacob," Leah finished with a sob. "And I fear my parents will be in trouble this time. I didn't want that to happen."

Jacob thought for a minute. "But Leah, since they did know, they had to have decided to take the consequences if it was found out."

Wiping away tears with the corner of her apron, Leah mumbled, "I don't know. I think they were just hoping to get me married before anyone discovered me reading an English Bible."

"It's done now. Nothing to do but face the music. Whatever the church decides, you know I'll be there with you, right?" He turned to Leah. "Let's pray about this when we get to town and we're safely off the road, okay?"

She looked at Jacob. This was the first time he'd mentioned praying with her other than at mealtimes. In spite of her fears and the confusion, a flutter of joy filled her heart at what his words could mean.

When they reached town a few minutes later, Jacob led Bingo to the first parking lot he saw with hitching posts. Jacob tied the horse to the post as Leah waited for him to climb back in the buggy. He took her hands in his and began to pray. Together, they turned the situation over to God and asked Him to give peace and guidance. They asked Him to allow the bishop not to deal harshly with her parents, but most of all, they prayed for her family's spiritual eyes to be opened through this troubling time.

When they finished their prayer, peace grew in Leah's heart. They completed the errands they needed to run, and when it was time to go home, the comforting spirit was still with her.

At home, no one met Leah at the door. She waved good-bye to Jacob. The house appeared quiet and normal.

As his buggy rolled off, Jacob called back, "I'll be praying, Leah. Don't worry. The Lord is in control still."

"Yes. I know. Thank you for praying with me, Jacob."

No one was in the kitchen or the living room as Leah entered the house. She went upstairs with the packages they had bought and spread them over the bed. She spent the rest of the morning sorting through the new things and revising her list for the wedding. Keeping out of *Maem* and *Daet*'s way seemed the wise thing to do.

The house remained unusually quiet. Leah worked on through the late afternoon, wondering now and then at the continued calm in the house.

At dinnertime, the family ate in tense silence. Leah did not press things with her folks. *Maem* was tight-lipped and solemn, and *Daet* refused to look her way. It was hard to swallow even the broth of the soup. Leah's heart raced as the strain in the room increased.

Oh, how I hate to be the cause of all this! When will I learn how to fit in, God? How do I obey You and keep the peace with the Ordnung? *How do I live among my people without causing this much conflict every time I read my Bible or try to witness to Your Son's grace? Where is the compromise?*

Dinner ended, and Leah and Ada stood side by side at the sink as they washed the supper dishes.

"What's going on?" Ada finally whispered.

Leah glanced around. *Maem* was bustling around, putting spread and apple butter away.

She leaned closer to her sister. "The bishop caught me reading my Bible at breakfast this morning."

Ada's eyes widened. Just then, *Daet* came into the kitchen on his way to the shop to finish up for the day. He eyed his daughters but said nothing.

Finally, they finished the chore and started for their rooms.

Maem stopped Ada. "I'd like you to help me with the hemming of these pants, Ada." Her eyes moved to Leah. "You should go on, Leah. It's getting late. Maybe you can work on wedding things more."

Maem's tone was polite, but weary. Leah nodded, obeying without comment.

She hurried up the stairs.

No time to chat with Ada. That's one way to keep her from my influence, I suppose.

Leah rearranged the packages from her morning shopping spree into a neat pile in her closet. The wedding seemed so very far away. There was no way the bishop would allow what he had seen that morning to go unpunished. There were bound to be repercussions for Jacob, as well. A meeting would be called. It was only a matter of when, not if.

As the late sun slanted through the window, her eyes grew heavy. The pillow looked inviting. She got ready for bed. There was no point in trying to join the family tonight. It would only upset her parents more than they already were. She said her prayers and changed into her nightclothes.

She settled onto the pillow and let her breath escape in a long sigh. In the morning, she would deal with whatever came.

⁂

When Leah went down to breakfast, *Maem* was at the table, and it surprised her to see *Maem* make eye contact, giving her a long, remorse-filled look.

Maem and Benny had their usual morning rush before she sent him off to school. And as Ada finished her work at the sink, *Maem* shooed her off with another chore.

Then she focused on Leah. She poured Leah a cup of coffee and asked her to sit beside her. Leah sat, but *Maem*'s kindness confused her. After what had happened, it was the last thing she had expected.

"First of all, Leah, I want to apologize for what I did to your Bible. That was wrong of me. I was mad. That's sinful behavior."

For once, Leah managed to keep her thoughts to herself. An apology from *Maem* was astonishing. Leah was not sure whether to be heartened or wary.

"I . . . I have some news to give you, and it made me think that what we've been upset with you about is really not as terrible as other things people do."

Again, Leah met this remarkable speech with silence.

"Did you know Martha has an English boyfriend?"

"I think she needs prayer," she replied simply.

Maem twisted her hands together and sat back with a sigh. "She left with him yesterday. And she abandoned her baby."

Leah stifled a gasp.

"*Ja*, it's true. It's so sad to think of the little one with no *maem*."

"Are her parents going to take care of him?"

Maem nodded. "But they aren't happy about it at all. I walked over yesterday afternoon to see if I could help out in any way, and Martha's *maem* was very upset. Said she wished the girl had taken the baby. No matter what Johnny had to live with, she wanted Martha to lie in the bed she'd made." Her eyes shimmered with tears.

"I'm sorry to hear that," Leah said, "but there's been something wrong in Martha's home from the time those two households joined together."

Maem studied her but said nothing more about Martha. She got up and asked if Leah wanted more coffee.

"Sure, but I can get it."

"No, it's all right. I'm getting another cup for myself anyway."

Leah watched as her mother poured the coffee and set out the cream pitcher. She brought it all to the table, and colored her coffee the frothy beige she favored. The cream created clouds again, just as it had that morning long ago when things hadn't been bad between them. A lump formed in Leah's throat as she remembered.

"So, Leah, I wanted to tell you I'm sorry. I don't want to say this to anyone but you, but I already miss seeing your head bent over that book every morning." She glanced up. "You seemed at peace while you read," she added wistfully.

Leah stared down at the oilcloth table covering. Her finger traced the familiar pattern of the checks on the surface, but again, she didn't know how to answer. This wasn't what she had expected the morning to hold.

"Where's *Daet?*"

Maem nodded toward the back door. "In the shop, of course." She stared out the window. "He doesn't know I wanted to say these things to you. As I was walking back from Martha's house, I thought of how much you've done for our family. In spite of all the things we don't understand about your new ideas, you don't do the things Martha has done. It's not been easy, I'll admit. We don't understand this born-again thing, not at all. And we've always heard how bad it is to take on the *Englishers'* religions, so of course it seemed terrible to us. And there's the miting . . ."

Maem gulped back a tiny sob. Her confession and emotions confounded Leah more and more. She hadn't figured her mother would ever say things like this to her. *Maem* regained control and went on.

"The mitings—I never wanted any of my children to feel the pain or bear the burden of having no family at all. It hurts me, Leah. I myself can't imagine not having a family to love and support me. I'm not the kind of mom who wants to bring trouble to her children, even if it is supposed to be rebuke for their own good."

She looked her in the eyes, and Leah believed her.

"I can't say it's been a happy time for me, either. The main reason I came home was because I missed you all so much, but I have to be honest with you; even though Jacob and I have taken the classes, we're not planning to stay in this church. We've tried to stay until after we get married, but our farm is in Holmes County. We plan to join a New Order church."

Maem took in the news, biting her lips and allowing a sigh to escape. She nodded slowly. "But you will still be Amish, right?"

"As long as we're allowed to be. I learned a lot in my time away from home, and some of it I really liked. The church services and the worshiping—it made me happy. I felt closer to God."

Maem averted her eyes and stood. "Don't tell me too much. I don't want to have to be the one to reveal truths to the bishop if I'm asked." She smoothed her apron and adjusted her *kapp*. "I've had my say. I think if you can convince the bishop and your *daet* the Bible reading is over, they'll ease off for now."

Leah stood, too. Her stomach was churning again. *I cannot give up reading the Bible.*

After a few seconds of silence, *Maem* turned. Her eyes met and held Leah's gaze.

In that moment, Leah knew the plans she and Jacob had made must change, and quickly. If Jacob agreed, they would not be staying long enough to be married here. Her wedding would not take place in this house. Mother and daughter never spoke the words, but the truth hung between them.

Leah went out to the shop to help *Daet* as usual, but she was worried about what he would say. For some reason, *Maem* followed her out. As she entered the door, *Daet* was talking to Preacher Weaver. They both turned to look at her.

"Leah, Preacher Weaver is here to ask about your intentions regarding the Bible reading." He glanced at *Maem*. "I mean, I know you don't have your Bible anymore, but if you did have one, what would you do?"

Weaver rocked back on his heels. "*Ja*, we need to find out where your heart is, sister. Do you mean to give up this dangerous practice once and for all?"

Leah kept silent, and *Daet* turned to *Maem*. "You talked to her—I saw you through the window. Tell me what she intends, Rachel," he demanded of *Maem*.

Maem glanced at Leah, but she turned without a word and left the shop. *Daet*'s face reddened, and he looked at Preacher Weaver.

"I think we can tell from my daughter's silence her heart is still hard, and she is being stubborn against the church. I'm sorry to say this, but I think we need to ask the bishop to send for the Amish counselor. I can't think of any other way to finally settle this."

"*Daet!*" Leah stood transfixed, her mind and body in shock. The Amish counselor? What she'd heard about his practice scared her out of her shoes. Rumors of drugs and mental facilities and all the things families whispered about. Surely her own *daet* would not do this to her.

"*Ja*, it's a sad day, but I think you're right, John. She has some troubles which will need deep help to mend." He glanced Leah's way. "If she changes her mind, send word."

Preacher Weaver left, and *Daet* stood staring at her. His eyes bored a hole into Leah's soul. This side of *Daet* was someone she just didn't know. She wiped hot tears from her cheeks.

"It's too late to be sorry now, Leah."

Daet flexed the muscles in his jaw as he ground out his words. "But as Preacher Weaver said, if you change your mind about all this nonsense, we can go on as though nothing happened. You and Jacob and the family can be happy again. You can have a *gut* life and *gut* home here. You can be a part of the church—"

"*Daet*, stop! I can't . . . I can't listen to this anymore. I tell you, I'm sorry now I ever came home. This is something I never thought my own *daet* would do to me. I have Jacob to consider, and he'll not allow you to send me to the Amish hospital."

"You listen to me! I'm still your *daet* and always will be. If you and Jacob marry, he will be under my authority, too. Don't you ever forget that!"

Daet stormed from the shop and slammed the door behind him. Leah whirled. Her world was collapsing. Fear gripped her heart. The rumors about the mental hospital flew through her mind. She would be at the mercy of endless sessions, all leading to acceptance and obedience of the *Ordnung*, the bishop, her community. It would be a nonstop process of pressure to get her to conform. And *Daet* had the power to place her there against her will.

Her thoughts raced. She had to get word to Jacob about this plan. She'd even heard of cases when members of the local church had moved into a house to keep the person who was under scrutiny from leaving. Supposedly this was done to keep the individuals in trouble from "harming" themselves.

Leah couldn't believe how fast things were happening. The news of Martha had set the community on edge. They wanted to be sure any more trouble was met with firm punishment for the sake of the other young people who might get ideas of leaving, too.

She was going to be a scapegoat, and one who wouldn't be around to cause more problems. The thought of being locked in a facility, drugged, and not able to leave filled her with dread.

She hurried to the house but stopped when she heard *Daet* yelling in the kitchen at *Maem*.

This was terrible.

She was trembling and didn't know where to go next. If she could get to Jacob, maybe they could go somewhere safe. Maybe the Schrocks would take her in again—maybe things would work out after all.

Just as she got to the barn doors to harness Sparky, *Daet* ran out of the kitchen and met her.

He pulled Leah inside the house and dragged her up the stairs and into her room, ignoring her tears and protests as she stumbled behind him, begging him to let her go.

Maem was crying, too, and Ada rushed up the stairs behind them, pleading with *Daet* to stop. The house was in an uproar. *Daet* locked Leah's bedroom door from outside and shouted at her through the door that he would do what it took to save her from sure hell. His footsteps pounded down the stairs. She heard *Maem* cry out to him, but then the back door slammed shut, and all that was left was the sound of *Maem*'s, Ada's, and Leah's sobs echoing through the disturbed house.

Leah sank to her bed. She put her head in her hands and called out to the Lord. "Please, help me! Help me! Help Jacob get to me, Lord—send me help—please send me help." She wept as she had never wept before. Her throat hurt and eyes stung.

"Please, God, help me. Show me what to do. Help me know how to change all this."

Leah heard a sound at the door. She opened her eyes. They felt crusty and dry. Her arms ached where her head had rested on them. Had she slept? She rolled over to the window. It was dark outside, but she could still make out the last remnants of sunset in the western sky.

"Leah—Leah," Ada whispered outside in the hallway.

Leah groaned as she sat up. Every muscle in her body protested the movement. She stood and went to the door.

"Yes, I'm here."

"Are you okay?"

"No, I'm scared! Ada, did you hear *Daet*? He's sending for the Amish counselor. I don't want to go—" She choked back a cry.

"Oh, Leah, what are we going to do? You can't go there; you can't!" Ada whispered fiercely.

"I don't know what to do."

"I've been thinking. I have to get Jacob. He has to be told what they're planning. I'll go right away. Okay?"

"Oh yes, but tell him not to let them see him. I know *Daet* won't allow him in the house."

"I'll tell him. We'll think of something. Don't worry."

Leah heard her head down the stairs. She sat back down on the edge of the bed. *How will Jacob be able to help me now?*

The sun slowly disappeared, and as the creaks and moans of the house settling on its foundation signaled the end of the day, she went to the window and leaned on the ledge. The moon was a sliver of pale yellow. Its head hung low, and its light, dim. Night crept in.

The world was still turning, wasn't it? Shadows shifted. A cat slunk away from the barn. It lifted its head and stared through silvery green eyes toward her window. She shivered and pulled away from the glass.

More time passed. She was puzzled about why Ada was taking so long to return. The night slipped slowly toward total darkness. Leah waited—and wondered.

A stab of morning sun woke Leah. She quickly rose and hurried to her bedroom door, fuzzy sleep still fogging her brain.

Had Ada ever returned? Did I miss her call as I slept so deeply?

Leah tried the knob. To her surprise, it turned easily and she was able to slip out to the landing at the top of the stairs. She stood and listened quietly but didn't hear any stirring downstairs. Leah had no idea what time it was but guessed it had to be close to seven since the first fingers of daylight were showing through the downstairs windows.

She crept down the stairs and walked quietly to the kitchen. Maybe she'd be able to sneak out the back door before anyone could stop her. Her thoughts were too jumbled to know what to do after that.

Inside the kitchen, a frying pan on the cook stove held sizzling bacon, but there didn't seem to be anyone near. As she ran to the back door, footsteps came from behind.

Leah hurried to open it just as a hand came around her shoulder and slammed hard against the door. The latch was put across.

She turned, expecting to see *Daet*. Instead Elsa Beiler, one of the ladies from church, stood looking at Leah with great sorrow, then turned on her heels, calling to *Daet* in Dutch.

Daet entered quickly from the front porch with Bishop Miller right behind him. Both men faced Leah, and *Daet* motioned for her to sit at the table. She was so surprised to see the bishop and Elsa in the kitchen when dawn had barely broken that she silently complied.

"Leah," began Bishop Miller, "we suspect you have plans to leave with Jacob Yoder. We've decided that the church community, who loves you and cares about your spiritual well-being, can help you best by keeping you here until the counselor can come to talk with you."

"What? I don't understand—"

"Just what I said, Leah. There'll be someone near you at all times until we have the chance to sort this out with the counselor."

"You mean, you're keeping me here as a prisoner?"

"Leah! You will *not* show disrespect to the bishop or to the church. You are *not* a prisoner," *Daet* interrupted angrily.

"But you're keeping me here against my will. Isn't that a prisoner?"

Daet clamped his mouth shut, and Bishop Miller shook his head. They looked at Leah as though she were the most pitiful creature on earth. *Clearly, they believe I've lost my mind.*

As *Maem* hurried into the kitchen, Leah could see she didn't agree with this, nor did she support it, but she didn't have a choice in this matter, either. The men had made their decision, and it was up to the women to help the men do what they thought best.

Leah looked slowly at *Daet* and then at the bishop. They had her here, and there seemed no way out. She shuddered at the thought of being sent to the Amish mental hospital.

Leah pleaded with *Daet*. "I don't understand why you're doing this to me. You have to know what could happen to me in the hospital, right? You've heard the same rumors I have."

Daet glanced down at his folded hands, and his hesitation betrayed his indecision.

"You've been given many chances to repent—to truly repent," the bishop insisted. "Your constant disobedience is a bad example for all the other youth in our community. We have to do what we think is right to save your soul from the Deceiver, who has built a stronghold in your heart." Slapping his hand against his thigh, he continued, "Can't you see we're trying to save your soul, sister?"

Leah got up from the table and paced the kitchen, fear wrapping around her like a heavy wet mantle. "Do you plan to let them drug me, to take me away?" she asked *Daet*, but the bishop answered.

"We won't know what the counselor thinks is best until he talks with you. We have to abide with whatever he decides; it will be the Lord's will if he decides you need treatment for your mental distress over being in the *Englisher* world for so long."

"What distress? I—"

"Yes, what other explanation could there be for such rebellion and unhappiness? We have seen the changes in you, Leah, and we know you must have suffered a great shock out there in that terrible world. Who knows what may have happened to you?"

"Nothing happened to me. Nothing! This is far worse than anything the English have ever done," she shouted. Leah could no longer hold in her frustration and fear.

Though hot anger rose, she knew if she allowed herself to continue ranting, they would have all the more reason to believe she'd lost her mind. She was trapped. She tried to calm herself and went back to the table. She sat down and clamped her mouth shut.

After a few minutes of silence, *Daet* and the bishop left to get on with their day's responsibilities. Immediately, several women came into the kitchen to prepare food. Though they looked busy, Leah could see it was a ruse to keep an eye on her.

Maem sat down beside her. She took Leah's hand and held it, her own fingers trembling against Leah's palms.

"*Maem*," Leah said quietly, "I'll go to my room. That way, you won't have to see me being watched."

Maem nodded, her sad eyes breaking Leah's heart.

"I'm sorry, *Maem*, for bringing all this into your home."

Maem's eyes filled with tears.

Leah spent the rest of the day in her room, and right on time, meal trays were brought to her door. After each woman left, she heard the key turn in the lock again. They fed her well, and a few of the women even tried to smile at Leah, but she didn't want their smiles. She could barely eat. Her stomach was roiling with fear.

She paced her room.

Where was Ada? What had happened to Jacob?

Leah knew if he even had an inkling of what was going on here, he'd not stand for it. Something must be wrong.

She went to the window and watched as buggies came and left. The women and men were coming to the house in shifts. *Unbelievable! All this because I read my Bible?*

Leah swallowed a huge lump in her throat. They were serious, and she could think of no way to get out. Would they go so far as to post guards at the corners of the house and barn? The idea seemed ridiculous. Yet it was nothing compared to the enormity of what tomorrow held: the Amish counselor.

She went back to her bed and curled up with the blankets tight against her chin, wishing for the comfort of her Bible—the very thing that had brought this penalty down upon her.

Closing her eyes against the shadows cloaking her room, Leah recited her favorite psalm, the words bringing an immediate calm to her soul. "Even though I walk through the darkest valley, I will fear no evil, for You are with me . . ."

Chapter Twenty-Two

Leah was startled out of a fitful sleep by a tap on her door. At first she thought one of the church women was bringing breakfast, but a glance out the window showed it was still dark. Then she heard Ada's soft voice whisper, "Leah?" as the door eased open.

Leah jumped out of bed and hurried to the door. Ada scooted inside and Leah quietly closed the door, trying hard to make no sound.

"They're all here, huh?" Ada asked, wide-eyed.

"Yes. There must be at least a half-dozen women in this house tonight, and I have no idea how many of the church men are sleeping in the haymow or other places. Can you believe this?" Leah asked her sister incredulously.

Ada shook her head. "I've heard tales of this happening, but I never thought I'd see it here in our own house."

"Did you find Jacob?"

"Yes—last night," Ada began, sinking down onto Leah's bed. "He went right into town to talk with the Schrocks about what to do for you, Leah, and I snuck back into the house. I've never been so scared! Then *Maem* sent Benny and me over to Daniel's house before sunrise to keep us from seeing what's going on here. Daniel won't have anything to do with it, and Sara cried all day. It's terrible, Leah, what the church plans to do to you! I know I treated you badly, trying to obey *Maem* and *Daet* and the bishop, but this . . . the hospital . . . this is wrong. If we can get you out of this house, you must leave."

Leah nodded. "Okay, but I don't want to get anyone into trouble."

"There shouldn't be legal trouble anyway. The Schrocks said that you're eighteen now and allowed under the law to make your own decisions. And if I'd known about this, I would have told Jacob earlier. He might have gotten you out if we'd known what the church and Bishop Miller were going to do."

Leah shook her head. "They were here when I got up this morning. I went downstairs and there they all were—Elsa Beiler even shut the door on me and locked it."

Ada sighed. "This is unbelievable, Leah." She suddenly got up and searched her apron pocket. "I almost forgot. Jacob sent you a note."

She handed her sister a wrinkled paper, and Leah opened it eagerly. In the note, Jacob promised to find a way to get Leah out of the house, and he ended his note: *Praying for you—keep your eyes open. We'll think of something, but you have to be ready to go when the chance comes. See you soon, Jacob.*

Leah stuck the note in her apron and looked at Ada. "Did he say when he planned to come?"

"No, but I think it will be sometime tonight."

She nodded. "I'll get ready then."

Ada stood and Leah studied her younger sister, seeing the dark circles beneath her eyes and the worry lines crossing her forehead. She could tell Ada, too, was thinking she might never see her again. She gave Ada a long hug. "Don't worry. I'll be all right."

"I know, I just wonder if I—"

"Don't think about that now," Leah interrupted softly. "If you ever need me, though, you know I'll be there for you, right?"

Ada nodded, tears bright in her eyes. "Things have changed, Leah. I wish we could move or get a new bishop. Miller is too harsh; he's part of the trouble."

Leah nodded but urged her never to say anything about their bishop to *Daet*. "My mistake was in trying to reason with them," she said softly. "It isn't possible to do that when hearts are hard and minds are closed tight against the truth."

Ada turned to go but stopped and turned back. "Leah, promise me you'll keep praying for all of us, okay?"

"Yes, always."

As she closed the door, Leah barely detected her sister's footsteps tiptoe down the hall to her room. Then Leah let the tears fall. Her last night at home and the sorrows she'd had before were there again. The dreams and hopes she'd had about things being different were just that—dreams.

Leah pulled herself together to prepare for Jacob. She washed her face with what was left in the jar of water one of the ladies had brought her earlier that day. Then she sat on the edge of the bed, waiting for what, she didn't know, but anxious to be ready when the moment came.

The noise of people getting ready for bed grew softer and then quieted altogether. The clock ticked in the downstairs hall. The old house creaked and moaned, and Leah's ears strained for any sound that might hint Jacob was outside. She sat rigid and tense. Waiting.

⚜

Leah must have dozed a little because she woke suddenly with a sound echoing in her sleepy head. She rose and crept quietly to the window.

Did I hear something?

She scanned the dark yard below, but nothing stood out. Her bleary eyes tried to sort the shadows into Jacob's familiar shape, but the darkness hid everything except the dull gray outlines of a half-dozen buggies lined up near the barn.

"I know I heard something," she whispered to the cold windowpanes. "What was it?"

She saw him. Standing by the corner of the barn, he held a lantern. It glowed softly, briefly, and he swung it upward just once toward her bedroom window. She gently moved the purple black-out curtain aside, hoping he would see it move and know she saw his signal.

Leah waited, hardly breathing, and when she glimpsed him melding back into the silhouette of the barn, she knew he was watching and would be ready to make his move soon. Leah went quickly to the door.

After a few minutes, a bell began sounding an alarm from a neighboring farm. Fire!

Leah waited and listened as one person after another awakened to the distress signal. No Amish man would ignore the community's call for help, especially when a fire could mean the end of a farmer's livelihood. Doors opened and shut downstairs, and she heard men running in the barnyard, calling to one another and hitching their horses to buggies. Leah heard *Daet* calling out as he thundered down the stairs.

Soon afterward, footsteps paused near Leah's door. The key turned in the lock.

"Go with *Gott*, dear daughter," *Maem* whispered. Then she hurried down the stairs, joining the other women gathering buckets out by the barn.

Leah brushed tears from her eyes, swallowing hard against the lump of sadness settling in her throat. Letting herself out, she looked around. The house was dark and empty; even Benny and Ada had left their beds.

Furtively, she slipped down the stairs and to the front door. She didn't dare go the back way; too many folks were out by the barn. Jacob certainly guessed what would get the attention of everyone.

The door groaned when she opened it, and Leah glanced around to see if any were still waiting at their posts inside the house. She saw no one until her eyes fell on Benny and Ada, standing together in the corner of the room. Ada had her arms around Benny protectively, but his eyes were wide with confusion and fear.

"*Daet* said I was to yell if I saw you, but Ada said it's okay if I wait a while before I start yelling." Benny dropped his gaze, his small shoulders slumped. It was not fair to subject her young brother to this chaos or put him between his father and sister.

Meeting her sister's gaze, Leah felt her heart break. Catching hold of his skinny body, she gave him a fierce hug. "Benny, my honey-boy, I love you. I always will. Please remember that in the days ahead."

Ada spoke quietly, tears clouding her voice. "And we love you, Leah."

In the commotion of the moonlit night, buggies, horses, and people flooded out of the driveway. The bell had stopped its warning peal, but the call for help lingered.

Leah slipped to the side of the porch and watched from the shadows as the buggies raced down the lane. She could actually smell smoke and wondered if this was truly a disaster or if Jacob had orchestrated a fire just to get her out.

Oh, Lord, don't let there be more trouble.

As she peered out into the darkness, Leah heard a buggy and horse racing toward the house. Jacob had his nerve.

She swallowed, said a prayer, and readied herself to jump from the porch. Just as Jacob pulled near, he grabbed her arm and helped her leap into the buggy, her dress billowing unladylike around her. She grasped his hand and felt her *kapp* slip to one side as he swung the horse back to the road. With a quick look at Leah, Jacob set the reins to Bingo.

They took off at a gallop, Bingo pulling the reins taut as his hooves struck the blacktop. They raced past the withered rows of last year's corn, the buggy rocking behind the horse's powerful motion.

"Did you set a fire?" Leah asked breathlessly.

He nodded. "In a field, fallow and empty. Dry as dust, but it looks dangerous until you get close enough to see it's last summer's bonfire site."

Leah looked back, the outline of her once-welcoming home fading into the distance. "Goodbye, *Maem* and *Daet*," she whispered. "Please, Lord, let them someday understand."

As Leah and Jacob veered onto the main road, away from the rushing crowd, she heaved a sorrow-filled sigh and nestled her head onto Jacob's strong shoulder. It was over, this life, but something new—a life she hoped and prayed would be blessed by God—had just begun.

Acknowledgments

Thank you to Joe and Esther Keim, whose encouragement and assistance have been invaluable. Their dedicated support to former Amish through the efforts of their ministry, Mission to Amish People, has been an inspiration. To learn more about the MAP Ministry and how to support it, please go to http://www.mapministry.org/.

Thank you to the former Amish who have shared their life stories with me. Together we have rejoiced and mourned, struggled and triumphed through many life experiences. Their perseverance is an amazing thing to behold.

Thank you to my writing friends for untold hours of support and cheer—Verna Mitchell (who believed in me from the first time I submitted a short story to Faithwriters.com), the Jewelers group, and the Marching Forward group, especially. So many times they were there to encourage me to continue when I was more than ready to give up.

Thank you to my family—my husband, Arlen, and son, Joseph. They put up with a lot of takeout and microwave meals so I could spend time writing. It's good to have built-in cheerleaders, and God blessed me with two of the best. To Rachel, Eli, Barb, Tim, Deanna, and my mom, Bernice: you being in my corner when times were tough was a huge blessing.

Thank you to the good folks at Kregel Publications for giving me the opportunity to share my story.

Writing often feels like a lonely journey, but along the pathway are those who love, encourage, and pray for a writer's success. To my heavenly Father I give thanks that He has blessed my life with so many wonderful people. His mercies are new every morning. His grace is the greatest gift of all.